Norah Hoult's *Poor Women!*

ANTHEM IRISH STUDIES

The **Anthem Irish Studies** series brings together innovative scholarship on Irish literature, culture and history. The series includes both interdisciplinary work and outstanding research within particular disciplines, and combines investigations of Ireland with scholarship on Irish diasporas.

Series Editor

Marjorie Howes – Boston College, USA

Editorial Board

Norah Hoult's *Poor Women!*

A Critical Edition

Edited and with an Introduction by
Kathleen P. Costello-Sullivan

ANTHEM PRESS

Anthem Press
An imprint of Wimbledon Publishing Company
www.anthempress.com

This edition first published in UK and USA 2019
by ANTHEM PRESS
75–76 Blackfriars Road, London SE1 8HA, UK
or PO Box 9779, London SW19 7ZG, UK
and
244 Madison Ave #116, New York, NY 10016, USA

First published in the UK and USA by Anthem Press 2016

British Library Cataloguing-in-Publication Data
A catalogue record for this book is available from the British Library.

ISBN-13: 978-1-78527-192-2 (Pbk)
ISBN-10: 1-78527-192-X (Pbk)

This title is also available as an e-book.

This edition is dedicated to
Cynthia Roman and Beth Eisgrau-Heller;
Audra De Paolo and Maryann Correll;
Lisabeth Buchelt and Julie Grossman –
all women who have made my life rich.

Norah Hoult's original dedication for *Poor Women!*
To Bob

CONTENTS

ACKNOWLEDGEMENTS

My thanks, first and foremost, are owed to the estate of Norah Hoult, Joyce Crozier Shaw, Roslyn Nicholson and Duncan Crozier Shaw for their permission to reprint *Poor Women!* Correspondence to Norah Hoult was obtained through the John J. Burns Library at Boston College. The letters of Oliver St John Gogarty are used by permission of Colin Smythe Ltd, acting on behalf of V. J. O'Mara. The letter of Brigid Brophy is used by permission of Sheiland Associates Ltd, acting on behalf of the estate of Brigid Brophy. I also thank Marjorie Howes, series editor at Anthem Press, for introducing me to the work of Norah Hoult.

I would be remiss not to thank the network of skilled library professionals who made this work possible. Deepest gratitude to Andrew Isidoro, Burns Library assistant, who provided me with remote access to the Norah Hoult collection; to Wayne Stevens, of the Noreen Reale Falcone Library at Le Moyne College, whose interlibrary tracking skills make virtually any project I undertake feasible; to Inga Barnello for her help with copyright issues; and to Kelly Delevan for assisting me with access to the archival *Irish Times*.

I also thank the Le Moyne College Research and Development Committee and the Office of the President, Linda LeMura, for backing this scholarship; Monica Sondej for her help with transcription; Melissa Short for her assistance; and my colleagues Miles Taylor, Julie Grossman, James Hannan and David Lloyd for their advice and suggestions. Any errors remain my own.

Finally, no work of mine is possible without the support and forbearance of my family – Tim, Thomas and Matthew – who tolerate my distractions and encourage my ambitions in the chaotic little world we call home.

INTRODUCTION*

Irish author Eleanor Norah Hoult (1898–1984) moved in prominent literary circles and corresponded actively with some of the leading Irish authors of her time, including James Stephens, Brigid Brophy, Sean O'Casey, and Sean O'Faolain. Oliver St John Gogarty sent poems and sketches to Hoult; he bemoaned that it was 'a damned shame that the most realistic woman writer living only can get a £100 in advance subject to their damned Federal Tax'.[1] Sean O'Faolain wrote in 1936 to congratulate Hoult on her novel *Holy Ireland*, observing that he 'admire[d] the strength of it […] and the sympathy of it'.[2] Critics today are often equally positive: they compare her not only to short story writers O'Faolain and Frank O'Connor, but also to novelists Kate O'Brien and Edna O'Brien for the insight of her work into the lives of women and the influence of the Catholic Church.

Despite her reputation and a 44-year publishing career, Hoult's oeuvre remains surprisingly neglected. She is generally recognized as a significant twentieth-century Irish author – yet reference to Hoult and to her work is often limited to indexes, biographical dictionaries and anthologies.[3] The need for a sustained critical and academic engagement with Hoult's canon remains.

---

* Note: All citations from *Poor Women!* in the present text and notes are from this 1929 edition.

1 'Partial TLS signed Oliver Gayaffo', Box 1, Folder 5, Norah Hoult Correspondence, MS2001-38, John J. Burns Library, Boston College. It seems evident from the address and correspondence that this is a letter from St John Gogarty, playfully signing with a nickname of unknown origin. Reprinted in appendix by permission of Colin Smythe Ltd on behalf of V. J. O'Mara.

2 'TLS from Sean O'Faolain to Norah Hoult, c. 1936' Box 1, Folder 16, Norah Hoult Correspondence, MS2001-38, John J. Burns Library, Boston College.

3 Hoult's inclusion in the *Field Day Anthology of Irish Writing* vol. 4 on 'Irish Women's Writing and Traditions' bespeaks her importance. However, of the 16 'studies' Karen O'Brien lists in her entry on Hoult in *Irish Women Authors, an A-to-Z Guide*, 13 are either biographical dictionaries, entries to *The Field Day Anthology of Irish Writing* (3 in vol. 4) or indexes of authors (or specifically women authors). O'Brien, 'Norah Hoult (1898–1984)', *Irish Women Authors, an A to Z Guide*, edited by Alexander G. Gonzalez (Westport, CT: Greenwood Press, 2006), 151–54.

This edition seeks to rectify that critical oversight by introducing Hoult's short story collection *Poor Women!* to a new generation of readers. Called Hoult's 'best-known and most widely admired work',[4] *Poor Women!* was nonetheless rejected 19 times before its acceptance and publication in 1928 by Scholartis Press in London.[5] Yet its release was marked by almost immediate critical acclaim: the 1929 American edition featured an 'Open Letter' from H. M. Tomlinson, who noted that 'there is no doubt, if she continues to write, that she is likely to be freely named whenever the best fiction is discussed'. *Poor Women!* displays Hoult's subtlety and humour as an author and her nature as a keen witness to human frailty – perhaps the combination of 'strength' and 'sympathy' to which O'Faolain would refer. Hoult sketches her characters in all their flawed humanity, thus creating individuals 'whose thoughts and language inspire both the reader's sympathy and a sharp awareness of their limitations'.[6] This remains one of the most commented-upon aspects of her writing.

At the same time, Hoult unflaggingly signals the restrictions imposed on these characters by society and its institutions: she thus provides a window into the social, literary, and political milieu from which the collection hails. Largely welcomed for its engagement with women's and religious issues, *Poor Women!* also closely examines its settings of place and time. It thus displays a less-recognized but nonetheless keen awareness of wider historical issues such as the challenges of war and cultural identity construction. Additionally, her characters' emotional paralysis, and the care with which she captures their self-delusions, invite further comparison to better-known contemporary Irish literary giants such as James Joyce and Mary Lavin. *Poor Women!* exemplifies the talent, and also the relevance, of this much-neglected author.

***

Norah Hoult was born in Dublin on 10 September 1898, to Anglo-Irish parents whose early deaths led to her being educated in various boarding schools in England. She worked as a journalist and book reviewer for publications including the *Sheffield Daily Telegraph*, *Pearson's Magazine*, and the *Yorkshire Evening Post*, and occasionally reviewed for the *Irish Times*. Hoult returned to live in Ireland from 1931 to 1937; she then lived in the United States until 1939

---

4 Marjorie Howes, 'Norah Hoult (1898–1984)', *The Field Day Anthology of Irish Writing* vol. 4, 'Irish Women's Writing and Traditions' (Cork: Cork University Press and Field Day, 2002), 933.

5 O'Brien, 'Norah Hoult', 151.

6 Howes, 'Norah Hoult', 933.

before returning to London. Hoult spent her last years in Greystones, County Wicklow, until her death on 6 April 1984.[7]

Although Hoult was Dublin-born, her relationship to Ireland was complex. As Janet Madden-Simpson observes in her introduction to Hoult's later novel *Holy Ireland*, 'she [...] belonged much more emphatically to the Anglo, rather than to the Irish side of her cultural inheritance'.[8] Considering she spent much of her life in England after being orphaned, this would seem to be natural. Hoult herself notes that her relationship with her Irish heritage was complicated by family history, and by an Irish worldview she described as 'boil[ing] down to one word, bigotry':

> I was very shocked to learn that my grandfather's house was locked against my [Irish] mother, who had eloped as far as the registrar's office on the quays, on the morning of her 21st birthday, to wed a faithful and non-Catholic suitor. [...] Then there were other instances of this bigotry. One was when my brother and myself went with my Irish grandmother on a charitable visit. We overheard the comment that it was sad to think that two such attractive children should go to hell as they were not being reared as Roman Catholics.[9]

As a result of these jarring experiences, Hoult's two novels focused on Ireland: *Holy Ireland* and its sequel, *Coming to the Fair*, both 'depict Irish family life from the end of the nineteenth century up to 1916 and particularly explore religious prejudice'.[10]

This interest in the consequences of restrictive religious practices – and particularly their cost for women – has been a central focus of what little critical attention Norah Hoult's work has enjoyed. Margaret MacCurtain observes that '[t]he Catholic hierarchy as authority, the Catholic school and

---

7 Information for this biography was drawn from Corban Rhodes, 'Biographical Note', Norah Hoult Correspondence, MS2001-38, John J. Burns Library, Boston College. Also see O'Brien, 'Norah Hoult'.

8 'Introduction', *Holy Ireland* by Norah Hoult (Dublin: Arlen House, 1985), i–vi (ii). After reading this novel, however, Sean O'Faolain observed, 'I could almost believe you an <Irishwoman'. O'Faolain, 'Letter to Norah Hoult'.

9 Norah Hoult, 'Preface' to the Arlen House edition, *Holy Ireland* (Dublin: Arlen House, 1985).

10 Rhodes, 'Biographical Note'. Of a later novel, *Cocktail Bar*, Brigid Brophy writes to Hoult: 'To my half foreign mind, you tell the whole truth about the Irish – but simply, by just writing literature'. Brophy, 'ALS (on notecard) from Brigid Brophy to Norah Hoult, Jan 17, 1954'. Box 1, Folder 17, Norah Hoult Correspondence, MS2001-38, John J. Burns Library, Boston College. Letter used by permission of Shciland Associates Ltd, acting on behalf of the estate of Brigid Brophy.

the boarding-school […], the stifling religiosity of the home, these were the memories of novelists such as Kate O'Brien, Norah Hoult and Edna O'Brien'.[11] Karen O'Brien similarly suggests that Hoult merits comparison to these authors 'not only for being a great Irish writer, but also for being an author who deals with the oppressive facets of Catholic culture'.[12] Considering *Holy Ireland* against a text like Kate O'Brien's *The Land of Spices*, the comparison seems evident.

However, Hoult's resistance to religious oppression is not limited in its scope. *Holy Ireland*, Madden-Simpson observes, considers

> the condition of family life when it is dominated, rather than influenced, by dogma. *Holy Ireland* is not an anti-Catholic novel. […] To Norah Hoult, the crime is not inherent in religion, but inherent in slavish devotion to it, whether it be Catholicism or Theosophy.[13]

Poor Women! illustrates the inclusive critique Hoult offers of misguided or 'slavish' religious practice, be it Catholic or otherwise. In the story 'Alice', for example, the main character, Miss Alice Jenkinson, a seemingly devout member of the 'Pexbourne-on-Sea Congregational Church', is notable for her self-congratulatory view of religion, as well as for her small-minded jealousies. Her 'smile of happy humility' at service contrasts ironically with her vanity and obsession with her appearance; her donation of a sixpence is matched by her observation that 'heaps of people in the choir only give a threepenny bit'.

In the same way, Alice's life with her sister is marked by rivalry and petty bitterness, and her inability to connect with others – owing to her own prudery, her sense of superiority and her obsession with appearances – leads Alice to be both vulnerable to the questionable advances of a bored vacationer and, perhaps even more piteously, wholly unequipped for what may have been her first (and only) chance at sexual intimacy. As a supposedly pious woman, Alice is not a spectacular failure: on the contrary, she is an all too common one.

Many of the religious characters in *Poor Women!* share this tendency to subordinate religious practice to their own desires. In 'The Other Woman', Monica, a mistress, attempts to strike a deal with God about the arrival of her adulterous lover, promising to 'be good' if God will only make George

---

11 'Religion, Science, Theology and Ethics, 1500–2000'. *The Field Day Anthology of Irish Writing* vol. 4, 'Irish Women's Writing and Traditions' (Cork: Cork University Press and Field Day, 2002), 459–63 (462).

12 O'Brien, 'Norah Hoult', 152.

13 'Introduction', *Holy Ireland*, v.

arrive – but she feels driven to clarify her intention, lest 'God […] wriggle out of it by pretending not to understand'. This wilful misuse of religion is consistent with Hoult's canonical critique of religious hypocrisy.

Similarly, in 'Miss Jocelyn', religion is used as a kind of rationalization by the eponymous protagonist, an older, single woman, as she tries first to deny her fate (losing her home and having to move in as a dependent of her cousin) – 'God, Who answered all prayers, would help her if she only had faith, complete faith' – and then, when she imagines a piece of luggage left on a train was intended for her, strives to use belief to create a desperate hope: 'The initials [on the bag] were "A. J.". The "J" seemed an extraordinary coincidence to Miss Jocelyn. [… S]upposing God, supposing Jesus had sent this bag to help her in her trouble!'. As entertaining as it is pathetic, Jocelyn's delusion not only suggests the self-deceiving nature of her faith, but also gestures towards the paralyzing effect of religion on women whose lives are devoid of other societal options.

'Bridget Kiernan', the final story, is about a young Irish maid in an antagonistic relationship with her English employer, Mrs. Fitzroy, and particularly foregrounds the issue of religion. Bridget questions the sinfulness of her actions in having had premarital sex and frets over the consequences of a possible pregnancy: she worries over her mother's possible response, gestures towards the history of Catholic priests' control of women's sexuality, and fears the potential to become an outcast. However, she also questions that same morality, contemplating women who have managed on their own:

> There was Margaret Callaghan of Carrickmore, that the priest had sent away out of the parish because she wouldn't tell him the name of the fellow that was after giving her a child. And she had just sailed off as cool as you please to Dublin, and, so they said, was seen walking down Grafton Street, dressed up to kill, with not a feather off her. Well, those girls might be bad, she wouldn't say they weren't, but didn't they have a better time than sticking on toiling and moiling day after day with no thanks from anybody? […] And hadn't many another girl had her trouble, and got through it, and nobody a penny the wiser?

Bridget's sense of the threat her pregnancy poses reflects a pointed critique of the religious and social consequences faced by women for pregnancies outside of marriage.

Like Jocelyn and Monica, however, Bridget also consistently negotiates with God, even while acting hypocritically. For example, she thanks God in the same breath as observing, '[I]t wouldn't hurt me at all to know that [Mrs. Fitzroy had] fallen down where she stood and died'. Similarly, even as she prays, she simultaneously downplays her own supposed sense of culpability: 'Sure, God would forgive her if she truly repented and offended Him no more. And she did truly repent. Perhaps He'd let her off having a baby'.

Finally, like Alice, Bridget clearly sees religion as a matter of appearances, and her morality is up for negotiation. Thinking of a sermon, she notes that she 'remembered the time well, because she had been wondering if it would be right to pray for a bit of money so that she could get herself the new cute hat in Murphy's'. She ultimately denies responsibility for her actions altogether: 'She had been brought up badly, and that was the truth. It was her father's blame. For ever cursing and swearing at the priests and saying they were the bane of the country. God forgive him!'.

Throughout *Poor Women!* Hoult thus makes a sustained and quite pointed critique, not only of individuals' hypocritical uses (and abuses) of religion, but also of the ways in which women are subject to, and conditioned by, religious ideologies that lock them into positions of subservience and social dependence. Hoult thus empathizes, yet holds her characters accountable for their behaviour; she simultaneously recognizes their weaknesses and the social and cultural circumstances at work against them, which they have often failed to interrogate.

In these sketches of women's responses to, and uses of, religion, we see another of the most prominent characteristics of Norah Hoult's work: her attention to detail and ability to capture the flawed humanity of her subjects. Consistently described as realistic in style and as 'focused on the small, quiet or unspoken intricacies of human relationships', Hoult's attention to detail is variously received.[14] For example, in a multi-novel review written for *The Irish Times* in 1952, one reviewer (identified only as 'B. W.') flatteringly compares another author to Norah Hoult, as both, he states, 'can, at times, turn [...] female characters inside out as easily as though they were so many gloves'.[15] In contrast, in his 'Biographical Note' prefacing the Boston College John J. Burns Library collection of Hoult correspondence, Corban Rhodes cites what he perceives to be Hoult's 'tend[ency] to overburden [stories in *Poor Women!*] with dull realistic details and thus to impede the action'.[16] This is notably true in 'The Other Woman', for example, in which Monica treads and re-treads the same anxieties and illusions for thirty-odd pages within the suffocating confines of her room, even though her abandonment is almost immediately clear to the reader.

---

14 Anonymous editor, 'Introduction', *The Persephone Book of Short Stories* (London: Persephone Books, 2012). She was also perceived, by at least one contemporary, as 'the most realistic woman writer living'. See note 1, above.

15 B. W. 'Recent Novels'. *The Irish Times* (1921–Current File): 6. 9 February 1952. *ProQuest.* Web. 19 March 2014.

16 'Biographical Note'.

The stories in *Poor Women!* are, however, less interested in action per se than in the movements of the mind. Monica's obsessive ruminations about her lost lover make for a somewhat claustrophobic read but, by detailing her mundane, fidgety movements about her home, Hoult recreates for the reader the suffocating despair, the abandonment, and the distorted and hopeless worldview from which Monica suffers. As a mistress – and a hopelessly devoted one – Monica lives in a Purgatory partly of her own making from which she is unable to imagine any escape, but the despair and sense of hopelessness she suffers are pitiful nonetheless: 'A Sunday morning like this: a wet chilly dreary London morning. […] That was Life, as it waited for you, underneath Things'.

Many of the stories in Hoult's collection focus in this way on the mundane details of everyday life, and on the tales people tell themselves to create just this effect – a sense of the realness and, hence, the fallibility of these characters. In the story 'Ethel', the main character, who ran off with a lover, seeks to win back her disillusioned husband following the lover abandoning her and the death of her husband's good friend. Absolutely unapologetic for her betrayal, Ethel instead feels entitled to husband John's unflagging devotion and the financial gain it could bring: 'This was the beginning of her great chance. If she muffed it! But she wouldn't. John was always a fool. Easy money. People didn't really change'. Ethel's resentment when John resists her (which she reads as 'selfish'), her materialism, and her meditations on what she believes she is entitled to mark her as incredibly vain and narcissistic.

Nonetheless, Ethel's lack of self-awareness or ability to see beyond her own (heavily gendered) desires simultaneously renders her pathetic: 'She had been a fool about Billy perhaps. But not again. She knew what she wanted. Security. A house of her own. A servant to order about. Other married couples dropping in for a game of bridge'. Moreover, Ethel's focus solely on her (supposed) attractiveness and on what she can attain through feminine wiles carries with it the echo of accustomed financial dependence. Ethel is thus not only self-absorbed and selfish, but also a product of the financial dependency her society has taught her to expect. In this way, Hoult effects a critique of the societal patterns that condition women's behaviour even as, with Wollstonecraftian bluntness, she mocks and pities women who succumb to such conditions.

The second story in this collection, 'Violet Ryder', shares these themes of self-delusion, financial dependency, and societal expectations.[17] Violet,

---

17 'Violet Ryder' was published separately as a novelette and was one of two stories not included in the 1928 publication of *Poor Women!* The present edition follows the 1929 American printing in part to include this story. The other story added in the 1929 edition was 'The Other Woman'.

an 18-year old woman working in an office and living with her mother, also suffers from a sense of entitlement. Scornful of the mother who supports her and looking forward to a 'future when there might be a husband to keep in hopeless adoration', Violet, like Ethel and Alice, agonizes about her appearance and views her attractiveness as the marker of her worth and the means to her future: 'Violet for the first time felt dismally that if she didn't look sharp, there was just a possibility that life might cheat her out of her dues'.

Similarly, her ignorant devotion to Miss Carey, an older co-worker, as a role model bespeaks her innocence and sheltered social life: although Miss Carey is described by the other office women as 'fast' and is 'reported to have a husband somewhere, and [to] be much older than she said', Violet sees her as sophisticated and mature. Violet's experience of having Miss Carey effectively prostitute them both for a drink and then of being assaulted herself by her 'date' in the taxi home betrays her entrapment between vulnerability and naiveté as a young unmarried woman, as well as her suffocation from the strictures of her single life at home.

Perhaps the most dramatic example of a woman reduced to a state of both mockable self-deception and sympathy by her social circumstance is the main character in the story 'Mrs. Johnson'. An aging prostitute, Mrs. Johnson is older and sick but maintains the illusion that she is better than the average streetwalker. She, like most of the characters in this collection, obsesses over her appearance: for example, she notes, 'The first thing was to look respectable, as of course in your way you were'. Similarly, as she begins her evening's work, Mrs. Johnson notes that she is 'too refined for this side of the Bridge'. She clings to this sense of superiority throughout: 'The action gave her the sense of being very much a lady, and for a few seconds the reflection that she was in reality superior to everybody else in the room comforted her'. Like Ethel, Alice, and Miss Jocelyn, Mrs. Johnson's distorted view of herself speaks to her self-deception; however, it also signals the severely limited currency women had to trade for advancement, acceptance, or recognition.

As the story progresses, the reader's critical recognition of Mrs. Johnson's delusions is tempered by an understanding of her sad financial and social straits. Recently recovered from the flu, she is nonetheless forced to go out to try to earn her rent for her impatient (but, thus far, forbearing) landlady. She uses drink and pubs as her only refuge, recognizing that she cannot compete with her younger colleagues, but too tired and dejected to leave the bar: 'She wouldn't be good enough for them. Too old! As a matter of fact she hadn't much of a chance sitting in this pub, at all. Too much light; too much competition. Still, she'd wait a bit. It was a rest'. Rest and the escapism of alcohol are her only comforts.

Finally, we learn that Mrs. Johnson (tellingly referred to by her married name throughout) has been brought to these straits by widowhood, having owned a pub with her husband until his death left her destitute: 'Poor Jim! He was generous with his money when he had it. Too generous! Better for her today if he'd have been the saving kind. Ah, well! What was had to be!'. Mrs. Johnson, like Miss Jocelyn in particular, but like all the women in *Poor Women!* generally, may be self-deluded and flawed, but her marginal societal position and the lifetime of financial dependence to which she was consigned are clearly causal factors in her straitened circumstances.

In a short piece entitled 'Mary, Pity Women!' (sometimes included in 1929 editions of the story collection), Norah Hoult directly addresses the financial factors that bear on her characters' fates:

> Most of us who are women, and particularly who are unsheltered women, have, I suppose, at one time or another, been moved to envy men the greater ease with which they can maintain their self-respect, and play their own hands without dissimulation; without niggardly fears for the future.
>
> These stories are not propaganda; they are not attempts to solve the unsoluble [*sic*]. I wrote about the individual women, young and old, whom I have written about, because, very briefly, each of them happened to come my way; and it seemed to me that I was able to understand, at least in part, something about them.[18]

Hoult's recognition of the social plight of women has drawn comparisons to Kate O'Brien and Edna O'Brien, as we have seen – but her willingness to expose the ugly realities of middle-aged prostitution, old-age dependency on male relations, and the costs of single pregnancy are, in her era, particularly pointed and aggressive.

It is perhaps surprising, given Hoult's specific emphases on widowhood, old age, 'spinsterhood', and the financial and societal constraints imposed on women, that she is so seldom (if ever) compared to another of her approximate contemporaries, short story author and literary giant Mary Lavin. In

---

18 Norah Hoult, 'Mary, Pity Women!' This short piece is included as a sort of pasted addendum or preface – sometimes numbered – to some 1929 editions of *Poor Women!* I have not been able to trace how it came to be included in only some printings, but I have included the passage in its entirety – along with a brief reading of its intertextual reference to Rudyard Kipling's poem of the same name – at the end of this edition.

large part, this may be because of Hoult's closer contemporaneity with Kate O'Brien and *Holy Ireland*'s direct address of the Catholic Church. Lavin's work also often stresses women's tenacity in the face of social and personal challenges, whereas Hoult's characters, at least in *Poor Women!*, are generally less aware of the forces at work against them. Lavin's prose is also more descriptive than that found in Hoult's short story collection.

Nonetheless, Lavin's canon of short stories has many parallels to this collection – a parallel that bears further consideration. Hoult shares with Lavin the tendency to create incisive psychological portraits of her characters. Just as Lavin often employs the kind of restrained prose and spare analysis we have come to recognize in much later twentieth-century Irish writing, Hoult allows her characters' blindness to invite analysis through their ironic lack of awareness, as we have seen. Lavin draws on her own experiences in her representations, as is perhaps best evidenced in the collection *Happiness and Other Stories*; Hoult also drew heavily on her own history, particularly in relation to her Irish subject matter.[19]

Finally, Lavin addresses issues of 'spinsterhood' in stories like 'A Single Lady', as does Hoult in stories like 'Miss Jocelyn'. Lavin's canonical, sympathetic engagement with widowhood is in some ways foreshadowed by Hoult's thoughtful treatment in 'Mrs. Johnson' some years before. As popular short story authors whose careers overlapped in early to mid- twentieth-century Ireland, and who share thematic parallels regarding Ireland, women's lives, financial and societal constraints, and the influence of the Catholic Church, Lavin and Hoult present exciting opportunities for further comparative study.

Unlike in much of Lavin's work, of course, in *Poor Women!* Norah Hoult does not focus on small-town or rural life in Ireland. On the contrary, her works consistently display a careful sense of urban setting and of London as geographical space. This tendency to be precise and locational in her stories associates her more closely with another literary contemporary to whom she is seldom compared: James Joyce.

It is probable that Hoult read and digested *Ulysses*, published in 1922 before she wrote *Poor Women!* in 1928. As John Harrington observes, when reviewing Samuel Beckett's *More Pricks than Kicks* after its publication in 1934, Hoult recognized Belacqua's similarities to Leopold Bloom and Beckett's indebtedness to Joyce's earlier novel.[20] It is entirely possible that Hoult's approach to representing setting – particularly city space – was influenced by Joyce.

---

19 O'Faolain wrote of *Holy Ireland*: 'It's good, Norah. With a great deal of yourself in it'. 'Letter to Norah Hoult'.
20 Harrington, cited in O'Brien, 'Norah Hoult', 151.

Like *Ulysses*, *Poor Women!* is meticulous in narrating the characters' various perambulations around town: for example, tracing Violet Ryder's travels with Miss Carey, or narrating Mrs. Johnson's journey through London on her night's failed excursion. References to sites like the Hippodrome and Westminster Bridge, and locations like Oxford Circus and Elephant and Castle, pepper the stories. In Hoult's canon, this focus on geography is not unique to *Poor Women!*: in a reference that could as easily be applied to Joyce, Madden-Simpson claims that *Holy Ireland* 'captures – as perhaps no other novel of its period manages to do – the vividness of Dublin life. The city itself is a tangible presence in the book, not a backdrop for the action'.[21] Written in the shadow of *Ulysses*, *Poor Women!* could easily be experimenting with the methods of Hoult's close predecessor, Joyce.

Hoult also shares with Joyce's canon the tendency to represent characters whose lives are marked by paralysis and self-deception, as we have seen. As in many of the stories in *Dubliners*, Joyce's own short story collection, published in 1914, Hoult's women suffer from erroneous or inflated self-perception undergirded by insecurity. The self-aggrandizement and insecurity, as well as the obsession with respectability and appearances, evinced by Violet Ryder and Ethel in their respective stories offer interesting parallels to Mr. Duffy in 'A Painful Case' and Gabriel in 'The Dead'. Just as Duffy initially greets Mrs. Sinico's death with scorn – 'The whole narrative of her death revolted him and it revolted him to think that he had ever spoken to her of what he held sacred'[22] – so, too, does Ethel see her husband's mourning only in light of her own worldview: 'John with his mind full of Dick Hempsall. Never seemed to think the accident mattered at all to her. [...] Such disgusting selfishness'. Similarly, Violet's obsession with her clothing and appearances parallels Gabriel's insecure posturing and his emphasis on sartorial reassurance: 'He was still discomposed by the girl's bitter and sudden retort. It had cast a gloom over him which he tried to dispel by arranging his cuffs and the bows of his tie'.[23] Violet's emphasis on her clothes and middle-class appearances heighten this echo of insecurity and obsession with self-presentation.

Unlike Joyce's characters, however, Hoult's do not reach a moment of paralyzing self-realization so much as a return to gendered self-deception. Violet scorns her mother and feels superior until her encounter with the Major, for example, just as Mr. Duffy in 'A Painful Case' feels superior to his would-be lover until her untimely death. Whereas Duffy questions his decisions, however – 'He began to feel ill at ease. He asked himself what else he could

21 'Introduction', iv.
22 James Joyce, 'A Painful Case', *Dubliners* (London: Penguin Books, 1996), 107–17 (115).
23 'The Dead', *Dubliners*, 175–224 (179).

have done' – and concludes that 'he was alone'[24] – Violet's self-delusions reassert themselves, and she stubbornly returns to a narrative of victimization and entitlement: 'But wasn't there somewhere something quite different? Romance, Love, beautiful shining things? [...] But perhaps somewhere, some day'. Similarly, whereas Gabriel in 'The Dead' recognizes his impotence and failure, seeing his 'own identity [...] fading out into a grey impalpable world',[25] Ethel in her eponymous story abandons her sense of despair to reclaim a sense of entitlement and ungrounded hope: 'Only thing was she'd have a bit more money; perhaps she'd go abroad; she might meet someone; a rich American; didn't look her age [...] still attractive [...] never knew your luck'. If Hoult's characters engage these same questions of self-deception, aggrandizement and despair, they ultimately reject the hopeless but nonetheless honest enlightenment procured by Joyce's male characters for the promise of a deluded, gendered lie. In this respect, Hoult's collection intimates a gendered response to Joyce's earlier collection.

Perhaps even more pronounced are the parallels between 'Miss Jocelyn' and 'Eveline', which offer intriguing implications for students of Hoult and Joyce alike. Both stories begin nearly identically, with a woman ruminating in the home she is soon to leave; both women are to leave with someone, perhaps not coincidentally, named 'Frank'. There, the juxtapositions and reversals become surprisingly pointed. Whereas Eveline, who is young, dislikes her home but ultimately finds she cannot leave it, Jocelyn, who is old, loves her home but cannot stay because of financial exigencies. Whereas Eveline ultimately is unable to break free from her familial responsibilities to pursue a new life abroad, Jocelyn is unable to *prevent* the assumption of her new, unwanted life in her cousin's home in an unfamiliar city, where she will be subordinate to Frank's wife and become a familial responsibility herself. In this respect, Hoult's story seems almost like a response to the earlier piece, serving as a kind of contemporary counterpoint to Joyce's work; Hoult's story explores not fear of an unknown country and a failure to imagine escape, but rather the real strictures, financial and social, on an older woman who imagines escape but has no means to effect it. As in the case of Mary Lavin, opportunities for more extensive consideration and comparison between Joyce and Hoult and their respective short story collections remain.

There is, however, one final and pronounced area where Joyce's canon and *Poor Women!* overlap – but this parallel is far more problematic. Joyce's representation of Jews in both *Ulysses* and *Dubliners* has long been a subject of study.

---

24 'A Painful Case', 116–17.
25 'The Dead', 223.

In most readings, Joyce's treatment of Jews in *Ulysses*, particularly through Leopold Bloom, has been considered recuperative. As Dermot Keogh argues in his important study, *Jews in Twentieth-Century Ireland*, Joyce 'created in Leopold Bloom one of the strongest and most enduring refutations of anti-Semitism in western culture'.[26] Marilyn Reizbaum concurs, arguing that 'Joyce is not merely documenting Irish antisemitism [*sic*] but creating a set of metaphoric identifications from certain historical apperceptions of Jews and Judaism'.[27] In both readings, Bloom is a response and rebuttal to the particular thread of Catholic Irish nationalism integrating a rabid form of anti-Semitism.[28]

Dubliners, however, is less clear-cut. As Reizbaum observes:

> While the stereotypes of Jews in *Dubliners* are continuous with those in *Ulysses*, Joyce's conception and use of them [...] differs markedly in the latter. Jews or Jew-*ish* figures appear or are mentioned in [various stories] and serve largely as convenient representations of qualities that become for Joyce closely associated with Jews and/or Jewishness. The most outstanding of these literary tags is a quality of otherness, often represented in Joyce criticism as 'the exotic'.[29]

Along with this exoticizing impulse, Reizbaum notes, Joyce eventually reverts to employing the standard slur of 'the moneylender/shyster, another configuration of the Jew within the symbology of otherness'.[30]

As is well established, the stereotype of the money-lending Jew is a poisonously long-standing one. Fr. John Creagh, the anti-Semitic priest who provoked boycotts and violence against Limerick Jews in 1904, particularly exploited this stereotype of the Jewish pedlar, suggesting that Jewish tradesmen (who previously had happily coexisted with their Limerick neighbours) were parasitic blights on the community.[31] Whatever the recuperative elements of *Ulysses* may be, representations of Jews in *Dubliners* are far more ambiguous.

---

26 Keogh, *Jews in Twentieth-Century Ireland* (Cork: Cork University Press, 1998), 56.

27 Reizbaum, 'A Nightmare of History; Ireland's Jews and Joyce's *Ulysses*'. In *Between 'Race' and Culture: Representations of 'The Jew' in English and American Literature*, edited by Bryan Cheyette (Stanford: Stanford University Press, 2006) 102–13 (104). Of course, Joyce was neither English nor American.

28 Both Reizbaum and Keogh provide excellent considerations of the Irish problems with anti-Semitism in the years around *Ulysses*'s composition, particularly in reference to the Limerick pogroms incited by Fr. Creagh and through leaders such as Arthur Griffith. See Keogh, *Jews*, 26–53 and Reizbaum, 'Nightmare', 104–11. Both also note contemporary nationalist resistance to such anti-Semitism, particularly from figures like Michael Davitt: see Keogh, 31–32 and Reizbaum, 113.

29 Reizbaum, 'Nightmare', 111.

30 Reizbaum, 'Nightmare', 111.

31 Keogh, *Jews*, 28–30, 32–35.

Like *Dubliners*, *Poor Women!* also includes a few stories that introduce Jews – but in each of these instances, the Jewish figure is either analysed through common stereotypes or, more disturbingly, subjected to a sudden and virulent outburst of anti-Semitism. In 'Ethel', for example, Ethel ruminates over the girl for whom her lover left her, noting, 'He was so impressed by that Jewess girl he had started taking to dances, though she had only her clothes to rely on and no looks at all. Of course she had everything money could buy her'. This obviously invokes what Reizbaum describes as the 'image of the rich and exotic Jewish woman', a type readily recognized in both English and Irish literature.[32]

Two other stories feature Jewish merchants. In 'Violet Ryder', Violet sees a young Jewish merchant, and her language is laden with stereotypes of Jewish Otherness and of the Jewish merchant:

> Outside Samuels, the jewellery people, a young Jew was standing in his shirt sleeves. Violet stared at his dark face, and black curly hair; not bad looking in his way. Jews were funny, sort of different from anybody else. How would it feel to be kissed by one? Miss Carey said they were awfully passionate; hot stuff with a vengeance. She had had affairs with several, but she had had to drop them, because they had been out for all they could get. They weren't content with just kissing and holding hands. 'Damn Jews!' Miss Carey had said contemptuously.[33]

Similarly, in 'Mrs. Johnson', the eponymous character and her acquaintance, another prostitute, clash with a local Jewish shopkeeper who objects to their presence in his shop:

> 'Can I get you anything else, madam?' he inquired with mock politeness. [...]
>
> 'Are you going to stay here all night then?' he said, changing his voice disagreeably.
>
> 'All right, all right', said Mrs. Johnson. 'You're in a hurry, aren't you?' [...]
>
> 'Wait a mo', said Agnes, [...] 'and I'll come with you, though the perfect gentleman here is so polite and pressing to me to stay with him'.
>
> [...] For a moment Rosenbaum took no notice. [...]
>
> Then he turned full on Agnes, who had vexed him with her tongue before.
>
> 'Well, I must say you're one as I'd rather see your back than your face', he said, turning full on her.

---

32 Reizbaum, 'Nightmare', 112.

33 It is interesting to read this against Little Chandler's description in 'A Little Cloud': 'He thought about what Gallaher had said about rich Jewesses. Those dark Oriental eyes, he thought, how full they are of passion, of voluptuous longing!' Joyce, *Dubliners* (1996), 70–85 (83).

'You may be a nice sweet little thing, but somehow I don't seem to see it'.

'Don't you insult me, you dirty Jew', said Agnes in a raised voice. 'I needn't put up with anything from you, and I'm not going to. You get your living mostly from us girls, don't you; and you'd better treat us proper. I've paid you, haven't I?'

In each of these instances, anti-Semitic stereotypes and slurs – the exotic Jew, dirty Jew, the usurious Jew – are spoken by characters who have already been treated with irony. Ethel is vain and self-absorbed, so it would be natural for her assessment of her female competition to be subject to ironic critique. Similarly, Miss Carey is a thoroughly unlikeable and unreliable character, as her example to Violet illustrates – and both Mrs. Johnson and Agnes are drunken prostitutes who are also subjected to dramatic irony for their world-views and self-deceptions. It is entirely possible that Hoult, like Joyce in *Ulysses*, seeks to critique a common form of bigotry – a trait she specifically would condemn years later after her first visit to Ireland – which was, unfortunately, all too well known in England and Ireland of the time.

It is, however, equally possible that Hoult was unself-consciously employing common stereotypes of the time, not unlike Joyce arguably does in *Dubliners*. There is no specific or compelling narrative reason for these Jewish characters to be included in the stories, particularly in the latter two, where it is secondary characters who malign the Jewish figures. Whereas Miss Carey's anti-Semitism might reflect on her bad influence on Violet, Agnes does not hold the same modelling role to Mrs. Johnson. Thus, while there is the possibility of dramatic irony, such virulence nonetheless seems arbitrary and gratuitous, at least to this reader.

Hoult also implies an exoticizing view of Jewish figures in other contexts, which suggests that she uncritically accepted this view of Jewishness. In a 1957 review of Mary McCarthy's *Memories of a Catholic Girlhood* for *The Irish Times*, Hoult notes that the author's father married '*strangely* to a beautiful Jewess', and later in the review she suggests that '[w]hat is likely to remain in the memory […] is the brilliant portraits of two such various *exotics* as the Jewish grandmother, and the Scottish schoolteacher'.[34] This analysis clearly and unself-critically endorses the cliché of the 'exotic Jew' that the character Violet Ryder also endorses. (Hoult's rare references to black figures also suggest a similar mid-twentieth-century tolerance for stereotype: Bridget Kiernan objects that 'Sure a black or a slave would get more decently spoke to' by

---

34 Norah Hoult, 'From Rough to Smooth'. *The Irish Times* (1921-Current File): 4. 7 December 1957. *ProQuest*. Web. 19 March 2014. My emphasis.

Mrs. Fitzroy.) Hoult certainly would not be unique in being influenced by the worldview of her contemporary moment, however problematic it may be for the modern reader.

Finally, Hoult herself was a known correspondent of Oliver St John Gogarty who, as Keogh bluntly observes, was a 'medical doctor, man of letters and anti-Semite', and who contributed racist articles to the paper *Sinn Féin* in 1906.[35] Gogarty does reference Jews in one correspondence to Norah Hoult.[36] However, association does not imply agreement: Joyce himself 'enjoyed for a time the patronage of Oliver St John Gogarty', but nonetheless created a figure like Leopold Bloom to refute such a worldview.[37] This leaves the question of Hoult's intention with these representations ultimately up for debate, but also sets her clearly in conversation with the literary and cultural concerns of the time. This, too, suggests that *Poor Women!* offers further opportunity for analysis and study.

In all, *Poor Women!* is thus an intriguing and engaging collection of short stories. At times ironic; simultaneously inviting and rejecting sympathy; and always provocative, these stories give a portrait of women's lives distinct from, but in conversation with, those of Hoult's literary contemporaries. Her thematic parallels to Mary Lavin and particularly James Joyce should provoke further discussion. *Poor Women!* is, to borrow from Tomlinson, a text 'freely [to be] named whenever the best fiction is discussed'.

---

35 Keogh, *Jews*, 56.

36 See Oliver St John Gogarty's letter to Norah Hoult, which claims, 'It may be that the Jews are making the wish father to the war'. 'TLS [signed Gayoffer?], n.d.' Box 1, Folder 6, Norah Hoult Correspondence, MS2001-38, John J. Burns Library, Boston College. Reprinted in appendix by permission of Colin Smythe Ltd on behalf of V. J. O'Mara.

37 Keogh, *Jews*, 57.

POOR WOMEN!

Norah Hoult

An Open Letter from H. M. Tomlinson[1]

Croyden, January 16, 1929

I have never before heard of Norah Hoult, but there is no doubt, if she continues to write, that she is likely to be freely named whenever the best fiction is discussed. There is nothing precious or superior about her writing. It is simple and direct; all its subtlety is in its observation, not the comment upon it. Her short stories are far away the best I have read this year – in fact, no comparison is possible, for I know of nothing written of late years with which to compare them. They are the unique manifestations which genius always gives us. Norah Hoult's gift for narrative is the right magic for storytelling. She begins casually, and goes on, apparently at random, and one follows her because one must. It looks so easy that it would deceive the innocent into supposing that anyone could do it; that means, I suppose, that both the fastidious and the omnivorous will read her – she may even be popular. What the uncritical would fail to observe, because they would be too interested in her story to bother about it, is the fact that she creates men and women, and that we are at once deeply concerned in their adventures; for we happen to recognize their common humanity. Norah Hoult's compulsion of a reader, in fact, comes of the virtue without which no writer can be great – pity. She would never have observed her frail sisters so faithfully without that quality; and she would never have aroused our interest in them so deeply if our instinct for fellowship had not instantly responded. She is not cynical, even over sinners. She belongs to a better and greater tradition. Here is not a new note in English fiction, but it is so rare today that, after the astonishing case of Thornton Wilder, one would venture to predict that the public will turn to it in relief, for its servitude to the harsh brutality of so much of the successful authorship in these years of disillusionment has been too long.

(sgd.) H. M. Tomlinson.

---

1 This introductory note was included in the 1929 American run of *Poor Women!*, not in the initial 1928 London publication. Henry Major Tomlinson (1873–1958): London-born English novelist, journalist, and essayist.

ETHEL

Mrs. Ethel Stone shut her bedroom door unobtrusively, and sat down in front of the dressing table. Her light blue eyes became cold and appraising as she examined her face in the mirror. But the front view, she decided, was really quite good. Her skin had kept wonderfully: only the faintest wrinkles under the eyes. No one could possibly think she was thirty eight. Unless they were the kind of people who put years on just out of spite. That lemon-flavoured cream was really excellent if it did cost four and six a jar. But thirty eight was only two years off forty. Still it was no good thinking of that.

"I must remember," she told herself, "to blot the figure thirty eight right out of my mind. Perhaps it would help if I put another figure definitely before myself. Say thirty. No, that's too obvious. Thirty two? Thirty two is all right. Mature and finished, yet young. But the thing is I must believe I am thirty two. We get old because we keep remembering our ages. If I think I am thirty two, I will be thirty two."

She paused to rummage in her mind for a quotation from Mrs. Besant[2] which, she seemed to recollect, bore out what she was thinking. But it failed her. Her New Thought[3] phase had been over three years ago; and she had not, after the first few lectures, taken it too seriously, since she had found that the average man was not impressed by New Thought. Most of the men she had told about the great spiritual help it was proving to her had smiled with some superiority as if it were a typical feminine weakness. And that line didn't suit her style one bit. She preferred being told – as Billy had told her once – that she had an essentially masculine mind in an irresistibly feminine body.

So she had dropped New Thought.

And now it had eluded her when it might have been some use. But there was the Coué school![4] Of course they were on her side. She rose suddenly and

---

2 Annie Besant (1847–1933): Well-known British socialist, theosophist, women's rights activist, and author. Theosophy: A branch of esoteric philosophy that stresses mystical experience and access to individual salvation through accessing 'divine wisdom.' (Theosophy derives from the Greek theos ('god') and sophia ('wisdom'). The Esoteric Section of the Theosophical Society was established in London in 1888. (*EB*))

3 A nineteenth-century spiritual movement associated with American Phineas Parkhurst Quimby (1802–66). Popular in England and America, it was based on the belief that illness was a state of mind and is sometimes referred to as a 'mind-cure' movement.

4 Reference to Couéism, a type of psychotherapy or self-help based on positive thinking. Founded by Émile Coué (1857–1926), author of *Self-Mastery through Conscious Autosuggestion* (published in England 1920), this school of thought is based on positive self-suggestion. Ethel's determination to talk herself into being 32 shows a basic misunderstanding or refusal of the Coué principle that what one thinks must actually be possible.

moved over to the long glass in the wardrobe, surveying herself with a smile which she mentally described as tantalising.

"I am thirty two," she murmured brightly to the looking-glass. It was good to be thirty two again! She pushed her sleeve down over her shoulder. Her shoulders were good, too. She caressed them with her hand. So soft, and warm, and white. She rarely beheld her bare flesh without feeling regret for the lovers who would have appreciated it so. It was bitter to think she had been wasted for so long. She, who had had such good times. Well, she determined she would have them again. Just a little management; a little playing up.

Her new black marocain[5] frock was certainly a success. What a mercy black suited her! It was just a touch like that which would be sure to appeal to a sentimentalist like John. When he saw that she had gone into mourning for his precious friend, he would think how much she sympathised with him, how well she understood.

Sitting down on the bed, she started to rehearse the coming scene. She would show John that she, too, was very cut up. After all she had known Dick a long while, and they had got on pretty well: though it had always amazed her what a young man like him could see in an old fossil like John. And he was so cold physically. She had tried and tried … well, not tried, of course, just attempted to show him that she was to be trusted, and was broad-minded and modern. But it was obvious that he didn't like women much. Seemed stupid, as if he didn't understand the simplest … perhaps a bit of a pervert.[6] There was usually something queer about it when two men were as fond of each other as John and Dick. Not that there was anything like that about John at least. He was frightfully passionate; he had always admitted he was the sensual sort.

Ethel unconsciously nodded. If he hadn't had a woman for some time … perhaps not since she had left him, then, all the better for her.

Perhaps she'd been rather a fool to want a separation. It had all been so different then, of course. John making hardly any money; and Bill crazy to give her a good time, if she would only come up to town to live. It had seemed a great idea to go back home, make John pay her a third of his income, and let Billy take her out.

She hadn't let herself think of Billy for months, but now that she was intending to go back to John she might allow herself to. Oh, it was a shame the way he had treated her, when she had given up everything for him. First, taking other women out as well. And now engaged to an insipid little schoolgirl.

---

5 A type of crepe (light, crinkled material) used in dresses.
6 'Bit of a pervert': Likely a suggestion that Dick might be homosexual. This usage of 'pervert' dates back to 1856 but is generally considered highly offensive today (*OED*).

Absolutely nothing in her at all. She had really loved Billy. So young and good-looking and gay. The way people used to look at him in the street.

Dancing together. It had been gorgeous. Close together. The feel of him, the sway of him. No one had ever satisfied her like Billy. "What happened after the ball? That's what I'd like to know," she found herself humming softly, and then her mouth grew slack in recollection.

She aroused herself, and gave her head a little shake. It was all over now. She had paid for her good time with a year of the most utter boredom; hardly spoken to a man, living as quietly as they did. Now it was up to her to get a home of her own again. This was her opportunity. It wouldn't be so bad living with John again after all this time. She'd settle down. After all she was nearly forty, though of course she didn't look it. If it were necessary she might perhaps have a child. It had been so awful the first time, and then the poor kid dying so quickly. She had vowed she wouldn't go through it again. Afraid of spoiling her figure. But in a way a child might keep her young. People would think she was younger than she was if she went about with a little boy of three or four.

Now for it! She rose and regarded herself once more in the mirror. Perhaps a little less lip salve.[7] It was safer to be on the quiet side with John. He might think she was heartless if she made up too much. She dabbed with her handkerchief, and then went downstairs.

Her mother was in the dining room laying tea. "I wondered where you'd got to," she said, turning. "You know he's about due now."

Ethel sat down in the arm-chair, and looked at the legs she stretched in front of her with approval. "I've been sitting upstairs thinking of things," she said. "You know, mother, I feel fearfully nervous. Fancy meeting a husband after two years!"

Mrs. Wright poured out lump sugar from a bright blue bag into the sugar bowl. With the bag tucked under her arm, she crossed to the fire. "The great thing, Ethel," she said with unwonted urgency, "is to think of his loss. I must say he always seemed to half worship that fellow."

"I know," said Ethel impatiently. "I know." She looked at her mother coldly. Did she think she was afraid that John wouldn't take her back? She'd show her that John would fall like a ripe plum into her lap.

Mrs. Wright's colour increased slightly, for she found speech on intimate matters difficult. "I know it's a little awkward your meeting him again after so long. But things will surely come all right now."

---

7 Salve: An ointment for the lips.

Ethel made no answer, and after moving the cups and saucers and then moving them back again, Mrs. Wright went into the kitchen, afraid she had said too much. It was against her habit to touch upon her daughter's relations with her husband at all. Some things were better left unsaid, was one of her practical tenets. As long as she could she had believed that John Stone was unable to live with his wife, as a husband should, because of the shortage of houses. He had sold up everything, Ethel said, because he wanted to go and paint in Italy. That was why she had come to live at home again. But then he had come back, and received an offer to be curator, as they called it, of the Castle Art Gallery at Battingham. That meant a regular salary, and, as it was only right he should when he had a wife to keep, he had taken the post. But that was two years ago. And he had just seemed content to live in diggings with Dick Hempsall. Well, it wasn't her business. Ethel was never one for talking – not to her mother that was. Though she hadn't behaved nicely with that Captain Byng. Staying out late night after night with him. It wasn't the thing for a married woman. It was a good thing that was over. But it was John's business to look after his wife.

Of course if Ethel went back with John, the money she paid for her board would stop. And it was useful with prices being so high.[8] But Ethel made a lot of work, and was never satisfied.

Ethel was the first to hear the taxi stop at the door. Her heart missed a beat. This was the beginning of her great chance. If she muffed it! But she wouldn't. John was always a fool. Easy money. People didn't really change. Not at the bottom of them. She peeped hastily at herself in the glass over the mantelpiece, and fluffed her front hair out a bit. She had a handkerchief? Be quiet and sympathetic. Poor old Dick, killed like that.

He was ringing. The maid would go. He would be shown in to her. The door handle turned.

Ethel let her lips fall apart. As her husband came towards her she turned in her chair, and then rising with hands outstretched swayed into his arms.

"O, John!"

The man drew himself back instinctively, then held himself rigid, tolerating her touch. He looked at her searchingly, yet furtively.

"John! Dear! I *am* so sorry. So very, very sorry! I couldn't tell you in a letter. You were so *fond* of him."

"He was my friend," her husband said quietly. "My only friend. But I'd rather not talk about it, if you don't mind."

Ethel was jarred. Just like John to put her on one side, to say all the wrong things.

---

8 Prices being so high: A possible reference to the economic challenges faced by England in the aftermath of World War I.

"But, my dear, I know. I understand. Even I, who always came second with him, who was just your wife in his eyes, I cried and cried when I heard. He was such a dear. Such an exceptional sort of man. So very clever."

John nodded. "I know, I know." He crossed to the window.

"Darling, tell me. I don't want to be a nuisance, but I've been wondering so. Poor, poor Dick! Run over, you said? Was he killed instantly?"

"Yes, thank God for that. And damn God for the rest, now and for ever."

Ethel felt uncomfortable. That was rather strong. Blasphemy really. John had such a habit of expressing himself violently. Coarse he was, at times, too. There was a pause before she persisted.

"A motor car, I suppose. And he wasn't looking?"

John made no reply. Ethel watched him staring out of the window. Part of her felt a surge of resentment against him. There he was standing, not thinking of her at all. Should she go to him? Perhaps safer not. He was not thinking of her at all. God! Men were selfish. Never attempting to talk to her: to ask how she was after all these years. It wasn't even manners.

He had gone balder at the back of his head. His hair had always been thin. Not the kind you wanted to run your hand through, and stroke. More hollow cheeked than he used to be, too. Anyone could see that he was a lot older than herself. But better dressed than he used to be.

He turned at last. She prepared a movement for him. He would come towards her, then drop on his knees and bury his head in her lap. Her letters had been affectionate enough to show him, though he hadn't liked to reply.

"I wonder if I might have a wash?" he asked her.

Ethel rose silently, and led the way upstairs. She showed him the spare bedroom prepared for him with its double bed. Had he everything he wanted? She so hoped he would be comfortable. Then she went back to the sitting room, and, after a moment's study of herself in the glass, on into the kitchen where her mother was. She would make some toast for him. That would be a good move. But all the while she had to repress her irritation. Really it was stupid, things happening like this. John with his mind full of Dick Hempsall. Never seemed to think the accident mattered at all to her. Yet, as a matter of fact, it had been her own sister who had introduced John to Dick. He'd never have known him if it hadn't been for *her* family. But he didn't seem to think *they* were likely to feel it at all. Such disgusting selfishness. He had never even kissed her. Or asked her how she was.

The little sitting room was clogged with misery. There was a clean table-cloth on the table, but it had been badly laundered, and its faint brownish tinge made it look mean[9] and ashamed. Mrs. Wright poured out tea, and

---

9 Mean: Shabby.

in her nervousness filled the cups over full. When she passed John his, some overflowed into the saucer, and she apologised in a little murmur of sounds which began brightly, and then faded into nothingness. There was a silence. The weather had already been fully commented upon.

Ethel, wearing what she knew to be a resigned and yet sweet look, found herself absorbed in watching her husband. She knew that each time he drank drops of tea fell from the bottom of his cup on to his trousers; and she felt the familiar bite of irritation against him because he didn't seem to notice. That suit must have cost ten, or perhaps twelve guineas. Was there any way of finding out how much money he had in the bank? He must have sold a picture for a decent sum. And of course he'd be too mean to tell her. Spend the money selfishly on himself. His tie was coloured; looked the sort of tie a woman might have given him.

Was there another woman somewhere? If so, it would make things more difficult. But then nobody could possibly attract him as much as herself. In the old days whenever she had wanted to soothe him out of a temper to get money she had only to put her hand on his knee, clingingly, the way she knew how, to be assured of her dominion over him.

And he had a great sense of duty, and all that stuff, too. He would never have let her go so easily had he not taken her at her word that she was sick to death of him, and their precarious way of living; plenty of money one week, and none the next. Why was it that he had refused to let her come and stay with him even for a weekend except that he was scared of her?

She met his eyes across the table and held them with determination. Her own, she felt, were filled to the brim with sorrowful understanding.

"You must be so tired, John," she said, modifying the natural shrill of her voice to a low, deep, and, she hoped, thrilling note.

He nodded. And added, impressed for the moment by the amount of white powder she had put on, "And you look tired, too."

Ethel smiled wistfully. "One doesn't think of oneself at such a time. When other people have to go through so much more. But it was a terrible shock to me."

To her pleasure Mrs. Wright joined jerkily in the conversation. Ethel was letting herself go too much, she said. It didn't do anybody any good to take on so. She would make herself ill, and then where would they be?

Ethel felt a sense of justification take possession of her as she listened. Perhaps John would realize now that she had her feelings too. After all, they had known Dick for years. And also that she was unhappy in herself as well. But he only muttered some polite agreement, and for the moment her eyes forgot themselves and became a little hard. He might at least press her to have some more to eat. Couldn't he see she wasn't eating anything?

The two women helped to clear away. Then they joined John round the gas fire. Ethel noticed with annoyance that the tap was only partly turned on, and that it was burning very low. Even if it was Spring and mild weather, it ought to have been turned higher to start with, and then if the room got too hot, turned down in front of John. There was something sordid about a half fire burning when there was a death round the corner. And John might think they were a mean household. She had always told him that she was no good at money, that she simply couldn't save and be mean. But with the curtains drawn, and the white narcissi on the green tablecloth looking, Ethel thought, sad yet beautiful, like poor Richard lying dead – he had been a nice looking boy, you had to say that for him – the atmosphere became easier. The hot tea had unloosened their tongues; and the recognition that the three of them had been known familiarly by the dead man sufficed for the moment to unite them. They sat, speaking in low voices, tasting the tranquility of resignation, and their faces took on the droop of endurance. At that moment all of them realised in their own degree that there was an inscrutable hardness underlying the mystery of life.

Presently Mr. Wright came in. Ethel was a little annoyed because his arrival dissipated the atmosphere of intimacy. Her father, she knew, was never able to say the right thing in the right way. It was frightful drawback, she realised once more, having a parent with a cockney accent who always managed to make you look more insignificant than you really were by virtue of your relation with him. Wright was a middle-sized, bald-headed man with a grey skin and a long shapeless mouth, now carefully compressed into an appearance of dejection. He never felt his real self unless he happened to be in an environment in which he could discuss business deals, comment on the strangeness of various facts, and use women and schoolboy jokes to provide the light relief; and he disguised his distaste for the present unpleasantly delicate situation from everybody, including himself, by interpolating vast tracts of silence, during which he sat stroking his chin in sad meditation, with brief questions and remarks about the time of the funeral and kindred matters. But in case there should be the least flavour of a lack of sensibility about his attitude – his family had often suggested he was lacking in sensitiveness – he had no sooner settled a point than he would emit an interjection as, "Bad business!" Or "Poor fellow!" Or just "Dear, dear!" followed by a shake of the head and a pursing up of the lips. These brief but assiduous lamentations had the effect of throwing John back on his own sad musings; and he sat passively like a hurt child.

On the whole Ethel was glad when bedtime came. The hour had not yet come for her to take the stage.

Sitting and talking there, in the house which had once been so familiar to him, John Stone felt the pain of the past had mingled inseparably with the pain of the present. There burnt again in his memory the humiliations he had endured when there had been so little money that Ethel had for periods left him, declaring that even the mortification of living at home would be more worth while than the pitiful fare he provided. And there she would wait till he had sold something, and then back she would come to spend it. But always he must bring her to London, since she did not like travelling alone; men would speak to her, insult her, she said. And though he seemed to himself to accept this explanation, for he had taken a pride in her good looks, there had even then been part of him which glimpsed otherwise. Sitting opposite her at those gloomy suppers, taking part in forced conversations, he knew that in some way her refusal to eat a good meal, the wearing of her shabbiest clothes were designed for the purpose of exhibiting herself as a pitiful captive to his impotence and failure. Her mother, he remembered, had always fussed over her, while her father had employed the hearty manner he thought suitable for invalids.

And once more Ethel seemed to be reacting to Dick's death as she had reacted to her husband's incapacity to make a fat living – by regarding herself as a tragic heroine. Sometimes she would seem to consider that it was her dear friend who had been killed, not his. He smiled inwardly: Ethel had always enjoyed a situation.

So he was more interested in the question than in its significance when, sitting alone together that evening, Ethel said to him softly, "John, I have something to ask you. Do you believe that people change?"

He shook his head. "No. Not fundamentally, that is. They grow a little maybe, or decrease a little. They may even believe that they forget, and someone has said that each man is himself a necropolis; that the old dreams, the old faces, the words we have said, the thoughts we have thought, are buried within us, buried deep. But if we carry our dead within us, it is only that they may be eternally resurrected. Pains which have fed upon us sink back appeased, and we think we shall feel them no more. But on a chance word or sight, they start the old prowl. And so till we ourselves die, which so often comes before the arrival of physical death."

He was talking to himself more than to Ethel, but she listened attentively and with pleasure to his words. Had she succeeded already?

"I am glad you think that we don't really forget," she said softly. "Because I never have. Not the sweet things. And I want you to believe, John, that I have changed. I have found out the real thing in life. I see that what matters is love. Faithful love!

"And I want to ask your forgiveness for the past. Because I know I was often frivolous and vain. I was young, you see, and wanted to have a good time. And you were very patient with me. More than I deserved.

"But I am not like that any longer. My life alone has taught me so much."

She paused. John asked dryly, "What about your great friend, Billy Byng?"

"Captain Byng? Oh, John! Surely you never thought there was anything in that. Billy and I were just pals."

"Oh, indeed! I had thought you might want to marry him."

"Never, John, dear. Never! Believe me when I say I never had any such idea. Billy, of course, was good to me. I mean I was all alone here: no friends much. No one I really cared about. And we went out a bit together. That was all. Now he's engaged. To a Miss Wilson. Quite a nice girl, I believe."

"Is that it?"

Oh, so he was sneering at her, was he? Well, she'd make him eat his words one day. Not now!

She waited a little till she was fully in control of herself. Then she said gently, "Whether you believe it or not, John, Billy Byng was just a friend. A dancing partner. Our steps went well together. You would never take up dancing you know, though I asked you. But I haven't seen him for a long while." Her voice trembled, and she added under her breath, "And I am all alone."

John stirred uneasily. Of course it was bad for her. It was true what she had been saying. If Byng was engaged, she was all alone – unless she had found some other man, because to him at least she was a stranger. He felt guilty.

"We must both be brave, Ethel. I know how you are feeling. It's a hell of a world, but somehow it's got to be lived through." He felt his heart contracting, and something within him cried out an appeal, "Dick, I'm sorry, old man. You loved life. You said, 'Never deny life. That's the worst treachery.' I loved it, too, when you were there. But now you've gone away. Dick, lad, I'm sorry. Can you hear me? Can you understand?"

But most likely he couldn't hear. Perhaps he wasn't anywhere at all. All finished. Ethel was speaking again.

"You are right, John. We must be brave. And I think I can bear it if I feel that you are beside me. The worst thing is suffering alone."

He looked at her unseeing. Suffering alone, yes, that was true, too.

"Yes, you are right. That's the most terrible part. When you watch an accident in a crowd it doesn't seem to matter nearly as much as when you watch it alone. And if it's your own self that's hurt, you suffer most when you realise that no one else can come in because no one but yourself knows."

Ethel suppressed a growing irritation. This was just the way John had always gone meandering on, absolutely missing the point of what one happened to be saying. Making a sermon out of it.

"Surely," she said plaintively, "you and I at least can understand and comfort each other. I quite realise how you will miss Dick. I was very fond of him, too. And I have had other trouble of my own. I've had a hard time, John, this last year."

"My dear, I am sorry you are unhappy. But you wanted to go back to your people, you know." He looked across at her almost imploringly. Why couldn't he catch a spark from her which would make him feel tenderly towards her, and not so wrapped in his own grief? It was brutally selfish if she were really unhappy.

She saw the look and rose and came to him. Kneeling down, she laid her arm across his knee and buried her head in it. A sort of fear and repugnance came upon him, but he ignored it, and stroked her hair. She began to cry, but quietly, and not, he felt, as a prelude to the hysteria into which she had often previously worked herself. Soon she raised herself, and slipping on to his knees hid her face against his coat, disregarding his passivity.

So they sat for a little while. Mrs. Wright opening the door and finding them thus paired, withdrew immediately, and they heard her say something in a low voice to her husband. Afterwards their footsteps retreated up the stairs. They were going to bed.

Ethel was quite quiet now, but more and more the weight of her body against his urged itself on John's attention. She was so close. It was as if she were smothering him. He felt his own body slipping away from him and coming under her dominion. Turning traitor. Yet not traitor, for this woman was not an enemy, only a stranger. A strange woman seducing him. Queer expressions came into his mind. But that couldn't be, not in decency with the words still sounding, "Earth to earth, ashes to ashes, dust to dust." Only death mattered. The rest was playacting.

"You had better go to bed, Ethel, hadn't you?" he said, stirring. "You need sleep, rest."

"I don't want to sleep," he heard her murmur. "I want to be with you. To comfort you. To make up if I can."

He made no answer: what was the good of all this? People must just be quiet when they are hurt. Not resigned, because it wasn't fair to strike down someone who had loved the world with a single heart. No, never resigned, but still.

"John," she said softly, "John, may I come to your bed? I would like to feel you were near me. I could bear everything better then. I dread lying awake thinking of you, of the mess I have made of our lives."

He made a movement away from her, and then checked himself.

"I will come and sit with you until you fall asleep," he replied with averted eyes.

She seemed as though about to say something, but stopped, and after a moment withdrew from him in silence. Slowly she went towards the door, but before passing through turned and looked at him. Her eyes shone with trust and sweetness as it seemed; and gazing back at her he felt that with that look she was giving herself to him, that between them she was insinuating gentleness and love. He sat down, burying his face in his hands. There was something he had to guard himself from. There was something unpleasant knocking at his thoughts. But once again all that really mattered was that they had taken his friend from him; he had no friend any more. A laughing, struggling, fighting, eager man. What had he felt? If he could only have been there.

The minutes passed by. He looked at his watch. Twenty five of them had gone. Better go up to Ethel. A nuisance! A damned nuisance! You didn't want women butting in when you had lost your friend. You wanted to sit quietly with the thought of him. It might be – for how, after all, could one tell anything? –that something of him was near. He could only feel emptiness, but . . .

Ethel! He would read to her, be kind to her for a little while. Then he could go back, and be alone, alone for ever.

He knocked at her door and went softly in. The room felt stuffily sweet with some sort of scent. There were too many things about. He stumbled over some slippers and noticed as it were an oddity that they had red heels. The bedclothes were turned back from the bed, and he saw a pink nightgown, soft and silken, spread out, but she was not there. Ethel was sitting by the gas fire in an easy chair. Her head rested against a pillow which she had taken from the bed. She was wearing white cami-nickers,[10] and one of the ribbon straps had slipped down her arm so that part of her breast was revealed. After the first glance he seemed to see nothing but her bare shoulder, and was irritated by its looming so large before him.

"My dear Ethel," he said, sounding a little annoyed in spite of himself, "why aren't you in bed?"

She answered without looking at him, "I sat down for a moment and then I got thinking."

His eyes fell upon a small bookcase, and he walked over to it with relief. Classy books, of course. She had them to impress people. Shaw, Poems by Drinkwater.[11] Stupid name, that! Wasn't she going to bed? Oh, hell! He was tired himself. But a lot she'd care for that.

"Much better to get into bed, Ethel," he heard himself saying.

"All right. If you think so, dear."

But she wasn't moving. He'd have to turn round. Hang the woman!

---

10 Cami-knickers: A one-piece undergarment combining a camisole and knickers. Knickers are loose pants that were worn as undergarments by women and children.

11 George Bernard Shaw (1856–1950), Dublin-born Irish playwright. John Drinkwater (1882–1937), English poet and playwright.

Immediately she rose, and began to slip off her garment. As he turned back, she stopped him. "What's the time, by the way?" she asked in matter-of-fact fashion, and, as he told her, she seemed to shine out upon him desirably not as Ethel, but as woman. But all the same, she was Ethel, he reminded himself, and before now he had judged her harlot, unfaithful, a light woman. These damn Biblical phrases!! Well, he could take her if he wanted to, as that. But he didn't want. No, emphatically no!

She was getting into bed now, thank goodness.

"John."

He came over to her reluctantly. She raised her arms, and he bent awkwardly, and kissed her. Still her arms enfolded him. He felt her hair on his cheeks, and the warmth of her rising to him. He released himself.

"John."

"Yes?"

"Don't you love me at all, any more?"

He was silent. It would be brutal to say no. It would be wrong to say yes. But she was waiting for an answer.

"It seems hardly the time to think of ourselves." (How priggish that sounded! Try again.) "We must have to a talk tomorrow when you are rested."

"How long are you staying?"

"I must go back tomorrow, some time."

The silence became uncomfortably prolonged. Ethel lay there gazing in front of her. She didn't look so attractive now. Showing signs of her age after all. But he was afraid of what she was preparing to say.

"Well, good night. You'll sleep better if I leave you."

Still she was silent. Her mind flowed in hate towards him. If she spoke she would scream words at him. Dying to get away. Taking no notice of anything. He was afraid of her, that was it. He had implored her often enough, and she had refused. He needn't think she wanted him. If she could only kill him. But there was nothing else she could do now. He could go, the weak maudlin brute.

"Good night," he said again.

"Good night," she forced herself to reply.

He switched out the light and closed the door.

Ethel lay in the darkness angry with herself. She had allowed her hate of him to get the better of her. She had missed an opportunity. Why hadn't she…. Oh, there were heaps of things she could have done. She knew men. She had been a fool. For the first time fear stole on her. Supposing that after all he resisted her. But there was tomorrow. Her mind began to work, revolving plans.

She had her breakfast in bed in the mornings. It was indeed her habit to breakfast in bed, and only her husband's arrival had disturbed her programme.

These last two mornings she had certainly been up early, helping her mother to get breakfast, and had been seen by John carrying in things for the table. But today after waking she had hurried to her mother's room, and finding her just ready to go downstairs, had said with hand clasping brow, "Mother, would you let me have a cup of tea upstairs? I have such a terrible headache. I haven't slept a wink all night."

Her mother nodded. Her mother always agreed to everything. Of course that was because she paid for her own board and lodging, and was quite independent of anybody. And she might have been a little sympathetic, asked about her headache, and suggested things.

Ethel, breaking the top off her egg, wondered with frowning brow if her mother had had the sense to tell John about her headache. She might be too stupid. You could never tell. But at that moment her eyes took in the agreeable picture of her new black hat resting on top of the chest of drawers, and her thoughts were pleasantly deflected. It was really a smart hat. It really suited her.

And so it ought considering the price. Three guineas! But then John was paying the bills for all the mourning, though he had seemed surprised at the idea of her going into mourning[12] at all. And she might just as well order a few more things while she was about it. He could hardly say anything at such time. Another frock. And what about black underwear? She had seen some awfully pretty black chemises at that shop in Oxford Circus.[13] It was the sort of solid expensive shop, too, where country folk went; good form, not merely smart. It wouldn't be likely to put black lingerie in the window if black lingerie (she wished she knew the absolutely correct pronunciation of that word) weren't quite the thing. Of course they would be frightfully expensive.

But John couldn't say anything. Anyway he probably wouldn't bother to look at all the items. If he did, she would tell him that not only her outside clothes, but every stitch on her must symbolize her grief. Perhaps she had better not say that. John was so queer and sarcastic about some things. Men were so sentimental, and yet at the same time so heartless and material. Oh, well, she would see how she got on with him today. But didn't Lady Diana Cooper[14] and those Society people go in for black sheets and things like that?

---

12 Going into mourning: A reference to the tradition of wearing mourning clothes for a period after a death.

13 Oxford Circus: The intersection between Oxford and Regent Streets in the West End of London. The West End is known for its shopping and entertainment venues.

14 Lady Diana Cooper (aka Viscountess Norwich, née Manners, 1892–1986): Socialite and author well known in London and Paris around the world wars.

Funny, too, how prostitutes, specially French ones, so often wore black. Black hat, coat, and flesh coloured stockings. There must be something in it. On the other hand, black was trying unless you put on a bit more makeup. Plenty of lip-salve. "Just lost a very dear friend, poor thing. And Ethel has always been so sensitive." That's what people would say. And they would be right too. Poor old Dick. It was a shame.

She dressed slowly, savouring herself agreeably. She felt and looked better this morning. How nice it was to have new clothes! If she could only have a dress allowance of, say, a thousand a year, how men would turn and stare at her as she walked along the streets. It was bad luck on her she had always been poor. Never had a proper chance. Married too young, and men never took you seriously after. If she had had more clothes she could have made Billy marry her —she was sure she could. He was so impressed by that Jewess girl he had started taking to dances, though she had only her clothes to rely on and no looks at all. Of course she had everything money could buy her – that gave her the pull – and Billy was so weak about women. Still now that John was really making a bit of money at last…

As she was brushing her hair, she heard him come upstairs, and go into his room opposite. A thought struck her, and she stood still with tightened lips, the brush suspended. Then she crossed the room and took a letter from her tray she had received that morning. Opening it out she laid it on the dressing table, then slipping on a silk dressing jacket, powdered her face rapidly. With a backward glance in the mirror she went to the door.

"Is that you, John?" she called.

"Yes; do you want me?"

"I want to show you something if you can spare a minute."

He followed her into the room, and she picked up the letter from the dressing table. "I thought you would like to see this; it's a letter from Nancy Legge. She was always so fond of Dick."

As she passed the letter to him her wrap slipped back from her throat, and hung away. Their hands touched, and it seemed to him that she had come very close. He could smell some warm sweet scent and see the line of her breasts, and there began to tingle within him a slow ugly desire. He pressed his elbows into his sides to keep his arms from drawing her to him. She saw that she had moved him, and her hands sought his and tightened upon them.

"John, dear! Love me a little. I am so lonely." Her voice was a hoarse enticing whisper.

He stepped back from her, and looked her in the eyes. Yearningly she gazed back, her mouth widened into a pitiful appealing movement. "John."

Why not take the woman? Why not take her, and then drop her: catch his train after half an hour's amusement? No, damn, her! No! He was through with the bitch! Abruptly he released himself and walked to the door. Then he turned:

"I'll take this letter away and read it while you dress. Then we'll have a talk." Without waiting for a reply he left the room, but as he went he knew that she was standing still; he knew that her arms were outstretched; he knew that he would have liked to have gone back.

He sat down on his bed after carefully closing the door, and lit a cigarette. So Ethel with her clothes carefully tumbling off her, and not at all bad-looking, still had an effect on him. Quite a narrow escape! There was need for him to fortify himself.

Doggedly he impelled his mind towards the old days. He forced it to seize upon one incident after another when Ethel had wounded his pride, his self-respect, his sexual vanity, his spirit – she had left no part of him untouched. He created them over again, brooded over them delicately, and having sucked their sting, called upon his brain to pronounce verdict.

No, not again. Never again. He had finished with being a fool. That particular sort of fool at least who let a woman walk over him and continued to grovel. His egoism had returned before it was too late. He would never forget, and never forgive himself, but anyway he had got clear. He had got clear even of being angry with her – except when his senses let him down. But that was only for a moment. It was not as if she had ever been a woman of any quality.

One of the eternal pains of life stirred within him. The pity was less that the sweets of life grew stale and tasteless, as that in reality they had never been sweet. In one's hunger one grasped so trustingly – and it was only a shadow after all. Shadows we are and shadows we pursue – that old tag! And sometimes worse than shadows; ugly common things that leered afterwards. All through one's life they raised their heads and leered and mocked because one had been fooled by them, taken in, humiliated, robbed … but what was the good of sitting there growing bitter? Poor Ethel, she wouldn't have too good a time of it. Impersonally he was sorry for her. Perhaps if he had been another sort of man he might have patched up some sort of life for them, together but separate. It would have satisfied her. But he couldn't go back. At bottom he took himself too seriously for that. And that was enough moralising!

Rising, he put his things together and packed his bag. He thought of his work with pleasure. He was glad he was going back to it. Work was the thing. It helped you to forget you were by yourself, living without Dick, living without a friend.

When Ethel came to him in the sitting room she looked as if she had been weeping. She had. Tears of rage they were, but they would serve their purpose. And her trump card was still to play.

He pulled out a chair for her, and looked at her with geniality. He felt kindly towards her as to a beaten foe. "About money, Ethel," he said, "if you will forgive my mentioning the matter. I shall be able to allow you the rather larger sum about which I wrote, and in the circumstances you won't be so straitened as I am afraid you have been. I would suggest you go away somewhere for a change – get a thorough rest somewhere.

"What do you think?"

She lifted her downcast head, and shot him the look of one who had been outraged in her tenderest feelings. "You are going to leave me alone? Quite alone in the world?"

John felt annoyed. There was going to be a scene then. "Hardly alone, my dear," he answered reasonably. "There is your mother ... and your father. And I cannot flatter myself that my presence was ever a great source of gratification to you. At least it did not appear so."

He was faced suddenly by a flushed indignant woman.

"You talk, you talk," she almost shouted. "But can't you think of me, of my position, left here by myself, a married woman with a husband in another place, who never comes to see her? I'm years off forty yet, much younger than you, and you condemn me to a living grave. Whatever I've done, if you don't love me any more – and you know you did at one time – have you forgotten everything? I don't deserve that. It's so cruel, it's wicked!"

He made no reply, only shook his head slowly; and at least something of his aloofness struck at her as if she had gone out to a cold place. Was she going to be beaten? By a man whom she had possessed as completely as she had possessed John? A man she had always despised because she could have her way with him?

Her excitement left her, and fear came into her heart.

"Aren't you a little sorry for me, John?" she asked after a pause. "Certainly I'm sorry for you," he answered promptly, and she could have killed him for the kindness in his voice. "I wish I could help you; but I know this, that no good would come for either of us in going back to the old life. It was too ugly. And I am afraid, Ethel, my mind is made up on that point."

"I won't persuade you. You must do as you think best. If you want to punish me! But there's one thing I'm going to ask you," she was speaking now with grave sadness, "let me have a baby to love, so that I shall not be left utterly alone."

He started and looked at her searchingly. A deep repugnance filled him.

"It's impossible," he said, and frowned unconsciously. What an indecent suggestion! And yet why? Perhaps she was sincere. Who could tell?

Ethel drew a deep breath. "Why is it impossible?" she asked with anger in her voice. It was so hard to keep her patience. "Why do you say that?" she asked again urgently, leaning forward. She trembled violently, and then burst into tears, whimpering weakly like a sickly child.

"You must, you must," she reiterated. "I must have another child. I can't be all by myself. I can't bear it."

He sat watching her with detachment. She didn't really want a child. She wanted to get hold of him. He felt suddenly tired.

With an effort he got up, and went over to her, putting his arm round her shoulder.

"Ethel dear, try and not cry. Life is very hard, I know. It is for us both. We made a mistake in the past, and now we must pay for it. But I can't do what you ask. I don't want any more to have a share in bringing some defenceless thing into the word for God and man to torture."

"You need never see it. I'll look after it entirely. I just want it to comfort me for all I have lost, for the terrible life you are leaving me to have."

His weariness deepened. "There are other things besides our own wants to consider," he said, turning away. "Anyway it's no use. I'm going out now for a bit. I want to get a timetable." He felt he was being brutal, but what other way was there?

Ethel ignored his last words. She was on him once more, gripping his arms, urging desperately. "Don't decide now. Let me have some hope. You can't live without hope. It's the wrong time to talk about it now. I see, I see! You can't think of anything but poor Dick. But later, later! Say you will think it over, and write to me. John! say you will! Else I believe I shall kill myself...." Her voice had risen to hysterical pitch.

Oh, to get away from this scene! "All right," he answered. "But remember I don't commit myself. I believe that what you ask is wrong. And now perhaps you will excuse me."

Left alone, Ethel quieted herself. He was a brute and a beast without decency or anything else. A man had no right to marry a woman and behave so. But she had done all she could. She had to face that. She had done all she could. It was difficult, but she must leave him alone now. This last hour or so she would have to be sweet and kind: yes, sweet and kind when she felt like murdering him! At least, thank God, she had given him some bad half hours in the past. But now, she had to leave a good picture: or else there wasn't an earthly [chance] of his turning up again. Viciously she went upstairs to bathe her face, and powder. Somehow, some day, she'd get her own back.

She played her final part efficiently enough, and her mother, watching, decided that at least she and John must have come to some understanding about the future. But as she stood, waving her handkerchief and watching the train gather speed and then disappear, a dull depression put out the fire of her rage. There was something so irrevocable in the way the train moved out of the station when its minute had arrived. She realised that nothing she could say or do would ever call it back. Things came – and went.

For a little while she occupied herself in wondering what chances she had missed, in rehearsing words she should have said, appeals she had failed to utter. She ought to have gone into his room at night, that was where she had gone wrong. She had nearly had him without that. Yes, she had been a fool.

But blaming herself was dreary unprofitable work. As she walked down the grey street which led to her mother's house, passing dull, grey, preoccupied faces, she felt herself grow old and tired. What use, after all, was Coué against life? Quietly she went upstairs to her room, locking her door behind her. Then she sat down and stared at the future. It might be, after all, that it held nothing for her. She had had lovers, heaps of affairs, married the sort of husband a woman ought to marry. A devoted fool. He had been blind for years to the way she had really diddled him. But now she had no lover, nor, for practical purposes, a husband. And every year reduced her chances of getting either. Even if she grabbed, took every chance that came, there would be more humiliations than triumphs, more rejections than conquests. And it was a husband, not someone to sleep with, she wanted.

Oh, it wasn't as if she was a fool. She had been a fool about Billy perhaps. But not again. She knew what she wanted. Security. A house of her own. A servant to order about. Other married couples dropping in for a game of bridge. Theatre jaunts. The knowledge that the local shopkeepers recognised her when she came in, and would come forward with a bright, "Good morning, Mrs. Stone. Now what can we do for you?"

She would like to entertain her friends, safe comfortable friends. She would leave the husbands alone. Just be the superior among them all. More looks, better figure, smarter in every way. To be consulted when they bought new clothes, and listened to with admiration. To have a good cook; plenty of cigarettes, sweets and magazines always about.

That was what she wanted now. And that was what she had a right to. What most women, inferior to her in every way, no looks, no brains or anything, had. But she had been cheated. She was nothing but a lodger in her father's house, with people always wondering behind her back where her husband was, and thinking that it seemed rather strange he never came to see her! Ethel clenched her fist, while her face took on an ugly look. Outside she heard a car approaching, the sound increasing and then dying away. She strained her ears to follow it, but now the silence was unbroken. Her mind followed its progress. She might be in it – ought to be in it. Being taken to a dance or show. The good times she and Billy had had together. Would she ever have any good times again?

Now with self-pity the tears came, and her body shook and shook. "Oh, God," she moaned and cast herself on the bed. She laid hold of the word, and kept repeating it as each wave of mortification broke. Sometimes she lay still, feeling nothing, and then, momentarily rested, she would writhe again, and even bang the pillow.

Her mother came to the door, knocked, and then tried the handle, but Ethel held herself still, refusing to answer; and Mrs. Wright, made wise by experience, went away. The room had become dark and her head ached. If only she hadn't taken so much for granted…

At last she arose and slipped out of her clothes, leaving them huddled and neglected on the floor. She wouldn't go down that evening; she wouldn't have any supper; she'd pay somebody back somehow; see, if she didn't; it was a beastly world … Only thing was she'd have a bit more money; perhaps she'd go abroad; she might meet someone; a rich American; didn't look her age … still attractive … never knew your luck. …

VIOLET RYDER

Violet Ryder got down quite punctually to breakfast that morning. The reason for this rare behavior was to be found in the new mauve crêpe de chine jumper she was wearing. For when Mrs. Ryder had banged her daughter's door on her way downstairs to light the fire and prepare breakfast, Violet had been arrested in the act of snuggling deeper into bed, as it might be into the last and therefore most tender embrace of a lover, by a sudden feeling that something pleasant attended on her waking. Then she remembered what it was: the new jumper; and eagerness came to her. She ought, she felt, to do the jumper the credit of allowing herself the full half hour for dressing. She was longing to see if she had really looked as well in it as she had seemed to do yesterday. Everything, including oneself, Violet remembered, had a way of looking so much prettier and more exciting by gas or electric light.

It was a chilly morning, especially when you were just forcing yourself out of bed; and so it was the jumper again which decided the daily question of whether just to wash the face, neck, and hands, or, stripping almost, but not quite, down to the waist, of having a really strenuous wash. In honour of the jumper – and even though she had washed thoroughly on the previous morning – Violet chose the more arduous course before hastening to put articles of clothing between herself and the unwarmed day.

But it was an unpleasant business, and Violet asked herself once again why couldn't hot water be brought to her properly in a jug? That was the least one might expect when you possessed the sort of bathroom in which the hot tap always turned on tepid water unless by special arrangement with mother, hours, or even days, before. And at this hour of the morning it would not even be tepid. Disgusting, washing the way she had to, Violet thought, sponging herself down with a screwed-up face of resentment.

She drew on her white woolen combinations[15] – another occasion for rebellion. (Why were they not at least opera tops[16] if she couldn't have silk vests for the winter? Like Miss Carey wore.) These were fitted, shameful to relate, with sleeves reaching nearly to the elbow. But since they were tight, Violet was able to roll them up, and thus minimise their offence. Sometimes she contemplated cutting them off; but since her mother washed her clothes as well as buying and paying for them, she only dared protest verbally.

Then she put on her two and eleven penny imitation silk stockings; then her band of cotton elastic fitted with suspenders; then her knickers, a sensible mixture of wool and cotton. Everything she wore underneath was repellant to Violet. There was a window of one of the small shops in High Street which about this time had no more ardent worshipper than herself. It was filled with silken lingerie of the most expensive kind; and as Paradise gains in splendour to the degree in which the world appears most foul, so did the contents of this window take on an unearthly, dazzling radiance to Violet standing without, arrayed in garments which the longer she lived the more she realised to be sordid and drab beyond bearing.

She cleaned her teeth hastily, another unpleasant task, and turned with relief to slipping on her white voile[17] petticoat. This she should really not have worn, for Mrs. Ryder had bought her daughter, the winter before, coloured skirts of thick cotton, directing that the white petticoats should all be put away for next summer. But Violet evaded this regulation with some success: the other petticoats were really too ugly, too old-fashioned, too unspeakable, to be borne.

Violet did not look at her best in her petticoat as she well knew. Her collar bones were too prominent, and her shoulders answered to the description of scraggy. On a November morning such as this her nose was condemned to

---

15 Combinations: An undergarment made of a camisole and knee-length drawers popularized in the 1880s.

16 Opera top: 'An artificial silk vest, with short or no sleeves' (*OED*).

17 Voile: A soft, sheer, cotton fabric.

redden, while her small childish face, always pale, looked pinched and sallow. It didn't matter much now, thought Violet, as there was only her mother to see her at such off times. But she had misgivings about the future when there might be a husband to keep in hopeless adoration.

Quickly then she hurried through the process of combing her hair, and fixing the slide in place. Now her skirt! Now at last the jumper! With tender fingers, Violet picked it off the chair, and slipped it on. It wasn't the jumper that was wrong, it was her face: she was too pale. That might be remedied. First she rubbed her cheeks hard, then she went to her handbag and took out a small green book of white powder leaves. One of these she detached, and passed over her nose, giving an extra dab to the corners of her nostrils as she had seen her great new friend, Miss Carey, do. Violet favoured that unsatisfactory method of powdering because powder still seemed rather daring to her; and she felt a little shy about passing a puff over [her] face in public, not to mention the circumstance that Mrs. Ryder would be horrified at the notion of Violet powdering at all. Only fast girls, girls who were no better than they should be, powdered, Mrs. Ryder always said.

She was better able now to receive the jumper; and with her looking-glass jammed, now backwards, now forwards, Violet began a prolonged scrutiny of herself. For a minute she stood close to the mirror; then she sat down and with the aid of a hand glass examined the back and side effect. Now up again, and alter the position.

"Hm!" she said thoughtfully. All her mind revolved round one tremendous question. "Did it suit her or not?" Not quite as much as it had seemed to do last night, certainly, but all the same it wasn't bad. Or was it? It seemed all right to her; but the depths of her cried out in appeal for sure and certain knowledge. Miss Carey, she reflected, always knew in a minute what suited her, and what did not.

Perhaps in a year, when she would be nearly nineteen, she would know too. Miss Carey said you could always tell if a new thing was right by the number of men who looked at you in the street. But the jumper was nearly hidden under her coat. It would be seen in the office chiefly.

She turned back to her bed and started to strip off the bed clothes. Should she wear it or not? Perhaps she looked a fright. And it was so embarrassing to go into the office with anything new on. The other girls would stare. But they might think she looked nice. She was drawn back to the mirror. But elation had gone, and in its place were only doubts and fears.

"Violet," called her mother from downstairs. "Hurry up! Breakfast!"

"All right," Violet called back. Her voice sounded cross, not so much because she felt cross, as because it was her habit to be always on the defensive with her mother. "That's done it," she thought. "It's too late to change it now. I may have time after breakfast if I feel like it."

Breakfast was served in the kitchen. Violet knew perfectly well that one should not eat breakfast in the kitchen, that if her mother had only possessed her own sense of fitness, it would be served in the dining room, and a maid kept to get it ready. Mrs. Ryder, however, was impervious to such a suggestion. She would merely say firstly that she couldn't afford a maid, and that as a matter of fact the girl who came in the mornings for three hours from half-past nine to half-past twelve was able to do all that was necessary in such a small house; and secondly that she was certainly not going to have two fires lit in the morning; and thirdly, and most crushingly, why didn't Violet herself give a hand instead of staying in bed while her mother did all the work? And at this point Violet, who felt uneasily that a girl in a book would probably have helped her mother as well as going to the office, usually grew absent-minded, thinking it as well not to pursue the topic further. All the same, she was convinced that it was simply meanness on the part of her mother to refuse to have at least one proper maid.

On this particular morning she found to her chagrin that she was likely to suffer for her virtue. Breakfast was not quite ready. It was, Violet knew, often not quite ready when her mother called, and usually she made generous allowance for such a circumstance. But this morning in her eagerness to get it over and return to her bedroom she had overlooked this probable state of affairs.

Mrs. Ryder was busy frying bacon, and the table was only partly laid. "Put on the cups and saucers, Violet," said Mrs. Ryder without turning her head. "And get the bread and butter from the cellar head."

Violet retraced her steps along the passage till she came to the cellar door without saying a word. "Good mornings" would have been considered an affectation in the Ryder household. As she returned and disdainfully planked the bread board, and the lump of butter in its green glass dish, on the table, she felt decidedly injured. Now the cups and saucers and plates. Why had she to *do* things?

Mrs. Ryder now saw her, and found something to say.

"Good gracious, what are you wearing?"

"That's the new jumper I told you about, mother. The one I got last night out of my own money that I had saved from the office."

"You are not going to the office in it, are you?"

"Why not?"

"Because if I know you, you'll get it mucked up in no time. And anyway if I were you I should have kept it for Sundays or when you are going somewhere special of an evening."

"*In* the evening, Mother. Not 'of an evening.'"

"Don't presume to correct me, Violet. If you knew a little bit better yourself how to behave, you'd do well."

There was a silence while Violet, arranging the table, set her lips stubbornly. It was no use explaining to her mother, of course, that while at home or on Sunday, horrible day, there was no one to see her except the chapel people, and old frumps, it was very different at the office. Her home was dull, untidy, and sordid; the office was clean and large and shining; a palatial place with people coming and going all the time. And it contained people of importance: girls who, most of them, were so much smarter than herself. And men, that exciting other sex, whose notice and banter were the rewards only of the attractive. Violet smiled inwardly with pity at her mother's ignorance as she had nowadays so often to do. Her mother just thought the office was a place to work in, where it didn't matter what you wore, so long as you were tidy!

They sat down. Mrs. Ryder said a short grace, which Violet disassociated herself from, first by staring out of the window, and then by taking up her knife and fork two seconds before the amen was reached. It was enough, you would think, that her mother didn't know how to do things, or even talk properly, without being religious into the bargain. Chapel, that was the worst of it! If it had only been C. of E.,[18] it wouldn't have mattered. No one hardly said grace nowadays. She would never be able to invite anyone she really admired, like Miss Carey, to the house while her mother said grace.

Frowningly she observed as she started to eat that the cups didn't match the saucers. Also the tablecloth was by no means clean. To vent her impatience she pointed out an ugly brown stain to her mother, the remains of spilt tea, and said impatiently, "Look at that! Can't we have a clean tablecloth? It's time, isn't it?"

"No, we can't," was Mrs. Ryder's sharp retort. "And considering it's you that did it, I wouldn't talk about it so much, I don't think. You must have slopped something at supper last night."

"No, I didn't," said Violet. "I only had a glass of milk, for one thing. And what's more, it was there before!"

"I wouldn't tell lies, Violet!" Mrs. Ryder poured herself out another cup of tea, and drank some down in silence. Then she spoke again.

"I really don't know what's come over you lately, Violet. Ever since you've started going to that office you've been unbearable. And let me tell you, Miss, I'm not going to have it. You'll speak politely to me or else I'll take you upstairs, and give you a good hard smacking just as I used to when you were little. You out to be ashamed the way you go on."

Uncontrollable tears stung the back of Violet's eyelids! She bent over her plate, and began to eat with feverish haste. The ignominy of being spoken to

---

18 C. of E.: Church of England.

like that. To have to put up with it instead of leaving the room immediately, leaving the house, for that matter, and for ever. Soon she regained her composure, but she herself would have described it as a bitter calm. She glanced at her mother. That grey wrinkled face with its unbrushed hair, still dark and plentiful! She malevolently noted the detail of an old purple velvet blouse with – would you believe it? – a yoke.[19] If someone came in now, they would think her mother was just a common elderly woman, untidy and slatternly.

"Why," she asked herself, "can't mother make herself look a bit more decent in the morning? Even if she has to light the fire her hair needn't be all wispy. And her blouse is all out at the back, though she doesn't know it. And I shan't tell her."

Mrs. Ryder, who preferred any conversation to no conversation, returned to the topic of the jumper.

"I don't think that mauve is quite your colour," she said. "Pink has always suited you better than mauve."

Violet kept on saying nothing. Her mother needn't think she had forgiven her for speaking to her like that. And anyway it wasn't as if *her* opinion about clothes mattered in the least. She didn't possess an atom of taste and never would.

Mrs. Ryder was aggravated by her silence. Her mind, which a moment before had been filled with thoughts of the day's occupations, now occupied itself with her daughter and her daughter's iniquities.

"I suppose you're not coming home this evening?" she said in a tone which expressed a grievance impatiently borne.

"No, I am afraid I shan't," said Violet, trying to make her voice sound remote and careless. "I am going to the Hippodrome[20] with Miss Carey."

"So I might have known," said Mrs. Ryder triumphantly. "So I might have known." Then, with a sudden change of key, "And might I ask does this Miss Carey, whoever she is, think it a right thing for you to go gadding about the town night after night while your mother has to sit at home by herself?"

Violet prayed for patience. She mustn't irritate her mother too much. "Why, you know perfectly well, mother, you nearly always have someone in. Mrs. Eiliott or Miss Lyons. Or you go and see someone."

"Yes, and it's a nice thing, isn't it, to have people asking evening after evening where you are, and that they never see anything of you nowadays, and me having to say that you are out again with someone from the office. Someone

---

19 Yolk: 'A part of a garment, made to fit the shoulders (or the hips), and supporting the depending parts, often of double thickness, of special material, or particularly ornamented' (*OED*).

20 Hippodrome: A London theatre and music hall founded in 1900.

that I haven't so much as seen and don't know whether she's fit company for a young girl like you."

Violet looked at her watch, and affected a preoccupied air. Now her mother was on an old unhappy topic, and one to which Violet had no effective retort. As if she were likely to ask Miss Carey to meet her mother! Miss Carey, who was used to champagne suppers, and things; or had been when she lived in London.

"If your poor father was only alive," said Mrs. Ryder, her thoughts turning down another accustomed channel, "I know he wouldn't allow such goings-on. Out most evenings a week at the pictures or theatre or something and sitting wasting your money in cafés. I tell you straight, Violet, you'll be talked about."

Violet went on munching busily. Silent disdain; that was how a lady would greet such talk.

Her mother gathered steam.

"It's all very well to sit there, not saying a word, and thinking you're very clever, I'll be bound. But listen to me. Whatever you're doing tonight, you must be home tomorrow night. I'm going out, it doesn't matter where, and someone must be left in charge of the house."

Violet thought for a second. Miss Carey was going out tomorrow with a boy: that fellow she had clicked with on the tram. Nothing else for her to do but come home, worse luck!

"All right, Mother. I'll remember."

"Mind you do," said Mrs. Ryder, unplacated.

"I'll have to rush now. It's nearly nine. Where are my shoes? In the cupboard? Right. I'll put them on after."

She went quickly from the room, while her mother lingered over the meal. She felt unhappy and irritated. How hateful every meal she took at home was! Instead of friendly charming conversation like you read about, nothing but nag! nag! nag! And then her mother complained that she liked staying out. Likely, wasn't it, that she'd rather be with her mother than nice people who didn't treat her like a little girl.

In the bedroom, her mirror made her forget her grievance. She looked at herself anxiously. One thing all this rowing at breakfast had done: it had given her more colour. She'd keep the jumper on. Going to the "hippo," it would look better than her navy blue dress.

She slipped on her coat, and then her pull-on felt hat. She didn't look very pretty. She wished she looked prettier. So that people would look at her, and think, "What a pretty girl," as she went along. Pull that hat more over the eyes! A little on one side! That looked better. It would have to do. She re-entered the kitchen noisily, and sat down to put on her shoes. Her mother was clearing the table.

"Now, Violet, you're not to be so late this evening. I won't have it. It's not fit for a girl like you to be out so late."

"All right, Mother. You'll see me at dinner if you've any more injunctions." ("Don't suppose she knows what the word means!")

"Goodbye."

"Goodbye."

She banged the front door behind her with a feeling of escape. She had left the sordid, the petty, behind her; and the world was in front: a world full of the most exciting possibilities.

Once in the street, she became, indeed, transformed. She was no longer a seventeen-year-old girl, named Violet Ryder, an unappreciated daughter of a dowdy and cantankerous mother, forced by unkind fate to dwell in one of the unfashionable suburbs of a provincial town. She was a charming creature, young and bright, to whom all sorts of things might happen at any moment. At least she knew she was young, and she hoped she was charming, or at least attractive; and when a man on the opposite side of the road looked across at her – not just a casual glance but a real stare – she was inclined to give herself the benefit of the doubt. She remembered that Miss Carey had said that what she lacked was self-confidence. If only she wasn't so shy, then perhaps she would be as successful with men as her friend was.

She mounted to the top deck of the tram car. The ascent still gave her a feeling of daring, for, before her office days, she had always gone inside. Her mother always went inside, and Violet used to have the feeling that men went on top, and that the woman's place was inside. But Miss Carey always went on top, and after all, why shouldn't she?

At the first stopping place a man with a long face, wearing eyeglasses attached to a black ribbon, got in. Violet had seen him waiting for the tram, and recognised him with a thrill: he was Mr. Arnold, who occupied a position of some importance at the office. Twice he had come to ask her to copy some mysterious figures, something to do with the advertising, she thought, into a book. The last time, Violet remembered, he had used her name, "If you wouldn't mind, Miss Ryder." Still he mightn't recognise her now. She hadn't known he had lived down this way. Or he mightn't want to see her. Some of these top men were awfully set on keeping their dignity. And though Mr. Arnold had the glamorous reputation of being separated from his wife, still he never took special notice of any of the girls. On second thoughts she had better pretend not to see him.

So she stared fixedly out of the window as she heard and felt him sit down on a seat well behind her. What a good thing he hadn't come and sat down in front of her! Because then he might have turned round suddenly and caught her eye. And she wouldn't have known whether to bow or not. And anyway she would have been sure to blush.

For some moments Violet thought disconsolately of her remarkable aptitude for blushing. There started into her mind one of those small "ads." From the back of *Home Chat*:[21] "Blushing. This miserable complaint permanently cured." Should she pluck up courage, and send for it? It was only threepence in stamps. Though, of course, you might have to send more afterwards. But how glorious it would be if she could only remain absolutely calm, and self-possessed; dignified and, perhaps, a little aloof, no matter who spoke to her or what they said.

Her thoughts took within their range another advertisement: "Lady Patty's Bust Developer." For a guinea this high-born person promised to send you in plain wrapper, and in strictest privacy, an instrument warranted to create pounds of flesh in the right places. Violet had an enticing vision of the disappearance of her collar bone, and in its place the appearance of –what did the ad. say? – firm healthy flesh. All the hollows would be smoothed out; and her salt cellar filled. And then when in the future, which would surely come, she wore evening dress, she would have no cause to be ashamed of her shoulders and neck. She ought to have more breasts, too. It was beginning to be fashionable to be slim, but men all seemed to admire Miss Carey much more than herself. And Miss Carey was what was called well-developed.

Violet looked absently out of the window. The tram was now nearing the town proper, and was passing row after row of small red brick houses led up to from the pavement by stone steps. Some of these front steps were undergoing the process of being cleaned. Violet's attention was caught by the ugliness of the position of the cleaner. "All feet and big behind," she thought. "Horrid dirty soles to shoes." She frowned, and thought a little. "I'll never, never marry," she decided passionately, "unless I can afford a maid to do that sort of thing."

The tram turned a corner, and entered the long thoroughfare which led to the centre of the town. Violet roused herself. Even at this comparatively early hour there were more people walking about; and the shops were opening, or had opened. Outside Samuels, the jewellery people, a young Jew was standing in his shirt sleeves. Violet stared at his dark face, and black curly hair; not bad looking in his way. Jews were funny, sort of different from anybody else. How

---

21 A best-selling women's magazine of the twentieth century known for focusing on cooking, fashion, knitting, etc.

would it feel to be kissed by one? Miss Carey said they were awfully passionate; hot stuff with a vengeance. She had had affairs with several, but she had had to drop them, because they had been out for all they could get. They weren't content with just kissing and holding hands. "Damn Jews!" Miss Carey had said contemptuously.[22]

They were just getting to that new hat shop. There it was! Now! Violet, peering eagerly, had a glimpse of a green velvet hat with a black osprey which seemed as if it would be just the thing for herself. She craned her head back in order to keep its appearance in her head as long as possible. Oh, if she only had enough money to buy a decent hat, a hat that looked sort of alluring and rakish, like that. It would make all the difference.

There was that turning which led to the Hippodrome. It was an unromantic red squat building, but Violet never passed near it without turning her head and gazing adoringly at its porticoed front. There had been a time, not so long ago, when the Hippodrome had been to her a magic pleasure ground, only to be entered on the most momentous occasions. Since Miss Carey had made friends with her she had gone nearly every week, and familiarity had almost accustomed her to its existence. But the rapture still remained. She stared at the huge poster opposite which displayed the charms of Miss Daisy Hood, comedienne. Miss Hood was wearing short white knickers, a white shirt with a red handkerchief scarf which showed her bare throat very effectively. And she sported a big white cowboy hat from under which she winked roguishly at all the passersby. Violet was filled with admiration. How dashing and thrilling she looked! Violet was glad she was going to see her that very evening. She liked comediennes best of all.

The tram turned another corner, and the town took on a more serious and solid aspect. Now it had grown from a rather shabby youth into a portly alderman wearing ribbons. There was the parish church, blackened by smoke, and surrounded by gravestones. And there was the fat round Yorkshire Penny Bank, and Poole's, the big drapers; and now, the square Town Hall with heaps and heaps of steps leading up to it. Also there were mostly men walking about now; men carrying bags, and walking hurriedly with down-turned heads. Violet became self-conscious, feeling that her share of the burden of the day was about to start. She pressed her lips together, and held her bag tighter as her thoughts went forward to the office. She remembered her new jumper, and saw herself returning from the cloakroom while heads turned to look at her. She wished now she hadn't put it on.

---

22 On this anti-Semitic moment in the text, see the Introduction.

The tram was coming to a standstill. Violet did not rise till she felt that Mr. Arnold had descended. Then she followed, keeping his back a safe distance in front of her.

She crossed the street, fixing her eyes on the imposing entrance to the office, which never ceased to gratify her as one of the members of the staff, and wearing what she wanted to appear an absorbed business-like look. The sort of look Mr. Arnold would be wearing as he entered. When she saw the commissionaire, who was tall and good-looking and rather romantic to Violet because he had lost an arm in the war, her heart tightened a little. She hoped very much he would smile, and say "Good morning, Miss," when he recognised her. He did, and Violet, smiling back, entered the office with renewed self-assurance.

But Miss Pringle, who had been on duty since nine at the front entrance desk for enquiries, was too busy talking to someone from outside to take any notice of her. Violet enviously noted her professional but smartly cut black coat frock, her waved hair, and her certainly rouged lips. Miss Pringle was one of the girls who always made her feel inferior. She was always getting off with the outside men who came to her counter; and Violet had been told that there was one awfully rich elderly man who took her out in his car, and bought her clothes.

She forgot Miss Pringle in savouring the pleasant feeling of bustle and important activity which greeted her on entering the main office. Miss Gillingham, the clerk who sat next to Violet, and who was always early, looked up from her place to nod, "Good morning," and Violet nodded back the more brightly because it was a patronising nod. It was the right thing and unavoidable to patronize Miss Gillingham because the poor girl was so very plain. And her clothes were awful. And her huge glasses made her look so odd.

Violet enjoyed, too, the sound of her feet on the marble floor as she went along to the cloakroom. As she left the main office, she met Mr. Jones, one of the advertising clerks, returning from the men's cloakroom; and though Violet did not theoretically approve of Mr. Jones – for all the girls agreed that he told too many dirty stories for it to be quite nice – she smiled up at him with the teasing look she instinctively put on when she met his eyes; and felt flattered and stimulated when, taking advantage of their momentary isolation, he squeezed her arm as he passed.

At the cloakroom mirror she found with approval that her cheeks were flushed and her eyes bright. She passed another powder leaf over and around her nose, and made her hair stick out round her face as much as possible. Now for it. She hastened back to her desk more rapidly than usual, and could not have told if she had attracted any attention or not.

But as she sat down she knew that Miss Gillingham's eyes had been caught by her jumper. Violet busied herself in taking out pen, pencil, and blotting paper, and took no notice. She suddenly felt that the right attitude was to affect a complete unconsciousness of anything she might be wearing. Women, wealthy women, who stayed in hotels, and went abroad, and got divorced, and had new or different things on every day, would accept their perfect apparel as a matter of course. Therefore it showed you weren't used to anything if you did otherwise.

All the same if Miss Gillingham was going to stare so, she might, Violet felt, say something about the jumper suiting her. Something like, "You do look well, this morning," or "I do like your jumper, if you don't mind my saying so, Miss Ryder." Just looking and saying nothing was ... well, not good manners. But then it was only Miss Gillingham, and it wasn't as if anything she thought mattered. Besides she was probably jealous.

For some time no one else showed any sign of taking notice of Violet. The first part of the morning always brought the office an air of deep absorption in pressing business which insensibly relaxed with the progress of time. But now clerks who had slipped in a few minutes late were working with an appearance of feverish energy designed to cover their personalities; and the steady light of the efficient punctual clerks, with their air of engrossment in their work, shone at its brightest. Others there were who disguised their early morning bad temper and dislike of their own kind by bending deeper than usual over their ledgers.

The men who walked along the corridor on their way to visit the manager or the cashier on some affair of importance strode along in business-like fashion, turning their heads neither to the left nor the right. In the distance could be heard the clicking of a typewriter, fast and furious. It was evident that it was transcribing some message of the utmost significance to the firm. Sometimes a clerk left his desk and with paper in hand went to consult one of his colleagues. Their heads would come together, and they would speak in short abrupt sentences. Then, with a short nod of agreement, one would return to his seat; and the other would bend his head over his desk once more, giving the visible effect of embarking again on a work of magnitude.

Violet reacted to the atmosphere surrounding her. She copied figures, of whose significance she was totally unaware, into a book; drew lines in red ink with assiduity; and filed letters that were from time to time handed to her with a deep gravity. Her work did not interest her in itself; it was not as a matter of fact very interesting work; but she still nourished the feeling of importance which being in a big office gave her. Besides, there were always thrills of a sort to be relied upon. The manager-in-chief, Mr. Pentwill, came into the office no less than twice, and spoke to different clerks. As soon as he was seen in their neighbourhood, Violet, in common with the rest, presented an appearance not only of working, but of offering up her whole life to her work. Nevertheless, she was aware of his every movement, and the exact moment when he retired from the scene. And when she heard his raised voice from the cashier's room, which was only built up half way, she nudged Miss Gillingham, and they both permitted themselves the half of a knowing smile. They all agreed subsequently that Mr. Pentwill had been in a fearful wax that morning, and that Mr. McDougall, the cashier, had been told off properly.

Then a little later, Violet observed Mr. Thornett, one of the outside advertising men, going past. Mr. Thornett was a handsome young man with deep blue eyes, dark hair, and a rakish air, who, Violet knew from the other girls, was considered a bit of a lad. But he had never so far taken any notice of her, and thus she was surprised and delighted when, sensing perhaps her gaze, he turned in his passage, looked her full in the face, and then gently let fall one eyelid.

Violet tried to administer a smile that should be at once encouraging and reproving. She found it hard for a few minutes afterwards to fix her attention on her figures; her mind was so confused. "Fancy!" she thought. "Mr. Thornett!" And then, "I wonder his daring to wink like that. Anyone might have caught him at it. Just like him!" As she ruled another line her mind asked, "Wonder whether the yarn Miss Carey told me about his having given a girl who used to go with him a baby is true?"

She thought how surprised her mother would be if she realised all her daughter knew about things. Only a little while ago, when she was at school, she had had all sorts of wrong notions. Being in an office made you understand about Life. You never knew what might happen. Heaps of people did that sort of thing before they were married (she wished she knew exactly what it was they did: of course, she guessed in a way; but she had to pretend she knew absolutely or else she'd be laughed at). And in London no one thought anything of people who lived together without being married. It was a courageous sort of thing to do. Defying convention.

She looked at the clock: twenty past eleven. She had nothing to do for the moment. It would kill time a bit if she went and washed her hands.

As soon as she was in the cloakroom, another thought occurred to her. No one would miss her for a little while if she slipped upstairs to see Miss Carey for a minute. It was better for her to do that than wait for Miss Carey to come and see her. There were too many bosses about downstairs; thought it was absolutely sinful, they did, if a girl stopped to have a word or two with someone.

Nominally Miss Carey occupied a secretarial post to one of the upstairs people. Actually she had very little to do; and in the mornings her chief, whose room she shared, could almost certainly be relied upon to be out. Violet knocked and entered cautiously, a carefully arranged sentence on her lips in case Mr. Lawton should be there. But she was fortunate. There was no one in the little room but the benevolent Miss Carey, and so she was able to relax from her business-like self, and turn from Miss Ryder into Violet, or, more accurately, "Vi.," as Miss Carey had christened her.

"Hullo," said Miss Carey.

"Hullo," said Violet.

"Got home all right last night?" asked Miss Carey perfunctorily.

"Yes. How did you get on with the man who spoke to you just when I was going?"

"Oh, him! He was a fellow who used to be about the place a lot last year. Before I knew you. I went out with him once or twice. But he bored me stiff. Coffee and cakes sort of person, you know, and always wanting to kiss."

Violet nodded understandingly. She looked appreciatively at Miss Carey's large white face, heavy jaw, and full throat. Miss Carey (it seemed more natural to think of her as Miss Carey than Joyce, somehow) had such an attractive air of good nature and easy-goingness. Violet on their first acquaintance had politely guessed her age at twenty five, and had confidently accepted twenty eight. A more experienced observer might have placed her at anything from thirty odd to forty something; but except at certain moments she could pass for much less.

"He's a traveler, I think," went on Miss Carey. "Not really a gentleman. But I used to get an occasional pair of stockings or something out of him, either for nothing or at cost price. So I stopped last night, as you had to go on account of your mother, as I thought he might stand me a drink in the Majestic. He pretended he had to catch a train or something; and wanted my 'phone number. So after we chatted a bit I just hopped it."

Violet was sympathetic. "I didn't think he looked much. But he might ring you up."

"I don't care if he does. Except of course for the chance of getting some clothes out of him cheaply. I'll remember you if I do."

Miss Carey leaned back and stretched her arms, yawning. Then she looked at Violet. "Oh, you've got it on, have you? It suits you ever so."

Violet felt warmed and comforted. "Do you really and truly think so?"

"Rather. Turn round a moment." Violet obeyed. "Yes, it fits you all right. Look here, we're going to the Hippodrome tonight, aren't we? We'll go to the Majestic and have a drink after. I'll treat you if no one turns up. I tell you why I'm being so generous. My aunt, you know the one in London I told you about, sent me ten pounds for my teeth being done. And the bill only came to six ten. Tell you how I got the extra. I got Hicks to make out a bill for ten – he's very sporting, I must say – and sent it to my aunt. Then he gave me a receipt and the change! Isn't it good?"

"Awfully good. You told me you were going to try that on, but I didn't know you'd really managed it. You weren't sure if Hicks would do it."

"No, I wasn't. But I talked him round. Told him what a close old devil she was, and let him kiss me. So he made the bill out for ten, and I sent it her. But I only got the cash this morning, and knowing how mean she is, I was afraid she mightn't send it all. It's all right now, though."

"That's great! I say, I'll have to fly. Pentwill was on the warpath this morning, and everybody's being furiously busy."

"Thank God, I don't work down there," said Miss Carey piously.

"You're damn lucky. Everybody knows that. Bye-bye."

"Bye-bye. Be good! See you this evening anyway."

Violet went back to her desk feeling much fortified. Saying "Damn," – she had said, "You're damn lucky" to Miss Carey – made her feel careless and dashing. None of the other girls in the office had Miss Carey's assurance and experience in dealing with men. Just treating them as things useful to pay for your meals and drinks and take you to shows. That was the way to get your own back for all the kissing and poking and pressing men wanted. At least they did from Miss Carey. The other girls thought it funny of her to go about so much with Miss Carey; they thought she was "fast." She was reported to have a husband somewhere, and be much older than she said. Violet didn't believe a word of it. It was just that they were jealous because Miss Carey dressed better than they did and had a little money of her own.

After twelve o'clock the pall of seriousness over the office lifted. The clerks who left early for their midday meal slackened in their work, or hurried to perform some final task in preparation for the coming of half-past twelve. The atmosphere of expectancy they generated corrupted the other clerks who didn't go out to lunch till later, but who felt as a consequence it was time they gave themselves some sort of a breather. Accounts and invoices and letters received a more divided attention while minds released into the channels most favoured. (What was there going to be for dinner? How was such and such a debt to be paid? Miss Grinstock had nice legs, but a little too thin. Now you could just see her garters! Was she doing it on purpose?) Affairs of the outside world noticeably intruded on the atmosphere, and disturbed its former calm. There was an epidemic of yawning.

Violet was told that a typewriter in the tiny office at the back wasn't being used, and that she had better go and practise. For a little while she applied herself strenuously to striking out over and over again, "Now is the time for all good men and true to come to the aid of the party." After a little fumbling, she was able to dash it off quite fast, and her attention wandered. She thought with pleasure of getting a pound a week as a typist to start, instead of her present ten shillings. Would her mother expect any of it? If she took ten shillings, she wouldn't be any better off than she was now. So that wouldn't be fair....

Going home to dinner in the tram and looking out at the shops, she felt more pessimistic over her future. After all, even if she did get to be typist; even took up shorthand and bookkeeping, and managed to earn two pounds a week in another year or two, what was there in it? Nothing at all! Her mother would have to have some of it for her keep; even if she was desperately daring, and left home, she could only just live on that. There wouldn't be any money left over for decent clothes, and going away for holidays, holidays where adventures might happen if you had another girl with you like Miss Carey instead of mother. If she could only go on the stage. That would be a real life full of thrills and adventures. How did one get on the stage? There were dramatic schools in London but they needed money. Hanging round stage doors; asking to see managers! That was what someone had told her was the best to do; to make oneself an absolute nuisance. But she wouldn't have the nerve for that. And then for musical comedy and revue there was dancing and singing: she couldn't do ballet dancing, and she hadn't anything special in the way of a voice. It was too bad, because heaps of girls on the stage hadn't even as much looks as she had. And she *was* young! But there it was.

Violet for the first time felt dismally that if she didn't look sharp, there was just a possibility that life might cheat her out of her dues.

She sighed aloud unconsciously, and looked out of the window. The road was grey and hard and dull: horrid little houses; neutral people walking up and down. Would her future stretch as sordidly? Perhaps she would end up married to some little clerk, and live in one of those beastly villas. Oh, never! She'd rather die.

After luncheon, which her mother *would* so tryingly refer to as dinner, Violet felt better. She only had time to eat very quickly, and her mother very properly was willing to let conversation take a back place to the main business of getting Violet back to the office by two. But, of course, there were the usual questions:–

"Have you been busy?"

"Oh, pretty fair. About the usual."

"What did you do?"

"Nothing special. Filing the correspondence for Mr. Raynes – that's the manager's secretary: and copying figures and things. And I practised typing."

"How are you getting on with it?"

"Oh, all right. Of course it's more difficult than it looks."

"Well, I hope you are trying."

"Yes, of course."

But before she left Mrs. Ryder had an order to give: "Now, Violet, remember I shall expect you home just after nine."

"Oh, mother! I can't possibly! You know I told you I'm going to the Hippodrome."

"Well, the first house is out before nine, isn't it? It must be, because the second house begins then."

"Yes, well….Just on nine. But Miss Carey and I always have a cup of coffee afterwards."

"I don't see why."

"Oh, well! I don't suppose you do. But it's jolly rotten not to."

"Sitting wasting your money in cafés! Well, half-past nine then."

"Ten, mother! It's an awful rush, you know."

"I shall expect you half-past nine, Violet. That's quite late enough. Goodbye."

"Goodbye, but I don't see how I can get back decently by then."

"You heard what I said, Violet."

Violet went out, banging the door as much as she dared. It was mean. Ten was her usual allowance. Anyway she hadn't promised she'd be in by half-past nine. If she got out of the Hippodrome at the usual time, about twenty to nine, she'd have nearly an hour in the Majestic. Miss Carey was going to treat her. That was really nicer than hanging round for men. You felt such a fool. At least she did. Miss Carey didn't seem to mind.

Her heart lifted in anticipation, and she looked smilingly out of the window. What a lot of different people there were in the world! There were too many not to provide promise that somewhere provision would be made for her. If not now and here, at least some time and somewhere. She wasn't eighteen yet. She had heaps of time.

The office also shared her hopeful mood, for the longer, most trying part of the day was over. The promise that freedom lay ahead, that no day lasts forever, spurred some to work harder; others, where it was possible, to regard their tasks with a detached interest. There were a few, of course, those to whom the time at the office provided the chief fulfillment of their being, who pursued their course untouched, their moral fibre neither weakened nor strengthened by the passage of time.

Violet was not one of these. Early in the afternoon the cashier had spoken curtly to her, and so darkened her horizon. She had copied a figure wrongly and caused, it appeared, a good deal of trouble.

"Please don't let that occur again, Miss Ryder. You must be more careful," he had said dismissing her coldly. This was enough to make Violet decide finally that she hated the office. She had for some time suspected that it was dull, so far as her work was concerned; now it seemed it could also be unpleasant. She resolved in her gloom that the best thing would be to get married as soon as possible. If not, she would get away somehow, and do something to show people she was not a fool. Perhaps she'd go to London. Making such a fuss over a figure! One little figure!

She was the first to leave her desk when the clock at last in its tedious progress came to the hour of freedom. She put on her hat and coat hastily, speaking to no one, and in a minute was in Miss Carey's room.

Miss Carey was a soothing spectacle. She was leaning back in her chair smoking a surreptitious cigarette. Her chief had gone some time ago; she had performed the scrap of work he had left her, and had just finished writing to one of her male acquaintances. She looked, and felt, on good terms with the world.

Violet watched her carefully adjusting her hair, and then rouging her lips. She could not help feeling that the lines had fallen to Miss Carey in more pleasant places than to herself. Admirers, the sort that attracted men, very little work, good clothes, an aunt who really seemed pretty generous in spite of all Miss Carey said – why, she had everything practically that a woman could want. Some women, most women perhaps, wanted husbands; but Miss Carey obviously had a much better time than if she was married. Perhaps she was married: It might be true: still, anyway, she didn't let her husband interfere with her freedom.

The only thing which she had better than Miss Carey was being ten years younger. And perhaps she didn't really score even there. It was better to be mature and self-confident like Miss Carey. Miss Carey hadn't a mother who was always ordering her about and treating her like a kid. And now the people at the office were doing the same.

She told Miss Carey about the disgusting behaviour of the cashier. Miss Carey sympathised, a trifle vaguely perhaps, but still she did administer consolation. The point she made was that it was no good worrying about what these people said or did.

"It's a pity," she concluded, "that these nagging old maids, because that's what they are with their botheration over trifles, haven't got something better to think about. Being cooped up in an office, a provincial office, all their lives, makes them narrow-minded, I suppose."

Narrow-minded and provincial were favourite terms with Miss Carey, and before now they had deftly explained away for Violet ideas, people, and customs, which in their previous darkness she had believed unchallenged. If you only kept on thinking of objectionable people and things as narrow-minded or, more deadly even, provincial, then you needn't worry much what they said. She went downstairs and out of the office, in the splendid company of Miss Carey, with an enjoyable sense that she was leaving her inferiors behind.

For splendid she felt Miss Carey was in her black tailor-made costume and small white hat. Other people couldn't afford to wear white hats in a town like this because of getting them dirty so soon: Miss Carey could! It was pleasant to be walking along the lighted streets of an early November evening crowded with people hastening homewards in company with someone who received the salute of so many masculine eyes. Sometimes Violet had felt just a bit jealous – a pang at her own comparative insignificance – at this moment she was too fond of Miss Carey to mind. Was not Miss Carey, Joyce, the only friend she had in the world? Her mother, with her perpetual nagging, "nattering," as she herself would have said, was against her, and now so was the office. It had pretended it wasn't; people had been decent when she first came; it admittedly had a superficial appearance of interest and glamour; but underneath it was just as much a tyrant: a cold, hard tyrant that exacted its perpetual pound of flesh under threat of disgrace and dismissal.

She would have liked to discuss the fundamental beastliness of the office with Miss Carey; but she felt her friend might be bored. Would think she was just like the other girls downstairs whom she had dismissed as absolutely brainless, and unworthy of her acquaintanceship. Violet was different; she had been to a boarding school, and had brains. It was necessary that she should live up to her reputation.

Anyway, Violet mentally agreed, it would be out of tune with their present freedom to go on yarning about what was left behind: done with for another day. Now was the time when they started to live. Now, when the street lamps were shining with pleased excitement; now, when the shops were putting up their shutters; now, when other girls in two's and three's were passing, talking eagerly, and often laughing shrilly; now, when men were walking slowly, many of them, with observant eyes.

Men did look different in the evening; it was as if they had left off being their ordinary selves; had been changed from men into representatives of Man, something inexplicable and exciting...

Oh, yes, the pulse of life was beating faster now; and all this expectant atmosphere was somehow centred in Miss Carey. She belonged to it; she was at home in it; and Violet was glad, *glad* to walk in her train, and pick up such crumbs as would be vouchsafed her. "Joyce, you do look pretty," she said, squeezing her companion's arm fervently, and Miss Carey replied, "I don't think!" and then, more seriously, "But this hat does suit me, don't you think so? I was afraid it might be trying, the white you know, but it's all right at night, isn't it?"

"Absolutely," said Violet, and then, eager to please, "Did you see the way that fellow stared at you, the one who passed in a bowler, with a brown face?"

Miss Carey nodded. Miss Carey saw everything. But Miss Carey was still good-humoured and frank. Not a bit stuck up!

They had passed the Town Hall now, and were able to walk more quickly. Violet sniffed the autumn air with appreciation. There was a faint mist abroad which made everything glow the brighter. The street lamps were tall and proud under the grey sky: it wasn't such a bad old city, after all.

Miss Carey drew Violet's attention to a pair of ankles waddling in front of them. "Hargreaves says that women with thick ankles ought to be exterminated."

Violet laughed appreciatively. A picture of Hargreaves, one of the upstairs men to whom Miss Carey had introduced her, appeared in front of her: short, broad, with a heavy reddish face, and small twinkling eyes, walking always as if he were pushing the lower of part of his body in dignified fashion in front of him. He had a deep rich voice which lifted his frequent judgments into the more rarefied air of profundity. Hearing his latest exordium, Violet felt it to be a criticism of life which directed her another step up the ladder leading from the utilitarian and moral standards of her mother and the office. It wasn't as if she herself were incriminated. Her ankles, thank God, were all right.

They crossed the road, and turned up the side street leading up the Hippodrome. It was pleasant to walk past the queue waiting for the cheaper seats. When her mother had taken her, she had often had to stand in a queue herself: her mother was so mean about that sort of thing; now she was exalted even beyond those who made their way regally through the front doors, but had to plank down coins before they were admitted. Miss Carey had been lent one of the office passes by Mr. Lawton.

She tried to look unconcerned as she followed her sumptuous friend through the front doors; but as Miss Carey showed the pass at the box office and received tickets in return, she could not help looking round, half guiltily, half pleasurably, to see if there were any watching eyes to be impressed or made curious. To be on the free list! To get stalls for nothing! As your right! The office certainly had its points, she grudgingly admitted.

A deep satisfaction with her immediate lot possessed her as she walked along the corridor, and felt her feet tread the crimson carpet. She loved the jazzy pattern of the wall paper too: so exotic, so barbarous, so, thought Violet, piling up her epithets, boldly artistic. There were pictures of actors and actresses on the walls: old music-hall favourites winking and curtseying, or looking soulful, and she would have liked to stop and examine them, but as usual there was no time. Now they were at the entrance to the stalls; the strains of the orchestra were fittingly ushering them into the feast; the programme-seller was Eton-cropped[23] and daringly made up, a fitting hand-maiden to the

---

23 A hairstyle popular in the 1920s, featuring close-cut, often slicked-back hair. Named for Eton students, who were known for wearing their hair slightly longer than was fashionable for boys at the time, this cut was also known as a 'boy bob'. Jazz singer Josephine Baker was likely its most famous wearer.

courts of pleasure. And the electric atmosphere of an audience prepared and eager to be entertained rose at Violet and took her into its warm embrace. She followed Miss Carey to their seats decorously enough, but with a dancing heart.

"I am sure it's going to be good," she said, as soon as they were seated. Miss Carey beamed amiably back, noting that her young friend's eyes were shining. "One thing about the kid," she thought, "if she hasn't much go, she *does* enjoy things." She felt benevolent, and proceeded to amplify the programme. Violet listened respectfully: Joyce had seen most of the turns before; she could remember when she had last seen a certain comedian at the Victoria Palace in London, and Violet was made to feel superior to the people around her. Was she not sitting next to a Londoner, which was the same as a cosmopolitan? One of Joyce's often expressed articles of faith was that she, Joyce Carey, was a cosmopolitan, which meant that she was at home anywhere, in any society. And Violet, listening to her easy talk of theatrical stars – who had married who; who had divorced who; who was living with who – would have been the last to deny her knowledge of the great world.

Suddenly the lights went down, and Violet thrilled to the immediate hush which followed. Unthinkingly, she leant forward eagerly, and then remembered that the first turn was only a card juggler. She had learnt from Miss Carey that the first turn was always negligible, and that it was a mark of a lack of sophistication to take any notice of it, that is, *special* notice. And card juggling demanded too much attention; besides, Miss Carey had seen the same tricks over and over again. Violet therefore converted her gesture into a jerk, and leant back, permitting only a bored glance to rest on the stage.

Miss Carey nudged her: "Look," she said.

Violet followed her eyes, and saw Miss Pringle from the front office entering, wearing beautiful white fox furs. Behind her and with her was a well-dressed man about forty with a clean-shaven long face, and a superior air of non-recognition of his surroundings which Violet noted with envy and appreciation.

Both girls watched Miss Pringle take her seat, and their gaze became more intent as they observed that Miss Pringle's escort was buying from the attendant one of her very largest boxes of chocolates. Two pounds at least!

"Who's the man?" whispered Violet to the all-knowing Miss Carey.

"Don't know. Not one of her usual, because I haven't seen him about."

"Wonder where she picked him up?" said Violet, in Miss Carey's phraseology.

"Wonder where she got that fur?" returned Miss Carey, in a tone of infinite meaning.

Violet giggled, because a giggle seemed the right answer. But she suddenly felt a little cold and troubled. Where had Miss Pringle got her fur? Of course she was jolly lucky to have it. Made her look like a rich girl, like a rich chorus girl. On the other hand, perhaps she oughtn't to have had it: Miss Carey seemed to imply she had done things for it. She would have liked to be able to dispose of Miss Pringle, but envy was her predominating emotion. Would anyone ever give her a fur, or expensive jewellery? She turned back to the stage, not quite so happily as before. Somehow Miss Pringle's triumphant entry had rather taken the edge off things; even off the free tickets.

The juggler went, bowing his thanks for a very moderate amount of applause. Violet picked up the programme from Miss Carey's lap, and examined it critically. Perhaps it wasn't going to be a good show.

The next turn was a girl of no outstanding gifts who, clothed in a kilt, sang a Scotch song; appeared again in a Welsh tall hat and sang a song that might have been Welsh, though it didn't seem so; was, as she was expected to be, on her third entry an Irish colleen in green and red, who danced even more vigorously than before; and, after having been scrupulously fair, became an exhilarated Yorkshire girl, in which rôle she received the most applause. Then a male dancer who was very tricky with his feet, as Miss Carey observed, but whose patter was poor; and then a woman ballad singer, whose most noticeable feature, the two girls agreed, was her lovely evening cloak.

Violet, sitting back, a little resentful at the way things appeared to be going, longed for some chocolates. Miss Pringle kept on eating them all the time. Not of course that she was jealous of Miss Pringle. Miss Pringle wasn't really a lady, probably had only been to a board school or something like that. Most of the girls at the office had only been to council schools; and the girls like that met heaps of boys and started going out with them awfully young.

Still, Miss Pringle was rather pretty. You couldn't deny that. When she turned sideways to say something to her man and was looking up. A good profile, much better than she, Violet, had. And lovely teeth. Was that why she was always smiling up at men at the front counter?

Violet suddenly felt ashamed. Wasn't she being rather horrid and mean? And thinking horrid and mean things? She turned back to the stage, and concentrated her attention on the singer. All the same, she rather wished Miss Pringle hadn't come in.

After the interval the programme started to brighten up. The first turn was a musical quartette; and the women were plain – Joyce was exceedingly amused by their looks and their clothes – and the men frightful sticks, but they had rather a nice setting; and the shaded lights and smooth black grand piano made the violin solo, and the piano solo, and the singing very soothing. The members of the quartette who didn't happen to be doing anything, bestowed themselves in graceful attitudes about the stage meanwhile, just as if it were a private drawing room. When one of the men was playing the piano, accompanied by one of the women on the violin, the third woman sat on the couch provided, gracefully leaning back and looking meditative. After a while the other man, who had gone off the stage, came back and stood behind the woman on the couch with his arms crossed, just like, Violet thought, a late visitor who had dropped in. They weren't perhaps very good – Violet wished she knew more about classical music – but they had a pleasant air of repose and dignity. She started to occupy herself with a vision of a tranquil, well-ordered, and well-off existence in which composed men and women in evening dress had musical evenings, and chattered politely to each other in low tones after beautifully served meals, with butlers and things just taken for granted. Such a life might be superior to any other more adventurous existence; for, though quiet, it was certainly aristocratic and beautifully superior to anything girls like Miss Pringle would ever have. People like that would think Miss Pringle very common. You would wear nice clothes, not just in the evening, but all the day, from the very moment you got up. And there would be a lovely garden, and people showing each other flowers quietly, no one ordering anybody about – except, of course, the servants. Speaking gently, discussing intellectual problems, and then saying, "What about a little music?" Or, "Miss Ryder, you recite so beautifully."

It was a pity the refined musical quartette broke up her picture when, for their final encore item, three of them advanced resolutely to the front of the stage, and sang "Land of Hope and Glory" vociferously to the pianist's accompaniment. They put much more gusto into it than she felt was quite suitable for such perfect ladies and gentlemen. She agreed with Miss Carey when the latter said, "That old thing!" in a tone of deep contempt. They also bowed themselves off the stage much too effusively, appearing before the curtain a great many times hand in hand. Still, there was a lot of applause, so they must have been very good, and Violet joined in the clapping to a moderate extent.

"A bit too classy for me," said Miss Carey. "Still, the little one hadn't a bad voice. What next?"

The number went up at the side of the stage. Violet consulted the programme. "Daisy Hood, the popular comedienne."

"Now we ought to get on a bit," said Miss Carey with relief.

The house seemed to share her opinion, for it relaxed, and then seemed to be reinforced, swollen with expectation, as the orchestra burst into a tune of the kind that, wily-nilly, sets feet tapping and voices humming. Now at last Violet could permit herself with some justification to sit forward eagerly, her eyes fixed on the rich rose-coloured curtain, waiting for the moment when it would magnificently swing back.

Now it was drawing apart, disclosing a painted woodland scene. From the wings sauntered on coyly, and yet with an exquisite assurance, a rakish figure with a wide white soft-brimmed hat turned up in front; a pink and white silk shirt, very much open at the throat, and pink silk shorts ending just above the bare knees. The most enchanting mixture of principal boy and coon costume[24] as worn by Miss Daisy Hood. And what roguish, rolling eyes, and what perfect white teeth, and what an intimate swagger!

No wonder applause broke out. Daisy advanced to the front of the stage, with a bow and the most comfortable and good-humoured of smiles. It assured everybody that someone had arrived who knew them, and was going to give them what they wanted; someone who could be relied upon not to let them down.

The conductor waved his baton, and the song started. It was just an ordinary song, which Violet had often heard sung, whistled, bawled, hummed, and played, even on the barrel organ, before. Now she heard it sung as it should be sung: a little yearningly, a little wistfully, full of a touching appeal, until you got to the chorus, and then off with a triumphant swing stirring the blood into joyous sympathy:

"I'm going BACK
To the SHACK
Where the Black-Eyed Susans grow,
They're all AROUND
On the GROUND
Where I left them
S'long ago.
The honey bees all seem to say
You'd better be (*what a gorgeous mouthful she made of those b's*) gettin' busy foolin'
   around.
To stroll AGAIN
Down the LANE (*now she was starting off, hat pushed well down*)
To that quaint old rustic seat
Will be a TREAT."[25]

---

24 Coon costume: Likely a reference to a rustic outfit, or possibly to the costume worn by blackface minstrels, white actors who wore makeup to represent black people. Popular in the nineteenth and early twentieth centuries such performances (as well as the slur 'coon') died out of popular usage with increasing racial awareness in the mid-twentieth century.

25 'Where the Black-Eyed Susans Grow', Words by Dave Radford / Music by Richard A. Whiting, 1917. The song was later popularized by Al Jolsen.

She sang the chorus twice through, and then started the second verse. All the time she was singing Violet was just longing for her to get to the chorus again. And so was the audience, apparently, for when she started to dance so lightly and buoyantly with the cleverest little runs and leaps, it took up the tune she softly hummed, and threw the words back to her, at first softly, and then gradually louder. Violet and Miss Carey joined in; and Violet could have gone on humming and watching Daisy's shrugs, her beckoning eyes, her twinkling feet, and listening to her warning, "You'll be losin' Yer little Susan," for ages and ages. But even a good number has to end, and Miss Hood, waving her hat in farewell, and displaying delicious auburn curls, raced off to change for her next song.

This seemed as if it would really and truly be a mournful one. For it, Daisy wore a blue taffeta silk frock, standing out widely at the hips, and sprinkled here and there with tiny, pale pink rosebuds. She looked very sweet and modest, and it appeared she had a grievance against her boy. He was neglecting her. He hadn't been at all like himself lately; and the audience would have felt properly annoyed on her behalf if they had not been reassured by the feeling that it was only a joke. As if any of Daisy Hood's boys could possibly neglect her for a moment! And they were confirmed in their faith that it was only a delicious bit of fun when, after singing the chorus for the first time sadly and meltingly, looking the sweetest of hurt sweethearts, Daisy suddenly gave one of her entrancing winks, and let herself go thoroughly, parodying the spirit of the words with exaggerated pouts and shrugs:

> "WHY do you leave all the LOVIN' to me?
> WHY can't you do yer little share?
> 'Tisn't fair! 'Tisn't fair!
> WHY do you leave all the KISSIN' to me?"

The audience loved Daisy like this. And she knew it. And suddenly she started to make love to one of their representatives. Leaning with divine nonchalance against one of the side pillars, with a deep blue spotlight turned on her, she pointed an accusing finger at a baldheaded man in one of the boxes opposite:

> "You used ter bill and coo
> Like other lovers do,"

She reminded him sadly; and then, plaintively, "WHY do you leave all the lovin' to me?"[26]

---

26 Possibly a contemporary song: title and provenance unknown.

The audience shook with delighted laughter as the cruel limelight picked out the man in the box. Nothing could have pleased them better. One of their number was being made a fool of. For their sakes! And the bald man, though at first inclined to blink and dodge the light, gave himself up to the joy of being fooled. He smiled fatuously back. He even wagged a beckoning finger, at which the audience roared and roared again. He leaned out of the box; but then suddenly, Daisy was away, dancing like an irresistible fairy.

Another song, a funny one this time, and then it was over. They recalled her again and again. She ran backwards and forwards and bowed. Then she just stood and kissed her hands to them. And finally, as the clamour persisted, she just slipped her head through the curtain and gave her celebrated wink. It was positively her last appearance. Alas, that it should be so!

After this, everything was a little in the nature of an anti-climax. There was a small comedian with a simple-looking face who made lots of jokes; and though sometimes Violet didn't understand them ("He's always very suggestive," said Miss Carey), she laughed when everybody else laughed.

And besides Miss Carey enjoyed him so much. Violet, listening to her friend's unrestrained mirth, could not help laughing more loudly than she felt inclined to do for companionship's sake.

The final turn was a company of trick cyclists, the best part of whose turn to Violet was the lovely valse[27] the orchestra played over and over again. A beautiful sighing sway it was. She hadn't much attention to spare for anything else, but she felt happy, and tolerant of all things.

She was disturbed out of her placidity by feeling that it would soon be all over. In two's and three's, the people who never waited to the end furtively left their seats, and made their way hurriedly to the door marked "EXIT." Glimpses of the backs of these vanishing forms started the mournful sense of disintegration. People averted the better half of their attention from the stage in order to fumble for hats, and other detached belongings. The cold unmoved air of the huge outside world trickled in, and performed its unsocial work of metamorphosing a snug well-warmed community into a crowd of solitary responsible individuals with trams to catch and suppers to eat.

The cyclists trooped off. The curtain fell for the last time. The band hastily turned from the seductive valse to the stern clang-clang of "God Save the King." Violet and Miss Carey occupied the time in adjusting their hats, and powdering their noses. The show was over.

---

27 Valse: Another word for the waltz.

They drifted in their turn towards the door. Violet remembered Miss Pringle, and turned to look, but she had disappeared. "Wonder where Miss P. has gone," she said.

Miss Carey gave one of her woman-of-the-world shrugs. "To have a drink, I expect. That is, first of all," she added.

The street was cold and dull after the theatre. It always was, of course. People looked shabby and discontented and plain. And Violet felt everybody was walking too fast. It was undignified, too, the way they pushed to get into the trams.

Violet took Miss Carey's arm as they walked back towards High Street. She, at least, felt and looked warm and comfortable. Nothing pinched and dowdy about her. "Where shall we go?" she asked her. "Remember I simply daren't be in later than ten. Mother said half-past nine."

"Well, it's only twenty to nine now," said Miss Carey. "Rather a short show. Don't worry, Vi. You've got nearly an hour."

They had arrived at the centre of the town, and some of that sense of anxious hurry which had oppressed Violet lifted. There were plenty of people here, mostly young, who appeared to be waiting like themselves for something to turn up. Couples strolled about; sometimes arm in arm, laughing loudly together; sometimes staring at other people with a kind of suppressed excitement. The girls in their two's and three's and the young men in their two's and three's were very conscious of each other; though at times they pretended a deep absorption in themselves.

Violet tingled again to a feeling of freemasonry.[28] It was not the freemasonry which had united the audience at the Hippodrome; it was less comfortable, and more exciting: you felt it in the pit of your stomach.

Miss Carey slackened her steps as they approached the Cinema de Luxe, and looked urgently about her. "I wish to Christ," she said, "I could see someone I knew who'd stand us a drink in the 'Met'."

The "Met" was the town's leading hotel. As expensive to stay at as the Station Hotel, and not nearly so stodgy. Violet still thrilled slightly when she heard it mentioned. It had a terribly bad reputation. All the leading theatrical stars stayed there. And the more affluent of the town's bad women – prostitutes, they were called, Violet knew, but they were too magnificently arrayed to be thought of as prostitutes – went there to "get off." Violet had never been, though she knew Miss Carey had often gone. She felt she was on the

---

28 A reference to Free Masons, who had a reputation as an organization for secret communications, signals, and meetings. Used here to suggest Violet's sense of involvement in something secretive, exclusive and almost illicit.

brink of a great experience; the Majestic had hitherto represented her highest flight.

"Don't you feel like the Cinema Café'?" she asked.

"No, I feel more like a real drink. Or a coffee and a Benedictine. I'll treat you myself all right as I promised, only we would get more if we saw someone."

They walked up and down before the Cinema several times. Its neighbourhood represented the great rallying ground of the town's youth and beauty of an evening, and there were plenty of loiterers. But so far as the male loiterers were concerned, standing and staring seemed all they required; and Miss Carey began to grow disgruntled.

"What a crew!" she exclaimed. "As mean as hell. They'd fall down dead rather than spend sixpence. Provincial louts."

Violet experienced sensations of mingled shame and boldness. At the curb stone there was a group of young men standing, whom they had just passed. One was staring after them. Miss Carey looked round and caught his glance, but Violet, watching, saw that he immediately turned away. Then a general laugh went up from the whole group. Violet wondered uneasily whether it concerned them. After all, it was rather beastly to be walking up and down in front of young men like this as if you were for sale. Specially when there were no buyers. Suppose someone like Mr. Arnold passed and saw them.

A woman standing in the shadow of the side entrance to the cinema with a very red mouth stared at Miss Carey, and then suddenly smiled at her. Miss Carey looked full at her but walked on without altering her expression. "Do you know her?" asked Violet. "Only by sight, of course," said Miss Carey. "She's one of that sort – you know. Like her cheek to smile at me. But she's often round there. Let's turn back just once more."

They turned, and Violet restrained her impulse to walk fast. After all, she and Miss Carey were quite different to other girls who did the same thing. They weren't trying to get off because they were bad, or even because they wanted to know men and didn't mind being kissed. They were just trying to get some fool, as Miss Carey would have said, to stand them a drink. Doing them down, and not being done yourself, it was. Therefore they were superior to these common-looking young men who stared them up and down, and even winked, but who never made a move. Still, Miss Carey *had* said she would treat her; and it would be much nicer to go in by themselves.

She felt her arm nudged. Two young men were coming towards them, one rather smartly dressed, wearing a soft hat. The other looked duller; fair and insignificant, wearing a light mackintosh. As they drew level, Violet, not daring to look herself, felt that Miss Carey was staring at the dark young man, and that he was looking back. They had passed now, but Miss Carey was walking slowly, and looking round.

Violet, looking sideways over her shoulder, saw that the young men had come to a standstill. The dark one was approaching; he was going to raise his hat. Lord! Now they were for it.

She stood still with Miss Carey, but stared hard the other way. It was really hateful, hateful and thrilling at once. Suppose anyone saw them from the office. But even if they did, how were they to know that the men weren't friends of Miss Carey's? Oh, well, perhaps it didn't matter anyway!

"Good evening," said one of the young men.

"Good evening," said Miss Carey affably.

"Where are you two off to?" said the dark young man.

"That's it," said Miss Carey. We were just wondering what we would do."

There was a brief pause. Violet felt the other young man was studying her, so feeling ill at ease, she looked at Miss Carey. She would have to do it all.

"We have just been to the Hippodrome," said Miss Carey conversationally.

"Oh, have you? What sort of show was it?"

"Not too bad. Daisy Hood is on, you know."

"Oh yes, Daisy Hood," said the other young man suddenly. "She's a bit of all right, isn't she?"

He had addressed his remark to Violet and, flattered, she felt that a reply was necessary. "I think she's very good," she said.

As soon as the words had fallen from her mouth she felt they had sounded still and prim, and her voice seemed to have chilled the atmosphere. The fair young man made no comment but removed his gaze to Miss Carey. It was generally felt it was up to that lady to take charge of affairs. And she responded.

"As a matter of fact," she said, "my friend and I were just thinking of going into the 'Met' for a drink."

The idea did not seem to arouse enthusiasm.

"What about coming for a walk?" said the dark young man, with an air of getting down to business.

"I'm sorry," said Miss Carey, and Violet felt proud of her friend. "That's imposs. My friend has to be home by ten."

The dark young man looked at Violet for the first time, and she was made to feel that he had found her wanting.

"Well, even so, there's time for a stroll," he said, turning back to Miss Carey. "And you needn't be in by ten, I suppose."

There was a slight emphasis on the pronoun which Miss Carey ignored.

"You see," she said, with a little laugh, "we're just dying of thirst. If I don't have something to drink, I shall expire."

"Will you come for a walk?" said the young man, ignoring her words and looking her full in the face.

"Only as far as the 'Met," said Miss Carey, gently but firmly.

"Well, we mustn't keep you," said the dark young man politely. There was a short pause. Hostility had evidently arisen between the opposing sexes, but it was difficult to break away.

"Come on, Fred," said the other young man, showing an unexpected determination. "We're not wanted."

His friend yielded to the inevitable. "Well, so long," he said jauntily to Miss Carey. "That is, if you won't change your mind."

"Goodbye," said Miss Carey coldly.

The dark young man felt there was something undignified about their exit, and tried to cover it up. "See you again, one evening, perhaps," he suggested as he moved off.

Miss Carey did not deign to reply. She seized Violet's arm, and turned her in the other direction.

"The bounders!" she commented, softening her epithet out of regard for her companion's youth. "Never mind, I'll treat you myself. We won't wait any longer. Go for a walk! I should say so! Remember what I've told you, Vi. Never go for a walk with any of these fellows. They're all out for one thing."

Violet nodded. "I didn't like them," she said.

"No, very common!"

They pushed open the heavy entrance door of the "Met" and walked along the corridor. Violet gloried in the feel of the carpet, thicker even than that of the Hippodrome – or at least better looking. And how pleasant it was to feel the warmth and repose of this palatial hotel after walking up and down the street! At the same time, she became exceedingly and unpleasantly conscious of herself as a possible target for surprised or scornful or amused eyes. She was all wrong from head to foot – she knew it in a flash. Her jumper was cheap and flimsy; not a dainty pretty thing, as she had hoped it was. "Don't' think about it," she advised herself, and remembered that an aloof or an abstracted air was the best guard against attention. But with startling clarity objects shot into her vision.

There was a girl behind the reception desk, who had beautifully waved golden hair, and a white high-necked shirt blouse with a black ribbon round the neck. She had a very white face and seemed to gaze at everything and everybody through half-open eyes. This made her look very superior and terrifying; and Violet looked away quickly, hoping to pass unobserved … two men in evening dress standing on her left talking together. One of them was thin lipped, with glasses, and looked very … was sardonic the word? Thank God, he hadn't seemed to notice her. She had got past them all right. Perhaps not interested in women … A splendidly dressed woman coming down the stairs; she looked beautiful seen through the palms. Lovely pink velvet cloak. The fair man with a moustache was with her; perhaps her husband. Taking her into dinner.

What a long long time they seemed to be walking. Would they never get to the lounge? What a mercy she was with someone like Miss Carey who knew where places were, and who looked large and well-dressed and confident even in this intimidating atmosphere. She would never, never, be able to come in here by herself, not all her whole life. It was quite as awe-inspiring as she had ever imagined, with people springing up here and there, and interpolating their low conversations with high unamused laughs. One lady was saying with exaggerated emphasis, "Don't tell me that about John Wilcox, because I don't believe it, "and Violet felt unhappily that she ought to be ashamed of not knowing who John Wilcox was.[29]

Ah, there was the lounge, not far, after all, really. And quite small and modest looking. But comfortable, with easy chairs surrounding small, glass-topped wicker tables. Miss Carey chose a table towards the back centre though Violet, seeing an empty corner table, would have preferred to sit elsewhere.

"No," said Miss Carey. "It's better here. We shall see people more easily."

Violet comprehended that she meant people would see them more easily, and felt a little disturbed. Surely Miss Carey didn't want to do anything vulgar like "clicking"[30] here. She herself would have liked to sit passively with Miss Carey to savour to the full this glorious experience, which, now that the worst was over, assumed a very satisfactory appearance. Still probably, however much Miss Carey stared at men, nothing would happen.

At the table next to them on the right there were a man and girl talking, and Violet, observing them, felt renewed courage. The girl was almost as ordinary looking and shabby as she was herself. Just a well-worn navy blue costume, and navy straw hat. Not specially attractive either. And the man was really rather common looking, like the ones you saw in the street.

Behind them, at the back of the lounge, there were three men, also very ordinary looking, just talking business affairs evidently, and having drinks. Luckily she had her back to them, but in any case they didn't seem to be taking any notice; they had hardly looked up when they entered, so their arrival couldn't be a matter of much importance.

And a woman in the corner by herself reading a book. Middle-aged and severe-looking, with a wing at the side of her hard black hat. There was nobody there she need worry about at all. Miss Pringle wasn't there with her man; Violet had been rather afraid of finding Miss Pringle again.

29　John Wilcox: Probably John Mitchell 'Jack' Wilcox (1886–1940), an English professional football player.

30　Slang term unknown: Probably suggests, a la forming a clique, the action of trying to form connections or suggest exclusivity.

She leaned comfortably back; took a cigarette from Miss Carey's proffered case, and tried to look as if she were in the habit of sitting in hotel lounges, and was, if anything, a little bored. A waiter came to their table.

"Port?" Miss Carey asked her, and she nodded. Port she knew and liked. Other drinks were still dangerous and exotic. "Two ports and a lemonade," Miss Carey informed the waiter, with the beaming smile she lavished on all men, whatever their status. "Schweppes."

The waiter, thought Violet, after a furtive glance, was very dark and very pale and very romantic. Though he couldn't be more than thirty, he seemed very old and wise. He did not glance at either of them, but only nodded. When he had gone Violet wondered uneasily if he felt that they, or at least herself, were not the sort of people he should be waiting on. She uncrossed her legs, and sat up more stiffly.

Suddenly strains of music gave the effect of lighting up the whole atmosphere. Violet lifted her head with delight. "An orchestra," she cried.

Miss Carey nodded and smiled. "It's further on," she said. "At the end of the passage. Raised. You can't see it from here. It's really meant for the dining room. But we can hear it as well."

Miss Carey wore the patronizing air of the proud proprietor towards a poor relation. She made Violet observe they were nearly opposite the entrance to the dining room. And Violet could just see to her left the red-carpeted wide staircase, running easily and gently, as well-ordered stairs should, up to a window where it divided to the left and the right. "The ladies' room is just on the right," said Miss Carey informatively. "It has full-length mirrors in it. You needn't pay the attendant if you just slip in to powder your nose. She can't tell whether you aren't staying here."

Violet thought privately that the attendant would be sure to spot she wasn't staying there, but she nodded appreciatively.

The port was brought to them in tumblers, and the lemonade in a green glass bottle; Violet was astonished at the sum asked, and relieved that Miss Carey paid and tipped without demur.

"Port and lemonade is a great actors' drink," said Miss Carey, pouring in the lemonade generously.

Violet liked it. Sweet and fizzy. It wasn't at all difficult to like wine, though heaps of girls said they only pretended to like it. She sipped and listened while Miss Carey embarked upon a long and scandalous tale about the hotel proprietor. He was a German, though all through the war he had pretended not to be. There was a woman, too. Of course Miss Carey, being broadminded, didn't condemn him, but there were people….

Violet listened eagerly, though she only took part of it in. There was so much to distract her. People kept coming out of the dining room and passing along the corridor. One or two were quite exciting. There was a dark woman, with a small pale face, in a red silk shawl who kept running up and down stairs. Spanish-looking and intriguing, she was. Perhaps she would be staying there with one of her many lovers. She would be bad in a daring attractive way. "Full of vivacity and aplomb," Violet described her appreciatively to herself.

The men behind them were laughing louder now. They had reached the funny story stage. And the girl kept staring at them, well, chiefly at Miss Carey. Other people came in, and Violet would have liked to watch them, but Miss Carey would go on talking.

But most alluring of all was the orchestra.

Sometimes it played little sweet sharp rippling notes that just struck into your heart. And sometimes it bore you up and up on a deep yearning wave of sound that seemed to reach out and out to the very stars and beyond them to something still more that was waiting. And then it wailed sadly away as if it just couldn't manage it, and was heartbroken at all the misery of its frustration.

Miss Carey finished her narration and disposed of Violet's comments. Her eyes, which a minute before had been shining with the excitement of her storytelling, now became cold and calculating. She moved restlessly, and gazed searchingly at the people passing in front of her. She also looked once or twice at the three men sitting there, but they remained absorbed in themselves. It was evident they had no need of other society.

Violet knew she wanted someone to pay for another drink for them. If she, Violet, only had some money then she could pay. But the jumper had cleared her out, and she hadn't anything till Friday. Oh, to have enough money to enjoy yourself properly! Then you could be independent of men and everything.

"Oh, well," said Miss Carey, giving up her pursuit with resignation. "In for a penny, in for a pound." She beckoned the waiter again.

"Would you like a liqueur?"

Violet gave an expressive nod. Liqueurs! She had read about them, of course, but never had one. And weren't they expensive? Almost as expensive as cocktails.

"One crème de Menthe, and one brandy liqueur," ordered Miss Carey.

"I say, it *is* good of you," said Violet earnestly. She knew what it must cost her friend to pay for her herself, when there were fools of men walking about.

Miss Carey smiled benevolently. "Your lucky day," she said, and then her eyes searched the corridor again.

The orchestra was now playing "The Indian Love Lyrics."[31] "Very hackneyed!" said Miss Carey, but Violet loved them. Lovely deep notes, which

---

31 A composition by Amy Woodforde Finden (1860–1919), published as 'the Four Indian Love Lyrics' in 1902.

made her feel happy in a beautiful sad romantic fashion. Life was full of pain and grief, but also, in a way, very beautiful. Her eyes shone.

A tall fair man going a little bald at the back of his head, with a large nose and blue eyes, noticed her as he came out of the dining room. He slackened his steps, and said something to his companion, a little black-haired sallow man with a toothbrush moustache. Both men turned and stared at the two girls. The fair man smiled at Violet.

Daringly she returned his smile; and then, taken with confusion, looked at Miss Carey. It was she who took charge of this sort of thing. But it was good of him to choose her to smile at.

Miss Carey had already noticed the two men, and though she wasn't actually smiling, there was nothing forbidding about her. On the contrary.

They were approaching. Violet experienced the funny feeling of excitement in her stomach again. Somehow she felt *she* was going to be in it this time. Wasn't it time she went home? Don't look at the clock yet.

"Have we your permission to join you, ladies?" said the tall man. He addressed Miss Carey, but it was Violet he was looking at.

"Certainly," said Miss Carey in the tone of mixed condescension and welcome she employed on these occasions. The condescension was perhaps a trifle too pronounced at this time.

The tall fair man sat down by Violet and his friend dragged up a chair and sat on the other side of Miss Carey. The waiter arrived with the liqueurs. He could not have chosen a better moment so far as Miss Carey was concerned, but Violet felt embarrassed. What would the waiter think? They had certainly given themselves away to him. She carefully avoided looking in his direction.

Miss Carey pulled out her bag, and made a pretence of fumbling with it. But the fair man stopped her with a gesture. "You must allow me," he said; and to the waiter, "Two small Scotches, waiter. And soda."

They were gentlemen, really gentlemen! You could tell by the way they spoke. Violet was ashamed when she remembered the two young men outside who had spoken to them. *Young* men were never any good. This was the real thing. Like in books.

They all exchanged names. Everything was done properly. And her man – she already felt he was her special property – whose name was Major something, Major Hinkson, or something like that, was very curious to know all about them. They worked in the same office, did they? That was very nice for them. But they liked a little fun in the evening?

He was very particular in asking Violet. Did this little girl like a little fun in the evening? Yes, of course, she did. He could tell by her eyes. They sparkled so.

Miss Carey had questions to ask in her turn. Yes, Major Hinkson lived at the hotel at present; he had just been entertaining his friend who had come down from Town. Miss Carey wanted to know how London was. "Dear old London!" She, of course, was a Londoner, and it was obvious that Major Hinkson's friend was pleased to learn this. He brightened up considerably.

"It must be lonely to live in a hotel," Violet said, seeking something to say. Major Hinkson agreed, and patted her hand. "It wouldn't be if you were here," he said, and Violet laughed, feeling rather foolish. She didn't know the cue to that.

Another liqueur had been ordered for each of the two girls, and now they changed into the corner seat of the lounge because Major Hinkson thought it would be more comfortable, unless there were any dissentients, and there had been no dissentients. She felt his arm was round her waist as they sat next to each other on the couch, and she wondered if she ought to object. Wasn't it behaving rather familiarly when you had only just met a person? But she would look so young and childish if she made a fuss. Like a village maiden! And it was, on the whole, rather pleasant and comfortable. Why worry?

They were talking about love now. The major said he was a bachelor, and no one had ever loved him. His friend was the lucky one; his friend was a Benedict,[32] as Shakespeare said.

"Oh no, I'm not," said the friend.

"Of course you both are," said Miss Carey. "Don't tell us the tale."

There was a lot of chat about marriage. The two men took their revenge by refusing to believe Miss Carey wasn't married.

"I can't find a husband," said Miss Carey.

They wouldn't believe that, either. And the major was sure Violet had a nice boy up her sleeve somewhere. Did she love him very much?

She hadn't! That was excellent. Perhaps a lonely old fellow like himself might get a look in. The talking and laughing went on, and Violet felt she was doing famously. She didn't feel at all shy. It was so easy to talk in this understanding appreciative atmosphere.

Heavens! What time was it?

"I shall have to go," she said, becoming very grave, while all her excitement went. Oh, it was a shame! She'd have loved to stay longer. "What time is it?" she asked Miss Carey, and then, as her friend was too deeply absorbed to answer, "Joyce, what's the time?"

The dark man answered. "Twenty-five past ten," he said with grave courtesy which even at that moment impressed Violet.

---

32 Benedict: A reference to the character Benedick (often misconstrued as Benedict) in Shakespeare's *Much Ado about Nothing*. Benedick is a confirmed bachelor who rails against marriage.

But the news gave her a sick feeling. It was as if you heard a bell pealing for a dead person. She had never been as late as this before. There would be the devil to pay.

"I am sorry, but I am afraid I shall have to go," she said rather desperately, standing up.

"You can't go yet," said Major Hinkson. "The night is still young."

"You see, my mother is expecting me," said Violet. She hated having to say it; it made her look such a frightful little ass; but it couldn't be helped.

It was extraordinary how difficult it was to get away. They didn't seem to think she was in earnest, but Joyce helped her out. Then the major man said he would come, too, and Violet both wanted him to come and didn't want him to come. It was very difficult.

At last she broke away and went out by herself. It was queer: you had to concentrate to get your legs to walk smoothly and straight in the right direction. But it was all right as long as you kept hold of yourself. And it was funny, she didn't mind the people she passed at all. They didn't seem really to exist. And there was a door straight in front!

Suddenly Violet felt her arm taken. It was Major Hinkson. "I'll see you home," he said.

What was this? He was signaling a taxi. She was going to be taken home in a taxi. What a night!

But it would be better not to drive right up to the door. Suppose her mother was standing by the door. She would be quite capable of making a scene even in front of Major Hinkson. And he would see that her mother was quite a common-looking dowdy person.

Somehow he seemed to understand her hesitation when she gave him the address. "I'll tell him to drive to the corner of the road," he said reassuringly.

The inside of the taxi seemed very dark and small. He sat very close to her, and moved up when Violet wriggled into a corner. Then he wanted her to sit on his knee, while what she wanted to do was to compose herself and think out a story to tell her mother. But of course she couldn't be rude to him when he had been decent and paid for so many drinks.

All the same it wasn't at all as it should have been, Violet felt. He seemed quite different now. Not nearly so nice. Those horrid smeary kisses which she couldn't escape, however much she turned her face away. And all the time he kept on telling her that it was all right, and that she wasn't to be afraid. "Anyone who knows me will tell you," he said, "that I've never taken advantage of an innocent girl." He knew an innocent girl when he saw one. She was innocent, wasn't she? But she oughtn't to go about with Miss Carey. It appeared that he didn't approve of Miss Carey at all. Which was rather a triumph for *her* in one way. But it wasn't right for her to listen to things said about her friend….

And all the time those kisses, those wandering hands to be restrained and avoided. She disliked him very much now. She hated being touched like this. It was vile!

What a mercy, the taxi was stopping! Yes, here they were at the corner of the street. Violet tidied her hair, and put her hat straight. Then she got out.

"Goodbye," she said. You had to say Goodbye. It was only polite. But she wouldn't say "thank you."

"Goodbye," said Major Hinkson. He didn't ask to see her again, and she felt both disappointed and relieved. It would have been a triumph to tell Miss Carey, but it would have been awful, of course. He had got out too, and was looking at her in a cold superior way as if he disliked her. As she turned to go, he raised his hat, and stood with his head uncovered. He was certainly a gentleman. You had to say that for him. Now he looked dignified and attractive again.

She heard the taxi driving away as she went up the street. Well, that was over. It hadn't been a nice evening after all. Not a bit like it had seemed at first. In the "Met" she had thought in a way – not really, of course, but in a way – that Major Hinkson might fall in love with her, and buy her things and so on. But he was just the sort of man Miss Carey talked about. Just Passion and nothing else. And Passion was a beastly thing. And men were beastly. They made you beastly. Everything was beastly.

Violet felt sobs rising at the back of her throat. She choked them back, and refused to think any more about him. There was her mother to face now.

She knocked at the door – oh, if only she had a key – and it was opened quickly.

"Well!" said Mrs. Ryder in an outraged gasp. "Where have you been?"

Violet brushed past silently into the dark hall. How small and dirty looking it was! And what a close disgusting smell of cooking! And her mother was a plain-looking angry woman of no consequence, who was always interfering with her.

"Violet!" said Mrs. Ryder, and the word was rapped out as sharply as a pistol shot.

Violet felt desperation rising within her. She couldn't stand any more. And what was more she wasn't going to stand any more.

"For God's sake, leave me alone," she answered fiercely, and started to mount the staircase.

"Violet come here," said her mother. Her tone sounded gentler, even a little alarmed now, and Violet stopped unwillingly.

"Aren't you going to have your supper?"

"Don't want any supper."

"Violet," and now Mrs. Ryder sounded sharp again. "What have you been doing? Why are you so late? Do you know the time? Getting on for eleven. Answer when I speak to you."

Violet advanced a few steps reluctantly. How sordid all this was! How ugly and meaningless! Her mother was wearing her blue dress with a red front. It was most disgusting, that smell of fried fish!

"Violet," said her mother, and her voice was almost a whisper, so slow and solemn it was. "Tell me! You've not been doing anything wicked, have you?"

Violet's imagination was arrested. In a way, of course, she had been wicked. But not in that mysterious fashion her mother meant. Hysteria threatened, and a memory of her novel reading came to her aid. "No, I haven't," she said quickly. And then, raising her voice, "How dare you suggest such a thing!"

Mrs. Ryder was suitably abashed. She had evidently been on the wrong tack. Thank God for it.

"Well, then, where have you been?" she said in her ordinary voice. "You know very well I told you to be back by half-past nine."

Violet thought quickly. She would have to say something. Miss Carey. Oh, yes.

"Miss Carey didn't feel well when we came out of the Hippodrome, so I went home with her and saw her into bed."

"I should have thought she could have managed to look after herself," said Mrs. Ryder. It was evident that she was suspicious, but not sure of her suspicions. "Well, come and have your supper. I kept your plaice warm for you."

"No, thank you," said Violet. "I couldn't eat anything." She felt contemptuous of her mother as well as being relieved. Half-formulated in her mind came the idea, "People will swallow anything. It's their fault if you tell them lies." She added carelessly, "I had some tea and bread and butter with Miss Carey at her diggings."

Her mother said no more. She went away without a word, and Violet realised that the scorned plaice was preying on her mind. Her mother was always hurt if she didn't eat her supper and enjoy it. What a fuss about nothing!

Wearily she turned into her bedroom, and started to undress. She had thought the mauve jumper a fine thing when she put it on in the morning. What a fool she had been! Cheap it was, and common. Soiled, too. She had spilt some wine on it; and she, too, felt soiled and cheap. Tears started in her eyes as she folded it up. What a long time it was since the morning! A long exciting restless day with a horrid ending. That was the way of it: if you were happy one minute you were miserable the next. There were always people spoiling things. On the whole most people were rather horrid. And the office was hateful. She would have that again tomorrow morning. And the day after ... perhaps for all her life until she got too old to be kept any longer. And probably no one would ever fall in love with her, ever.

"Life is rotten," she told herself passionately as she brushed her hair. "Rotten to the core."

In bed she thought about Major Hinkson again. Well, anyway she must have attracted him. Only he didn't go on liking her because she had struggled, and wouldn't kiss him back again. That was what Miss Carey had told her about men. That was why you had to get them to pay and then run away. It was queer and rather mean – all of it....

But wasn't there somewhere something quite different? Romance, Love, beautiful shining things? Wasn't there? Miss Carey didn't believe in love. She was a cynic. Another name for Passion, was what she said. But perhaps somewhere, some day....

"Dear God, make there be someone soon to fall in love with me, and me with him, and make it all beautiful not like ... You know, all beautiful," she prayed, half-unconscious of her prayer, and soon fell asleep.

ALICE

The Pexbourne-on-Sea Congregational Church were having their customary Bright-and-Cheerful-Visitors-Heartily-Welcome Sunday Evening Service. As a matter of fact there were not many visitors present because it was towards the end of the season; and Miss Alice Jenkinson, scanning the pews with apparently unseeing eyes, noted few faces there were not familiar to her.

Nevertheless it was quite a good congregation. And what was more important it was being a successful service. There was that zest in the air which emanates from any body of people who are enjoying themselves, and pleased that they are enjoying themselves. Electric currents of warmth united each pew in fellowship and kindliness. One appreciated the fitness of the expression when the Reverend Joseph Hawthorne, M.A., addressed his hearers as "My dear brothers and sisters." Quite a number of people assembled that September Sunday evening did really feel themselves to be brothers and sisters in Christ; they knew so much about one another, who had married who, and what their good and not so good points were; and it was a pleasure to see the same familiar faces every Sunday in the same familiar pews, and to be certain that you also were being recognised. Besides, this was a small homely chapel in which it was not difficult to experience a cozy "When-Two-Or-Three-Are-Gathered-Together-in-Thy-Name"[33] sort of feeling.

So young people sitting next to elderly people occasionally found the hymns for them, and the elderly people smiled and nodded in return. And everybody was careful that the few strangers, members from other churches worshipping with them, should be made to feel at home, assured that they were welcome. They were looked at with kindly interest, and could have had their pick of their neighbours' hymn books.

It was all very agreeable, and Miss Alice Jenkinson sitting in the choir felt herself becoming happier and happier. She was conscious that she was looking her best; and it had seemed to her, perhaps wrongly, that the few words and smiles she had exchanged with her acquaintances in the front pews had been less perfunctory and more prolonged on their side than usual. She felt that when her own eyes had slid away, theirs had returned and stayed on her long enough to receive a clear impression, and that that impression had been favourable. Not that she was wearing anything smart. She only had on her navy blue costume that Miss Dixon, the dressmaker, had made up for her at a charge of two guineas – quite a reasonable charge, because everybody said that Miss Dixon was very clever with her fingers – though, of course, thought Alice, pulling herself up, it was a duty as well as a pleasure to support chapel members. And she was still wearing the brown straw hat with a wreath of small pink rosebuds round it which had done duty for best all through the summer months. In a week or two she would really have to get a winter hat; a felt or perhaps a velour. Except that velour was so expensive. She'd have to think it over.

Oh, well, she knew, or, at least, it was perhaps that which made people look at her tonight rather specially: it might be the old pink woolen scarf she had put on as an afterthought because the evenings were really getting rather chilly. It had lain at the back of a drawer for ever so long, and she had forgotten all about it. But when she had taken it out before going to chapel, and put it round her neck, she had seen that it suited her. It made the hat look different somehow; the rosebuds stood out and appeared unwontedly gay and saucy. Also it seemed to have lent her own pale cheeks a touch of its pink, and her eyes looked dark and quite shining. She felt they were bright now; she generally looked at her best in chapel of an evening. Why was it? She asked herself a little uneasily. Of course, because she was happy there. She could really and

---

33 'For where two or three have gathered together in My name, I am there in their midst'. Matthew 18:20.

truly say that she never felt happier than when she was in God's house, show-ing forth His praise with her voice.

Her lips dropped a little apart in a smile of happy humility. Her long sallow face with its aquiline nose and thin mouth seen thus appeared not unattrac-tive; and she was right in assuming that her eyes, large and deep set, were dark and shining. With the pink scarf concealing her scraggy neck, and softening her prominent chin, she might have been roped in under that usually charita-ble verdict, "about thirty," instead of her real age, which was thirty four, and revealed to all her friends, with a lot of laughter. How she was getting on!

The Rev. Joseph Hawthorne had finished giving out the announcements of the week, and Alice, disturbed from her musings by the rustlings which meant that people were diving into bags and pockets, and surreptitiously passing coins to junior members of the household, felt rather ashamedly aware that she had not heard a word he had said. Still, being one of the leading church workers, she knew it all beforehand. She knew, too, that the reason why the meeting for church members only on Thursday evening was not going to be held was that Mr. Hawthorne had been asked to give a special address that evening to young people in the neighbouring village of Seabrook. Thus, when Mr. Taylor passed her the plate, the smile she gave him as she laid her sixpence down (heaps of people in the choir only gave a threepenny bit or sometimes even coppers, but she always managed sixpence) was prompted by the sudden proud glow of consciousness that she was one of the few who moved behind the scenes, who even pulled strings from behind the scenes. Mr. Hawthorne had said to her over and over again, well, *at least* three times, "What we should do without you, my dear Miss Jenkinson, I really do not know."

Now Mr. Hawthorne was giving out the hymn before the sermon. It was "Nearer My God to Thee."[34] Alice loved "Nearer My God to Thee." It was one of her favourite hymns, and she stood up with the rest of the choir, before the congregation, while the first verse was being played, with her happiness sharpened almost to ecstasy.

> Nearer my God to thee,
> Near . . ah to Thee . . e,
> E'en though it be a cross
> That raise . . eth me,
> Still all my song shall be . . e,
> Near . . ah my Gaud to Thee . . e,
> Near . . errah to Thee . . e.

---

34 A nineteenth-century Christian hymn by Sarah Flower Adams.

She sang the words with much feeling while her heart quickened its beat. She felt that God was stretching out His arms to her and drawing her upwards to Himself. It was such a beautiful thought to have!

She was disappointed when the last verse came to an end. She longed to go on singing for hours – there was so much rapturous praise in her heart. But now they were all sitting down, settling into their pews with a fidgety determination which told their seats they had come to stay for a while. As Mr. Hawthorne stood up, some of the lights in the body of the church were put out, and then a golden light shown out just over the pulpit. The preacher had pressed the switch of the overhanging electric lamp, and his ruddy face glowed impressively underneath it. Wandering eyes stayed themselves on his face obediently. The sermon was about to begin.

"I take my text," Mr. Hawthorne started, "from the thirteenth chapter of the Gospel according to John, the thirtieth verse: 'He then having received the sop went immediately out: and it was night.'"

Mr. Hawthorne lowered his voice as he repeated the final phrase, filling it with solemnity. Miss Alice Jenkinson having composed her face into that attitude of reverent attention which she reserved for the most casual utterance of her minister, heard his voice echoing arrestingly in her mind: "And it was night." Gradually the words swelled up till, though their substance was lost, the whole of her mind had adapted itself to their shape. Night! Unexpected queer things always happened at night: burglars breaking into houses; hushed footsteps; people being ill; asleep in bed; husbands and wives together.... Hush! Listen! What is Mr. Hawthorne talking about? About Judas!...

"It is the custom, the acquired habit of thinking, to blame Judas for the sin of avarice. It is claimed that he denied Our Lord for thirty pieces of silver. Now to me it seems utterly inconceivable that this, the greatest betrayal of history, the most infamous treachery known to man, should have been inspired by paltry greed. It is impossible to think that Judas was swayed merely by the itch to acquire such a paltry sum. I do not believe it for a moment...."

Wonderful, thought Miss Jenkinson, the way Mr. Hawthorne was always getting new ideas about things. He really was a clever man; everyone admitted that, saying that he preached such a thoughtful sermon that made you think afterwards, even if it wasn't so ... well, exciting as some. There was young Mr. Harvey, who had preached on the laxity of modern life four Sundays ago, the increasing wickedness there was about ... still Mr. Hawthorne was human, he had his human side. There was that time when they were coming home from the school; for a moment he had put his hand under her elbow, and had let it remain for few seconds before he let go. He would have hardly done that if he hadn't, well, rather liked her.

Emptied, her mind sank back into vagueness as she sat staring at the figure in the pulpit. At length his voice, grown to a deeper earnestness, arrested her attention:

"So, then, my friends, I want you to picture to yourselves the figure of this wretched man who had expected, with what lively anticipation we can all imagine, to see his Master entering Jerusalem with all the grand pomp and clamour which attends the progress of an earthy potentate. But what did he see instead? Christ standing mute before Pilate, unable apparently to save himself from the terrible, the unspeakable torture and death by crucifixion which awaited Him. And, so we are told, he went and hanged himself. Finding that his plan to make Our Lord reveal himself as an earthly emperor had failed, he made the only reparation that it was possible for him to make. We must, I think, take into consideration, that black as was the sin of Judas, black beyond all compare, yet his remorse, the remorse of that unhappy man, was also deep. We can see him hurrying away with despair gnawing at his heart, turning his back upon lighted houses, upon all the things that make life dear to us: love, the laughter of little children...."

His voice retreated from Miss Jenkinson. "Love, the laughter of little children," were the words that were pressing the springs of her thoughts. Mr. Hawthorne had been in love, and he had four children. They were nearly grown up now, but there had been a time when they had only been little: a time even before they had come, a time when he was making them come....

Fascinated, she gazed upon the large round face, from which words came rolling out. He was an elderly man now, with almost white hair. It was impossible to imagine him and Mrs. Hawthorne – Mrs. Hawthorne, large, pink, benevolent but vague – feeling thrilled by each other. Kissing, and all that! Funny, unless you actually saw people kissing, it was so queer to think of them ever kissing at all. The people in the congregation, for instance. She had a slight, almost imperceptible, peep at the front pew: Mr. and Mrs. Sidebotham, the deacon and his wife. Mrs. Sidebotham, small, with yellow faded skin, and tightly pressed lips, gazing stiffly upwards. Mr. Sidebotham, rather stout, inclined to be rubicund, but not cheerfully rubicund, always rather grave and solemn. Never made jokes, or anything; referred to his wife always as Mrs. Sidebotham, and addressed her as if she were a rather distinguished acquaintance. Her name was Joan, wasn't it? Yes. "Yours very sincerely, Joan Sidebotham." That was how she had ended that letter about the harvest festival. Did they kiss? Surely not! They hadn't any children; perhaps they had never ... or did all married people? They were supposed to, of course. You couldn't tell. No one outside could tell. Mr. Hawthorne was still explaining about Judas. Dear Mr. Hawthorne. Such a kind comfortable sort of man. She watched him affectionately, till gradually her mind tightened to take in the sense of what he was saying. It was his concluding peroration:

> "We are all Judases, sometimes, my friends. We betray Our Dear Lord not in actual words perhaps, but in our hearts, by denying Him entrance. For if we do not think constantly of those we love and venerate, how can it be said that we really love them? In spirit and in truth? And I say to you that unless you make God and the Spirit of God your constant companion, you are betraying the Divine Master, your greatest Friend if you did but know it. The One Who said those words of comfort, and wonderful hope, 'Come unto Me all ye that are weary and heavy laden, and I will give you rest!' If there are any in this church tonight who feel that their walk has been away from God, I ask them in His Name to return to Him, for with Him is all love and joy – and away from him, what? Nothing – less than nothing."

Mr. Hawthorne sat down abruptly as if overcome by the despair of his final thought, but immediately dispelled such a suggestion by rising again to announce the number of the hymn. His voice now sounded flat and perfunctory. It was evident that to him the service was really over.

But Miss Jenkinson liked the hymns best of all though she would not have admitted this; and when her hymn book happened to open in the exact place it struck her as a strange and beautiful occurrence. Her exaltation returned, and she stood up a trifle in front of the other members of the choir. She felt as if she had been specially noticed, specially picked out from the others, who, good Christians though they might be, were yet perhaps a little commonplace, a little unseeing, incapable of experiencing certain of the finer emotions.

It was not a very well-known hymn, and the singing dragged a little. At the end of each verse came a chorus:

> Behold me standing at the door,
> And hear me pleading ever more,
> Say weary heart, oppressed with sin,
> May I come in – may I come in?[35]

The comparative apathy of the congregation prompted Miss Jenkinson to sing the more fervently. When it came to the repetition her voice could be heard above those of the other members of the choir. She sang with head uplifted and shining eyes, pouring out her entire self. Her mind was forming a

---

35 'Behold me Standing at the Door,' written by Frances Jane 'Fanny' Crosby, (1820–1915). Originally published in *Sacred Songs and Solos, 888 Pieces*, by Ira D. Sankey (London: Morgan and Scott Ltd.).

picture of Christ with hands dripping blood raised in supplication. Everyone turned from Him, except herself. With every repetition of the verse the picture became more glowing. She saw herself, heedless of taunts flung at her, drawing Him in; and now His face was turned on her with gratitude and love. A warm glow made her skin tingle. She and Christ! She and Christ alone against the world. She would sit at His feet and tend Him like Mary Magdalene. Oh, if she had only lived then!

As the last strains of the organ faded out, she sat down feeling extraordinarily happy, and a little giddy. She had a queer feeling that something was going to happen to her, something beautiful and wonderful; and she bowed her head low as Mr. Hawthorne pronounced the Benediction, thanking God for his mercy and love towards her.

The congregation, after carefully allowing a suitable interval for prayer to elapse, lifted their heads from their hands, or from close contact with the pale shiny surface of the rest which bore their hymn books, an occasional Bible, and an occasional pair of gloves or handbag, and settled themselves back in their seats for a few seconds while Mr. Hawthorne left the pulpit. Then, to the accompaniment of whispers to their neighbours, they rose and straggled out of the pews, many intent on having a word with someone else. The girl who sat next to Alice thought a remark would be seemly.

"It's been a nice Service, hasn't it, Miss Jenkinson?"

"Yes," replied Alice warmly. "And such a fine sermon, didn't you think? I feel now that Judas is so much more a living person to me than before. I never thought about him in the way Mr. Hawthorne said until tonight."

Miss Evelyn agreed, but not so insistently as to give Miss Jenkinson any encouragement to go on chatting. She felt indeed not quite at her ease. It was all right to say a sermon was good, or agree when older people said it, but if you made a song about why it was good, it made you appear awfully religious and stuffy. As she waited for her special friend, Marjorie Lawless, who sat in the pew behind, she reflected that there was sometimes something rather weird about Miss Alice Jenkinson. Of course she did a lot for the church and all that and she didn't usually talk about things. But you often felt uncomfortably that she was keeping herself from bursting out about things just because she thought you wouldn't understand. She wasn't quite a lady either; she and her sisters took boarders in the summer and were quite poor; they didn't look [like] ladies, hadn't the style or way of talking.

Some of this criticism she passed on to Marjorie as they walked down to the front together to hear the band.

Marjorie agreed. "And I thought she sang most frightfully loudly in that last hymn," she said.

"Yes, she did. And she was a bit out of tune on the high E."

There was a pause, and then they permitted Miss Jenkinson the benefit of their tolerance. "You have to expect these old maids to get a bit cranky and religious."

"That is so. And her voice isn't bad, I must admit."

"Alice had felt Evelyn's lack of response, but it merely had the effect of increasing that unwonted unconsciousness of superiority, a superiority which caused her to hurry over the customary end-of-the-service conversational exchanges, to which she usually looked forward.

Several people stopped her to enquire after her sister whom she had left at home with a cold. She replied, "She is a little better, thank you very much, but thought she wouldn't venture out," and smiled with a sweet gravity which chilled effusiveness, and caused her questioners, eager to repay like with like, to murmur, "Quite right, better to be careful," and turn away quickly so as to give the whole thing the air of a casual contact. There were more important matters to be discussed after all than Miss Minnie's cold.

Leaving them, Alice went out of the side door of the chapel, walking with a quick springing step, and holding her head high. She took the familiar path home, but it did not seem to her that she was going home. Sometimes she imagined that she was setting out on a long journey, to meet and overcome dangers and difficulties; sometimes that her Beloved Saviour was with her, featureless and insubstantial of outward aspect, but nevertheless walking by her side. It was strange to her when she turned the key in the lock, and went through the narrow hall, hung with a man's hat to frighten burglars, into the room they called the dining room, to find her sister sitting by the fire, and supper laid on the table, just as if things intended to go on in the same way. She hesitated a moment inside the room, looking not at her sister, but round her with a thoughtful air.

Miss Minnie Jenkinson was two years younger than Alice; she had more flesh, and more colour in her cheeks and lips; and her fair hair was abundant. She laughed readily, and, in company, frequently, showing good, regular teeth; and liked cheerful colours in her dresses. For one thing, she thought, this emphasised the fact that she was younger than Alice. Another of her social assets was an appealing way of looking up at the married men of her acquaintance with her head on one side in quite a pretty attitude. So she had her share of popularity, and when she called in the evening for subscriptions or to ask after someone's uncertain health, was often made very welcome and teased in a jocular fashion that was much to her liking. Alice was not such a success, even though she did much more church work; she either overdid the deference or went to the opposite extreme and appeared a shade condescending.

Also it was recognised that she was the quiet one of the two. When two sisters lived together one was generally labeled "the quiet one" in Pexbourne.

But tonight Minnie did not look her best, while Alice did look her best. Minnie's nose was very red, and all the redder because she was wearing her Sunday frock of a rather bright shade of blue. Her skin looked rough and porous, and her mouth sagged. I am sure she looks older than I do now, thought Alice. I wish Mr. Hawthorne could see her.

"Well, you're back early," said Minnie. "Who did you see?"

"Oh, the usual people. Mr. Sidebotham asked after you, and so did Miss Pallister. Mrs. Dixon hoped you'd be all right for the lecture on Thursday. And Mr. Dixon said that if you didn't turn up, he'd have to come round and pour quinine into you himself."

Minnie's eyes lightened, and she gave a little gasp of laughter.

"Did he really? He does say some things, doesn't he? He has got a great sense of humour, I always think."

Alice made no reply. What a fool Minnie was! Still! She walked over to the mantelpiece, and picked up an ornament with a bored air. "Who else did you see?"

"No one special. Mrs. Hawthorne was there by herself. Hardly any of the family turn up in the evening nowadays. Mrs. Vaughan had brought her little boy."

"He's a dear little boy, isn't he?"

Minnie looked into the fire with some elation. Fancy Mr. Dixon! *He* had missed her then all right. She looked up at her sister, hoping to draw out some more plums, and became disapprovingly aware of Alice's remoteness.

"Aren't you going to get your things off? Supper's all on the table. I thought I'd have it all ready for you when you came in."

Alice surveyed the table. The cold beef from dinner: a lot of gristle about it. The half cut loaf of bread, and glass dish of butter. Nothing else? Oh, yes; she had put the tinned fruit out on the sideboard. But there were not many left, only apricots, too. It was hardly worth it.

"I don't feel specially hungry," she said, her eyes going back to the mantelpiece.

"Fancy! You generally have such an appetite after evening service. Of course being in all the time like me takes your appetite away. Then this cold, too!"

Alice thought: she wants me to ask about her cold. Why should I? I can see it's the same. Oh, well!

"Doesn't it feel any better?"

"No, they say colds are always worse at night, you know."

There was another silence.

Through the window came the sound of a man's voice, followed by a woman's laugh. Alice raised her head, and looked at herself in the overhanging mirror. Yes, she still looked well. Still had her colour. Of course you needn't expect Minnie to say anything nice.

"I am worried about Mrs. Coleman," she said suddenly. "She wasn't at church. I am sure her neuralgia must be worse."

Now Minnie refused to reply. Why didn't Alice take her things off and let them start supper? At intervals, while she had been sitting by the fire, her thoughts had gone pleasantly to savouring the apricots. Now was the time for them. She would have hardly any meat. It wasn't a very good joint. Then it would look all right having a good plate of fruit.

Alice turned upon her eyes grown gentle and candid.

"Minnie dear, do you know, now that I've seen how you are, I think I'll just step round to Mrs. Coleman's. It must be very lonely for her by herself, especially if she feels poorly. She always lets the servant out on Sunday, and it would be too bad if she suddenly felt very bad, and no one there."

Minnie couldn't speak for a moment. She felt something really violent occurring inside her. Mrs. Coleman might have neuralgia! But what about her? Charity didn't begin at home, did it? Sitting there by herself all evening; no one had come to see *her*. And now her own sister rushing off to be an angel to someone else. Just a trumped-up excuse. Not that she would demean herself by saying anything. Then she'd be made out to be selfish. Oh, Alice wouldn't trap her.

After a moment she spoke in a carefully colourless voice:

"Just as you like, Alice. How long shall I keep supper then?"

"Minnie dear, of course you don't wait for me. And don't bother about keeping any either, because really it's funny but I'm not a bit hungry. I'll be as quick as I can. Anyway I'll be back to do the washing-up. But don't you think I ought to go?"

Minnie allowed some of her irritation to leak out.

"Well, Alice, since you ask my opinion, I can't quite see how it's necessary. You told me yourself that you saw Mrs. Coleman out on Friday afternoon, and that she told you that her neuralgia was much better. As for not being at church, you know perfectly well that she often doesn't come to church on Sunday evening because she's nervous at leaving the house with no one in it. But you have to do as you like, of course. I wouldn't say anything to prevent you."

Alice was still tactful.

"I hate leaving you, Minnie, when you feel so poorly. Otherwise I'd have gone straight from chapel."

"It doesn't matter about me," said Minnie. She wasn't going to be caught like that. She breathed through her nose with a sniffling noise, and then took out her handkerchief.

Alice ventured recklessly: "If you don't want me to go, I won't."

"Oh, I don't mind. It doesn't matter as far as I'm concerned." Minnie put her handkerchief away with an air of sullen hardihood.

"Well, then, I think I will run round while you are having your supper, just to see if she's all right. I shan't stay."

"Please don't hurry on my account," Minnie shot in quickly.

Alice said nothing. If Minnie wanted to be nasty, she wouldn't. The sense of being patient under provocation made her feel happy again. It was Paul, wasn't it, who endured all things for the Name's sake? It was perfectly true, as she had heard many ministers say, Christianity was an everyday matter as well as being in the Bible.

She put her hat straight in the glass, and her eyes smiled back at her kindly and steadily.

"Now get your supper, Minnie, and I'd make myself a cup of Bovril[36] if I was you. Feed a cold, you know."

She smiled warmly on her sister, who didn't respond, being engaged in fetching out her handkerchief, and moved to the door.

"Bye-bye!"

"Bye-bye!"

When Minnie heard the door really close, she sat back, forgot about her handkerchief, and did some thinking. Mrs. Coleman's son couldn't have come home for a holiday; no; if so she'd be sure to have heard. Had she seen Mr. Hawthorne after the service? Pretended to have something to ask him about and was going to slip into the Hawthornes' on the chance that he would take her off to his study. It was a bit out of the way though – her doing that on Sunday evening.

Ah, well. She didn't care. She rose, walked over to the sideboard and looked down lovingly at the dish of apricots. She set it on the table carefully, and drew up a chair.

Out in the street, Alice walked along in the direction of Mrs. Coleman's house, shutting her mind against any thought of arriving at her destination. It was lovely being out; it was lovely walking along by herself with her pink scarf; she felt so well and happy; and that was queer, because usually she didn't feel specially well or specially happy. But tonight was different. Surely, surely God would let something happen to her tonight! But when she walked up the little stone flagged path that led to Mrs. Coleman's semi-detached villa residence she recollected that she was on an errand of mercy. Unconsciously she arranged her face in ingratiating lines as she rang the bell.

---

36 Bovril: 'The proprietary name of a concentrated essence of beef, invented in 1889 by J. Lawson Johnston'. (*OED*).

There was a pause, which deepened into silence. Alice, stepping back, noticed what she had been too engrossed to perceive, that there was no light in the front room where Mrs. Coleman generally sat.

She rang the bell a second time, but without any real belief that it would be answered. She rang the bell a second time for two reasons: the first because one did always ring an unanswered bell at least once more before permitting oneself to assume that no one was at home; and the second in order to give her mind time to get into working order again. People couldn't stand plunged into deep meditation outside a street door. It looked suspicious to anybody passing if you didn't seem to be intent on getting inside.

Well, then, thought Alice, gazing hard on the glass panel at the right side of the door, Mrs. Coleman being out meant that she was having supper with someone … most probably Mr. Hawthorne and his family, who lived only two doors away, and with whom she was on very friendly terms. Mrs. Coleman was said to be the only woman to whom the minister's wife really ever talked. And she never felt that Mrs. Coleman cared for her, Alice, very much. Still, don't bother about that now. She had come all this way after service to ask about Mrs. Coleman's health. And Mrs. Coleman was a few doors away with the Hawthornes.

Should she go on there? If it were only just the three older people! Mrs. Hawthorne was always quite nice when she met her. But there were the two Hawthorne girls and young red-haired Fred Hawthorne, who weren't very friendly to her, stared at her in a sort of bored amused fashion, had jokes of their own when she was there. They always made her feel uncomfortable, though she had tried her best to make Mary Hawthorne, who was the quieter of the two girls, like her. No, their cold inquiring eyes would kill all her precious happiness.

She walked slowly down the path and, after carefully latching the gate, stood a moment gazing up and down the road. It was a beautiful evening, so nice and clear. The sky was darkly blue as far as she could see: a blue so opulent that it reminded Alice pleasantly of the infinite riches of God. How solemn the trees looked against it.

Alice jerked her head sideways. From her left had come the strains of the esplanade band interpreting succulently the love duet from "Samson and Delilah."[37] They came to Alice as an enticing mixture of loveliness and wickedness. Tempting somehow. But, of course, music wasn't wicked. Books and pictures and statues … no, not statues, because that was art, but books and

---

37 Samson and Delilah: A grand opera based on the biblical story. Music by Camille Saint-Saëns, words and story from a French libretto by Ferdinand Lemaire. It was first performed in Weimar, Germany on 2 December 1877.

pictures could be bad; not music. You never heard of banned music; even jazzy stuff and comic songs, fox-trots and the rest were not thought of as wicked – just considered a little vulgar and beneath the consideration of really musical people. "Samson and Delilah" was an opera, and therefore quite like classical music. She rather thought it was classical music. And she, who had always been considered musical, appreciated it for that reason.

Somehow she found her steps turning in the direction which led to the front and away from Minnie and supper. It wasn't that she was going to listen to the band, she told herself, only just to take a few steps and get perhaps a breath of the sea. For listening to the band was a thing she hadn't done for years. Not even when visitors who became friendly had asked her to go. There had been that Miss Lowe only two Sundays ago, ever such a nice girl, who worked in a big office in London. A responsible position. "Do come, Miss Jenkinson," she had said – she had seemed to like her better than Minnie for some reason, though Minnie had always tried to get hold of her as she did of everybody else – "I should feel conspicuous like if I went by myself." And she had replied, "I am so sorry, dear. It isn't that I am narrow-minded or anything like that, but you see doing so much chapel work, and everybody knowing us, you have to be so careful. Spiteful people are always looking for a chance to criticise."

That's what she had said to Miss Lowe, and the girl had seen her point at once, and stayed in and had supper with them, and been interested to hear about Mr. Hawthorne, and how they had never thought Mrs. Hawthorne was quite the right sort of wife for so clever and bookish a man … Mr. Hawthorne had once preached, many years ago now, upon the importance of keeping the Sabbath holy, and she had thought how she would always carry out his ideas in that one thing at least. It had made her so happy making that resolution. But all the other girls in the choir went during the season, and so did the Hawthorne children.

The music could be heard quite distinctly now, and it sent little thrills of pleasure through her to listen to it. Imperceptibly to herself she quickened her footsteps. The road she was on took her straight down to the front on the right of the esplanade where the band was playing. She would perhaps just stop and listen for a few moments, unperceived by anyone, and then she would turn in again, and home through the town. Minnie would have eaten all the apricots in any case now.

People, mostly in couples, wandering home from the front, were meeting her, and passing by. Alice rearranged her scarf, burying her chin right in it, and pulled her hat a little more forward on her forehead.

Now she could hear the dreary beat of the sea, and see it stretched in front of her so grey and dark and wide that it seemed to send its chill to her heart. That mustn't be. Quickly she looked away, and went, trying to make her approach appear casual, toward the arc lights which advertised the great open hall where the band was playing.

But not too near! She wouldn't go too near. Already she could glimpse the faces of those who sat in the deck chairs surrounding the open windows through which they could see the band, and the interior audience who had paid ninepence instead of threepence for their seats in order to escape the cold of out-of-doors. She stood still. Oh, she was happy now! She was very happy. It was a beautiful moment in her life. She had always wanted to listen to the band on Sunday evening when the season was on.

It was while she stood so that she attracted the attention of Mr. Alfred James. Mr. James was feeling, as he told himself, more than a little fed up. He had chosen Pexbourne for his final weekend at the sea because he had never been there before. He knew Brighton, Margate, Eastbourne, Hastings, Broadstairs, Littlehampton, Bognor[38] and he had been for a char-à-banc trip[39] to Bournemouth, but he did not know Pexbourne. He had, there, taken a weekend ticket on the Saturday after a hurried lunch, and descended upon it in a spirit of adventure and hope. He was clad, he considered, in a manner which should prove to any observer that he was at least as good as they were. He wore a grey flannel suit that had been perfectly new in May, and which was none of your ready-mades, but had been carefully fitted by a well-known Strand tailor and made to specification for three pounds ten. Sometimes music hall jokes were made bringing in the name of this tailor; and this caused Alfred to feel a little uncomfortable. But he didn't really mind, for everyone had admired him in it, and said it was an excellent cut.

His blue striped tie had been chosen from a whole bunch of similar ties which bore across them a little notice, "Tasteful." The description had impressed Alfred, who didn't like loud things. "Gentlemanly," "For the Fastidious," "In Perfect Taste," "Correct Neckwear": such were the epithets which appealed to him far more than "Smart," "The Very Latest."

And he had a white cotton shirt, soft white collar, no hat, but a sufficiency of dark hair, good teeth, and adequate features. He was generally reckoned quite a good-looking young man, and he was not unaware of this circumstance.

But somehow he hadn't felt at home in Pexbourne. It was, he felt, quite different from any other seaside town of his acquaintance, and he couldn't classify it as one thing or another. It was not common and hilarious like Brighton and Margate; but neither was it really classy like Bournemouth, nor superior like Eastbourne. There were no obvious "nobs" driving and

---

38 Coastal towns in England known as beach locales/vacation spots.
39 char à banc (aka charabanc): An open, horse-drawn vehicle with bench seating used in England in the early twentieth century for sight seeing.

walking about, or women dressed up to kill. The Pexbourne visitors were a rather dowdy lot taken all together, but, on the other hand, they sat on the beach, and walked up and down with that air of seeing nobody and nothing in particular which Alfred had observed was one of the insignia of the governing classes.

And there was nothing much to do at Pexbourne, specially on a Sunday. There was no pier; there was no regular promenade; the three picture palaces were, surprisingly, closed; there was nothing but the band.

It was not that Alfred minded a place being quiet; he often said he liked them that way; he was a fairly quiet sort of chap himself compared with some of the fellows he knew. But in that case he liked someone to talk to. Someone perhaps to cuddle. A girl.

But the right sort of girl hadn't turned up at the boarding house. There were two friends staying there, and one wasn't bad looking (you could see her breasts under her jumper; they were the sort you wanted to squeeze): but they hadn't been very come-alongish. And he wasn't going to push himself where he wasn't wanted. He wasn't that sort. But it had been a bit lonely yesterday evening with no getting off; no one at Pexbourne seemed to think about getting off. And now it was Sunday night. And he would have to catch the early train tomorrow without having spoken to anybody. No story to tell the fellows at the office. Nothing to do but listen to this rotten music.

It was in this mood that Mr. James observed Alice standing with shining eyes listening. At first his attention was merely casual; then he observed that this solitary woman muffled in a pink scarf was in a state of some excitement, mingled with a desire not to be seen. Alfred, though a realist in practice, was not without the perception of romance, and he began to find Alice intriguing. A governess crept away for a bit of fun? Too pleased looking to be wanting to commit suicide. She didn't look particularly passionate, but with women you could never really be sure till you got to close quarters. Was she meeting someone? Anyway, he didn't seem to be turning up.

Feeling someone's attention fixed upon her, Alice turned suddenly, and gazed straight at him. She saw a pale good-looking young man with dark eyes, which seemed to be devouring her with rapt attention. They made you feel you were terribly interesting, and also as if all your secrets were known. She felt colour rising in her cheeks, and turned her head away. A queer nervous sensation started to thrill inside her. For a bit it was as if she couldn't seem to hear properly what the band was playing.

Alfred noted the blush with the eye of the professional in such matters. He considered her appearance more intently. A bit scrawny, the soap and honest water sort; but not too bad when she blushed. Not a flapper, of course. But still! He coughed experimentally.

Alice heard, and wondered deeply. Was that meant for her? Don't look! Oh, of course, he didn't mean anything. Just turn round, and glance casually through him to make sure. He was staring at her in a meaning a sort of way. What should she do? Move away? And yet … he must admire her. She was all right standing there. Ignoring him. Her heart beat uncomfortably. She stared fixedly in front of her, seeing nothing.

Alfred sat still for a minute, making up his mind. It seemed as if he could get her if he wanted to, though she was the shy sort. Left it to you to do everything. Of course she wasn't a beauty; but then she looked almost like a lady. She was quite likely to be willing to go for a walk, and not expect him to buy her a coffee. Anything was better than sitting there all evening not saying a word to anybody. "Buck up, old fellow," he told himself. "She can't kill you." And slipped off his perch on the wall.

Alice heard him approach, and felt a little sick and giddy with excitement. Now he was just behind her! Now he was at her side! He was saying something.

"Good evening! Looking for a friend?"

With an effort Alice turned. This was the moment to snub him; to turn away haughtily. To show him she wasn't that kind of a girl. To tell she thought he was making a mistake. There might be someone watching, even if they were well behind the crowd.

"Good evening," she heard her voice saying. Well, after all there was no harm in being civil. He probably didn't mean to be disrespectful. "No, I was just stopping a moment to listen to the band."

"I must say I'm tired of it," said Alf. "There's a much better one at Eastbourne, you know. This strikes me as a very tuppenny-halfpenny affair."

"Oh, certainly the one at Eastbourne is much better," said Alice, resolutely summoning to her mind the picture of one summer three years ago when she had been for a day to Eastbourne. And she had been before, once or twice. "But then it's so much bigger a place – you expect more, don't you?" The way she was talking to a strange man! Quite brightly, and at her ease. As if she had known him for years.

"Well, I can't say I think much of Pexbourne," said Alf. "Just come down for a weekend, you know – from London. It's my first time here, and I wouldn't say that it won't be my last."

"Oh, don't be so hard on poor Pexbourne," said Alice taking hold of all her courage, and looking straight into his eyes.

"Care to come for a stroll?" said Alfred abruptly, returning her gaze with some meaning.

His direct glance recalled Alice to a sense of the enormity of her conduct. She couldn't go for a walk with a strange young man; if he had only been a member of the chapel it would have been different.

"Come on! There's a good girl."

Alice turned and walked by his side hesitatingly. She didn't mind a few steps, but ... "I really oughtn't to ... you see my sister has a bad cold. She's expecting me back ... I really mustn't be more than a minute or two," she added with a nervous laugh that pleaded don't be angry with me.

Alfred did not trouble to reply. She was coming; that was the point. Get her away from the people; then she'd be all right. They walked away from the lights along the sea front in silence. With the consciousness that danger of discovery was being left further and further behind her, Alice started to feel happy and exultant again. A little too excited perhaps. All the same something had happened to her as she had expected it would. She thought of the service in chapel. She had had such beautiful sacred thoughts. And wasn't this a beautiful thing, too, if you looked at it truly? She and this young man walking along in friendship, though a few moments ago neither of them had known of each other's existence. It must be meant. It must mean something.

She turned her head and peeped at his profile. Extraordinary how familiar his face seemed to be already to her. A strong face you'd call it. Quite a good chin. Had he been an officer in the war? Well, perhaps he didn't speak quite like a gentleman; not like Fred Hawthorne, who had been to a public school. But in any case she hated snobbishness.

Alfred turned and caught the warmth of her glance. It encouraged him to take her arm, and press it close as he guided her; and he felt a little shiver run through her at his touch. Really he was beginning to feel quite fond of the woman. She didn't seem at all a standoffish sort.

"You live at Pexbourne, don't you?"

"Yes."

"One of the idle rich, or otherwise – like me?"

"My sister and I take in a few paying guests in the summer; then we just have a very little money of our own which helps us tide over the winter." Strange talking like that; but she felt she could tell this man anything.

"You might do worse. I suppose you find things a bit quiet though?'

"It is rather, yes. Of course we know plenty of people, and all that, but ..." Alice let her voice trail wistfully away. She must make him understand that she wasn't satisfied, that there was no one in the way if he ... suppose they got engaged, how would she explain where they had met? Oh, think of that later! Easily make up something.

"Yes, we all get lonesome at times in spite of our friends. I was feeling quite in the dumps till I saw you."

"Really and truly?" questioned Alice with a coy upward look. Then she felt herself getting hot all over. Ought she to have said that in – in that way? Was it immodest?

"Really and truly," said Alfred. "But as soon as I saw you I said to myself, 'I'd like to know that wo….that girl.'"

This was wonderful. "I felt the same when I saw you," said Alice, speaking very low. That was true, the way his eyes had gone right through her!

They had reached the end of the path along the sea front now. To the left was a track leading inland to lighted houses, and safe respectable pavements. Before them a little path wound up a stony slope and then through a gate to the downs, dark and silent, holding in their mystery all adventure.

Alfred glanced around. There was no one behind them in sight. "What about going up here a bit of way?"

Alice shook her head without speaking. Part of her wanted to go on, oh, ever so much; but no, she couldn't risk it. She'd be absolutely alone with him. And what must Minnie be thinking? No, her adventure was over.

"I'm very sorry," she said, summoning firmness in her voice, "but I must really get back now."

Alfred put his arm round her waist with a sudden movement, and held her to him. "Must you?" he questioned urgently. And then softly, "But you don't want to, do you?"

Alice made no reply. What was she to do? While she hesitated, she felt herself kissed on the lips, at first experimentally, and then long and closely. It seemed as if he would never take his lips away from hers again.

When he did, she felt that the strength had gone out of her. That was how it felt then to be really kissed. Beastly and horrid, but oh, God, it was worth it. She ought to tell him not to, but she couldn't speak. The commercial traveler she had gone to the pictures with years ago had kissed her, tried to kiss her like that; but then she had only felt repelled, and disgusted. Now it was different.

Alfred kissed her again; and this time his kiss burned through her, leaving her whole body weak and hungry. She heard him murmur as if from very far away, "Kiss me."

Resistance had been burnt out of her, and she fastened her lips on his. Like for like. As he had kissed her.

"Let's go on a bit," said Alfred. With his arm round her, he guided her up the slope, and opened the gate. Without his help she felt she could not have moved. She noted her own powerlessness as if it were the only thing that had any reality; when he took his arm away from her to close the gate after them, it was as if everything she desired in life had been taken from her, leaving her cold and a sleepwalker.

"I ought to be going back," she repeated as if to herself, standing still.

"Not yet," said Alfred. And there was determination in his tone. Alice surrendered to the pleasure of giving way to that determination. If he really wanted her to stay with him what could she do?

Triumphantly Alfred led her on. Now his blood had been lit, and he was determined to have as much as he could get. After all, wasn't she old enough to look after herself?

"You like me a little, don't you, dear," he said in her ear gently.

Alice nodded. Oh, yes she did. That made it all right. If they liked each other.

"And you do trust me, don't you? You know I'm a gentleman?" Couldn't always risk that, he thought to himself, but if you could it was always impressive.

"Yes, I know you are," said Alice. Her heart gave an upward leap. She wasn't doing anything wrong really. Narrow-minded people who didn't understand might think evil, but she knew herself ... God knew ... God seemed a long way off now.

"Well, let's sit down here, if it isn't too cold for you. There's a place just over here."

He directed her off the path. His eyes had noted that just to their left the ground dropped sharply a little way and then paused before starting a gentle decline. The curve would make a tolerable hiding place.

"Let's slip down here," he said, his voice rather thick.

Without waiting for a reply, he slipped over, and turning held out his arm to help Alice.

She went to him blindly. A queer sensation of panic caught at her as soon as he went, if only a few yards away. There was only him between her and the world, between her and thinking. She just wanted to be with him. They sat down together.

How dark and cool it was sitting there by themselves. Beyond and below there were little lights shining out of houses, but it seemed to make it all the darker in that little hollow. The ground on which she was sitting felt rough but friendly to her touch. Everything was still, so still that behind them she could hear the mourning lap of the sea. And that, too, made everything so much the more remote. It wasn't herself, Alice Jenkinson, at all, sitting there with a strange young man. It was a dream. She shivered.

"Are you cold?" said Alfred. "Better come close to me. *Close*, I said."

She was very close now, and his arm was round her waist. She knew it was better to keep away, but it made her more afraid if she didn't have the sense of his nearness to lay a warm exciting muffling hand over her thoughts.

Now he was kissing her, again and again. His hands were moving about her ... they were lying down now; her body was limp. It was as if it no longer belonged to her, as if it had become just a Thing. That made it so that you had no responsibility for anything that might be happening to it. Further and further her mind withdrew, averting its attention from everything. No more thinking; a rest at last from thinking … let the Thing have what it had wanted for so long, what now it seemed it had been waiting for.…

A sound called back the departed sentinel.

What was that? Voices! People passing! And she, Alice Jenkinson, she *was* Alice Jenkinson, Mr. Hawthorne's best helper; she could never look Mr. Hawthorne in the face; what was she thinking of? What was happening to her?

She jerked away, and sat upright. "Don't," her lips were saying angrily and sharply. "Don't dare, you … cad!"

How could anyone take such advantage? She was just resting. She had lost her head, but now she understood things. She had been attacked by a man with whom she had just exchanged a few casual words. It was dreadful that such things should be allowed to happen in Pexbourne.

"What's the matter?" said Alfred, startled. Then he added reassuringly, "It's all right, you know. I'm not … it's all right. Honest!"

"You cad!" said Miss Jenkinson again. It was the only word which came to her; and she used it with a sense of satisfaction. Her memory assured her that it was the right word for such an occasion.

Alfred felt aggrieved. Evidently she had finished. No doing anything with a woman once she had made up her mind. As he hesitated, uncertain how to end things with some credit to himself, he heard fresh voices. After a moment he stood up. People were passing through the gate – a woman, two men. No use risking a scene. Better be off. Leave her … If he hurried he might get a bit of supper at the boarding house. Apologise when he got there. Tell the old girl he had been for walk and lost his way. It would be cold meat. The roast beef they'd had for dinner.

"Well, Goodbye. Must be off, or I shall get locked out," he said to Alice with assumed jauntiness. She stared at him blankly. She had not expected him to say that. He couldn't be going!

Alfred lingered uneasily. If she would only call him cad, or something again, it would really make it better for him to hop off. Women who sat silent like this one, and women who shouted and yelled, they were both pretty bad.

"You'll be able to find your way home all right, won't you?"

"Yes, thank you," said Alice coldly. The cad, the bounder!

Alfred felt relieved. Now he had got his cue. "Well, cheerio!" he said, and walked rapidly away. Alice tried not to turn, but after a moment she did so, and saw him go through the gate, and disappear.

Two figures sprang up from the grass only a few yards away. A man and a girl. They must have been somewhere near all the time, or she would have heard them come. Had they heard anything? Heard her cry out? She mustn't let them notice her, in any case. She turned her back quickly, and fumbled in her handbag.

She became conscious that her hat was all pushed on one side, and her coat disarranged, and started to tidy herself with uncertain fingers. When the couple had disappeared, she stood up. There couldn't be any mud sticking to her because the ground had been quite dry. And they hadn't really stopped there very long.

But still it must be late. As if in answer to her question she heard a church clock start to strike. Carefully she counted the strokes. It couldn't be eleven? No, ten! She had been away from home about an hour and a half. Somehow it seemed longer. All the same Minnie would be in a state.

But still she stood there. It was as though if she once moved, she would have planted her feet once and for all in an ugly threatening unfriendly world from which hereafter there would be no escape. If she waited a bit, perhaps something would happen to save her. Perhaps even, he might come back and apologise. If he would only do that it would be so much better.

In the distance she could just see the three people who had startled her. Two men and a woman. She remembered that they had had that drawly upper-class sort of voice when they had passed by. The kind of people who would be staying at the Queen's. What would they have thought about her if they had seen anything? No, don't flinch! They would think her a vulgar cheap person, someone perhaps who ought to be locked up. Or perhaps because she wasn't very young, or very – may as well face it –very nice looking, they would find something amusing about it. Were both those men in love with that woman? They might be. Women in books always had a least two men wildly in love with them.

Now she couldn't see them any longer. They had gone, gone forever. She shivered…. What on earth was she thinking about? What had those people to do with her? She must be getting home to Minnie. He wouldn't be coming back now. And if he did, why then, of course, she would threaten to send for the policeman. After the way he had tried to take advantage of her. Disgusting! Horrible! Still she had pulled him. She had told him he was a cad. She had sent him away.

How blue the sky was. So deep and rich. You might go into it for miles and miles, flying on and on and on. What was the sea looking like? Queer the way she wanted to see things!

She climbed on to the path, and looked down over the cliffs. Oh, how cold-looking, dark and grey and still. She didn't like looking at it. When it was blue and there were waves topped with white foam, that was the time to look at the sea. Not now. When you listened to it breaking on the shore, and then falling back, again and again – it would never stop, all through the night – perhaps she was fanciful, but it sounded so lonely and sad. Or perhaps not sad. For it didn't care about human beings at all. It didn't care about what happened to her at all.

Of course there were lots of women like her, women who had never been loved; who had never had chances of meeting men. This town was packed with spinsters, and heaps of them were much better looking and could talk and dress better than the other women you saw married. But in a quiet seaside place where no one came but families, and an occasional tripper, what chance was there? Mostly it didn't matter. You did your work, were useful to people, respected, quite important in your way. Mr. Hawthorne had really and truly said three times that he didn't know what he would do without her, and heaps of other nice things. Perhaps she was silly to think of what he said so much, but it *did* help.

Oh, it was all right, mostly! Just sometimes in the night when you couldn't get off to sleep; or when you came across a couple in a shelter making love to each other; or when people in the church got married – she had subscribed five shillings, more than some of the other people in the choir, when Mary Riddell had married Fred Read – or when there was a sunset – Minnie never really appreciated sunsets, she only pretended she did – just a few times there were when it seemed a bit unfair that you hadn't been loved and married in the ordinary way.

It was chilly now in spite of her pink scarf. Dark, too. The summer was over. It wouldn't do to say; but she liked the winter better than the summer. Quieter and more restful.

If she ever saw that young man again, she would cut him. If he dared speak to her, she wouldn't listen. The sea looked cold as cold. Queer, how when you lived by the sea you never noticed it much. But, of course, it was there all the time.

She would have to get back. The band would have finished. It finished at ten. She could tell Minnie something. Not quite everything. Say she had been accosted, had to go out of her way. It was true enough. And Minnie never understood anything properly. She was awfully stupid and greedy in little ways, was Minnie, if people only knew.

With an effort of will she moved, and went through the gate, and back to the front. An hour ago she had come that way with him. She dismissed the thought from her, and squaring her shoulders walked briskly. She had had an unpleasant experience, that was all. Heaps of girls would think nothing of it. And women too. It didn't do to brood over things. She might get to think she had really encouraged him. Some women might have done. But she certainly had given him no cause to take any liberty. Let him kiss her? Well, that was nothing after all. No one said anything to a kiss nowadays. She had just been polite and friendly till he got objectionable. It was the pink scarf perhaps. She must be careful and not wear it again.

In any case, no good thinking about it. It was all over now, and as long as nobody knew, there was no harm done. No one had seen. She was sure of that.

Nothing had happened. There was really nothing she need blame herself for at all. Let's see now! There was the Guild of Help meeting tomorrow evening. That was something nice to look forward to. She must remember to say a few words to Mrs. Hawthorne in the school room about the decorations.

Was that Mr. and Mrs. Telford in the distance? Yes, just turning in at the gate after a stroll. Good thing they hadn't seen her. She would have had to stop and speak; they would have asked her what she was doing out so late. Mr. Telford was the joking sort, a bit vulgar.

Nearly there now. She wouldn't say anything; she couldn't be bothered with all Minnie's questions tonight. She had a headache. So she had! A really bad one! She could feel it pressing on her temples.

It had been a very good sermon that evening. All the hymns had gone well, except the last one. Mr. Hawthorne had been very interesting about Judas. It was terrible to think of the way he must have felt when he went out into the night and hanged himself. She must tell Minnie about it the next morning. Though she often couldn't help thinking – course, she might be wrong – that Minnie wasn't really religious.

She put her key into the front door. Hearing the sound, Minnie came to the front door.

"Alice, where have you been? Do you know it's after half-past ten? I've been terrified out of my life wondering what had happened to you."

Alice went past her into the room. "I am very sorry," she said. "I've been [on] quite a walk."

Minnie started. "A walk! Why, whatever for?"

"Mrs. Coleman was out. So then I went for a bit of a walk. I had a headache and I thought a little fresh air might do it good. I didn't want to tell you in case you might be worried. And … well, a man followed me. I had to go miles out of my way. It was awful!"

"A man followed you! Really, Alice? Did he speak to you? Why didn't you turn back home?"

What stupid questions Minnie asked! As if she didn't believe her, too. Alice struggled with the temptation to tell her how Alfred had come up and spoken to her. Asked her to come a walk most politely as far as that went. Better not. Minnie would keep her talking all night.

"Minnie, do leave me alone! Can't you see I am all upset? I'm going to bed now. Sorry about the washing up. I'll tell you everything in the morning. He didn't speak or anything. Only called out and walked after me, and of course

I was far too nervous to turn round and face him, so I just hurried on and on as fast as I could. He was such a big man."

She started to move away. Minnie showed her disappointment. "Well, you are queer, not telling me. Don't you want anything to eat? A cup of tea? … Was he a young man? He must have been drunk. Whereabouts was it?"

Drunk indeed! "No, he wasn't drunk," said Alice sharply, opening the door and viewing the staircase as a way of escape. "Not at all drunk. And young. Rather good looking, I should say, though I didn't stop to notice him much. Good night! I hope your cold will be better in the morning."

"Good night," said Minnie. Her voice was noncommittal.

She sat down and gave herself up to thought. There was something very funny about this business. It was not likely that any man would follow Alice. Yet she was certainly upset. Looked queer, and acted queer. It was an odd idea going for a walk, too. Pretty cool leaving her the whole evening! And not helping to wash up. So much for Alice's religion! She had probably been to the band. That was it! Could someone have spoken to her there or something? But how was it she acted as if it were such a mystery, instead of telling the story? Perhaps she had been followed. … Alice of all people!

Grudgingly she mused on the miracle. Then she stood up, and gazed at herself in the piece of glass over the mantelpiece. "I have got a cold tonight," she reflected, "but I'm certainly much better-looking than she is even with a cold. And younger!"

She looked at herself from various angles, her face intent and thoughtful. Then she put out the light, and went upstairs.

THE OTHER WOMAN

It was twenty past eight on Saturday night. Monica sat in her bedroom with a book she wasn't reading in front of her. She was waiting; she had been waiting for some time, and she couldn't settle to anything any longer. He was late; he was twenty minutes late; he had never been late before. Did that mean then he wasn't coming?

She wouldn't, she justified herself, have felt that little tug of fear which was now pulling at her – because that seemed as if she didn't trust him – only things hadn't been the same lately. They hadn't been the same since George's wife had found out about them; and had been so very noble over it all. If only she hadn't been so noble; if only she had made a scene, been horrid … anything! But she had just cried a little, and then offered to divorce George, to efface herself; said she would always let him see the children, behaved in fact most perfectly. George said she had been wonderful. He had kept saying that over and over and over again. And she, Monica, had just to smile and agree.

She knew George thought now that he had misjudged his wife; that perhaps she did love him after all. That made her own love not so important as it had been to him.

It was half-past eight now. What a queer noise the gas made sizzling! It always made that noise of course, only you never heard it unless you were listening. That was a funny thing to think: the heaps and heaps of noises that went on sounding all the time, and heaps of people had never really listened to them once in their whole lives.

Then if he didn't come, would that mean that at last he was giving her up? But then she had asked him; she had said that they had better not see each other again if the thought of his wife gave him such pain. And he had cried out, "Don't say that; don't say that!" And clung to her. He had asked her to hold him tight, never to let him go. And she had put her arms so tightly round him and promised that she would always stay with him while he wanted her. "And I shall always want you," he had said. She knew he loved her, too. You couldn't make a mistake about love when it was really there. Books were often so silly about that. The real thing was so big that you always knew. But there was something lacking. It was, she thought, because he didn't put her first, in front of everything. He wanted always to do the right thing. Dear George!

Surely that was a knock at the door of the flat. Everything stopped inside Monica, and then went on lightly, dancing as if they had been let out of an airless cage. She ran through the little landing to the door. What fright he had given her by being so late! She would tell him that.

There was no one outside. But someone was just passing through the door of the adjoining flat. That had been the knock she heard. It hadn't been her own door after all. And anyway, she remembered now, George never knocked; he always rang.

She returned to her seat, and sat down, feeling a little sick: just the way she had felt when she had been sent to school for the first time. She was beginning to be afraid that something awfully horrid might be in front of her. She tried to compose herself, and leant her elbow on the side of the chair with her cheek resting on the knuckles of her hand.

After a little while, her intent attitude won her own observation. She thought drearily, "I wonder how many women are waiting in London tonight, waiting for the men who never come. And men, too, I suppose, waiting for women who never come. Walking about with their hands in their pockets, whistling, pretending not to care. And getting more and more afraid. And God doesn't care. God laughs perhaps, because He sees what the other person is doing. And He enjoys a good joke."

She heard a taxi in the distance, and jumped up. "O God," she prayed, "I'll be good. I take back what I said now. I'll do anything. I'll never complain any more if You make that taxi stop at the door."

"With him in it, *George*, you know," she added in desperate haste. God might wriggle out of it by pretending not to understand.

The taxi was very near now. It made a loud buzzing noise of cheerful defiance, and ran on, getting fainter and fainter. Its going seemed heartless, like a train that went on running for a bit after it had just run over a man. Of course the train didn't know what it had done, and the taxi didn't know that it should have had George inside it, instead of the horrible person it probably had.

Monica struck her knee. "I can't bear it," she said aloud to the stillness of the room. "He isn't coming, and I can't bear it."

Shocked at herself, she sat up straight, and frowned. She was being silly. George might easily have been delayed by something, some business matter perhaps. When he did turn up, she would feel no end of a fool at having got herself into such a state. She consulted her watch.

Five to nine. He wasn't an hour late yet. And you really couldn't say that a person was late until ten minutes after the appointed time. Ten minutes or even quarter of an hour. That made him just over half an hour late. Anything might happen to keep a person that late. She was really getting hysterical. Stupid, it was! But if only George hadn't a wife; hadn't got that awful woman.

Some people might call her pretty. She didn't. A very obvious type. Dark hair, parted in the centre, and plaited in those knot affairs over the ears. Everybody who thought they were artistic did their hair that way. Ear rings. Languishing! But didn't quite bring it off. "No, my lady, you don't quite bring it off," murmured Monica to herself with satisfaction. And her legs weren't half as pretty as her own. Just sticks. No shape. Nothing but sticks.

As for the nobility stunt. Did the woman really think that she was fool enough to be taken in by it? It was just the usual woman's trick for holding on to her own property. She knew that George was a bit of a mug.[40] Found it easy to marry him probably. And now she intended to hold him by hypocrisy. Lord, how easily men were taken in by women!

Yes, she might as well face it. It might be that his wife was keeping him. Had burst into tears, or something, just as he was going. And George had felt bound to console her. Kissed her, perhaps, taken her into his arms. Oh, it was damnable, damnable!

40 Mug: A fool or gullible person.

It must be that woman. What else could it be? What kept people from their appointments? An accident?

Heavens, that might be it, and she was misjudging him. After all, he was her own dear George. And he might have got run over. Perhaps he was dead; dead, or suffering awful pain.

She rose, and walked half blindly about the room. "I must go to him," she said to herself. "At once."

Swallowing hard, she reached for her coat and hat from the peg. Pulling on her hat in front of the glass, she saw that her face was twitching queerly; and there was a look in her eyes that she couldn't bear to meet.

She turned away, and stood still, her hand gripping the top of the bed post. "Control yourself," she insisted in a hard strained voice. "Control yourself, you poor idiot! What do you think you're doing? Aren't you making a fool of yourself? Think now."

She forced her mind to work. Of course he might have got run over, but the chances were against. All the same he *might* have got run over. Heaps of people were. Well then, presuming he had got run over–presuming! That was a funny word to use – what would happen to him? He'd be taken to a hospital. That's where people were taken when they were hurt or fell down in the streets. An ambulance was sent for by the police (she averted her mental gaze from the picture of a white ambulance tearing along while people stopped still to stare after it) and the man, or woman, of course, was lifted into it and taken to a hospital. What hospital, now, would it be? She tried to think of the way he would come.

Wimbledon. That was where he lived. Yes, but the accident wouldn't happen till he got out of the District at Charing Cross.[41] Crossing Villiers Street? Or just by the Strand? That might be it. He would be struck by a taxi as it turned into the station. Not looking where he was going, but thinking of her. Yes, well, in that case he'd be taken to Charing Cross Hospital. Charing Cross Hospital rose up in front of her, pale and yellow, with its hundreds of secretive windows. It had, perhaps, taken her lover, her child, into its cold sanitary efficiency.

But then he might have got out at Victoria. That was almost as near for him. Killed in Victoria Street. Killed in Victoria Street. She repeated the words, seeing them huge and staring as if written on a newspaper placard. Well, not *killed*. It couldn't be *killed*. People who were run over were not usually killed, or not immediately. She didn't mean killed. But supposing an accident had happened – yes, that was what she was trying to get at: supposing an accident

---

41 District: A reference to Charing Cross tube station (on the District line) with entrances located in Trafalgar Square and The Strand.

had happened in Victoria Street, what hospital would the body … not the body, that wasn't the word … well, where would he be taken to? There was St. George's Hospital. But perhaps there was one nearer. Wasn't there one in the Vauxhall Bridge Road? Or there was Westminster Hospital, not too far away. It all depended where exactly the accident had happened. And then, of course, there were cases of hospitals being too full to take anyone else in. No more beds! Hadn't she read in newspapers about serious cases that had died because they were so long in getting to a hospital?

She sat still, and watched herself going from hospital to hospital, asking questions of porters: fat comfortable men they would be, who would stare her up and down, gravely putting two and two together; or else thin with black moustaches, inclined to be bullying or indifferent. "No, Miss! No one of that name."

It would be awful! But she would do it. Yes, she would do it. She would spend all night doing it, because George was hers, hers to look after and protect. But was it the best thing to do? That was the point. Was it the best thing to do? Because she didn't really know that there had been an accident. You had to admit – it was silly not to – that people who didn't keep their appointments, who didn't come when they said they would, had not usually been run over, or killed, or anything like that. Besides if there had been an accident to George, they would send for his wife. Not her. They wouldn't know anything about her. And if they did they wouldn't care. The wife was the person to be by the bedside in the last hours; she, Monica, had no right at all: she was only "an affair." "Another woman has been seen hanging round the hospital; his bit of fluff; really smitten on him, I believe." "Ah, old George wasn't so quiet as he looked!" Those were the sort of things they'd say. It was all right; she wouldn't give them the chance.

She took off her hat, and laid it on the bed. Then she went over to the washing stand, and poured some cold water into the basin out of the white jug that she had always loved because it was so plump and comfortable and inquiring. Filling the palms of her hands with water, she splashed it over her face twice, three, four times. Then she dried her face, and going over to the dressing table re-creamed and powdered herself, and combed her hair. Doing all these things would brace her up to think better. There was no use getting in a panic; there was no use rushing round to hospitals or asking policemen. If George didn't come, why then, he didn't come, and that was all there was to it.

All the same he might still come. She looked at her watch with a sort of fear. Twenty past nine. The time was going with extraordinary slowness, and with extraordinary rapidity.

He might still come, and there she was sitting ready to receive him. To receive him? How stiff that sounded. Why was she thinking in such queer phrases? It was true he might have had an accident. But it was, on the whole, unlikely. She felt she'd have known at the very moment it occurred if anything terrible like that had happened. What was more likely was that the other woman – how she hated her; God, how she hated her! – had kept him.

A fierce hot misery gripped her. It was different from the pain that had caught at her when she thought of him being knocked down and lying help-less, with crowds of strangers gazing gloatingly. Then she had gone soft and weak, melted away in an agony of longing to be with him, to put her arms round him, to hold him, to comfort him. This was different: this was love's hard ache; a fretting for something that had been taken away from her, that was deserting her, leaving her desolate forever. And this was the worst sort of pain. She tried to turn from it to the thought of some evil which had happened to George; but now this evaded her. The other pain was the truer one. It was that which she had heard in the distance before, claiming her as its own. Only she had never listened, never admitted it. Now she would. She had never been sure of him, never when she was with him, and never when she was away from him. He was kind, and was afraid to take, and wanted to do what was right. Well, perhaps that was inevitable in the circumstances. Men were different from women. Was any woman sure of her man, even when he told her, and she knew that it was true, that he loved her? Not when there was even the shadow of another woman floating round. And when the other woman was the wife, the lawfully married wife, whom he had sworn to love and cherish, "for better or for worse, for richer or for poorer, till death do us part" – something like that it went –then it was the most difficult, the most humiliating, the most damnable of all! Yes, it was damnable, that was the word.

Monica sat up and clenched her fists. Her face grew dark and frowning. She thought of all she had given up. Why, she could have been married sev-eral times! She was pretty, she was intelligent, she could talk … it wasn't as if she was a cheap little girl of no account; the kind that usually solaced mar-ried men. George had never really appreciated all the sacrifices she had made for him. People had criticized; how she had disturbed and hurt poor Auntie Connie! And she hadn't minded; she had never denied him, never cut him in the street if she had been with anyone; always put him first, always been ready whenever he wanted her. And this was her reward! She was left waiting here, sitting in her bedroom, a whole evening wasted and spoiled. And no word of explanation or apology. That's what she complained about. "I don't want him to come now," she muttered to herself, "except that I'd like the chance of tell-ing him exactly what I think of him, his cowardice and weakness. I won't go on with it any longer. I'll give him up. I'm through! I'm finished. There can be

no satisfactory explanation for this evening. And it's the last straw." She nodded and set her lips.

A barrel organ[42] came and started to play outside the window. She listened
to it fascinated, as the sick mind takes hold of anything to divert itself.

She knew what it was playing. It was playing a valse tune called, "What'll
I do?" The chorus went round in little moans, and finished by jerking upwards,
right into your heart. Such a tawdry shameful little song it was! What were the
words? Something like:

"What'll I do
When you are far away,
And I am feeling blue?
What'll I do
When I am wondering who
Is kissing you?
What'll I do?
What'll I do?"

"Oh shut up," her heart cried out in resentment. "Shut up, can't you?"

But the barrel organ went on and on and on. Heartbreaking it was, playing out there with everything round it so hot and restless and seeking. Women
calling to each other; men in public houses: public houses which took on these
autumn evenings an exaggerated look of warmth and excitement; a baby crying and someone scolding it. The way babies and little children cried was so
disturbing. They cried as if their whole hearts and their whole selves were in
it: no reserve at all, yelling on and on as if watching their world crashing down
around them. And yet you knew all the time it would pass: a great clamour
about nothing. But what a great noisy clamour it was!

How it went on, that barrel organ! Over and over again, its plaintive little trickles of sound! Was there warmth, and ease, nowhere? No satisfying
warmth anywhere? Only desire and pain?

The barrel organ went away. Far down the street it could be heard starting its melancholy little round of tunes all over again. On and on from street
corner to street corner. From public house to public house the whole evening
through. Asking everywhere, "What'll I do?"

She took her mind away from it. Here was she then, sitting in her bedroom,
because so she could hear the bell better; sitting by her gas fire, waiting for
someone, for her lover, who didn't come. Twenty to ten! No, it wasn't very

---

42 Barrel organ: A mechanical musical instrument played by turning a crank, often used
   by street musicians (called barrel grinders) in Europe.

likely he would come now. He was staying with *her*. Being good! She laughed a little to herself.

With one hand she stroked her hair, looking round the room with parted questioning lips. There must be a way of escaping from the awful thing which was thrusting itself slowly, but very surely, in front of her.

What was that thing? Hush! Don't say it! Not yet. Wasn't she after all being very silly? Morbid, they called it. Of course she would see George again. There would be a long loving and ever so apologetic letter in the morning explaining everything. He had tried to get away till the very last moment, and then it had been too late to send a telegram.

"How stupid and childish I am!" she said to herself with an effect of cheerful calm. She got up, holding in her ears her own assurance, and walked into the sitting room. She re-arranged the papers and books on the table. She put the cushion on the chair straight. She looked at the flowers, and thought of taking them out and doing them again. But that would be stupid; that would be giving the show away because she had only bought them this afternoon. She had bought them this afternoon because George was coming. And he hadn't come after all.

Unconsciously she put her hand to her heart. It was a little stab of pain she had felt then. She stood for a while staring at the flowers. A little grisly they looked now, those big bright golden chrysanthemums. They had been ready to dance, and there had come no piper. Perhaps it was a funeral now they would celebrate.

Her eyeballs went hot and dry, but no tears came. She couldn't cry. It was a pity, she thought, she couldn't cry. She felt so lonely. They had meant to sit close together and make love,[43] warming and soothing each other. But now she was by herself. A girl alone in a flat with no one to love her.

She went slowly back to the bedroom, and sat down by the window. Listen! Steps coming up the street. Steps that rang out loud and clear. They belonged to a person who knew where he was going, and meant to get there. Perhaps ... all of her subsided into a listening. She was poised ready to be at the door at the first ring. She saw herself in his arms, crying: she knew she would cry if he came now. The steps went past the door. Still loudly and firmly they echoed on down the street.

Monica nodded her head slowly twice. "Of course," she said to herself, "of course, he's not coming now. I wasn't really expecting it."

Her watch said it was nearly ten.

---

43 Make love: This is in the sense of the older usage, to pay romantic attention to, not to have intercourse.

No good waiting any longer then. Sitting round and doing nothing except getting worked up. Should she cook herself some food? An omelette? But she didn't want anything to eat. Well, how about a cup of tea? She didn't really want it. It was silly to have it if she didn't want it. She had thought she would be making some for George. He loved her to make tea for him, to sit drinking it alone together in her own place. Or should she get into bed? It would be something to do to take off her clothes, and have a good wash.

But if he should come. If he should manage to slip round just for a moment and say good night. She wouldn't undress till eleven anyway. That was another hour. Sixty more minutes of sitting there waiting. Minutes were sometimes very important when you had to live through them.

Another taxi in the distance. Monica moved quickly to the window, drew the curtain, and stood watching. Here it was! Just turning the corner. A black car running on smoothly and eagerly. It was going too steadily for it to stop. She must prepare herself for it not to stop. It hadn't stopped. That was that!

She stared after it. It would be good to be in a swiftly moving car like that, going on and on, always on, right out of the world, out of time and space and consciousness and people: escaped for ever from having to face life … things, something in particular that she might have to face very soon.

For a little while she stood staring out of the window. A misty night it was with people walking up and down very intent upon themselves. She knew nothing about them, and they knew nothing about her. Happy or miserable, it was all the same. Each lived their own lives, and went down to the grave leaving no record. And what good would it be if they did tell? Such faint whispers against the bustle and the hurly-burly.

God! Who was that turning the corner of the street? It was like him. Monica resolved all the life in her into a desperate urge. God! make it be him! Make it be him! Make it be him! She concentrated on the fierce appeal, while she peered at the approaching figure. Surely the intensity of her desire must make him turn into George as he approached, even if it hadn't been he to begin with. Surely it must be George coming!

No, it wasn't George. Not the least like him really. Just something in the walk that had suggested him for a moment. How silly of her!

The strength left her, and she felt cold and dull except for the heavy ache that laboured within her. "No use standing here," she said to herself. "Playing understudy for the Blessed Damozel."[44] She pulled down the blind, and went

---

44 Blessed Damozel: A reference to the poem of that name published in 1850 by Dante Gabriel Rossetti. The poem describes a damsel in heaven yearning to be reunited with her lover. Monica's comparison of herself to the blessed damozel shows how she perceives herself as faithful and blameless in her affair.

in a resolute spirit to sit by the fire. She spent some time fighting against the temptation to consult her watch. At least she yielded, looking at it furtively. The time had gone a bit quicker. It was twenty past ten: a little after twenty past, really. "He won't come now," she muttered to herself, and stretched out her legs to the fire. Then she gave a little nod and repeated the words, "He won't come now." She must finish with any idea of expecting him once and for all. Why not read?

But she didn't read. Instead she sat very still with her head bowed. There was a silence. Then as if in protest against the unseemly quietness the gas began to flicker. It demanded another shilling to keep it going. It jumped about a bit friskily, and then, turning sulky, burned lower and lower. But no one heeded its descent; and after a little it was provoked to a final flare of anger, then it went so low that the room was almost in darkness.

Monica, unaware, sat on. No movement came from her till, suddenly, a sound pulled at her attention. Someone seemed to be fumbling with the lock on the front door below. She raised her head and listened, her hand going to her throat. For a brief second the noise came again and then stopped: Monica went on listening urgently but there was only stillness.

Then, cut by a sharp fear of being given a chance and missing it, she rose, and ran out on to the landing. There was no one outside her front door. She ran on down the stairs, and stood in the dark entrance hall leading from the street, her ears trying to strain through the front door, which was usually shut at ten o'clock. Everything seemed quiet. With lips tightly set, and wide staring eyes, she stepped forward and drew back the latch, opening the door. Nothing! Nothing was there!

She stood for moment staring up and down the street. Two young men went by, and one turned his head to look at her. He smiled and murmured something to the other. They both came to a tentative halt; and Monica, uncomprehending, gazed back at them. Her disordered fancy was just beginning to suggest that they might have brought some message from George when the one who had first looked at her raised his hat and said, "Good evening." The direct address restored Monica to a consciousness of her surroundings. She stepped back and shut the door to. Then she went slowly upstairs.

It puzzled her to find her bedroom almost quite dark when she returned, except for a golden glow that suffused one side of the mantle. Mechanically she went to her bag and took out a shilling which she remembered having placed there, wondering gaily if they would use it. Sometimes it was pleasanter to sit in the dark. How long ago it seemed since she had thought that over her tea! After she had put it into the meter, she went back to her chair, covering her eyes with her hands.

Then that noise hadn't been George. Or if it had he had gone away again leaving no message. But she was sure there had been a noise at the entrance door. There were often sounds you couldn't explain, especially when you were by yourself. She sometimes thought they were ghosts, spirits of the dead. Well then ... suppose – only suppose, of course – that George had been run over and killed; or suppose – she wondered why she had not thought of that before – suppose he had killed himself (she remembered that he had once suggested that they should both kill themselves as a solution, and she had wondered then how seriously he had said it), well, suppose George had died, somehow. And suppose, he had tried to come to her on his way into the ghostly darkness. That might have been the knock she had heard!

Pain in full tide swept over her, so that she rose and walked up and down the room, sometimes beating the table or other hard objects as she passed in her effort to try and think. But for some time nothing came to her but a wild cry of protest, "Not George dead! Not George killed himself! O God, don't let it be that!"

It was too much. She went down on her knees and with her head in the counterpane strove hard to regain control of her thoughts. At last this came to her: if George was dead and had tried to come to her, he might be in this very room trying to tell her something.

Instantly she rose and went back to her chair, sitting very still, with all her senses alert, looking round her expectantly. First there was, it appeared, a rather embarrassed silence on the part of the room; then came the noise of the gas again; a steady hum that seemed to contain a sneer of derision. She rose and turned it very low. Then sitting again: "George!" she said. And then insistently, "George, my darling, my dearest, I am here. Waiting!"

From outside came a loud burst of talk which reached into the room. The people were being turned out of the public house at the corner of the street. They were struggling out in reluctant one's and two's and three's; and stood in little groups talking. Two men were having an argument and one shook his fist in the other's face. It was their voices that Monica found it difficult to brush away. She sat hearing them in a spirit of agonised hatred. Would they never get on? Drunken fools! Would they never stop? Damn the blasted fools!

There came a spell of quiet. But, with her eyes searching from corner to corner, she could only see the familiar motionless objects. The room was empty. Except for her it was empty. Terribly empty.

She tried another way. She put her fingers over her closed eyes and pressed her thumbs to her ears to keep out sight and sound. And all of herself was concentrated into a question. First she summoned George to her with a deep urgency, pushing back all that came between. Then she asked him, "George, where are you? George, tell me! Are you dead?"

Only silence. Still silence. It was as if he didn't care to answer. As if he couldn't answer. He had, she felt, his back turned to her, and was refusing to look.

She would ask others then. She would ask God. Thrusting the words into the darkness in front of her with all her strength she asked, "Is George dead? Or ill? What has happened to him? I have to know." Every ounce of concentration in her went to maintain the cry, to maintain its appeal through the darkness. No one could desire knowledge so much as she did and fail of its possession.

At last a wordless reply seemed to come to her. The conviction grew within her that George was not dead: that he was not even ill; only that he had gone from her. She realised him as moving about the same world as herself, but not feeling her as she was feeling him. It was as if he had put a barrier between them, and was occupied in turning his attention away from it. Also it seemed to her quite definitely that, Sunday though it was, she would receive news of him in the morning, but not good news.

With a long sigh and a shiver Monica took her hands away and opened her eyes. The light hurt them so that she had to close them again. She was as someone waked from sleep into the cold bleak morning when the evil that has haunted, springing backwards and forwards through restless dreams, assuming strange and bewildering disguises, now stands up clear and naked, showing itself as something from which there is no escape. In that moment Monica was sure, however quickly her mind might start to retreat, turning this way or that, seeking refuge, that George did not really belong to her; and that he was separating himself from her while she waited there.

It was clear, then, that her business was to face this. George gone from her – what did that mean to her? How did it leave her? Oh, she was too tired, too beaten to think of it now. It was too big. Much too big. It was all her life; all the life she had been conscious of for months past. It was too hard; too hard. It couldn't really be true. It was George's name she had said when she woke up in the morning: like stretching out her arms to something so warm and sweet that nothing else mattered. It made you able to jump out of bed and not care a bit about what the post brought you or anything that might happen outside of George. You went about all day hugging a mighty piece of comfort that shielded you from everything.

Well, yes. That was what it had been, and now it was there no longer. Without George, life was remote and unpleasant, silly and meaningless like a play you stared at from an uncomfortable seat at the back of the gallery, unable to see or hear anything of moment while hard knees pressed into you, and you got hotter and more uncomfortable. In the end you went out thinking it wasn't worth the money you'd paid....

Pretty comparisons to keep her from thinking! George had gone – that was the plain fact. And it was mean, it was wicked, it wasn't fair! She would like to kill him for it: coldly and with a contemptuous smile she would like to kill him. To pay him back. She understood now why girls brought breach of promise cases. Why they so far "forgot themselves"! When people had loved you, or pretended to love you, and then took the arm of their love away from you, it was mean and ought to be punished. They ought to be punished, condemned as unfit to live.

The anger which had flamed burnt down and out. She was being silly again. Talking of punishment! Making little faces and grimaces at a thing which was hard and stern and terrible. A vast wheel going on and on, crushing and killing, and you tried to raise yourself and shake your fist after it, uttering little squeals, little threats.

A ring at the bell! Quite loud and firm. She couldn't possibly be deceived this time. Hurrah! It must be George; and as long as it was George nothing mattered. If he talked about leaving her, she'd persuade him out of it. Oh, she would kiss him so that he would never leave her. She'd make him understand that she adored him, that she worshipped him, that she'd die for him. George! George! To feel him! That was all she wanted. Just to see him, and feel him.

She was running down the stone stairs now, with love and longing raising their wild hosannas in her head. Her welcome went before her through the door she couldn't open fast enough. She peered past a woman who was standing there. George must have gone. Where was he?

The woman was saying something to her. She must listen and understand. "Mrs. Hobson?" Oh, yes, Mrs. Hobson had the flat next to her own. Would she come upstairs? It *was* a very cold night.

She was back in her own room now, and she felt pleased that her voice had sounded so collected. But there was a choking feeling at the back of her throat; a sob that wouldn't come. So God wasn't tired of making a fool of her yet! Of course she didn't believe in God; never had believed in God since she was a kid, and never would believe in Him. But she was being made a fool of.

Mrs. Hobson had never had a caller so late before; she had never known her [to] have any callers much at all. What time was it? Twenty-five past eleven. It was lucky for that woman that she had been able to get in at all. It was a very queer time to go ringing on other people's bells. "I hope she will die of a most horrible loathsome disease, and go to hell," she muttered.

Half-past eleven it was. For three and a half hours she had been tortured. She'd go to bed now. She didn't care any more about anything. They could do their worst. She didn't mind.

Of course it would be a good thing to see George's wife, that horrible filthy cad of a woman, paid out. The woman who had spoilt her life. Doing it with a noble smile on her rouged lips. The hellcat. The ugly devil. Never mind. Some day perhaps. She would show her. But now, she didn't care. She was going to get undressed, get into bed, and finish with them all.

It was when she was undressing that the long choking sobs came. She wanted George so. That was it. "My dearest, my sweetheart, my darling; my own precious dear darling, I love you." "My darling, can you hear me? I love you." "Dearest George, I love you." "I will always love you, darling." "George dear, my dear." "Oh, my dear. My dear."

And in bed, hiding her head in the pillow, she called to him again: "George, my dearest, didn't you know how I loved you? Didn't you know, my sweet, my darling, my little boy? My own little boy, dear. Didn't you know, sweetheart? My precious sweetheart! I do love you so, my darling. My dear, dear darling! More than anybody, dearest. My dearest! Dearest George!"

In the morning there was a letter waiting with her milk outside. She saw it as soon as she opened the door, and her heart, that had bidden her laugh at her terrors of last night when she woke first, grew still and cold in its fear. He must have left it very late on the previous evening, she thought. Perhaps if she had waited up all night, she could have stopped him. But it was too late now. She opened it, and read it, standing very still. It said that George felt they couldn't go on; that his duty was towards his wife; he and Monica were not the sort of people who could hurt anybody else; that he would always remember her, and love her, but that he hoped she would forget him, and forgive, if she could, the wrong he had done her; that he thanked her for all the joy and happiness she had brought into a life that had been very lonely, and now would be lonely again except for memories....

The other woman had won. That was that. Monica folded it up carefully, put it back in the envelope, and laid it down. She had been quite right last night after all. George *had* given her up.

Of course she had always expected it would end some day. Affairs, this had been just an affair, always did end some time or another. All the same it was rather queer. To think that she and George wouldn't love each other anymore; wouldn't see each other, perhaps, any more.

She went to the window, drew the curtains, and looked out. A rainy day: rain falling gently, but with unostentatious determination, from a grey sky on to greasy brownish pavements, and a black road with little puddles in it. It must have been raining a long, long time.

The people who were setting out to church had umbrellas and wore mackintoshes. They walked with heads down. Going to say prayers, sing hymns, listen inattentively to sermons, and then go home to a hot joint. It was really surprising how the world went patiently on and on and on doing the same things. Tomorrow it would be Monday.

Tomorrow it would be Monday. And she wouldn't be seeing George. She had better think out something else to do some time. They had thought of going to the Old Vic.[45]

She had a headache; a horrible headache. That was worrying last night, and then crying, and not going to sleep. She wasn't going to think any more about George. It would only make her headache absolutely unbearable. After all, did it greatly matter? People went on falling in love, and then getting tired or disappointed, and falling out of love; seeing each other a lot, and then not seeing much of each other – they went on doing that all the time. And it was really rather futile, childish.

What a perfectly filthy morning it was! She would make herself some tea, have some aspirin, and get back to bed. As she waited for the kettle to boil, the Sunday morning harmonium came, and, as always, started to play "Abide With Me."[46] It thumped out the tune in weary gasps of sound. Monica listened frowningly. Why should anybody choose to make such a horrible noise – on Sunday morning – in the rain – and even expect to get paid for it! The man who played was probably frightfully poor. But she didn't mind how poor or starving he was. She didn't mind at all. She didn't mind what happened to anybody.

This was a great triumph for George's dear wife, Veronica, who loved him so all of a sudden. Well, let her have her triumph. She was quite welcome to it.

She lay in bed with closed eyes waiting for the aspirin to drive the pain in her forehead away. The world was a bare place. It was best to be alone in bed, under the bedclothes, where no one could get at you.

That was an idea! She might marry Frank Westcott. He had asked her a year ago, and he hadn't got engaged since. She had never seen him with any special girl. Look him up, be sweet and sympathetic and bright and interested. Monica Westcott. It went fairly well. Marry, have a house, and then a baby, and play bridge. It was best always for women to marry. She was tired of affairs, something restful, something permanent was what she wanted.

The rain was falling harder now and a wind came up and rattled on the windows. Sometimes there came a hideous morning like this one which showed up life for what it really was: underneath all the trappings, the loud noises it made on Saturday night, its pretence of being in a hurry and having a very good time. A Sunday morning like this: a wet chilly dreary London morning, when ugly people in ugly coats walked hurriedly, having the wet blown right

---

45　Old Vic (aka Royal Victoria Hall): A theatre in London on the corner of The Cut and Waterloo Road, established in 1818.

46　'Abide with Me': A Christian hymn written in 1847 by Scottish Anglican Henry Francis Lyte, usually sung to English composer William Henry Monk's 1861 piece 'Eventide'.

into their faces by the malevolent wind. That was Life, as it waited for you, underneath Things. That was why people cowered beneath umbrellas and houses, and had fires and husbands and children and everything they could think of to keep the cold and damp off them.

She was talking to herself too much. Her headache wouldn't go like that. If she looked as plain as she felt this morning, she must be a sight. Well, it didn't matter. Women thought a lot too much of how they looked. She did. Be quiet, that was the thing. Hold herself quite empty and still, deep inside the bedclothes, and perhaps she would go to sleep. Then she would feel better when she woke. Her eyes ached so.

…. It was odd not having George to think about any more. Odd and lonely. Don't think about that now, though. It really didn't matter a great deal. The thing was to rest tranquilly. Tranquil as dreams. But dreams weren't always tranquil. There was no doubt George had been very unkind. He might have come and said Goodbye. But perhaps it was best so. Never mind about it. Never mind, poor Monica!

Damn and blast! That piano next door. Started again. Now there would be no peace. "In a Monastery Garden."[47] Damn and blast! Oh, curse!…

MRS. JOHNSON

Mrs. Emily Johnson opened her eyes suddenly. The clock belonging to St. Matthew's Church had begun to strike. She moistened her dry lips and started to count:

"Two, three, four, five, six….not surely seven? Yes: seven."

Seven o'clock! Just fancy! She must have dozed off. It was only just after five when she had come in with a loaf of bread and quarter of margarine, and thought she would take a little rest before going out. And she had meant to be off early. A bad beginning! She must stir her pins now, and no mistake.

She threw off the blankets, and sat on the edge of the bed for a moment while her mind took stock of her body, searching to know how it felt. Her limbs were heavy and weak, and there was the same dull pain at the bottom of her back as there had been when she lay down.

"I don't feel a bit rested," she murmured. "Not a bit, I don't."

She sighed heavily, and went across to examine herself in the wooden looking-glass that was propped on her chest of drawers. She took it off, and held it close to her eyes.

---

47 'In a Monastery Garden': A famous piece of light classical music by Albert Ketèlbey, written in 1915.

She was wearing a pink jumper of artificial silk over a magenta coloured petticoat. Her skirt she had slipped off when she lay down. Her hair, which was a peculiar grey-brown, the result of many sousings in guaranteed colour restorers and improvers, was greasy looking and part of it had come down, for Mrs. Johnson still fought shy of shingling.[48] Her skin was a sickly yellow.

Mrs. Johnson gazed at herself with solicitude. "I do look bad," she thought. And then, not without pride, "No one could say as how I don't look bad."

But now another instinct put out its feeler and she searched the mirror for some more encouraging indication. She did not find it, and propped the mirror up again. "I look my age," she reflected with resignation as she took out hairpins. "Leastways I look forty something though neither fair nor fat. Except," she added as an after-thought, "where I shouldn't be."

She set the kettle on the gas ring to boil. Feel better after a cup of tea, she reflected, as she had reflected many times before.

She took it hot and strong, together with a piece of bread and margarine. Towards the end of her repast she fell to considering whether she should have a good wash or not. Custom and inclination insisted, "It's not as if I hadn't washed today," and "After just having the 'flu, you can't be too careful." On the other hand, perhaps it freshened you up. She decided she would bathe her face and neck and leave the rest.

She did so. She even cleaned her nails, and found a pad with which subsequently she polished them. Afterwards she surveyed herself more hopefully: the tea and hot water had brought a little colour to her checks. She'd keep on her jumper after all. If you could only stand it there was nothing like a little bit of colour for making you look young.

She dabbed on some lip salve, both on her lips and cheeks. Not too much! The first thing was to look respectable, as of course in your way you were. And then white powder over her little chin and short broad nose. On her neck as well, to hide the creases. She had a genuine double chin tonight; that was lying in bed so long. Ah, well, it didn't show much if you remembered to hold your head well up. Now her hat pulled down; now the grey coat.

At the door in spite of her hurry she was filled with misgiving, and turned back to have another look at herself. She certainly looked very far from her real self; it had to be admitted. No one could look really well, even if they happened to be raging, tearing beauties, if they felt as ill as she did. Perhaps after all it would better to wear a veil – not mind them being out of fashion.

With the veil attached she stared at herself keenly. Did it make her look older or younger? She wished she knew absolutely and for sure.

---

48 Shingling: Likely a reference to the skin disease shingles.

Still, she had had it on when she got off with that fellow in Hyde Park last week, the Tuesday wasn't it? On the whole, perhaps, she'd stick to it. She really did feel so poorly.

She drew it up to bestow a parting lick of powder, and then, after listening a moment at the door, went softly downstairs. Yet not too softly, for though she wished to slip out unseen, she didn't want to be caught looking as if she wished to slip out unseen.

She was unfortunate, for the door of the front room opened as she reached the bottom stair, and Mrs. Lytton, the landlady, came out.

"I thought that was you, Mrs. Johnson, quiet though you was. Going out, are you?"

Mrs. Johnson licked her lips unconsciously, and then gave a propitiatory smile.

"Yes, I thought I would, Mrs. Lytton. It's a nice evening, isn't it?"

"I thought," said Mrs. Lytton starting her lodger full in the face, "you was maybe coming to pay me what you owe me."

For a brief second Mrs. Johnson thought of essaying injured dignity. But she was hopelessly outmatched, for, besides being large of bust and determined of feature and countenance, Mrs. Lytton was all dressed up. She was wearing a frock of black taffeta silk cut very low to display an expanse of pink chest, and round her neck hung three rows of pearls. It was evident, too, that her bright yellow hair had been newly waved.

Must be expecting someone, thought Mrs. Johnson. I wonder … Aloud she said: "Now Mrs. Lytton, dear, you know yourself I 'aven't been able to get out for more than a week. You can't do much when you're sick in bed with the influenza, can you now?"

"Oh, I know you've been ill all right," retorted Mrs. Lytton. "Who should know it better than me that 'as 'ad to carry your meals up. You still owe me for that Bovril I got you."

"I know well how kind you've been," said Mrs. Johnson, rapidly. "And when my lad sends me the usual, you shall 'ave it all. If I don't get a bit of something from somewhere first – and I'm sure I shall –you shall 'ave that."

"Thank you for nothing, Mrs. Johnson. I know well enough when your son sends you the money, that is *if* he sends you it. He's missed, you know. And anyway it's not till Friday week. And you owe me three weeks' rent besides the ten bob I lent you because you was ill, or said you was, and the one and three I spent myself on the Bovril."

"Said I was ill," interjected Mrs. Johnson more in sorrow than in anger.

"And let me tell you straight and fair, from the horse's mouth, that I've no intention of waiting a fortnight to be paid. With one thing and another, Emily Johnson, I have put up with you till I am sick and tired. For friendship's sake. I'd not 'ave stood it from no one else. But there's reason in everything and I've my living to make, I suppose, same as everyone else. I could get more than I'm asking you for your room as you know well. Giving it away I am out of kindness."

Mrs. Johnson recognised her cue.

"Now, Rose, I've always said to everyone that there's no kinder nor more generous woman than yourself," she stated with dramatic emphasis.

"Don't Rose me! And listen. Things can't go on no longer like this. They gotta stop. D'you understand me?"

There came a knock at the hall door.

Mrs. Lytton's attention left Mrs. Johnson, and went eagerly to the other side of the door. Then she turned back to Mrs. Johnson but only to dispose of her.

"I'll see you again, Emily, when you come back, and if there's no rent or nothing coming from you you'll have to make new arrangements. I have to see a friend now about a business matter."

She stood back, and Mrs. Johnson opened the door and slipped out past the man who was standing there without a word or a look back. It would never do to appear inquisitive with Rose. And in any case she had always been one to mind her own business and not interfere with other people. "Live and let live, that's my motto," she thought with satisfaction which terminated in a touch of bitterness. "If it had only been other people's I wouldn't be where I am today."

She had now turned into the Camberwell Road, and the shouts of children at play, people passing hurriedly, the lights, the trams, and the coloured enticing patches made by picture palaces and public houses began to invigorate her. She forgot the pain in her back and stepped out fairly briskly, shooting little sideways glances about her. The familiar life of the streets, the easy security it gave, warmed her blood. There were so many things and people about: surely she could hardly miss going into something lucky. She had, she thought proudly, always been one for a bit of life and excitement; and even if she wasn't as young as some of the girls, she wasn't as old as others: no, not by a long chalk she wasn't.

Inevitably her mind began to turn over other considerations. Mrs. Johnson was not one of those who never knew quite how much they carried in their pocket or bag. Circumstances made such a fine carelessness impossible. And so without any need to refresh her memory by a look her thoughts went inside her imitation leather handbag, and added together the silver sixpence, the penny, the halfpenny, and the farthing which lay there together. It was all she had left of the ten shillings Rose had lent her. It would be better, she decided, to walk to the Elephant[49] and get a penny 'bus from there over Westminister

---

49 The Elephant: A reference to the Elephant and Castle, a major road junction in London.

Bridge. Or, would it save her more if she walked as far as Westminister, and then got a penny 'bus to the Circus? Once at the Circus she could slip into Long's, and see if there was anyone there she knew. A Guinness would do her no end of good if she only got the chance of one.

The picture of the foaming brown glass which might be awaiting her quickened her footsteps. She walked at a steady pace down the Walworth Road, taking little heed of passersby. Experience had taught her that the busy streets of South-East London were no lucky hunting ground for her at that time in the evening. As she put it to herself, she was too refined for this side of the Bridge. And though she rarely took the recollection out of its pushed-back corner in her mind, it was in the Walworth Road, returning home with empty pockets late one night, that a man, a very low-down sort of man, had stopped suddenly in front of her and said, "Give you a bob?"

Mrs. Johnson had not come to that, as she also told herself with regard to other unpleasant incidents from time to time. Yet its effect was sufficient to make her tread the Walworth Road with special circumspection. She was above it, at least when it took its pleasures.

So she walked primly along, her fairly red lips and whitely powdered skin thrown into shadow by her veil; and if she scorned the Walworth Road it cannot be said that the Walworth Road, in busy mood just before the shops closed down, took any more notice of her.

At the Elephant she stood on the edge of the pavement for a moment undecided. She had been walking twenty-five minutes, and the pain at her back refused to be lulled any longer. She also felt a little dizzy in her head, and she thought petulantly how very noisy, how much more noisy than usual, everything was. For now the glamour had left the lights and bustle, and what had been gay and seductive appeared only harsh and clamourous. How hard the pavements were! Her toes felt hot and constricted and a corn began to throb. "Them patent shoes!" thought Mrs. Johnson with resignation. And then sorrowfully, "My poor feet!"

Meditating there upon the question of whether or not to take the 'bus, her wandering eye perceived a young woman approaching from the right towards her.

A young woman it was, who unlike Mrs. Johnson, attracted a fair share of attention as she walked with airy indifference in front of 'buses, whose drivers' heads turned to watch her progress. For Miss Florrie Small possessed both an appearance and a figure, and showed the latter to advantage in a tightly-fitting costume of green velour cloth. Curves were, to a degree, out of fashion, but they still continued to possess an attraction, and Miss Small allowed herself a certain freedom of plumpness above her waist. For the rest she was careful about both her corsets and her diet. And on this occasion her little black felt toque[50] with ear flaps combined smartness and becomingness in an exceptional degree.

But what drew the eyes of many women to Miss Small was the genuine skunk fur, large and magnificent, which hung regally over her shoulders. Tired, shabby women, of hen-like outline, as they pushed perambulators or plodded slowly on weary feet, let indifferent glances drop from Miss Small's pink, red and white countenance (for everyone made up in these days) to her fur. Then the glances, returning to her face, were no longer indifferent, but disapproving and even malevolent. One woman coming out with another from a public house observed Miss Small for a fraction, and then nudged her companion, saying violently, "These 'ere tarts, they make me sick, they do!"

But Miss Small was inured to stares, and even to the occasional comments of her neighbourhood. She accepted them quite properly as a tribute to her exceptional smartness, and had they not been forthcoming in their customary degree, she would have hastened to the nearest public lavatory, there to expend, if need be, even a penny at the mirror in order to inquire after the cause. It was not that she appeared to take any heed, for, like Mrs. Johnson, the neighbourhood of the Elephant did not interest her professionally; but if she aroused no attention in the Walworth Road there was little hope of her doing so in more competitive areas.

Mrs. Johnson also observed Florrie's fur with interest, but when she raised her eyes to the wearer's comely, if somewhat artificial, countenance they contained only admiration and delighted interest, modified to a close observer by a rather uncertain appeal. As Miss Small arrived on the pavement, she raised her veil and advanced a little towards her.

"Why, it's Florrie!" cried Mrs. Johnson in a burst of joyful surprise. "Well! Fancy running into you!"

For a second Miss Small returned Mrs. Johnson's regard impassively. She knew the lady was apt to prove a hanger-on, and wisdom counseled her to walk on with a nod. On the other hand, in [the] face of Mrs. Johnson's effusion, this would have been tantamount to a snub, and Florrie was temperamentally averse to snubbing people. After all, she reflected, she could easily shake her off later. There were points of etiquette that even Mrs. Johnson could not disregard.

"Hullo! Haven't seen you about lately," she said affably enough.

---

50 Toque: A small cap or bonnet.

"No, you 'aven't," said Mrs. Johnson in the tone of one who confirms a great truth. "I've 'ad the 'flu. 'Ad it shockin' bad! I ain't been out of bed for a week."

"You don't look too bright."

"I don't. Nor I don't feel it."

There was a short silence, while Mrs. Johnson watched Florrie, and Florrie watched for a 'bus. It turned the corner.

"I was just waiting for a 'bus up West myself," said Mrs. Johnson. "If you don't mind my company, dear?"

"Not at all," said Florrie politely, if rather absently.

They got into the 'bus, Mrs. Johnson making a great show of drawing back politely to let Florrie mount first. They sat down on the left-hand side, and Florrie began to fumble in her bag.

"Going all the way to the Circus?" said Mrs. Johnson, trying to make her voice appear indifferent.

Florrie nodded.

"I'll have a tuppenny, too," said Mrs. Johnson brightly, surrendering her sixpence to the conductor. But as she took the four coppers handed back, she experienced a pang. Cut into her sixpence she had, and she only meant to have a penny fare. Suppose it was an unlucky evening? Well, it couldn't be helped. And a bit of company was worth it. You never knew.

She looked sideways at Florrie. Better not say anything about her fur. She didn't seem very talkative, and it was no use giving offence. It was certainly a new one. She would have liked to know who had paid for it.

But Florrie suddenly relented. She had realised that the conductor had half anticipated that she would pay for Mrs. Johnson, and it had made her feel a little mean.[51] After all she was in funds. She might stand the old girl a drink later.

So she asked for details of Mrs. Johnson's symptoms, and soon became really interested in the topic.

"It makes you feel so down in the dumps," said Mrs. Johnson.

"A friend of mine," replied Florrie, "once killed himself after having the 'flu."

"You don't say!"

"He did. Nice fellow he was, too, in his way. Very cheerful. Great sense of humour, you know. Always had a joke whenever you met him. He used to be in the Regent a lot with a lot of other chaps night after night. And always free with his money, you don't know! Why, he'd think nothing of taking on three girls at a time. And he wouldn't expect you to keep to beer. 'Order what you

---

51 Mean: In this context, poor or stingy.

like, and how you like,' was what he'd always say. Well, after a while I missed him. He was never there. Of course I just thought that he was away or something." Florrie paused.

"Of course you would," agreed Mrs. Johnson, anxious to show her appreciation.

"So I was talking to a friend of his one evening, Jack Hulton, his name is – very like the fellow with the band, isn't it the name I mean? –and I just happened to say, 'What's got Billy Richards these days?' – that was his name you know, Billy Richards. 'Where's Billy Richards?' I said, and he said, 'Haven't you heard?' and by the way he said it I knew there was something in the wind. 'No,' I said, 'What's up?' I said.

"Then he got [to] telling me about it. Threw himself out of the window of a hotel or boarding house or something in Torrington Square. At the top of the house it was. And when he was picked up he was as dead as frozen meat, poor fellow!"

"Dear, dear!" said Mrs. Johnson.

"And believe me or believe me not it was just that he'd had 'flu. Everyone said so. Had it real bad, you know. And never got over it. Moped and wouldn't go about with his friends. Though he had no money troubles at all. Very good position, I believe, in something or other. Isn't it queer what people will do when they get as low as all that?"

Mrs. Johnson agreed. The story depressed her slightly. "Well," she started, "I always fight against it myself. What I say is…"

"And there was someone else I knew," interrupted Florrie.

With an expression of rapt attention Mrs. Johnson gave her ear to Florrie, while her eyes occasionally wandered past through the window. They had left Trafalgar Square, and there was plenty to see.

Mrs. Johnson noticed many men unaccompanied, some walking fast making for a dinner appointment, others strolling slowly with a watchful eye. Solitary women there were, too, walking slower or a trifle faster than usual because of their recognition that it was pleasure time. Mrs. Johnson marveled, as she never ceased to marvel, at the number of taxis there were about, returning, many of them, from the theatre, others still busy taking late arrivals. And over all the uneasy throng, passing their various ways a little more self-consciously than earlier in the day, the impassive sky stared down indifferently. It had watched men and women repeat themselves too often; or perhaps it was too far away to understand.

Mrs. Johnson felt lonely and chilled. She would have liked the evening before her to have been blotted out. Or if only it could have been all over, and she was going back to snuggle down in bed, and lose herself and her aches and pains in rest. I do need a pick-me-up, she thought self-pityingly.

"Here we are," said Florrie, breaking off from her narrative, as the 'bus drew up.

They crossed Piccadilly Circus[52] together, going up the south side of Shaftesbury Avenue. Florrie had resumed her social air of nonchalance, but the gulf between her and Mrs. Johnson had lessened. True, the glances that came their way rested on Florrie, but the glances were casual, and both of them felt less like duchess and poor dependent and more on the equality of two members of the same overcrowded and hard-working profession.

But when Florrie had mounted the stairs leading to the lounge of the public house that was their destination, the dividing line between them became again tightly drawn. Men, men and women together, and women alone, looking each of them up and down as they entered, classified them by professional standards. Florrie, it was evident, was a force to be reckoned with: she had smartness, she had an air, and she thus received the compliment of thoughtful appraisal. But the room passed over Mrs. Johnson in uninterested silence. She was easy to place, and her place was a low one.

Glancing round, Florrie received and returned a nod of recognition from two men sitting in the right-hand corner. But they were with two girls, and she did not choose to go over to them. She sat down at a table by the wall, facing the bar, at which one girl was already sitting. This girl was small and thin. She had applied a high colour to her sallow skin; her red mouth drooped; her brown eyes were sharp; and she appeared both sulky and on the defensive.

At Florrie she directed a suspicious glance, gathering her personality together against a rival better-dressed and better-looking than herself. Her pose endeavoured to suggest that she remained unimpressed. Mrs. Johnson she ignored after one glance.

Florrie, refreshed by the feeling of power the room had given her, expanded. "What are you going to have?" she asked Mrs. Johnson. "A Guinness?"

"Thank you very much, I will," said Mrs. Johnson. And then added, for she could not afford to leave any vestige of doubt about the matter of paying, "It's very kind of you, dear."

"Well, that's that," said Florrie, and beckoned to the waiter. He came with celerity. Florrie was a good customer.

"A couple of Guinnesses, George, as quick as you like."

The waiter nodded and smiled. Before going away, he stared at the almost empty glass in front of the table's first occupant, whose name was Lily. It was a hard stare, and Lily, pretending not to notice, cursed inwardly. She had

---

52 Piccadilly Circus: A road junction and busy public square in London's West End. As with Oxford Circus and other such London place names, 'circus' is used here in the older sense simply of a circle.

been sitting with the glass of bitter in front of her for nearly half an hour, and she knew she couldn't make it last out much longer. She gazed with an increased intensity at a man at the next table talking to two others. He had looked at her once; if he gave her the least bit more of encouragement she decided she would go over and sit at their table. It had a vacant seat, and there was no use missing the slightest opportunity. She was sick to death of walking about the streets with a headache, and being looked at as if she didn't exist.

Mrs. Johnson had also observed the waiter's look. She was sorry it was his night on, for he was a difficult person with whom to deal. She liked the other man with the long drooping dark moustache much better. He was good-natured, and had sometimes exchanged an affable word with her. But this man allowed her no grace in the way of time; and his manner always made it perfectly clear that he regarded her as an intruder. "Get off or get out" was his motto.

He returned with the glasses of stout, and Florrie deposited a shilling and a sixpence on the red wine-marked tray as she asked him some question which Mrs. Johnson was unable to overhear. He replied reassuringly.

Mrs. Johnson started to drink, darting little birdlike glances at the people around her. When the waiter returned, Lily stared at him boldly. "A Bass, please," she said in a low hoarse voice. It would be the last drink she could afford to treat herself to tonight, but perhaps it was worth waiting a little longer.

There was little conversation between the other two women. Florrie sipped her stout slowly and watched the door. Mrs. Johnson, who comprehended much of the art of the living, concentrated on savouring her drink. Every time she raised her glass she experienced a thrill of satisfaction, and she followed the progress of the liquid down her throat with a tender observation. It didn't exactly warm you, but oh, how satisfying it was! Every time she placed her glass down she felt she had done much to add to her well-being. Two or three bottles a day, and, she thought, she would feel herself in no time. Self-confidence came gradually as her glass diminished, and she crossed her legs, and looked round boldly. She wished now she hadn't put the veil on when she had gone out. Men would have seen her in it when she came in, and it would certainly have given her age away.

Meanwhile Florrie became a little restless. She hated wasting time, and she knew she was not in the *milieu* to which her gifts entitled her. Sitting in a pub., a common pub., with an old hag of a finished and done-with prostitute was not suitable. But she had fixed up with Hemp to be free for him if he came along before nine. She finished off her drink in three large gulps and considered the question of ordering either another of the same or a Bass. The waiter was moving near, and, as she caught his eye, she remembered Mrs. Johnson, and hesitated.

She glanced at her companion, who in her engrossed enjoyment of her beverage had nearly come to the end of the glass without remembering that it was her bounden duty to make it stretch out to the utmost fraction of possible time. Now, however, she remembered, and raising the glass to her lips for appearance['s] sake, set it down untouched.

Florrie noticed the action, and was moved by it. After all, she thought, the poor thing had been ill. Who could tell? She herself might one day be in Mrs. Johnson's shoes, and then she'd be thankful for any small mercy. Besides, the little bitch opposite who looked at her in such an ugly way would be impressed. It would teach her that she, Florrie Small, was not one of those who never had a few shillings in her purse. And didn't mind spending them on others.

"Have a Bass with me?" she said to Mrs. Johnson with well simulated carelessness.

Joy and surprise caught at Mrs. Johnson. What amazing luck! It was a long time since she had been treated to two drinks running. She could hardly believe it.

"Ta!"[53] she said, her amazement making her briefer than usual. But gratitude in rich profusion flowed from her to Florrie. She looked at her with shining eyes. What a fine smart girl she was! There wasn't another one in the room to hold a candle to her. She deserved her luck with the men, her lovely fur; she did indeed. And she, Emily Johnson, didn't grudge it to her, if anyone else did.

As the waiter left them with Florrie's order, a newcomer entered, and Florrie, seeing him, jerked into animation. Her face radiated welcome, and as he came up to her she held out her hand to be shaken, and inclined her head coyly to one side in an appealing attitude. Florrie knew how to behave, as well as what was due to her. Mrs. Johnson, glancing at her unobstrusively, noted the gleam of a gold side tooth with covetousness.

She also unobtrusively took stock of Florrie's friend, and summed him up as sufficiently well off to be of importance, even though undistinguished, and not altogether at ease. He hadn't a hearty way with him, and Mrs. Johnson was inclined to be suspicious of the quiet ones. You never knew where you were with them.

After a few remarks, Florrie withdrew with him and her Bass to a table a little distance away which had just been vacated. Mrs. Johnson expected to be ignored, and she was. She was left alone with Lily.

---

53 Ta: 'An infantile form of "thank-you", now also commonly in colloq. adult use'. (*OED*).

They glanced at each other for a moment: Lily's gaze was hard and contemptuous. It was an unmistakable answer to Mrs. Johnson's vague expression of would-be friendliness. They both sat very still and aloof, slowly swallowing their ale, and watchful, at least so far Lily was concerned, for every stray glance and every newcomer.

It was not long before Mrs. Johnson felt very much like talking to someone. She glanced at the table next to her. Two small girls, tightly costumed, tightly hatted, and made up in precisely the same way and to the same degree, were sitting there talking earnestly. One, however, was dark and more vixenish than the other, and when her friend had finished what she was saying she leaned across to her, and said as one voicing a grave problem:

"But I thought he was very fond of you."

The other girl made no answer. She turned and looked over her shoulder; then, catching Mrs. Johnson's sympathetic eye, looked through her.

"I thought he was fond of you," said the other girl again, but more urgently. Still met by silence, she sat back and raised her glass.

Mrs. Johnson's attention went to the other side of the room, where she saw a girl called Kate, very vivacious, bright of eye and flushed of cheek, sitting close to a table at which were two men, both rather grave and watchful. Kate was swinging a pretty leg, and at last she caught the eye of her neighbor. "Swing me just a little bit higher," she said gaily to him, adding, "I bet you don't mind how high."

Mrs. Johnson sighed. There was no denying some girls had the gift. She watched Kate, now engaged in conversation, with admiration till her attention was called away by the appearance of two men at her table.

They were both quite young: one had a smooth-skinned, round face, and a small dark moustache. His hair was oiled, and his eyes sharp and closely set together. He appeared to be the leading spirit of the two, but the other one, Mrs. Johnson decided, was better-looking, with nice wavy fair hair, well marked nose and jaw, and a frank boyish look. "A bit like Cecil would have been, had he lived," reflected Mrs. Johnson, gazing at him with undisguised approval.

While they ordered whiskies she pondered on whether there was the remotest chance that she would be able to get off. Not much. She wouldn't be good enough for them. Too old! As a matter of fact she hadn't much of a chance sitting in this pub, at all. Too much light; too much competition. Still, she'd wait a bit. It was a rest.

Their conversation concerned racing matters, and Mrs. Johnson had to watch Lily's success with the dark man. "Would you like a cert. for the 3:30 tomorrow?" he had asked her.

"I know those certs," replied Lily, showing her teeth, which were white and even. She giggled and glanced coquettishly at the other young man. She also favoured him. But she took care to look quickly back at the man who had first spoken to her, and giggled again.

"Well, take it or leave it," he said. He pulled out a bit of paper and pencil and wrote something upon it. "I'm not a tipster. Am I, Frank?"

His friend shook his head.

"But I've put more money in the way of my pals than any blinking cheat of a tipster. Now then, do you want this?"

"I'm sure I'm much obliged," said Lily, accepting the lip of paper. She read it, and put it away in her handbag.

Mrs. Johnson felt neglected, and she also felt sociable. She decided that this was the time to force herself into action. "I'd like to get hold of a winner myself," she said, smiling at the dark young man.

He looked at her ungraciously. "A bob's my charge," he said.

Mrs. Johnson was not quarrelsome, but neither was she devoid of spirit, and the dark young man became oppressive to her.

"Didn't see *her* pay you," she said, jerking her head towards Lily. Then, alarmed at her boldness, she gave a deprecatory smile, intended to turn her remark into a joke. But the smile was a little late, and it was ignored.

"She's a friend of mine, aren't you darling?" he said, staring coolly at Mrs. Johnson while he patted Lily's arm.

Lily giggled again.

"Course you are," she said, not troubling to glance at Mrs. Johnson. "I've known you for donkey's years, haven't I?"

"But you didn't find me a donkey, did you?" He answered meaningly.

Lily went into a shriek of laughter. Pleased at his success, the young man beckoned her, and then bent and whispered in her ear. Again Lily shrieked with laughter.

Mrs. Johnson tried to catch the other young man's eye, hoping for a spark of sympathy, but failed. It was evident that, feeling somewhat uncomfortable, he was engaged in absenting his real self from the table. He was staring blankly at the wall; he hadn't bargained for women, and he was determined not to get involved.

Mrs. Johnson felt her mood change. The whole place became distasteful to her. She looked hard at the ash tray just in front of her, fighting against a dangerous impulse to turn on Lily and shout at her.

"Some people do think they're someone," she muttered. But no one took any notice. Indeed no one heard her except the good-looking young man, and he was still determinedly engaged in not being drawn into anything.

Mrs. Johnson took a resolve. She swallowed the last drops of her Bass, carefully took out a handkerchief from her bag, and wiped her lips with exaggerated precision. The action gave her the sense of being very much a lady, and for a few seconds the reflection that she was in reality superior to everybody else in the room comforted her.

She pulled down her veil and rose, darting as she did so a look intended to convey scorn and contempt at Lily, who did not observe the gesture. Then she looked from her round the room, including the rest of its occupants in her dismissal. Which of those girls had had a devoted husband, the same as her? She asked herself. And a little public of their own with garden and field at the back. None of them. Nor ever would. Prostitutes, that's what they were, and always would be.

As she passed across the room she noticed that Florrie and her gentleman friend were very much engaged in themselves. She half paused as she passed near them, hoping for glance of recognition, which would have warmed her. But Florrie did not look up.

Mrs. Johnson felt a little queer as she walked down the steps. She had had, she reflected, only a couple of drinks, but then her stomach had been almost empty. "Wonder if I could run to two pennyworth of chips or something?" she muttered to herself, and paused at the door to consider the question. But the cold stare of the commissionaire standing there sent her on into the street.

The lights of Wardour Street blinked heartlessly at her. Instinctively she turned into the comparative quietness of Gerrard Street, her mind going back in hostility to the place she had just left.

To herself she expressed the hope that that dirty little whore wouldn't get the young fellow; they had only come in to get a few drinks, and exchange compliments with the girls to make them feel big. As for Lily herself … her thoughts lingered round the girl in bitterness. Then suddenly she felt herself to be old and tired, and the hatred left her. She tried to remember the special grudge she had had against the occupants of the table and it seemed no longer important. After all she had got two drinks out of Florrie. How much had that fur she was wearing cost?

"Let me see," she asked herself. "How much did Jim give for that fur he bought me out of his winnings at the Lewes races? A real good skunk it was."

She stood for a few minutes by the gallery entrance to the Hippodrome, her mind reconstructing the event. She had been in the field, tying the goats to a fresh bit of grass, and he had called to her. There was a parcel for her, he had said. Yes, he had had it sent by post for surprise. And how rare and pleased he had been at seeing her in it. Everybody, or nearly everybody, who came into the bar that evening he had called behind to have a look at it. It was fourteen pounds he had given for it, and that was cost price, because he had got it through a man he knew in the trade. Poor Jim! He was generous with his money when he had it. Too generous! Better for her today if he'd have been the saving kind. Ah, well! What was had to be!

She looked up and down the street. She would have liked to tell someone about her husband. How good he had been to her, never denying her anything if he could help it! What would he say if he could see where she had got today?

There was nobody about: the two totties who had passed her had turned into Charing Cross Road. Wait! Wasn't that a man standing on the opposite side turned in her direction? She looked back, and then turned and walked slowly towards him.

As she drew near, he crossed, making a line that led past her, but looking hard at her as he came abreast. She coughed and stood still.

No! He had sheered off. Not to his liking evidently. Not much use following; he was walking quite fast now. Mrs. Johnson sighed and walked slowly on. She ought to have gone to the Park first of all. Perhaps she would go now. But she couldn't walk all that way without a bite. She weighed the claims of 'bus fares and a snack. The latter won, for she might feel equal to walking when she had got something inside her.

She hurried across to the other side of the road, and walked rapidly along. It was cold, and she shivered. A whisky now! A whisky would be the thing to give her help in getting hold of someone. It was no good trying to be gay and enticing without food or anything. Leastways not at her age.

Withdrawing into a corner, she took twopence from her purse ready to pass over the counter. It was against her practice to let anyone see into her purse; some people were nosey; liked to see how much you had; some of those girls, them that hadn't been brought up at all proper, were a bit too ready with their remarks.

Now she had only threepence halfpenny left. She felt a sharp pang of regretful kindness toward those meager brown coins. They'd be gone before the night was out, she'd be bound. And then where'd she be? Not a sou in the world! Not a bloody sou![54]

At the door of the café' she paused, almost relinquishing her intention. Fivepence halfpenny was, after all, a lot more than threepence halfpenny. There was the farthing, which came in for loaves of bread. But the smell of hot food caught at her nostrils too alluringly to be resisted, and she went inside.

There was nobody there she knew, for the place happened to be fairly empty at the time. Two girls were at the table eating heartily, and drinking out

---

54 Sou: A French coin, equivalent to five cents.

of big cups of coffee. A man and a girl were in a corner, and there was a girl sitting by herself smoking.

Mrs. Johnson ordered her sandwich from the white-jacketed young Jew behind the counter, and thought regretfully of the chips she might have had in its stead if she had only happened to be the other side of the river. These sandwiches were the best you could get up West for their price, and held a proud position among those who were initiated; but, after all, thought Mrs. Johnson, what she really needed was something spicy and hot. And a cup of coffee. Should she blow it all in, and order a cup? It was a difficult decision.

If she ordered a cup of coffee she would also feel entitled to a seat. Of course there was nothing actually to prevent her from sitting down with her sandwich, upon which she had liberally spread mustard; but Mrs. Johnson knew that she was in the bad books of the young Jew, and she hoped to placate him by standing. Once he had told her that you couldn't be expected to get a whole evening's rest for tuppence. "Was it," he had asked her with mock politeness, "reasonable?" And the resort was too convenient for Mrs. Johnson to wish to burn her boats entirely.

Eating as slowly as she dared, Mrs. Johnson had nearly come to the end of her sandwich when a young woman entered, quietly dressed in a grey flannel suit with a white jumper. She was pale, and though her dark eyes were lively and good natured Mrs. Johnson did not know how to place her since she sported very little makeup.

She ordered two ham sandwiches, and much to Mrs. Johnson's pleasure remained at the counter to eat them. For it was evident that she was disposed towards conversation, and not particular with whom she held it. So when Mrs. Johnson assiduously passed her the mustard, she was thanked with warmth.

"Very cold tonight," said Mrs. Johnson, encouraged.

"My God, isn't it! Cold as hell! Or I suppose hell isn't? What do you say, Tommy?"

She was addressing the Jew, who took, however, no notice. He knew Miss Agnes True, and did not care for her style.

As a retort to his silence, Agnes raised her eyebrows, and then turned down the corners of her mouth ludicrously, jerking her head back from Rosenbaum to Mrs. Johnson, who tittered, feeling that she was getting her own back to some extent. She decided she liked Agnes: not one of your stuck-up ones, she wasn't. A real nice girl. And it was plain that she had had a few drinks. That might make her generous. You never knew your luck.

For a little while Agnes was silent, concentrating upon her food. Then she turned to Mrs. Johnson again.

"I've been in the old hole. You know where I mean? Right! Got in with a chap what was as tight as an owl, and went on putting it away, too. 'Now my dear,' he says to me. 'I'm not going to ask you to take me home. I wouldn't insult you,' he says. 'But you can have as many drinks as you want.' And he meant it, too. He ordered a double Scotch straightaway. Some girls might have been too – you know what I mean – to take it. But what's the odds? That's what I say. A short life, and get through it as best you can, that's what I say."

"I wish I'd been there," said Mrs. Johnson. "I was just saying to myself that a drop of Scotch is what you want, my dear. I miss it, because you see my husband – he had a public house of his own. And I've just had the 'flu something awful. I couldn't tell you what I feel like. It's as much as I can do just to stand up."

She raised her voice slightly in the hope that Rosenbaum would get the benefit of the last remark. Not though, she thought to herself, that his sort have any decency in them.

"You do look off it," said Agnes sympathetically. "You've come out too soon. That's what it is. You ought to have given yourself another day or two in bed."

"So I ought," said Mrs. Johnson. "I know that. But there you are. I've my living to make."

"That's right," said Agnes. "That's what it is. No time to stay at home and say your prayers. Go forth into the highways and byways and compel them to come in. That's our game. For better or for worse. For richer or for poorer. And mostly for poorer."

She laughed loudly, and not being sufficiently applauded proceeded to make her point clearer.

"That's a quotation from the Bible, though you may not know it. But I know it. Oh, yes! I know my Bible. When I went to Sunday School I got the prize. Believe me or believe me not, I got a bew-ti-ful prize."

"You are a lively one, you are," said Mrs. Johnson.

At the sound of her voice, the Jew suddenly turned.

"Can I get you anything else, madam?" he inquired with mock politeness. Mrs. Johnson shook her head.

"Are you going to stay here all night then?" he said, changing his voice disagreeably.

"All right, all right," said Mrs. Johnson. "You're in a hurry, aren't you?"

Agnes's presence had emboldened her, and she recognised her own courage with approbation. Funny how you never feel up to yourself when you're alone, she thought.

"Wait a mo," said Agnes, cramming the last of her sandwich into her mouth, "and I'll come with you, though the perfect gentleman here is so polite and pressing to me to stay with him."

She laughed again, and Mrs. Johnson joined in her merriment. For a moment Rosenbaum took no notice, giving an attentive ear to a male customer who had just come in.

Then he turned full on Agnes, who had vexed him with her tongue before.

"Well, I must say you're one as I'd rather see your back than your face," he said, turning full on her. "You may be a nice sweet little thing, but somehow I don't seem to see it."

"Don't you insult me, you dirty Jew," said Agnes in a raised voice. "I needn't put up with anything from you, and I'm not going to. You get your living mostly from us girls, don't you; and you'd better treat us proper. I've paid you, haven't I?"

Mrs. Johnson realised that they were rousing attention from the other occupants of the café. She became a little frightened. If Rosenbaum got really offended, he might refuse to serve her again. Complain to the police or something. It would be like him.

"Get out of here, both of you," said Rosenbaum. "Get out of here, or it will be the worse for you."

"How do you mean, it will be the worse for me, you bloody Jew?" shouted Agnes. "What do you mean?"

"Come on, dear," said Mrs. Johnson. "Come on. Don't take any notice. It's beneath you."

Agnes hesitated. The temptation to have a really good row, turn and address the whole café, to relieve herself once and for all in glorious fashion was strong. But she sensed that Rosenbaum was waiting for her next move. And he had the authorities behind him.

"All right. But you shall hear from me further," she said with dignity. She looked round the café with a thoughtful air. But it did not appear as if anyone was coming to her aid. Mrs. Johnson was already out in the street. So she shot a last arrow. "There's nothing I hate and despise more than the Jews who betrayed Our Lord, and who are responsible for every mean and dirty action under the sun," she said clearly, and went out to rejoin Mrs. Johnson.

They walked away from the door in silence, and then Agnes said as a final comment: "The b....! The bloody b.... of a Jew![55]

Mrs. Johnson did not reply: she only shook her head once to imply that things had come to such a pass that they were beyond her. Pulling down her veil had turned her mind to another topic. She decided to consult Agnes.

"Do you think," she said after a short interval, "that wearing this veil makes me look old?"

---

55 On anti-Semitism in the text, see the Introduction.

Agnes glanced at her without bothering to give any careful survey, and then reassured her heartily: "Old, not a bit. You look as young as ever you were."

This was not exactly what Mrs. Johnson wanted.

"But would you say," she said, pushing her veil up, "that I look better without it?"

But Agnes was in too expansive a mood to give herself to any survey of details.

"Christ!" She said. "What does it matter? If your name's up to click tonight, you'll click, veil or no veil. If it isn't well then you won't, and that's all there is to it. Let's go and get a drink and hope for the best."

"I'd like to," said Mrs. Johnson, "but honest, dear, I'm cleaned right out."

Agnes looked at her searchingly. "I have heard that said before."

"It's the blessed truth," said Mrs. Johnson, stung into vehemence. "God strike me dead, if it isn't! 'Ere! Look!"

Agnes looked indifferently at the opened bag thrust under her eyes. A stick of rouge, a key, a box without a lid of compressed powder, and a very dirty small powder puff were its visible contents.

"Well, I suppose I shall have to treat you," she said. "If I wasn't on the streets already, I soon would be, what with all the things people get out of me for nothing."

Mrs. Johnson thought it wiser to be silent. Agnes was evidently in a mood when she might choose to quarrel with her at any moment. She followed her into the public house lounge selected a little wearily. The snack she had eaten had not had the effect she hoped, for her back was hurting, and her head beginning to ache. Urgently, too, it came to her that it was time to get to business. She ought really to leave Agnes and walk about a little. She would never do any good as long as she was with someone young. But then perhaps a glass of something would pick her up.

The room they entered wore a subdued, almost dejected air. There were plenty of men, but they were men who had come to drink and talk, and only casual glances rested on Mrs. Johnson and Agnes as they sat down.

Agnes looked round searchingly. "That fellow I told you about isn't here," she said. "He said he'd come back here, and pick me up later. Much hopes of that, I don't think! Well, we'll have a bottle of the usual to keep us going."

She gave the order, and it was not till they had drunk a little that Agnes regained her former cheerfulness. "If I don't work myself off on someone tonight," she said loudly, "I shall run all the way home smiling at every man I see. And then I shall dance round my room. Why not? You get what's coming to you, and if it doesn't come, why worry?"

"That's what I say," said Mrs. Johnson. "It's no use meeting troubles half way. No use at all. And that's a fact."

She emptied her glass; and then putting it down, fortified to have a good stare round, found that it was impossible to remember the faces of anyone after she had looked away. They were far off, and didn't seem at all important. Nevertheless she had to make them important. She kept her eyes fixed for some time on a fair boyish-looking young man in a corner, who grew more and more uneasy under her half unconscious leer; and told herself that she must remember to keep a clear head. This was only her third drink: showed the way illness and starvation had affected her. Thinking of her hardships, she removed her gaze from the young man, to his great relief, and shook her head sadly as she studied the red tiled pattern of the table which glowed up at her with rich warmth.

Then, "Never mind," she told herself after a few moments. "You're as good as any of them here anyway."

She looked round again defiantly, and the young man, catching her eye, removed his regard hastily. She would have liked to find an occasion for asserting herself, for all at once it came to her that she had been far too meek with people. The way Rose had grown to ride roughshod over her lately! After all she had done for that woman in the past! When you had money and a home and a husband, people loved you. But if you were down, they'd all of them like to give you another push. If she only had Rose here now, she'd tell her what she thought of her. Such a mean fuss over a few weeks' rent. She turned to Agnes with an idea of telling her the story of her wrongs, but the girl began to speak first.

"I tell you what!" said Agnes, with the effect of uttering a new truth. "The matter with us is that we're too refined. It's the painted bird that gets the worm every time. Much more important than being early."

Mrs. Johnson felt her mind grasp with astonishing clarity the immense significance of this utterance.

"That's right," she said, nodding her head several times. "We're too refined. Too quiet-like and decent for most of them."

"Decent's the word," interrupted Agnes. "Do you know what I was asked to do the other night? And for two pounds. Two pounds! I was supposed to make a beast of myself, if you please. Wait now, and I'll tell you the way it happened." Turning towards Mrs. Johnson, her eyes met those of a young man just coming into the room. He came towards her, and Mrs. Johnson, looking to see the cause of the delay in the narrative, saw with mixed feelings a young man standing by their table.

"Good evening, Mr. James," said Agnes, looking up with excitement flavoured by something resembling contempt in her eyes. "Or isn't it James tonight? You never know, you know. It might be one of the other holy apostles." She laughed loudly.

Mrs. Johnson reflected that Agnes was certainly a bit on. Seemed as if she cared for nobody. So flushed, too! And ordinarily she was such a pale girl.

"What's your poison?" said Mr. James, ignoring the sally, and pulling out a chair for himself.

"Just a wee drappie of the malt," said Agnes, adding absently, "as Harry Lauder[56] says."

Mrs. Johnson looked hard at her empty glass, and then turned a fixed smile towards her companions, directed neither at Agnes nor at Mr. James, but hovering between them in the hope of winning some sort of recognition from one or the other.

Mr. James, as he called himself, pink and round faced, with thin hair already receding from his forehead, began to realize for the first time the presence of Mrs. Johnson, and glanced uneasily from her to Agnes, waiting for a cue. He didn't want to treat that elderly person, and because of her lack of attraction became suspicious. Perhaps she was the girl's mother. Perhaps he had been unwise in sitting down straight off. What he ought to have done was to sit down at another table, and wait till Agnes joined him, or the old woman sheered off. He withdrew himself a little and became thoughtful.

Agnes realised the cause of his uneasiness, and hastened to reassure him. "This lady here has just 'ad influenza. Do you know the joke, 'How did you get it?' 'I opened the window, and in flew Enza!' She has just done me the favour of having a drink with me till you turned up – for somehow I thought it might be little Jimmy's night out tonight. But she's saying that she can't keep away from her by-bye much longer, she feels so bad."

Mr. James looked at Mrs. Johnson for confirmation. Mrs. Johnson was a little disappointed, but she admitted to herself that it was to have been expected.

"Yes, I'm just off," she said, preserving her smile, though the glow of expectancy went from her eyes, leaving them rather like that of a hurt child determined not to cry.

Mr. James understood that there was nothing to be feared from this quarter, and in his relief expanded benevolently. After all, giving the old girl a drink would only mean another eightpence, and it would look well with Agnes, who was almost the only one of her profession with whom he felt at ease. In talking of her to his chosen intimates, he would close by saying solemnly, "And to look at her you would never know she was that sort. Just a quiet-looking wholesome sort of girl, you'd think, if you didn't know her."

---

56 Sir Henry 'Harry' Lauder (1870–1950): An internationally known Scottish singer and entertainer.

To which someone or other could generally be relied upon to say, "But you know different," and then there would be a burst of laughter very flattering to him. Oh, Agnes was certainly an acquisition, if she did rag you rather when there was anyone else about. So he turned to Mrs. Johnson, and said graciously, "Have a whisky before you go. It'll do you good."

"It's most kind of you. Thank you very much, I'm sure," said Mrs. Johnson, affecting a ladylike precise voice which somehow seemed natural to her at the moment. She finished up with a little bow, thinking to herself with a gleam of pleasure, "Refined, that's what I am."

The whiskies having arrived, Mr. James decided he might dismiss Mrs. Johnson from his mind. Agnes was leaning towards him now, talking rapidly, her face close against his. He did not follow all she was saying, and laughed rather as his instinct prompted him than by the light of his own appreciation. For he considered he was well away now from the safe shore; and sometimes he felt a little thrilled by his own bravery and would glance round to see what attention he was attracting; and sometimes he felt uneasy and afraid, and his eyes grew absent as he thought of what lay in front of him. But whenever Agnes paused he nodded, looked thoughtful for a moment, smiled, and then renewed his grip on what she was saying.

Meanwhile Mrs. Johnson, sipping her whisky, watched them passively. Her mind remained tranquil, for she was not jealous of Agnes, and in so far as she thought at all, she felt glad that Agnes was evidently fixed up all right. At the back of her mind, as yet unformulated, was the realisation that her evening was running out, and that very shortly indeed she would have to try and do something about it. But she did not spoil the few precious moments in which she had a right to a comfortable seat, and was regarded with tolerance if not with approval, by taking thought. People came and went; occasionally a burst of laughter or a raised voice struck her attention; her head became heavy; and she felt further and further away from the world of struggle and discomfort.

Abruptly her pleasant coma was dispelled. "Time, gentlemen, time!" came the harsh voice of the waiter, intruding on conversation, shattering reverie, disturbing observation. To Mrs. Johnson it was the strident voice of reality shouting at her to get a move on, and remember that she had her rent to pay.

"Eleven o'clock, and I haven't spoken to a man yet," Mrs. Johnson warned herself in something of a panic. She swallowed the last of the liquor remaining in her glass, and pushing back her chair rose to her feet, frowning and determined. One predominating thought mastered her: she must get out into the street and accost someone, anyone, quick. But she remembered her manners. "Goodnight, dear," she said to Agnes, who nodded and laughed, and "Good night to you," she said to Mr. James, who gave a half nod, and shuffled uneasily in his chair. She went out of the room and, a little unsteadily, down the stairs, followed by a long high laugh, over whose significance she pondered vacantly.

Coming into Leicester Square, the bright lights, as they seemed, and throngs of hurrying people, confused her. For a moment she wondered irritably if there was an accident or something, to account for so many people. And there was such a noise. Faces shot by her, gleaming with astonishing clarity, as if lit up by a powerful white light, and then in a moment vanished as if they had never been. There were two men arguing angrily outside the Empire; just past them three girls coming along arm-in-arm, their red mouths opened by laugher. Again, a placard bore down upon her suddenly and impressively, "The Wicked Shall Be Turned into Hell" it shouted at Mrs. Johnson, and passed by; while in its turn the unshaven face of a matchseller standing at the curb rose at her, and fixed her attention a few seconds owing to its all aloofness. The matchseller was apart from the pushing staring talking people; he was too apart even to be a spectator. But he stayed his place like a sceneshifter who stands in the wings without a thought for the play, waiting till the end.

Crossing the road, Mrs. Johnson made her way down the short cut which leads into the Charing Cross Road. The fresh air steadied her a little, but she felt very tired and suddenly very lonely. It was easy because, she thought, there were so many millions of people about all talking to someone else except her alone. Outside the picture palace she paused, and laid a hand on her back.

"Christ! My back doesn't half ache," she said aloud, looking for sympathy from the commissionaire, who was impatiently awaiting the expected exit of the audience so that he could get home. Meanwhile he stared up and down, anxious not to lose any spectacle which he might add to his day's store before retiring into private life.

He was a big fellow with a fine moustache, and though he made no comment with regard to Mrs. Johnson's plaint, she continued to pause expectantly, for of a sudden she had become convinced that there existed a strong likeness between him and her dead husband. He gave her a glance at last, having failed to find anything or anybody else worthy of his attention.

"Cheer up, mother," he said consolingly, "you'll soon be dead."

"It's very strange," said Mrs. Johnson, disregarding this piece of comfort. It's strange indeed, but you're just the image of my husband. The absolute spit of him!"

A page boy coming out from the cinema heard, and a grin twisted the corners of his mouth. That was a good one to tell against Big Jim. The commissionaire, aware of him, said loudly, "Well, I'm not your husband. No. Nor likely to be if I can help it. So don't get ideas."

The boy laughed loudly, and two or three people passing paused and stared with expectant grins. Mrs. Johnson felt she was being made game of, and the mixed assortment of liquor inside her lighted a spurt of indignation.

"Don't you suggest anything against my husband," she said with tones that gathered loudness. "He owned a big hotel, he did, and took more money in an hour than you do in a month: for all you stand there as if you thought you was in a beauty competition." The crowd was increased by the first arrivals from the audience, and this time the laughter was against the commissionaire, who became annoyed.

"Here, none of your lip! Move along or I'll tell the police." And then added, instinctively finding the softest place in Mrs. Johnson's armour, "You're drunk, and at your age, too!"

Mrs. Johnson did not care, even at her most irresponsible, to have the police brought into the conversation, and slowly she started to move on, saying, but not too loudly, "Don't be so free with your drinks, my fine fellow, or else if there's a law in the land, you'll be made sorry for it. Libel it is! The law of libel!"

She left him behind, and walked fairly fast. But she still continued to mutter to herself, and a few of the crowd hoping to be provided with further entertainment, followed. Mrs. Johnson, turning suddenly, saw the white face of one of them, a young man, looming close by, and mistook his avid expression for sympathy.

"My husband was a fine man," she confided to him. "A fine big man; could have knocked down that whipper-snapper as easy." She shook her head in sad reminiscence. "But he died. He died of cancer."

The thought had suddenly flashed upon her with the vividness of a great discovery, and it seemed to her as if she was recounting for the first time a fact of the utmost moment. "Yes, dear! Cancer was eating his stomach out, month after month, so as he couldn't keep a bit of food inside him; and there he was looking as yellow as a Chinaman, him that 'ad never 'ad a day's illness in his life, so that it would a break your heart to see him…" She stopped, for the face had vanished, the young man's prudence having conquered his curiosity.

Mrs. Johnson crossed to St. Martin's Church, and then to Charing Cross Station, for the young man's presence had aroused her to a sense of her calling. With an effort she dismissed the pictures of her past which had occupied her mind. Better have a look at myself, she thought; and in Charing Cross Ladies' Room, she remembered, there was a full length mirror at which you could powder and have a good long view of yourself without being charged. In some of these places you would get your head eaten off if you so much as took a peep in the looking-glass without paying the attendant. It was a miserly grasping world!

Mrs. Johnson made her way into the station through the waiting room, and proceeded downstairs. She stood in front of the mirror, and powdered her face generously while she debated within herself the question of paying out yet another penny in order to satisfy a demand of nature. She had forgotten that there was no free convenience provided her: always a catch, she told herself, somewhere. If she spent a penny, she'd only have … how much was it? Twopence half-penny, or two pence three farthings, to be precise. On the other hand, if she waited till she got outside and then took a risk, she might get a policeman on to her. The commissionaire's threat had brought a sense of police persecution home to her. The way they walked so silently round corners just when you thought you was safe from observation! Besides, she had always kept herself respectable in those sorts of ways: not like some she could name. But then, they'd never known any better; never been legally married and had a place of their own. She had.

Before leaving she had another long look at herself. There was no denying that she did look yellow. She turned to a smartly-dressed young woman who was standing beside her, and, moved by the craving to receive some sympathy, coughed loudly, and put her hand to her throat.

The young woman, with a broad pink face and a lot of fair hair bunched outside her ears, happened to be feeling pleased with herself, and therefore benevolently inclined. She was just about to set off in a taxi with a gentleman who was going to pay for a really smart hotel, and then some more: so meeting Mrs. Johnson's appealing eyes in the glass, she responded.

"Got a bad cough, haven't you?" she said.

"Oh, terrible," replied Mrs. Johnson eagerly. "I've just had the 'flu. I never felt like I feel now in all my life before. It's cruel, that what it is. Have you ever felt like it, I wonder? There's a pain that's just eating into my back, here. I feel sickish; my head aches that bad; and the soles of my poor feet make it so that I can hardly put one foot before another."

"Oh, yes, I've felt like that in my time," replied the girl, replacing a stick of rouge in her hand-bag, a beautiful expensive handbag it was, Mrs. Johnson noticed admiringly. "Scores of times, if it comes to that."

"Fancy that!" said Mrs. Johnson gazing at her in a blend of admiration, wonder and appeal. Her mind worked rapidly. This girl seemed a friendly sort. No harm in trying it on.

"And the worst of it is," said Mrs. Johnson, "I haven't even got the price of my 'bus fare home. I was dying for a___, and it's took my last penny. Now, what I'm going to do I don't really know. I'm not young and good-looking and smart like you, dearie, and it's hard to live. I suppose I shall have to walk all the way back to Camberwell, that's where I live, though I know I shall drop down in the street long before I get there."

"Nothing doing," said the girl briefly. She started to ascend the steps, and then with the thought of her own immediate lucrative future before her she repented, and pausing for a moment opened her bag. Perhaps God would see that *she* never knew want, if He saw her being generous to other people who hadn't her luck.

"Here you are," she said, going back and handing three coppers to Mrs. Johnson, who had come to meet her, after a glance round to make sure that there was no attendant watching. "That'll pay your fare home anyway. As a matter of fact I'm pretty well cleaned out myself."

"Thank you very much, dear," said Mrs. Johnson, effusive and polite to the last, though a little disappointed. "Wouldn't have hurt her to make it a tanner," she commented to herself.

All dressed up as she was – pearl necklace and a beautiful cloth to her costume. Well, have to be thankful for a small mercies, I suppose.

She stared at herself with mournful interest a little longer: her mind occupied with the old problem, to veil or not to veil. It looked so old-fashioned. But it did hide her wrinkles. Leave it perhaps.

At last she dragged herself away, and slowly and heavily ascended the stairs, not even pausing for a final glance at herself in the mirror in the wall at the top, for a deep weariness not to be evaded or forgotten any longer had captured her whole being. It was true what she had told her late acquaintance: she ached all down her back; her stomach was a little uneasy; her legs felt so heavy that it was a weary business dragging them up the stairs. It wasn't fair, she told herself, to expect her to try and do anything. If Rose had a heart at all, she couldn't deny her a few more nights' rest. She had fivepence halfpenny now; whatever remained from her bus fare she would take to Rose. "See," she would say, "this is all I have, but if it's any good to you have it. Have it!" she would say. Perhaps Rose would lend her another ten bob if she got her in the right mood.

As she left the station, keeping close to the pavement, somebody pushed into her, nearly causing her to lose her balance. She waited a moment to steady herself, and then proceeded on her way, without enough heart in her even to place in his proper category the man who had shoved her. At the end of the Strand stood crowds of people waiting for their 'buses, almost, it seemed, blocking her way on purpose, as she moved pace by pace towards Trafalgar Square. She felt blinded by voices, the jostling rush, and whimpered a little out of tiredness as she moved through.

At the doorway of a chemist's shop at the corner she paused, and stood still thinking that she might give the world a last chance to do something for her. She waited passively, now and then recollecting herself enough to turn her head and single out the approaching figure of a man walking by himself. At these moments her lips would expand in an effort of invitation which remained fixed some time after the object which had inspired it had vanished from sight.

Before very long she felt someone pause beside her. Mrs. Johnson turned hopefully. But it was a policeman who confronted her. "Now then," he said "hadn't you better be getting along?"

Mrs. Johnson looked for a moment – which seemed to her a long while – into the red face which loomed above her. Vast and meaningless it appeared to her until gradually its significance reached her brain. Then she turned without a word, making her way mechanically across Northumberland Avenue. Arrived at the other side, she looked behind to see if he were following her. No, he had turned the other way.

It's no use, she reflected, not without satisfaction. Everybody and everything was against her. It was Friday, too, an unlucky day Friday had always been for her. Better go home while there was still a 'bus to get. It was nearly twelve, and there wouldn't be one if she waited much longer. Hadn't had any luck. But she couldn't be expected to when she was feeling as she was. No one could!

Her 'bus came, and she watched it drawing up with satisfaction. Nice friendly 'bus, that would take her home to bed. She was lucky in getting a corner seat, but, as she drew out tuppence for her ticket, a sense of the tragedy its giving up signified overcame her once more. "That's almost my last copper gone," she said aloud, looking round at the other passengers in the 'bus, and making her last bid that evening for a look or smile of sympathy, with her child's eyes half terrified, half proud. To be in such a hole!

But no one answered her. Any gaze that met hers withdrew with uneasy speed. The woman who sat next Mrs. Johnson nudged her neighbor, and exchanged with her a smile full of meaning. The man opposite gazed at his boots with great solemnity. Next to him a portly grocer thought with disgust, "Is the woman going to start begging? Here! In a 'bus! Scandalous!" And he frowned at her heavily in order that she should be discouraged from creating any such scene. And then one by one the eyes of the people who had overheard Mrs. Johnson returned to her, filled with carefully prepared impersonality. If she went on talking or addressed someone it might be amusing, the boldest thought. But be careful not to give her encouragement to pick on them.

But the flicker of life had died in Mrs. Johnson. She offered no more entertainment, but sat awaiting the time she would get out and creep home to bed. It would not be safe to risk going past her proper fare stage, she decided. She wasn't going to pay another penny, no, not if she knew it. So that meant dragging herself along the dark close-smelling Camberwell Road, which seemed to stretch itself out for ever. Sometimes she had to stop and lean against a wall to get a moment's respite. "Christ!" she would mutter at such times, and once, when she felt very exhausted, "Lord Christ!" Perhaps she had knocked herself up proper. It was disgraceful that she should have been forced to go that evening. A fair scandal it was! And nothing had come of it. Nothing had come of it.

At last she turned the corner of her street. As she approached she thought of Rose, who might even be waiting up for her, and her steps faltered. The thing was to be very quiet going in: not let the old cat hear her. Very quietly she slipped the key into the lock and slipped in, closing the door noiselessly behind her. Holding her breath, she tiptoed upstairs, pausing ever and again to listen. But there was no sound. Rose must be asleep. Thank God for that!

Inside her little bedroom, she closed the door, and cautiously turned the key in the lock. She was in now, and she'd not be turned out again that night at least for anyone. Not if Rose came and shouted ever so. Now she was safe. There was a whole night between her and the recurrence of unpleasantness. Florrie; Lily; the face of the dark man who had been rude; Agnes, a gay sort that girl! the good-looking fair boy; Mr. James; the big commissionaire: old beast he was; the girl who had given her threepence: dressed up tart; flickered in her confused head as she undressed. Then she dismissed them. It was all over now. The evening was over. She'd get a little rest and peace now. Feel better tomorrow perhaps.

"At least," was her last coherent thought, "I got a few drinks for nothing. Some of those girls, prostitutes though they may be, have good hearts. I will say that for them."

MISS JOCELYN

Miss Elizabeth Mary Jocelyn sat down to breakfast just as her silver watch said five minutes past eight. She lifted the little brown teapot, and then tilted it so that it would pour into her cup. The teapot had a broken spout, which necessitated a very gentle flow if you didn't want to make spots on the cloth, so Miss Jocelyn had time to think of something else while she waited for her cup to fill. Things being as they were it was not surprising that the thought which came was an unpleasant one. It was that this was the very last time that she would pour out tea for herself in her own little room.

Today was the day on which she was going to stay with her cousin's wife, and their children, and, of course, her cousin, in Hull. "Stay" was the word that had been used, and would probably go on being used, but deep down inside her, Miss Jocelyn grappled miserably with the fact that stay meant live, and not live *with* but live *on*. Miss Jocelyn had tried not to think of this more than she could help; and the best way of getting away from it had been to hope to the very last moment that somehow she would be able to get work, regular work, bringing in another ten shillings a week.

She could have just managed with that, because Mrs. Stack, of 10 Stanhope Terrace, was still employing her for four mornings a week, at half-a-crown for the three hours. Only for a long while there hadn't been anyone else, and so Miss Jocelyn's savings in the Post Office had dwindled to seven pounds ten shillings, and then seven pounds, and then six pounds ten, and then six pounds, and then five pounds fifteen, and then five pounds ten, and then, after two weeks, nothing could prevent it from reaching the five pound mark. It was then that Miss Jocelyn had forced herself to write to Frank, as he had told her to do if things got, well, difficult, and ask for his advice. It had been a difficult letter to write, and when it was written it didn't say very much.

But Frank had been so very good. She thought again with gratitude of Frank's goodness, as she spread her piece of bread thinly with marmalade, and cut it daintily into four little pieces. He had written that he was coming to Nottingham on business, and that they would have luncheon together. Then they could talk things over. It was true that Miss Jocelyn would never be able to think of that luncheon with pleasure. She had indeed felt very uncomfortable because of the quick abrupt way he had thrown questions at her. They seemed to have the effect of muddling her, and then making it very clear that she was much worse off than she had really thought. If Mrs. Moss had only not gone to live in London. She at least had found her useful, and Mrs. Stack often praised her; it was only that other ladies who interviewed her seemed so positive that she was too old to be worth paying. If they would only give her a chance! But they never did. Certainly she was sometimes able to get a little mending to do. And last Christmas two ladies had given her an order to knit a silk jumper for a present. But Frank seemed to disregard little things like that, which, after all, made some difference. He just reduced the whole position to the one circumstance that she could only earn ten shillings a week, and had only five pounds left in the bank.

He also told her, in a rather annoyed voice, Miss Jocelyn could not help feeling, that she didn't look at all well. "You want feeding up," he had said. At that a little red patch came on each of her cheeks, and it was very difficult to swallow the fish that was before her. The fact that she had to leave a good deal of it made her feel ashamed. It was such a nice piece of plaice, so nicely browned, and it seemed ungrateful to Frank not to appear to enjoy it when he had been so kind as to ask her out to lunch. But there were, too, so many people about, and Miss Jocelyn felt that some of them were staring at her. She was almost sure that two very smartly dressed girls at the table next to them were talking about her.

Nor did Frank appear as cheerful as usual. It was, of course, a very awkward position in which to have to put him. After her last reply he had become
very silent, and Miss Jocelyn was silent too, not wishing to disturb him. It was
when the coffee came that he had spoken.

"Well, Auntie Elizabeth," he had said. "You must just come and pay us a
long visit, and get a little fatter. Besides, Joan has only one maid now, and you
will be no end useful to her. She isn't very strong, you know, and the two children take a lot out of her."

It's very good of you, Frank," Miss Jocelyn said, "but…" She stopped.
What was there she could say? She didn't want to go. She remembered Joan.
Joan was a very grand person, and Joan always spoke to her as if she were a
child. Joan certainly wouldn't want her. She knew that. And she had so hoped
that Frank would have known someone, an invalid, say, who wanted a companion. That was what she had really expected: that Frank would have found
her some work.

"But what?" Frank had asked, rather impatiently. No, there was nothing to
say. There was no one else who would or could help her … the workhouse of
course.

"Thank you very much indeed, Frank," she had said in a low voice. She had
really to make quite an effort not to cry in front of Frank and all the people in
the restaurant. It was silly to feel so upset.

"Well, that's settled. And now Aunt…."

He had excused himself. He had to rush away. These business appointments! His voice was hearty again though he did not meet her eyes. Oh, Frank
was very kind and good. He had such heaps of important matters to attend
to. Settling her affairs was just a trifle to him. And so big and so strong. How
proud Joan must be of him!

Well, that had been ten days ago, and it had been a very busy ten days for
Miss Jocelyn. She had walked miles and miles of hard pavements in answer to
the advertisements in the *Nottingham Guardian*, but it had been no use. Nobody
thought she would suit them. It was evident that she was too old.

Then two days ago she had fainted when she had returned home. She had
lain quite still on the floor in her cupboard of a bedroom. When she came to
herself she had been startled by the sight she presented. She had looked so
very queer about the eyes, and her skin was quite yellow. The next morning
she started to pack.

On this, her very last day, she lingered over her breakfast, making her second cup of tea last out by taking very small sips. There was no hurry because
the train didn't go till ten forty-five. Even if she allowed an hour to get to the
station and buy her ticket, as she had done, it wouldn't mean starting till a
quarter to ten. She had the thought that if this breakfast time would only last

forever, then she would always just be going to live with Frank and Joan, but never really get there. The cab – it was generous of Frank to send her money for a taxi as well as her fare – would always be setting out to take her to the station, but it would never reach the door.

A knock came, and Mrs. Dixon, the landlady, entered. In the morning she was white-faced and slatternly with dark hair that wanted combing. In the evening she was pink-cheeked and red-lipped, with bright eyes and the prettiest of curls. In her girlhood, she had had her gay times promenading Long Row with the brightest and best of Nottingham's daughters: now a husband, whose employment was erratic, and a sickly baby had taken some of the glow from her. But she still had her rouge box and sometimes a little bit of fun; and because she was good-natured and curious, enjoyed herself more often than not.

"A letter for you, Miss Jocelyn," she said.

Everything stopped inside Miss Jocelyn. She saw the letter was from Frank. Perhaps they couldn't have her! Perhaps she needn't go after all! Conscious of Mrs. Dixon's watching eyes, she held herself from tearing open the envelope, and used the bread knife instead. It was an instinct with her not to lose such small opportunities of doing things that people like Mrs. Dixon would not think of doing. She knew she kept her rooms far cleaner than Mrs. Dixon kept the rest of the house, and it was one of her fundamental tenets that only a lady could really keep things as they should be kept. Mrs. Dixon was not a bad-hearted woman, even though at this very moment she was showing far more of her chest than was really respectable, and a good deal more than was nice, but she was not a lady. It was not, of course, the fact that Mrs. Dixon was poor that did not make her a lady. She, Miss Jocelyn, was poor, and had done work that she was well aware was not the right sort of work for a lady, but it was for the sake of her independence, and her two tiny rooms. It did not make he feel any more at home in the company of those who were not ladies.

Mrs. Dixon, for instance, used some not very nice words sometimes, which made her feel quite uncomfortable, even though she knew Mrs. Dixon could not be blamed. Since she was not a lady she did not know any better.

So now she started to read the letter quite calmly, without making the comment for which she knew Mrs. Dixon was waiting. It contained no reprieve.

It read:

75, Exeter Road, Hull.

May 27th, 19–.

Dear Auntie Elizabeth,

Here with I enclose £1 (one pound) to cover anything you may wish to buy for your journey, etc. It was very remiss of me not to have sent it before, but

I have been more than usually busy this week. I hope you will have a pleasant journey. Joan will meet the train.

Your affectionate cousin,
Frank B. Jocelyn.

Mrs. Dixon saw the enclosure, but couldn't quite make out whether it was a pound or a ten shilling note which Miss Jocelyn had rapidly slipped back into the envelope. Her curiosity made her linger, for she was aware that she had gleaned very little information as to Miss Jocelyn's future or her feelings with regard to her future. She had been going to a dance last night when Miss Jocelyn had come down to settle up finally, and she had been too pressed for time to try and draw her out.

"Well, Miss, to think this is your last morning," she started when she saw that Miss Jocelyn had laid the letter down, and was staring at the tablecloth.

Miss Jocelyn smiled a pale and ladylike smile.

"Yes, Mrs. Dixon. That is so."

"Well, well! But after all it will be nice your going to live with your relatives, won't it?"

"*Stay* with them, Mrs. Dixon. My future plans are uncertain."

"Oh, indeed, yes. Just a visit like?"

"Yes."

"Your nephew, did you say it was?"

"No, not my nephew. My cousin and his wife."

"Really. And I suppose there'll be children."

"Two children." Why didn't Mrs. Dixon go? Of course the woman meant well, but while she was standing there the minutes were rushing by: rushing along so as to cheat her out of the last few moments she had in her rooms, her own little home, by herself.

Mrs. Dixon sensed something uncomfortably rigid in the pale little woman with soft gray hair that was arranged prettily round the small face. She wouldn't be surprised if the poor thing didn't want to go. It was just, of course, that she couldn't make two ends meet any more.

"Well, it'll be company for you, won't it? I've often thought you must feel lonely sitting here of an evening all on your own."

Miss Jocelyn recognised that there was more of interrogation than affirmation in Mrs. Dixon's tone, and organized her wandering mind to meet it. Not that a woman like Mrs. Dixon would be able to understand.

"Of course I shall be glad to see my cousin and his wife, and their dear children, Mrs. Dixon. But I have been very happy here."

Miss Jocelyn smiled, but this time her smile was more pitiful than ladylike; Mrs. Dixon warmed to it, and to what she took as a compliment to herself.

"Well, I'm not surprised at that, Miss, because, as everyone has always said, they're two nice rooms, so convenient like, and nice to have the bedroom, if it is small, separate from the other. Cosy and yet all the difference from these bed-sitting rooms. A real home to a person, as you say."

Mrs. Dixon gazed round her property admiringly while she projected herself into the future, and saw herself confronting the next lodger. She ought to be able to get more. Another half-crown at least. She had been a bit soft with the old woman.

Miss Jocelyn said nothing, so Mrs. Dixon spoke again.

"Well, I'm glad you've been comfortable, and real sorry you've got to go. They're not many of them, I must say, as give as little trouble as you, never want anything done for them or anything. Now the man as was here before you, of course I charged him more, only right to with having attendance; but a regular terror he was for shouting downstairs at all hours of the day – and night, too, as you might say. I told you about him, an actor he was, and never got in till all hours, but expected something hot ready for him all the same."

She paused for sympathy, and Miss Jocelyn summoned a small, vague smile. "Well, I hope you will be more fortunate in your next...er...let, Mrs. Dixon. I know how busy you are with your own children–"

Mrs. Dixon nodded gloomily. Miss Jocelyn's words had reminded her of the baby kicking his heels in the pram down in the kitchen. He'd be making more work for her if she didn't get back to him.

"Ah, well, no use meeting trouble half way, that's what I always say. Keep smiling! And Goodbye, Miss, and the best of luck if I don't see you again. I'll send any letters on to the address you gave me, so don't worry about that."

"Goodbye, Mrs. Dixon. And thank you very much."

"You're very welcome. You don't want Johnny to run along and get you a taxi? I'll send him if you like."

"No, thank you, Mrs. Dixon. I ordered it last night. It's to be here at a quarter to ten."

"Right. Well, ta-ta!"

"Goodbye."

Mrs. Dixon went downstairs a little more thoughtfully than was her custom. Poor old lady! It wasn't all honey going to live with relations who were probably as mad as hatters at having to take her. Of course you couldn't blame them. Having a prim old dame like her dumped on you for the rest of her days. She herself wouldn't be sorry to get someone a bit more lively in the house; someone you could chat to. All the same she wasn't a bad little thing; no bother, you wouldn't know she was in the house.

The baby was whimpering. Oh, yes, just as she had guessed! Sopping wet! Who would be a mother? Well, he'd have to wait a bit. Get the breakfast things washed up first.

Upstairs Miss Jocelyn was considering Frank's letter. It was really most thoughtful of him to have sent another pound. But there was no need. He had already sent her the money for the journey. It must be that he was afraid of her arriving quite without a penny at their house ... well, well, it had come at last.

The room looked so bare without her photographs. She rose and looked in the bedroom. There was just room for a dressing table up beside the bed; and now there was nothing on it but a little pile of paper and rubbish. Gone was her green handkerchief sachet with its hand-painted pink tulips. Gone was the brown holland case with her brush and comb. Gone was the little bottle of eau-de-Cologne Mrs. Stack had sent her at Christmas. Gone was the white china pintray with its pattern of pink rose-buds. Of course in a few hours she would be taking them out, and putting them on a different dressing table. Probably a much nicer one with a glass that you didn't have to prop up by sticking in bits of paper. But still it wouldn't be the same; it wouldn't be her own as this had been. At least her own in a way, because she had paid to have it.

Miss Jocelyn shook herself. She really mustn't get so depressed. It wasn't grateful. It wasn't even right. She scolded herself a little as she went back to her chair.

She knew very well that it didn't matter where she lived, not really, so long as she was right with God. Things might be, might seem inharmonious for her, but it was just an appearance. God, Who answered all prayers, would help her if she only had faith, complete faith.

"Come unto Me all ye that labour and are heavy-laden, and I will give you rest."[57]

She couldn't help not wanting to give up her rooms. It was the first real home of her own she had had since father had died when she was thirty. Being a companion in other people's houses was a very different thing. And the Jocelyns had always liked their independence. But she must remember that it was very good of Frank to offer her a home. And she might be really useful to Joan if she would only let her. But in any case it was right to accept gladly every outward condition that was sent. God had sent His only Son to endure all the apparent pain and sufferings of the world so as to show that these

---

57 Biblical reference, Matthew 11:28.

things were only illusions. God, the All Good, Kind, Wonderful God, which Christian Science[58] revealed so beautifully. And he cared for her.

"Ask and it shall be given you. Knock and it shall be opened to you."[59]

Miss Jocelyn sat comforting herself with thoughts of the Love of the Divine Purpose which shaped all things. Sometimes, as for example when she looked at the clock, the world rose at her and confronted her with a hard malicious stare which for the moment isolated her from her consolations. At these times slow difficult tears would rise behind her eyes, and she would have to brush them away with one of the real linen handkerchiefs one or two distant relatives remembered to send her at Christmas. Quickly then she would have to call to Mary Baker Eddy[60] and God, but they did not fail her, and when at last she braced herself to rise and perform the last rites, her eyes were restored to their patience.

Still, it was somehow something of a shock to hear the cab drive up and then stop; and realise that it had really come to take her away. There had been a hope at the bottom of her heart, though she had never voiced it – that would have been too presumptuous – that even though it might be at the very last moment, God would have sent some sign, done something which would have allowed her to keep her own little home, her own independence. So many times other members had borne testimony at the Wednesday evening meetings of how God had interfered on their behalf. But in her case it was evidently not to be.

After the taxi came, things rushed on very quickly. Mrs. Dixon ran upstairs with the baby in her arms, and stood smiling and waving, and looking so kind that for the first time Miss Jocelyn felt her heart go out to her. She leaned out of the window, and waved her linen handkerchief for as long as she could see, and then sat back visualising Mrs. Dixon as her only true friend. She was a most kind-hearted woman, there was no doubt about that. Of course she belonged to a different class, but all the same if ever she went back she would be more encouraging to her landlady's talkativeness. She was a thoroughly nice woman, if a little untidy; while the baby, who had always seemed to Miss Jocelyn a revolting, because evil-smelling, little object, had really beautiful eyes. For quite a little while Miss Jocelyn occupied herself with encouraging thoughts about the baby. He would, if his mother only kept him a little cleaner, and didn't leave him alone so often at night, grow up a really nice good man. She hoped he would do well, and obtain regular employment.

---

58 Christian Science: A religious practice that believes sickness is an illusion that can be cured by prayer; part of the New Thought movement.

59 Biblical reference, Matthew 7:7.

60 Mary Baker Eddy (1821–1910): The founder of Christian Science.

Then, suddenly, she was at the station, and holding tightly on to her two suitcases which a porter wanted to take from her. Now there was her ticket to get. Where was the booking office? She felt very [flustered],[61] and it seemed that it no longer mattered that she was leaving her home at Nottingham for a strange destination, but that the important thing was to get herself safe in the train. She must have her money ready for the booking clerk or he would be annoyed….

She learnt, however, that she was not allowed to go on the platform yet. The train was not in. It appeared that for the moment there was nothing for her to do but to sit down and watch time going by. It was impossible to think because everything was so bustling, and yet at the same time possessed by that air of aloofness from individual concerns characteristic of stations.

It was an atmosphere which put one in one's place as a traveler among scores of other travelers, all undoubtedly going for far more important journeys than Miss Jocelyn. So she sat quietly, gripping her bag and umbrella, and occasionally glancing at the suitcases beside her to make sure they were still there. Almost she was persuaded by the remote, intent, shadowy faces passing that there was nothing extremely odd and momentous in her sitting on a station bench waiting to depart by the next train for Hull. It was true she might never see Nottingham again. Probably she would not. She had indeed already left it, because, after all, a town's stations could not be said to belong to the town. They were just places where one got off and got on. Still, what did that matter? Nottingham was a nice place, but it grew insignificant and remote when viewed in the light of the indifference and separateness of its terminus. She had nothing to do with Nottingham any more. She was going to Hull now. Well, and what of that? The station seemed to sneer. Other people were going to really important places like London, perhaps even abroad? People did!

She wondered whether it would not be better for her to sit in the ladies' waiting room. No, she was too afraid of missing her train for that. While she was there, at the very centre of the station, watching the clock, the train could hardly go without her. But she knew she would be uneasy all the time if she withdrew to a comparative seclusion. So she sat on, and looked frequently at her suitcases. There were some rough looking people about.

But as every ordained event will surely come in its season, as surely pass, so the time came when Miss Jocelyn was permitted to go on the platform. And then the train came triumphantly round the bend and impressively drew to a standstill, and Miss Jocelyn had hardly time to feel [flustered] again when she

---

61 Editor substitution for 'fluttered', as 'flustered' is used earlier in the chapter.

was in a corner seat of a third-class non-smoking carriage with her two bags on the rack over her head, and her umbrella propped behind her in the corner. Yes, she had everything; she was in the train; and it was the right train!

Then, just as she was feeling rather pleased with herself because she had managed so well, the guard waved his green flag, and the train responded by gathering itself together, and starting to move with a delusive air of leisure and unconcern. Before you realised it, this merged into a steady run, and the seat opposite Miss Jocelyn which had said Nottingham couldn't say it any more, because it had been left behind … perhaps, Miss Jocelyn thought, for ever so far as she was concerned.

She looked out of the window, and watched rows of houses and streets give place to wider spaces. The train had started to run away with her, and she recognised that she would not be allowed to descend from its clutch till another station seat or notice board announced definitely and inescapably "HULL."

She thought about this for a little while, and then looked out of the window once more with a sinking feeling in her stomach. As she watched cabbage-patch, field, row of houses, bridge, field again being caught up, briefly recognised, and passed ruthlessly by, hope died within her. There was no mistaking the train's determination.

There was only one other woman in the compartment. She was a pale person of no particular age, clothed in a brown costume and brown hat, who sat at the opposite end of the carriage reading *Nash's Magazine*[62] with absorption. The interest she was putting into the printed pages almost removed her from reality. Even Miss Jocelyn, who would have liked to say to Frank and Joan later, "I travelled with such a nice lady, most interesting," found she could not make any significant picture of her. She was just a lady reading a magazine, nothing more. There was nothing therefore for Miss Jocelyn to do but sit and look out of the window at the invincible passage of time.

After a while, she was disturbed in this occupation by the top one of her suitcases falling off the rack, knocking her hat sideways and hitting her shoulder in its clumsy rush to the floor. Startled, Miss Jocelyn fixed her hat straight, and then looked timidly over at the lady in the corner with words of apology and smile ready to appear. But though the lady had looked up to inform herself of the cause for the noise she had heard, she immediately turned back to the magazine, her countenance unawakened by any gleam of sympathy.

Miss Jocelyn realised that she was left to deal with matters by herself. She bent, picked up the bag and, after a second's hesitation, decided to thrust

---

62 *Nash's Magazine*: A British magazine controlled by the Hearst corporation that merged with the *Pall Mall Magazine* to become *Nash's Pall Mall Magazine*.

it under the seat. Putting it back on top of the other was evidently not safe. Laying it alongside on the rack would seem as if she were taking more than her fair share of the accommodation. Thus she reasoned, without knowing that thus she reasoned.

As she pushed the bag in, it struck against some hard obstruction.

She stooped to investigate, and found that the object which had delayed her bag's progress was a small leather attaché case. Did it belong to the lady in the opposite corner? Apparently not. And it was hardly likely she would place one of her possessions under the seat at the opposite end of the carriage to where she was sitting. What could it be doing there?

In uncertainty and some perturbation Miss Jocelyn looked across at her companion, hoping that she could encounter a glance which would give her courage to speak. It didn't come. The lady only smartly turned another page. Miss Jocelyn decided to place the stray bag on the seat opposite. Her own she pushed underneath. Then she sat back in her corner bothered and exhausted.

The train went running on, and even with a shriek of mingled challenge and despair took a dark tunnel in its course, but Miss Jocelyn was no longer a despondent observer of its progress. She couldn't take her mind off the little brown leather case opposite. Its existence disturbed her. She was the only person who knew it was there, and knew that it had no business to be there. The responsibility laid itself as a burden upon her, and refused to let her mind wander for long.

What ought she to do … if anything? Tell the guard? But the guard wasn't there to be told. She couldn't be expected to explore the recesses of the guard's van in order to find him. If only that woman –for so Miss Jocelyn was now thinking of her companion –had been a more approachable person, then she could have shared the problem. But all the same, she simply had to be told, or asked if it were hers, or something. You couldn't leave a strange bag, which might contain valuables, about without saying anything. It wasn't right.

She cleared her throat, and turned a determined look upon the lady in the corner. To her horror she found that she was no longer reading *Nash's Magazine*. It was lying with both its covers turned upwards on her lap, while her eyes were closed in oblivion. She was probably not really asleep, but she had taken on herself, most inconveniently, the appearance of sleep, thus making the outer world impotent to thrust itself on her except in a case of real urgency.

Miss Jocelyn looked at the bag, and it looked back at her. It was plain that they were meant to be alone together.

She observed for the first time that it bore initials upon it in little square black lines. The initials were "A.J."

The "J" seemed an extraordinary coincidence to Miss Jocelyn in her tense mood. The surname of the bag's owner began with the same letter as her own. If it had been "E.J." it would have been really too remarkable.

She recollected after a minute that her own mother's initials would be A.J., if you left out the Mary. Her mother's name had been Mary Anne Jocelyn.

The bag, and especially its initials, seemed to become larger than life to Miss Jocelyn. In order to stop herself from seeing it she closed her eyes; but her mind went busily on making up names to fit in with "A.J."

In her occupation she arrived at the thought that J stood for Jesus. Something inside her was arrested by this discovery, though it was some time before she had the courage to pluck the idea out of her mind which the recollection of the circumstance had suggested.

It was this: supposing God, supposing Jesus had sent this bag to help her in her trouble! It wasn't very probable, of course, but then things did sometimes happen like that. On most Wednesday evenings, Miss Jocelyn had heard her fellow Christian Scientists telling of how, when things had been most difficult, they had been shown a way out. It was only last week that Miss Carter, the librarian, had stood up to tell them about one of the books that had been missing for ever so long. It wasn't Miss Carter's fault that the book had gone, but it was an inconvenient thing, because they would hold her responsible. And then the head librarian, who must be a very strict sort of man by the way Miss Carter had referred to him, had come and said he must have the book by the next morning. And when Miss Carter, who had searched everywhere to no purpose, had gone home and laid her trouble on God's shoulders, she had received a wonderful feeling of assurance that things would be all right. And her faith had been justified, for the next morning Miss Carter found the book back again in its usual place all ready for the "chief." It was absolutely a miracle how it had got there, for it certainly was out of place when Miss Carter had gone home the previous evening.

Miss Jocelyn remembered how Miss Carter had quoted the words, "God moves in a mysterious way His wonders to perform."[63]

She looked at the bag again, and then shook her head. No, God would have shown her more plainly if He had any message for her. She would have liked to know what was in it, but you couldn't tamper with other people's luggage – if it was other people's – without a definite sign.

The train wasn't running so fast now. Suddenly the engine gave forth a shrill noise, an ugly fierce scream it seemed to Miss Jocelyn. It was the sign for

---

63 'God Moves in a Mysterious Way': A Christian hymn written in 1773 by William Cowper.

the train and time to take hold of Miss Jocelyn again, and they did so roughly, like a policeman saying, "Now, then! Move along there." She forgot about the bag, and only remembered that she was going to Hull, where the menacing figure of Frank's wife awaited her. She was unwanted, and she was old and tired.

She looked out of the window. The train ran through one small station, and then another, with proud indifference to such small fry. It didn't even give Miss Jocelyn time to see the names on the seats and lampposts, though she peered. They must certainly be coming to a large town: a church and little red villas, then a gap, then more houses pressing closer and closer together.

The train and everything in it knew that it was coming to somewhere important. The pulse of life changed to a more lively beat. Peace and lassitude departed. In all the carriages people roused themselves and fixed their thoughts on the present. The train no longer swayed and rumbled to deaf senses, but was accompanied by a hundred conscious minds where there had been only a few to observe its progress.

Miss Jocelyn, thus rendered uneasy and unhappy, bethought herself that one porter had surprisingly told her at the last moment that she would have to change at Doncaster. The first porter she had asked had said, "No, there was no change," and he had such a comfortable voice, such a pleasant red face, that he had brought an assurance to Miss Jocelyn which the warning of the second man had not seriously dispelled. But now she was uncertain again. She realised that she was alone, and that anything might happen to her if she did not maintain a careful guard. She must ask again at this station, and she had better get her bags ready in case she would have to move.

She stood up, and lifted the suitcase off the rack on to the seat. Then she bent underneath the seat to capture the other one. Hardly were they both on the seat beside her, hardly was her umbrella firmly in her hand, and her bag underneath her arms, when the train drew up under a dark roof which frowned gloomily upon a scene of fretful confusion.

Voices called out imperatively: "Doncaster, Doncaster," and her heart beating, Miss Jocelyn let down the window. A porter stopped beside her. "Do I change for Hull?" Miss Jocelyn asked him with strained eager eyes. "Change for Hull? Yes. Platform 4."

The porter passed on. He was out for higher game than shabby little elderly ladies with their inevitable tuppences.

Miss Jocelyn got out in a great hurry. For all she knew the train might only be waiting a few seconds. Her two bags were not very heavy, and in any case she would never have dreamt of incurring the expense of a porter. The taxi had been extravagance enough for one day. On the platform she stood uncertainly. She wasn't going to leave the shelter of the train which, now that it didn't appear to be going to Hull after all, seemed warm and friendly without being sure that it was necessary.

She accosted another porter. He confirmed his predecessor. Yes, she had to change. Platform 4.

There was no help for it. Travelling was really a dangerous and fatiguing business. Reluctantly Miss Jocelyn started to move down the platform when she felt an imperious something bidding her stay. She turned her head. Her travelling companion was leaning out of the window and beckoning to her.

Miss Jocelyn, alarmed, returned. "Have you left your bag?" said this lady, thrusting the little leather case upon her.

"It isn't mine," said Miss Jocelyn. "It was here before."

"It must be yours," said the lady a little impatiently. "It isn't mine. There's no one else."

"It's not mine," repeated Miss Jocelyn.

"Are you sure? Well, then I know. It must belong to the woman who got out at Nottingham. You had better take it to the Lost Property Office if it isn't yours."

Miss Jocelyn hesitated. Why should this complication be thrust upon her of all people? It wasn't as if she were an experienced traveler.

"Here, take it!" said the magazine person, now transformed into a very urgent and efficient woman, with thin mouth and cold eyes. "I don't get out till Leeds. The owner must have it returned as soon as possible."

Brought into submission by the last sentence, which sounded to her as the voice of the law, Miss Jocelyn took the bag. She had to put down one of her own to do it. The nondescript lady had become very much alive to her. She had a sallow skin, and a very good set of artificial teeth. Miss Jocelyn knew definitely that she didn't like her.

A porter came along slamming the doors, and the lady sat back and watched Miss Jocelyn endeavoring to cope with the difficulties presented by carrying three bags, one umbrella, and a handbag at the same time. As Miss Jocelyn having fixed things, if somewhat precariously, began to move away, she poked her head out once more.

"Take it to the Lost Property Office," she called in a voice of command. "They'll know what to do."

Miss Jocelyn made no reply. "Don't think about the bag now," she said gently but firmly to her harassed self. "First see about the train to Hull. Platform 4, he said. But when you see another porter ask again. And ask what time it goes. *You must not lose the train.*"

Platform 4 it evidently really was, since two other porters so assured Miss Jocelyn. One of them was the same she had asked the first time, but of this Miss Jocelyn was fortunately not aware: she would not have liked to hurt his feelings. She also learnt that she had thirty-five minutes to wait. The question of the bag had now to be faced. There was no excuse of lack of time. Anyway she could hardly abandon it in the middle of the station. Someone would be sure to hurry up to her with it the next moment.

She looked round. If she could only see *Lost Property Office* written up somewhere, then she would take the nearest course and leave it there. No such words came to her assistance.

Her next alternative then, in such a perplexity, was to consult the ever-present Creator and Father. Miss Jocelyn sat down on an empty seat at hand. She didn't close her eyes, as she would have liked to have done, because she had to retain their service to look after all her property. But she took her mind away from the distractions and bustle round her and left it open to receive Divine Guidance. "Seek and ye shall find."

It was a little difficult to concentrate fully in the circumstances; she mustn't lose her bags whatever she did. But after a few minutes, she thought an answer to her consultation was forming in her mind. She listened intently, and it seemed that words took definite shape, "Open it!" "You may open it."

Suddenly and desperately Miss Jocelyn made up her mind. It might be a sign for her, or it might not. But she would not pass it by untested. There would be no harm in having a look at the contents of the bag. It bore one of her initials. She rose with tightly pressed lips, and turned her steps towards the ladies' first class waiting room, which she had perceived near at hand. As she went she had to remind herself that the magazine lady would now be safely on her way in the train to Leeds.

There was no one inside at all: almost it seemed as if the coast had been cleared on her behalf. Was she about to receive some revelation? As she put her luggage on the round polished table an attendant poked her head out of the further door, but when she perceived that for the moment Miss Jocelyn proposed to stay where she was she withdrew. Miss Jocelyn was not a person whose appearance attracted either interest or suspicion. Nor did she appear as one who had largesse to bestow.

Not that Miss Jocelyn would have minded had the woman stayed to watch her. She was now lifted above self-consciousness by a deep sense of the purity of her motives. If you had asked her what she expected to find in the bag, she would not have known what to answer, but all the same she approached the opening of the little brown case marked with the strange and significant initials A.J. – for by now Miss Jocelyn conceived them to be very strange and significant initials indeed – in the spirit of a priest ordering a solemn rite. She had not sat through the testimony meetings on and off for the fifteen years she had followed the lights of Mary Baker Eddy without receiving the assurance that with God all things were possible; and the signs He sent, which the people who didn't quite understand called coincidences, were proofs of this truth.

So with her mind composed to quietness and reverence but with her heart beating just a little faster, Miss Jocelyn, having disposed of her other belongings, took up the brown case. She was familiar with the way it opened: you just pressed back the little raised keyhole of white metal and then the clasp slid out.

Miss Jocelyn pressed. Nothing happened. More urgently than she knew Miss Jocelyn pressed again. Still nothing happened.

Miss Jocelyn straightened herself, and studied the case. Was there any other way of opening it? No! In the next second the truth stung her. The case was locked.

It was perhaps odd that this eventuality had not struck Miss Jocelyn before. But it had not done so. She had probably believed more than she had realised in the notion that the bag was ordained to be opened by her. Also, it happened that the two bags belonging to herself had locks, but no keys. It seems reasonable to suppose that in the past, their locks had possessed such justification for their existence, but it was so long ago that the idea of locking one's luggage had slipped from Miss Jocelyn's head.

It was with her at that moment as if she had run her head against a brick wall of astonishing solidity. It was as if she had been knocked out, finished and done with, very neatly and very efficiently, in the most imperceptible fraction of time. There was nothing more to be done. Nothing remained to her. No way of escape. Nothing at all. She must be careful to get the right train for her destination.

She picked up the bags, and put the case once more under her arm. Outside on the platform she sought the counsel of yet another porter. He explained to her adequately where she was to go.

At the cloakroom she was interrogated. Where exactly had she found the bag? What train did she mean? Oh, yes! Where had she got into the train? Who else was in the carriage? What was her name? And her address, please?

All such questions Miss Jocelyn replied to clearly if in a rather low voice. She even remembered to tell the man about the lady in the same carriage who said it must have belonged to the other lady who got out at Nottingham. Only when she had to leave her address, it seemed rather strange when she remembered to write Frank's address at Hull instead of her own at Nottingham.

When she was released she returned to the seat she had formerly occupied. It was easier to walk now that she only had her own bags. And there she sat very still waiting for the train that would take her to Hull to come in. Dark figures moved about: some strolled and stared, some hurried. A woman with a baby came and sat next to Miss Jocelyn and the baby cried. But Miss Jocelyn did not notice anything. The few people passing who troubled to glance at her saw a neat little elderly lady with pale, rather hollow cheeks under a heavy black hat. A little, elderly spinster: a lady probably, but not at all well off. And there are so many of her kind about that they wouldn't have been struck by the fixed expression in her eyes.

Not that sitting there Miss Jocelyn felt unhappy. She really didn't feel anything at all. Nor, and this was stranger, did she feel disposed to worry about the train; if she were on the right platform, if there wouldn't be some alteration with regard to it at the last moment. On the contrary she waited for it in the knowledge, so certain that she didn't think about it, that the train would come; that she would get in it; and get out of it at Hull. And at Hull, of course, other people would take charge.

Time ceased to run forward for her. At one moment she was sitting on the platform, with her bags on the seat beside her, her umbrella and her handbag firmly gripped; at another she became conscious of anticipation and movement round her, and rose to meet the train as it ran suddenly and swiftly into her vision; at another she was getting into a fairly empty, as it appeared, third class carriage; at another she felt the train start again into motion, and Doncaster left in the path of the past.

Inside the train she sat as passively, her head a little down, her hands clasped. Two people opposite her were carrying on a conversation; that was all Miss Jocelyn knew about them. After a while the train stopped at a station. Miss Jocelyn put her head out of the window, and saw that the station wasn't Hull. She sat back immediately. Since it wasn't Hull, it held no further interest.

Two people got out. One, a man, got in. On again the train went, running smoothly and serenely towards Hull.

Slowly the pattern of the material with which the carriage was upholstered formed itself before Miss Jocelyn's eyes. The little black lines on the red were sharp and lively; but the red was kind and comfortable; only it must be very dirty. People ought really not to take off their hats in railway carriages. From it she turned, fulfilling it as a duty, to a brief stocktaking of her fellow passengers. A young man and a girl talking intimately, the girl glancing around observantly to see what impression they were making; a husband and wife, elderly and respectable, in the opposite corners, each with a newspaper; next to Miss Jocelyn the man who had just got in, also with a newspaper, five other people, possibly going to Hull, too. Though probably the train went on past Hull, further and further north, travelling through the afternoon? It didn't concern her.

But she heard the young man opposite say to the girl with him: "I don't want to stay past the weekend," and saw her nod agreement. That meant they were only going for a visit. How pleasant it would be if she were just going for a visit!

The thought having uttered itself was succeeded by a stillness, having arrested the passage of other thoughts. This gave it room to swell, and made it seem very loud and clear. It hammered in Miss Jocelyn's mind till it beat her into consciousness. She knew, and admitted boldly that she didn't want to go to Hull, that the thought was making her very unhappy.

What was that? Someone in the carriage had said that they were due in Hull in another five minutes. That affected *her*. In five minutes she would see Joan. She must go and make herself look neat and tidy for Joan.

When she returned to the carriage the noise the train was making seemed unusually insistent. People were stirring themselves, and somehow the carriage seemed to have grown much more crowded. There was no mistaking the sense of preparation. To her surprise Miss Jocelyn suddenly felt that it was all very sudden, much too sudden! Could they be really getting into Hull? The time had gone, must have gone, very quickly since they left Doncaster … Doncaster, where the bag was. For a few seconds her thoughts stayed on the brown case. When she visualised it lying uncared for in the cloakroom, perhaps with lots of other suitcases and things pressed round it, there was tenderness in her regard. Perhaps it had really been her bag after all? But that was silly, very silly, and it was too late now. Hull was coming.

There was no mistake. Hull was springing up to meet the train's approach. No more fields or quiet-looking roads rambling with an easy indirectness to placid villages, but hard, frowning, efficient roads that went where they had been put; gas works, lots and lots of little houses, people, shops, motor cars, a flaring theatre bill, advertisement hoardings....

It had been a quick journey. Remarkably so. She would tell Frank what a good journey it had been. The train would be almost punctual. Men were always interested in train services. Her father had been, she remembered.

Quite slowly and very smoothly the train drew alongside the platform. Having run with Miss Jocelyn for many miles very purposefully, it now relaxed its grasp with graceful indifference. It was as if it had suddenly become bored by her. It had nothing to do with her any longer. No waggon of destiny any more was it; only a train standing blankly at a station while people hurried away from it as quickly as they could.

Miss Jocelyn looked back at it, and saw that it had no hope for her. She would have liked to feel at least that it regretted her going, that it was a little sorry for her, but it stood impervious to appeal. Then she looked round the platform. What a lot of faces there were! What a lot of people there were in the world! Where was Joan? Supposing she didn't meet her, what would be the best thing for her to do? It was no use getting flustered....

Someone tall and dark in a still brimmed black felt hat, and tailor-made navy blue costume bore down upon her. Yes, it was Joan.

"Here you are! I do hope you haven't been waiting. I had such a rush. Most extraordinary. The train was actually punctual, wasn't it? Well, how are you? Have you had a good journey? I do hope so."

Miss Jocelyn replied. Her voice was low and timid. Colour had come into her pale cheeks. Whenever Joan started a new sentence she turned to her with a little smile that appeared anxiously and hurriedly and petered out unobserved.

Joan took one of the bags, and Miss Jocelyn tried to make her return it. "Really, you mustn't," but Joan insisted, and, while she smilingly warded off Miss Jocelyn, reflected, "It's not very heavy! We won't take a taxi. No use giving her the impression we are made of money at the start."

She bustled Miss Jocelyn away to a tram, talking with increasing rapidity and brightness as the other's diffidence and quietness made itself more apparent. Her companion began to irritate her mildly: she was evidently the sort that had always to be shown and guided; no conversation of her own at all. Any form of weakness, or what she considered weakness, always annoyed Joan; but she knew it was the right thing to make an effort to put the old thing at her ease.

So she plied Miss Jocelyn with the sort of questions that didn't require much answering, and if there was any delay in response just passed on to something else. Joan prided herself on her tact. She told Miss Jocelyn about Frank and the children, the troubles she had in looking after their health, and so on. Sometimes she seized occasion to insert little remarks which she hoped Miss Jocelyn would store in her mind for future thought, since they contained cues to the part she wanted her to play in the household.

They got off the tram. As they turned to walk along the pavement, they were passed by a cortège of small girls dressed all alike in navy blue dresses of rough serge and stiff straw hats. Their hair was tightly brought back from their small faces. They walked in silence.

To Miss Jocelyn the crocodile[64] appeared the first significant thing she had seen in Hull. Pity sprang up within her for the children, and it demanded expression. "Poor little things," she said impulsively, "I suppose they are orphans?"

Joan glanced behind her. "Yes, they come from St. Faith's Orphanage, just behind us. They are turning in now."

Miss Jocelyn gave a long look. Unfortunate little mites. Some of them were so small. No mothers! No one to love them. How sad it was!

---

64 Crocodile: 'A girls' school walking two and two in a long file. Also of a boys' school, etc'. (*OED*).

"You know they have a pretty good time really," said Joan. "Well fed. Good, plain food, you know, and all that. And, then, you know children don't really feel things as much as some people think." She stopped, her silence occupied with dissatisfaction as she thought of her own children. Phil was really much fonder of Frank than herself, or often made it appear so when visitors were there. Always hugging him, and having pretence fights, though it looked absurd, and really not quite nice, for a great girl of fourteen. What was it that book on psychoanalysis had said? Anyway it meant that it was really most disgusting, and could hardly be worse, this clinging about and kissing between father and daughter. She'd really have to say something to Phil if it went on. No use speaking to Frank…. And Bobby was getting more and more off-hand with her every day. School did change boys for the worse. So casual with her now, he was. So lacking in affection of any kind.

Well, no time for thinking now with this other worry on her hands. Just ahead was the house; and so she turned to Miss Jocelyn, and said brightly, "Well, here we are at last," thus putting an end to Miss Jocelyn's silent occupation of preparing herself to enter each coming gate in turn and, when they passed, greeting the next house with dismal conjecture.

At Joan's words both women exchanged smiles: Joan allowed hers to stay exactly the suitable time for such a gesture, and then it disappeared promptly and efficiently, leaving no trace; but with a swift call to God for assistance, Miss Jocelyn preserved hers both carefully and gallantly as they went up the garden path. Resolutely she thought, or thought she was thinking: "What a nice house! What a nice bit of garden! How nice and well cared for it looks! I have always been fond of those blue flowers."

Her smile gradually disappeared, to be replaced by an expression of pleased anticipation, as she followed her hostess up the stairs, up quite a lot of stairs, for her room was at the top of the house. Here it was, here she was at last! No way out! No way at all!

"I thought you would like it better up here," Joan was saying as she introduced the attic bedroom. "You see you are absolutely on your own. Away from everybody. I thought you would like the quietness of it."

Miss Jocelyn agreed eagerly, and when the last echo of her spoken gratitude had fallen from her lips, she went on repeating it to herself. How kind Joan was! So thoughtful! What a nice big attic, or rather bedroom, it was! And what a pretty wallpaper!

"Dinner will be ready as soon as you are," said Joan, leaving her with a nod. Outside the room she stopped a second, and then descended the stairs slowly, jerked into attention by a sense of omission. Oh, yes, nothing serious. Just that she had said dinner. But it didn't matter explaining to *her* that they dined in the middle of the day because of the children. She would only be puzzled. To anyone that mattered at all, of course you explained the circumstances of dining in the middle of the day, in case they placed you wrongly. But to Jocelyn!…

Left to herself, Miss Jocelyn looked round with a quite unconscious abandonment of her pleased expression for a more searching one. A plain deal chest of drawers for her clothes. Three pegs on the door to hang up things. No washing stand. That would mean she would have to wash in the bathroom. Well hot water, or water with the chill off at least, would thus be provided. She must remember to find out what times Frank and Joan and the children used it in the mornings so as not to get in their way. Quite a nice little dressing table. It was a little like the one she had had at Nottingham. There would be room to put out her handkerchief sachet and photographs. Her mother and father could go one on each side of the looking-glass, and then the one of Phyllis (Joan seemed to call her Phil: an odd name for a girl, surely!) and Bobby, taken together, on the chest of drawers with the shell-studded box for pins and her brooches. Oh, everything could be made to look quite nice. It wouldn't be very different from her rooms at Nottingham. Of course, only one room, and that rather a small one, and a camp bed, and her other bed had been so very comfortable, but still….

And it really *was* kind of Joan to spare her two bedroom chairs. She only needed one. She might, later on, mention that to Joan, in case Joan was stinting herself elsewhere.

Warmth stole a little way into Miss Jocelyn's heart at the feeling that generosity had been shown her. She mustn't be ungrateful. God was very good to her. Then soon, quite soon, Sunday would be here. She would make enquiries where the Church was. It might be better not to ask Frank or Joan. It would come out later, of course, that she was a Christian Scientist, but people who didn't understand were always inclined to be so argumentative. Better not have arguments at first. She would ask a policeman sometime when she was out alone, perhaps on an errand for Joan. Policemen were usually very helpful.

How much time had gone? She mustn't keep dinner waiting. Miss Jocelyn hurried over to the glass, and arranged her hair. She would have liked to linger, and unpack her bag, but dinner must not be kept standing for her, and she went to the door. But when she had opened it, and saw in front of her the unfamiliar stairs and strange wallpaper, and heard unaccustomed sounds, fear caught her hard. There would be the children to meet, Bobby and Phyllis. And perhaps they resented her coming. She ought to have bought them presents. Even little things might have been better than nothing. She was really nothing but a dull old woman. It wasn't to be expected that they would take to her at first. Afterwards, perhaps. If she did all she could for them; and didn't interfere with anything. At first everything might be rather difficult.

Joan didn't really like her coming at all. She had known that in the first few minutes they met. She probably had been very angry with Frank for asking her. Joan talked so fast; of course she was very clever; it was a little difficult to follow what she was saying always. She was afraid she was getting a little deaf.

As she stood hesitating between the door and her bedroom she heard the gong starting below. It was faint at first and far away, just like any sound that didn't seem to mean anything in particular. Then it grew in volume till it appeared to fill the whole world with its imperative clamour. To Miss Jocelyn it was deafening, it was hideous, it was terrible. She listened to it with one hand pressed tightly against her heart. As it died away she relaxed. That would be for dinner. Perhaps they had sounded it specially for her. She could not delay her going among them any longer. Henceforth her own life was over.

Yet for a few seconds she remained there while she threw all of herself into one voiceless appeal – "God!" The call was for courage and help. Then, with her lips made ready to smile apologetically, and her mind rehearsing the sentence, "I do hope I haven't kept you waiting," she went forward.

BRIDGET KIERNAN

"Bridget! Bridget!"

Bridget Kiernan answered before she was fully awake, some automatic impulse propelling her.

"Yes, ma'am."

"Are you getting up?"

"Yes, ma'am. I'll be down in a minute."

"Well, be quick. It's twenty past seven. You ought to have been ready long ago."

Bridget raised herself reluctantly, and sitting on the side of the bed, reached for her stockings. Listening, she heard Mrs. Fitzroy's door close. Isn't that the devil's own luck now, she thought. That one would be as cross as two sticks all day because she had had to shout to her to get up. It was queer she hadn't heard the alarum: she must have been sleeping very heavy....

Merciful Jesus! For the moment she had forgotten....

Bridget stood still, holding her vest in her hand. Full consciousness gripped her with a cold squeeze. Jim! Jim had gone. And what was worse, she was beginning to be afraid she might be going to have a child. Nothing had happened yet. And she had been awake half the night with the worry of it.

Well, there was no time to think about it now. Pull on her clothes quick to keep out the creeping November cold. She'd have to hurry or there'd be no breakfast for the master. But all the same it was nearly dead she was for want of sleep.

"Bridget! I thought you said you were nearly ready."

The mistress again!

"Yes, ma'am. I won't be a moment, ma'am. I'm coming now."

"Why *don't* you come then? Half-past seven, and not a sign of you. It's disgraceful."

With fingers made fumbling with haste, Bridget twisted up her hair into a knot, and stuck in two hair-pins. There was certainly no time to wash; anyway it was too cold. There wouldn't be time either for her to kneel down and say a mite of a prayer. But she remembered to cross herself hastily and murmur, "Jesus, Mary, and Joseph, I give you my heart and soul," before she opened her door. SHE was waiting with her bedroom door open. SHE'D be shouting at her again in another minute. It was terrible the way that hard thin voice made her lose her poor head altogether.

As she came out of her attic bedroom, she felt a little dizzy with cold, excitement and haste. But there was no time to stop and collect herself. Just keep on walking down the narrow stairs, holding the balustrade for support. As she passed the front bedroom, Mrs. Fitzroy poked her head out. "That's right, Bridget," she said with bitter sarcasm. "Take your time. It's only getting on for eight."

Bridget quickend her steps without replying. She was in the kitchen now, and the first thing to do was to rake out the fire. If only she'd done it the night before. But she had felt too tired and bothered, small blame to her.

How cold it was! She felt her body trembling with cold. And her hands hadn't any feeling in them at all. The air being full of dust and ashes made it all the colder. Cold and dirty. Just shove the cinders into the grate and leave them. No time to take them away now.

She eased herself and rubbed her hands together for warmth. Now she had to go down to the cellar to bring up coal and sticks. It was colder than ever in the cellar, and dark and ghostly. Wasn't that a rat she heard scurrying in the corner? Perhaps only a mouse. Never pay any heed. Shovel the coal into the bucket and bring it up. It would better when she had got the fire set and lit.

The sound of the sticks crackling and the look of the flames as they tried to push their way up comforted her. Nothing was so bad after the fire had been lit, and you were sure it was going. And it was going well today. Who knew but that that mightn't be a good sign for herself. She mightn't be going to have a baby after all. Sure, it was only a few days yet over the time. No need to fret herself.

She went into the scullery to get the breakfast things. She ought, she knew, by rights sweep out the kitchen and the kitchen passage first. But it would be just like Mrs. Fitzroy, the old devil – "God forgive me," murmured Bridget under her breath as she heard the bad word come –it would be just like herself to hurry up with her dressing and come running down posthaste to have the satisfaction of saying, "And the table not laid yet, Bridget!"

Well, she wouldn't give her that pleasure anyway.

The dining room was very mournful-looking with the yellow blinds still down. It hadn't woken up yet, and it didn't want to be woken yet. But the Fitzroys got up so early! Much earlier than the Gallaghers in Dublin, where her sister was. You wouldn't think the gentry would want to get up so early. But you wouldn't call the Fitzroys gentry. No style about them at all, there wasn't.

Those white cups and saucers and plates on the white tablecloth were terrible chilly-looking. Why wouldn't she have a few flowers on her cups, something a little bright? Bridget let her mind survey disapprovingly all Mrs. Fitzroy's crockery. So little there was of it, too! Why wouldn't she have a fire in the dining room this bitter cold? It wasn't much comfort for the master setting off on a morning the like of this. Not that she minded. It would make much more work for her, and that was the truth. Carrying up coals. And before breakfast. But it was hard on the master never to have a proper warm before he went off. And it just showed the meanness of her.

She ran down to see to the fire, and then reloaded her tray, thinking of Mr. Fitzroy. A nice quiet man, he was. One who'd always pass the time of the day with her when the mistress wasn't by to hear. A little stiff, perhaps, but that was the way Englishmen were.

If he heard she was going to have a baby how would he behave? Pass her by with eyes turned down, most likely. Pretend not to have seen her at all. That was what another man would do, if he had proper feelings, and wasn't the kind that would be encouraged immediately to think he could do the same with her.

Stop thinking, now, about that! Herself would be down and in the devil's own tantrums at finding no kettle on. She ran downstairs again, and her quick arrival in the kitchen gave her the impression that she was getting on rapidly with her work: she took the bread out of the bin, and banged the lid down, pleasantly conscious of the bustle she was making. What about making some toast? Wouldn't that be a way of getting the mistress into a good temper? Ah, but the fire was not good for toast yet. And it was ten past eight, a bit after. She'd better be cutting the rind off the bacon for frying.

Bridget jabbed at the white fat with an over-blunt kitchen knife, and once again questioned her mistress's ideas. What was in her head, now, that she made her cut the rind off before frying it in the pan? Because wouldn't anyone know that it was much easier to cut it when it was cooked: that is if you were so particular, and couldn't cut it off when it was on your plate.

That was Mr. Fitzroy in the bathroom. SHE'D be down any moment now fussing round, and chattering about how late it was. For God's sake! Wasn't that her step?

No! It was all right. There was no one. But she'd better be quick and get the rinds shoved into the dustbin in the yard, or else she'd be complaining that she'd cut off too much of the rasher with them.

She returned from the back door with a relieved feeling. Three eggs, for himself, herself, and Miss Paula. They wouldn't spare one for her, of course. Only bacon! Did anyone ever hear the like? Eggs regarded as though they might be a great luxury, and held away from the servant!

There! SHE was calling out to Miss Paula. Now she was on the stairs.

Bridget rushed for the frying pan, and was laying the rashers in with an intent face when Mrs. Fitzroy came in. She was interrupted by a cry of horror from her mistress.

"Bridget! For Heaven's sake!"

Bridget was confounded. What was it she was doing wrong?

"Your filthy black hands, all over coal dust, Bridget. Touching the food we are going to eat. How *can* you?"

Bridget was still perplexed. What was it that she was meant to do then? She looked at her hands, and then at the pieces of bacon.

"Use a fork, girl, can't you? And look at the fire! Nothing but smoke. How can you expect to fry anything on that? And there's no good leaving the kettle on." She removed it with a firm hand. "It would take an hour to boil like that. Can't you see?"

Bridget couldn't. She was conscious that she knew nothing, and that since the appearance of Mrs. Fitzroy the cooking of the breakfast had become surrounded by immense difficulties.

"Don't stand there doing nothing. Get a newspaper; there's one in the sitting room, under the armchair cushion; and hold it in front of the fire."

For twenty minutes the atmosphere was heavily charged with vexation and turmoil. Bridget no longer thought. She became merely what she appeared to Mrs. Fitzroy to be –an evildoer, who had made breakfast late, and was far too stupid to be capable of atoning for her transgressions. She had done so many things wrong that now Mrs. Fitzroy was standing in front of the fire cooking the bacon herself, and only occasionally uttering a command, or asking in a carefully restrained voice that denoted the pitch of fury at which she had arrived, some question which revealed all the things Bridget had left undone. There were one or two terrible moments when Bridget was left standing with idle hands. She dare not remain still, yet there was nothing, she felt, she dare do. Her guilt, symbolized in the figure of Mrs. Fitzroy cooking her own breakfast, seemed then too heavy to be borne.

To avert disgraceful tears, she went over to the kitchen table, and began to lay her own cloth. Anything was better than standing like a fool. But Mrs. Fitzroy, watching her out of the corner of an eye, reflected bitterly: "That's all she's thinking about. Her own breakfast. I've got a good mind to throw her piece of bacon into the fire."

But she did not go so far. She only disassociated it from the rest by thrusting it viciously into the side of the pan, where only a minor degree of heat could reach it. Then triumphantly she noticed an omission.

"If you can spare a minute, Bridget" – Bridget, startled, turned apprehensively – "get me the bacon dish cover. You have only got the plates and dish warming here."

Bridget went hastily to the pantry. She wasn't supposed to be setting her own breakfast, then. What she ought to have done, perhaps, was to go upstairs, and give the sitting room a dust? But it was too late now. Would she ever do anything right for that one, with her face like a thunderstorm?

Paula came running into the kitchen. She was a pale child of seven, with fair bobbed hair, heavy cheeks, and hard staring light-grey eyes. "Mummy, I'm ready. So's Daddy. He wants his breakfast."

Mrs. Fitzroy turned from the fire, and spoke with the terrible calm of the martyr. "Tell Daddy, breakfast is just coming. I'm cooking it myself."

At last it was over. The tea had been mashed and taken up, and Bridget was free to get her own breakfast. She gave another turn to her rasher. There wasn't any dip left. Well, thanks to the mistress being in such a temper, she had lost all her appetite. A cup of good strong tea was what she wanted, and she wasn't going to spare the tea either.

As she was washing up her own cup and plate in the scullery, she heard the front door bang. That was the master gone. A minute later Mrs. Fitzroy bore down like an avenging angel.

"You can clear, Bridget. Your master hasn't been able to have a proper breakfast because it was so late. Do you see now all the trouble you cause by not getting up in time?"

"Yes, ma'am."

The two women stood facing each other. Bridget saw through downcast lids a tall thin woman wearing an old skirt, and yellow-brown cardigan. Mrs. Fitzroy never dressed properly till after breakfast; and her brown hair, badly shingled, had a greasy matted appearance. Her rather large nose was reddened at the tip by the hot tea she had been drinking, and she wore a fretted expression. She was a woman who always gave the impression that she was only in her present place for few moments, and that it was not worth while to unbend and settle herself comfortably. But to Bridget at the moment her appearance resolved itself into a matter of cold blue accusing eyes, and an

ugly red nose; while she listened to the precise English accent which made her
feel she was dealing with someone she could never approach as an ordinary
human being; one who must be an inhabitant of a quite different world from
herself.

And Mrs. Fitzroy viewed Bridget with an equal distaste. She saw an exceedingly slatternly servant girl with a dirty pale face and untidy dark hair that was
always falling over her face. It was true, she had previously admitted, that the
young woman mightn't be so bad looking if she would only keep herself clean
and tidy. She had large clear eyes, and thick black lashes – if she only had not
had such a disconcerting habit of dropping them, which gave her a deceitful
air. But then her mouth was always a little open, a thing which always irritated
Mrs. Fitzroy in anybody. "Makes the girl look half-witted," she decided. But
it wasn't so much her appearance as her way of dragging herself about as if
there was no such thing as time in the world which annoyed Mrs. Fitzroy. "And
she looks," reflected Mrs. Fitzroy again, "as if she has been crying. That seems
her usual occupation. Though I'm sure she gives me far more to cry about
then ever I do her."

Leaving instructions, Mrs. Fitzroy went away to get dressed in a spirit of
acute dissatisfaction. It was a reflection on the house, she thought, to have such
an untidy depressed-looking girl about as Bridget. And Irish people were supposed to be bright and witty! Sooner or later she'd have to give her notice, and
start the search all over again. Or move into a flat with a gas stove, and manage herself with a day girl. This servant problem was really driving responsible
women like herself mad.

Bridget cleared the upstairs table, and washed up. Then she laid a fire in
the study, where Paula had her morning lessons from a visiting governess. As
she dusted the room, Paula sat on a chair, looking at a book. She kept calling
Bridget to show her pictures and to tell her about the story they illustrated.
Bridget went on saying, "Is that so?" and "Yes, Miss Paula," with mechanical
regularity. It was hard to keep her attention alert that morning, but alert it
had to be while Mrs. Fitzroy was still in the house. For you never knew when
SHE'D be coming in with some question or other, just an excuse, of course, to
see what you were after doing. And if you were taken by surprise, as well you
might with her flopping softly round in bedroom slippers, and started, then
she'd say, "Dreaming again, Bridget," or look very suspicious as if she thought
you had just stolen something.

So Bridget kept listening all the while she was turning out the dining room.
The dirt rose from the carpet and settled in her hair and all about her. Her
hands were swollen and purple, and she felt stifled for want of a breath of
clean fresh air. She wished she was back home, back where the air was soft
and people moved slowly.

At last Mrs. Fitzroy went out to do her shopping, and Bridget came thankfully back to the kitchen fire for a comfortable warm before going up to do the bedrooms. She disliked doing the big room, because she always felt the mistress didn't really care for her being in there at all. It was the most unfriendly room in the whole house to her, and her eyelids were downcast when she entered. Yet all the same you couldn't help being impressed by it in a way. All those silver things on the dressing table, and the lovely blue eiderdown that was so rich-looking. And the big real mahogany wardrobe must have cost something, that must have. Then there was that picture of a lady in evening dress, real evening dress, that showed a bit of her bosom like grand ladies did when they were off to a ball of an evening. A bit like the mistress this lady was, only lashings better looking. A sister, it might be, who had married a richer man than the master, and had a motor car, and lived in the real London you read about in stories, the London where there was a real gay life, not like this Ealing[65] place! Sure, Dublin itself was a hundred times as lively.

Now there were the potatoes to peel in the scullery. It was work that gave her a few minutes to think of herself before Mrs. Fitzroy came back, and there was the usual set-to about getting the bite she called lunch.

Well, here she was, Bridget Mary Kiernan, aged twenty five, in a pretty plight, and she might as well face it here and now. She had committed a mortal sin, fornication, and unless she had a piece of luck she might be going to have a baby. All because of that good-for-nothing fellow, Jim – Jim, with his lovely blue suit, and smart figure, and wavy fair hair, and laughing blue eyes. And his warm lips that held yours till they seemed to draw you out of yourself into a great fire and confusion. Stop now! That was no way to be thinking. Where was her pride? A likely-looking lad enough, maybe, but he had gone now and left her for ever. Deserted her! Deserted – that was the word they called it.

And there was no way of speaking to him, a boy that she'd met in the pictures three months gone, and had never got to know anything about, though he had met her regular every Thursday evening up to four weeks ago. No, three weeks. It was month now that *that* had happened between them, God forgive her! ... She ought to have known the sort of fellow his lordship was when he had started hinting. But there it was. It was her own fault in a way, because she hadn't chosen to take heed of his free style of talking. She had liked the feel of his arms about her in the pictures too much to frighten him off with being prim and proper. And there was an ache in her all the time till he was with her again, and she felt him touch her. Sure, no one with a heart

---

65 Ealing: A suburb in the Greater London area.

in them could blame her too much. Wasn't he the only friend she had in London? And everybody wanted a bit of fun now and again.

She hadn't really known, before God she hadn't, what he meant when he suggested going to a restaurant instead of to the pictures that Thursday. And she had felt shy even in her best clothes, and glad to know that it was in what was called a private room they were going to have dinner, where there'd only be the two of them.

It was true she had felt there was something wrong when he was muttering so long with the waiter. And it was such an odd dirty place, not like a proper restaurant at all. She had felt all queer when she saw the big sofa. But all the same she was dying to know what he was going to do. And he must have spent some money to get that room all to themselves. Half a bottle of expensive wine, too. She had laughed a lot. Wine always made her laugh a lot. But afterwards, in his arms … it just didn't seem to matter at all. Give him his way … She couldn't really see now that it was such a terrible thing as the way in which people talked about it. But, of course, it was badness, and she'd been bad; she had so.

All the same it was difficult to understand anything one way or another, and all that a poor ignorant girl the like of herself could do was to be good and leave the matters to the priests and learned people to settle. She had done wrong, and there was no use her trying to get out of it. Her mother would be terrible upset when she heard about it – that was if she had to hear – and there was no one at all to help her.

She ought to go and make her confession. Who would she go to? She had never been to confession the whole long year she had been in England, nor the five months she had been in the Isle of Man, nor the six months, as it nearly was, that she had been with Mrs. Fitzroy. It was so different here, where no one seemed to have any religion at all. Even Mass sounded different, and had different things in it. And she had never been very particular about religion. Perhaps it was a pity she hadn't.

Jim had no religion, any more than that fellow she had gone out with in the Isle of Man – Frank – had. Perhaps if Jim had had religion, been a Catholic, he'd have behaved different. He had thought light enough of what they had done. Just laughed when she said they had been wicked, and then got cross when she wouldn't let him kiss her. Walking away like that in the street when she had told him what she thought of him. She was an Irish girl, and wasn't going to put up with being treated any way. Walking away and leaving her like that in the street! She'd never forgive him for that, never. Ah, well, no good exciting herself with thinking of that all over again. But she had her pride, and even if he wanted to marry her she wouldn't. No one might believe it, but she wouldn't, not if he went down on his bended knees.

The potatoes were finished now. She carried them into the kitchen, and at the same moment she heard the latch of the front door turn. Her High and Mighty-ship was back. There'd be no peace now for a while.

Mrs. Fitzroy brought down the parcels she had been carrying. "Here, Bridget, is the chop I got for your dinner. And the potatoes are in the basket. Those are tomatoes that I've got for tomorrow to fry with the bacon. We've got eggs, haven't we? Miss Rowbotham and Miss Paula and I are having scrambled eggs. And coffee. Can you do the eggs?" "Yes, ma'am." "You ought to, considering the number of times I've had to stand over you to show you."

"Have you laid the table?"

"No, ma'am."

"Well, go and do it now. It's twenty to one. And I don't want lunch later than one because of Miss Rowbotham."

Miss Rowbotham came out of the nursery as Bridget passed on her way to the dining room. She had curly brown hair, a small round face, and bright brown eyes that peered over her plump little body with an air of being willing to meet everybody half way.

"Good morning, Bridget," she said with an air of cheerful benevolence. You-always-have-to-be-so careful-with-the-servants was one of Miss Rowbotham's maxims.

"Good morning, Miss."

The girl seems respectful enough, thought Miss Rowbotham, and, by way of rewarding her, she gave a little shiver and said, "Isn't it cold?" in a little upward rush of words.

"Indeed it is, Miss."

They parted, and Bridget, laying the cloth thought: "The English are always saying, 'Good morning,' or 'Good afternoon,' or something like that. And that teacher will be washing her hands again before her dinner. Is it to please Mrs. F. or to suit herself that she's so particular? I wouldn't be surprised but that she's scared stiff of her, like the master, and every blessed one in this house."

Paula came silently in, thrusting her under lip forward as was her habit when she was in a bad temper, and stood watching Bridget arranging the knives and forks. "You do look dirty and horrid, Bridget," she remarked after a thoughtful pause.

Bridget made no reply. "Mother says you are the dirtiest girl she has ever had, but that all Irish people are dirty. Is that true?"

Bridget thought it politic to refrain from uttering a direct denial. She'd only be making trouble with her mother, the little brat, she thought.

"The dirty Irish, the dirty Irish!" cried Paula in sudden excitement, dancing up and down, and then pulling Bridget's apron strings loose before springing away.

"Ah, go away now, Miss Paula, and leave me alone," said Bridget, the blood mounting to her cheeks.

"Shan't, shan't. The dirty Irish!"

Bridget felt an angry despair surging up. They were all against her, shouting at her and mocking at her. Very well, she'd stick up for herself. She had some spirit left in her, thank God. She turned round smartly on Paula.

"Do you hear what I say? Go out from here. This minute."

"Don't speak to me like that. Or I'll tell my mother of you."

For a moment the two stood confronting each other: Paula, pouting and lowering, Bridget with flashing eyes, and a look on her face new to the child. After a moment Paula, discomfited, ran out of the room, turning at the door to make a last thrust: "I hate you, you horrid girl."

Bridget stood still for a moment with a hand pressed to her rapidly beating heart, and then went on setting the table. But when she went back to the kitchen, Mrs. Fitzroy observed on her face what she described as her mulish look, and deemed it better to postpone a complaint that too many potatoes had been peeled till later.

"You go on making the toast, Bridget. I've beaten up the eggs."

The task of getting lunch proceeded silently, the two women ignoring each other's presence as far as possible. At last it was done, and taken up, and Bridget was left to fry her own chop.

She ate absent-mindedly, occupied with the new feelings which Paula's attack had aroused in her. Now they'd got her blood up she wouldn't care what she did, and she wouldn't be asking help from nobody either. If she was going to have a baby, what need was there for any great to-do? They'd have to take her in at the workhouse anyway, and then she'd go on the streets … steal. Get put in prison? What matter?…

There was Margaret Callaghan of Carrickmore, that the priest had sent away out of the parish because she wouldn't tell him the name of the fellow that was after giving her a child. And she had just sailed off as cool as you please to Dublin, and, so they said, was seen walking down Grafton Street, dressed up to kill, with not a feather off her. Well, those girls might be bad, she wouldn't say they weren't, but didn't they have a better time than sticking on toiling and moiling day after day with no thanks from anybody?…

The great thing was not to get in a stew or to be put on by anybody. If there wasn't anyone to help her, there wasn't anyone, and there was an end of that. And hadn't many another girl had her trouble, and got through it, and nobody a penny the wiser?

She washed the dishes, with her thoughts repeating themselves in gestures of defiance, and she became almost happy in her new boldness. Now she could think of Jim with indifference and even contempt. A poor ordinary

skulking fellow he was, doing an ordinary mean sort of thing, and then afraid
to face the band. In love with him? Not a bit of it! A bit of a fancy perhaps,
but she was well out of it and over it now, thanks be to God.

It was as if she had suddenly grown a year older, having come to read
things aright that an hour or two ago had been confused and dark. She went
about the house, finishing her work with a determination that perplexed Mrs.
Fitzroy, and made her suspicious. "It's not her afternoon and evening off," she
pondered. "What's she up to now, I wonder?"

It was almost strange to Bridget, so conscious was she of this change in her
outlook, to find that the streets outside looked just the same when she went out
to take Paula for her walk.

She went up the long stretch of Pitshanger Road, staring with unwonted
curiosity about her. It was, she thought to herself, as if in the usual way you
went along never looking up to take more than a pennyworth of notice of
anything about you, and thinking your own thoughts about the things that had
happened to you, and the things that might happen to you, and then one day
you got a shove when you weren't expecting it, and you were startled into taking heed of things that had been there all the while only you hadn't bothered
your head about them.

Those houses now, big and dark and silent, frowning away there they were,
as if the devil himself had taken possession of them. Sure, no one would
know who and what lived in a house the like of that one there unless you went
up and knocked and were shown in. And the cracks in the pavement stones,
streaks of black amid grey, hadn't they the queer way of shooting up in to your
eyes, so that having noticed them you had to go on noticing them. And in front
the wide hard road stretching on and on with an errand boy bicycling down.
There was the red 150 'bus just turning the corner; and, coming towards
them, a white dog rooting along with its nose to the pavement. A nice garden
that one was, with its yellow chrysanths.; and there was a woman in blue with
dark hair sitting by the window. More cheerful-looking than the other houses
it was, and she did right to be proud of her garden as surely she would be.
Then, if you looked up, there was the still grey wintry-looking sky over everything … no change in it as far as your eyes could stretch.

Bridget puckered her brows, feeling suddenly tired.

What did these things stand for? What sense was there, after all, in them?
They were things that went on, and would always go on whatever misfortune
happened to a girl like herself; but what meaning was to be got out of them it
would take a wiser girl than she was to find out.

Paula, who had been walking on a little in front to make Bridget think that
she didn't choose to own her, or have anything to do with her, got tired of her
own company, and decided to talk. "Bridget, did you see that lady with the red

face and the fur coat who went by on the opposite side? Mother knows her. She's Lady, Lady … something, I forget what. That's a very important thing to be, you know," she added condescendingly.

"Yes, Miss," said Bridget dreamily.

"Do you have ladies in Ireland? Like Lady Jane Grey, and Lady Duff Gordon? And Lady Astor?[66] You don't do you?"

"Ah, sure every country has them. You read about them in the papers."

"Not every country. You *are* ignorant, Bridget. You couldn't have them in France, because in France they talk a different language. They talk French. I learn French with Miss Rowbotham. But you're too stupid to understand things like that."

"Haven't I told you not to speak that way to me, Miss Paula?"

"Mother does."

"Aren't you brought up the way you know how to speak nicely?"

"Yes, if I want to."

There was a silence. Bridget thought without resentment that it was a pity Paula wanted so much pleasing, and was so unfriendly. But there was no use taking to heart what a child would be saying. A spoilt little madam she was, and no mistake. But then she was an only child, which was an unnatural thing for a child to be.

As she turned home the melancholy of gathering dusk took possession of her. Paula, who had chattered more than usual, disturbing Bridget with her questions and comments, and achieving a triumph in being the one to remember they had forgotten to buy more eggs, was now quiet; and Bridget realised that in her growing weariness something had escaped from her. This was the time when she was most put in mind of her own country with its creeping mists that counseled resignation. She heard the doleful cries of the grey birds that would be wheeling in from the mountains, and saw the tree in the middle of the field at the back of her mother's cottage. It would be bare looking now standing lonely against the sky. Inside, there would be a warm fire, making the red patchwork rug look gay and snug. And the little statue of Our Lady smiling down from her niche on the wall. Her mother would be chatting as likely as not to Mrs. Connolly over a cup of tea, bragging, for all that she knew to the contrary, about one of her children or another. Bridget herself, maybe, it would be, who had a grand post as a help in London, where

---

66 Lady Jane Grey (1537–1554): Temporary queen of England in 1553 after the death of King Edward VII; executed by Mary Tudor in 1554. Lady Duff Gordon: Lady Duff-Gordon (aka Lucy Christiana, née Sutherland) (1863–1935): A leading English fashion designer. Lady Astor: Nancy Witcher Astor (aka Viscountess Astor of Hever Castle, née Langhorne) (1879–1964): First woman to sit in the British House of Commons.

everyone was rich and there were more people than anywhere else in the whole wide world. Except perhaps New York, in America, where Kevin was. Ah, well, her mother was an old woman now, and she ought to be allowed her bit of romancing.

It was queer and lonesome when you got thinking of home. It was a pity in one way that she had crossed the water, though two fortune tellers had told her that that would be her fate, and that she would marry a handsome fair man, and keep her own servant. Well, there was a laugh to be got out of that bit. She had certainly thought Jim might be her fate when she met him. She had never been very partial to the one in the Isle of Man, and he was dark and small, but Jim had really been the spit of the fortune teller's description. Well, she had had her wish to travel, and now she was landed with one of the crossest women you could ever meet, a bold forward child, and nothing but cross words, however much she killed herself dead with trying to do work in new ways that no one had ever heard of before.

She sighed gently, and raising her eyes murmured under her breath, "Blessed Virgin, help me. Sacred Heart of Jesus, have pity on me!" It was no use her getting worked up. There was nothing she could do. That was a certainty. She hadn't the price of her fare home till the end of the month. And home was no place to go to anyway if it was a child of badness she was bringing with her. Bringing scandal into the parish and disgrace on her poor mother. Ah, well, what did they say? That there was no use crossing a river before you came to it.

That policeman was taking a good look at her. The cheek of him! Now he was turning his head to stare after her. She knew it without looking round. Would there be any harm in her glancing back casual-like and giving him a bit of a smile? Better not. Paula might notice and then come out with it. She was cute[67] enough to watch her even when she seemed to be seeing nothing at all. But, all the same, the knowledge of the policeman's interest pleased her, as if a sore place had received balm, and as they turned in at the house, she said cheerfully to Paula, "Here we are. Now you'll get your tea that you've been wanting."

There was a light in the kitchen! That meant the mistress was down there. It would be just like her if she had been prying into the drawer where she kept her paper-backed Smart Novels.[68] Three of them, Bridget remembered,

---

67 Cute: Acute, shrewd.

68 Smart novels: Probably a reference to novels by Henry Hawley Smart (1833–1893), an English army officer and novelist. 'When Love flies in at the Window' is not, however, the title of any of his works.

there were. She might even have thrown them out as rubbish. And she hadn't finished "When Love Flies in at the Window."

Mrs. Fitzroy said nothing to her maid, but welcomed Paula expansively, "Well, darling. Had a nice walk?"

"No," said Paula. "Just ordinary. Up to the shops. And Bridget forgot to get the eggs till I reminded her. So we had to turn and go all the way back when we got to the Underground."

"That was my clever little girl to remember for mother."

Bridget carefully deposited the parcels on the table. She didn't like to say anything to the mistress unless she was spoken to. Mrs. Fitzroy was so different from Mrs. Reynolds, who had kept the Isle of Man boarding house, and who was always ready for a chat. She might as well go upstairs and take off her things. But when she was half through the door, Mrs. Fitzroy called her back: "Oh, Bridget! Put on the kettle before you go up. And when you come down make some buttered toast. Three rounds. I've laid the table."

Bridget put on the kettle ungraciously. "Why, I wonder, couldn't she have done a little thing like that without calling me?" she asked herself. But when she came downstairs again she found the kitchen empty, and kneeling in front of the fire she looked round and took pleasure from the warmth and familiarity of the scene. She liked the room best in the evening, when Mrs. Fitzroy only came in for a few moments just to see if her dinner was going all right. Then each item became definitely hers. The light shining on the plates on the dresser, and the firelight warming the blue and red tiles; the clean-scrubbed yellow deal table. Oh, it was a pleasant enough room when the little red curtains were drawn across the window. Quite friendly like. She liked looking, too, at the shiny red bread bin with its big black-painted letters; and the tin tea caddy that stood by its side with its picture of an Irish girl and an English girl and a Scotch girl all joining hands. And there was the old basket chair that she would be able to give herself a rest in later.

The day was getting through, thank God for it; and the furniture and crockery and tins that had been pushed and banged about were now given a moment of peace, so that they took on a quiet and solid look that was never theirs in the morning, but which was the one natural to them.

Look at that now! She'd been and burnt the toast. Smoking away in blackness. No good doing anything with it. SHE would turn up her nose at it, however much it was scraped. She'd best hide it behind the clock on the mantelpiece, and do another piece. Perhaps she'd have it for her own tea. Or else throw it in the dustbin when the mistress was off out of the way.

Mrs. Fitzroy was already in the dining room when Bridget took up the tray. "You've been a long time, Bridget. I suppose you burnt the toast or something. I thought there was a smell."

"No, I did not, ma'am."

"Why have you been so long then?"

"Was I long, ma'am?"

Mrs. Fitzroy made an impatient movement, and then lifted the teapot towards her.

"Is there anything else you're wanting, ma'am?"

"No. Oh, yes. Bring up the biscuits I bought, please. They're in the pantry. And put them in the biscuit jar first."

Bridget enjoyed her tea. She made herself more toast, and buttered it generously. It wasn't as if she had had much to eat that day, she thought to herself, noticing her appetite approvingly. And she wouldn't be having anything for her supper beyond a cupful of cocoa. Mrs. F. was very close with food for the kitchen, and the meat didn't taste like good Irish meat at all, it didn't. She'd probably be taking a good look at that loaf, the old skinflint. It couldn't be helped. Didn't she have to keep up her strength some way? And she wasn't going to be treated worse than a dog all of the time, even if that one expected her to find nourishment out of the smell of what was cooking for herself and the master.

That put her in mind. She pulled out the drawer in the table. No, the three of them were there safe. If they hadn't been, she'd have asked straight to her face, so she would: "I see you've borrowed a book of mine, Mrs. Fitzroy." Or, "Might I trouble you to give me my book back, ma'am?" "I think you have interfered with my property, ma'am. Might I ask why?" Quite easy and polite, but enough to show that she wasn't intimidated by HER. That she knew her legal rights, which she did. There was the bell! Ah, she could wait. She wasn't going up till she had finished her tea comfortably. Wasn't she ever to be allowed a bite of food quietly?

When she was washing up the tea things, she heard Mrs. Fitzroy go into the kitchen, and she also heard the breadbin being ransacked. A moment later her mistress came into the scullery wearing her gravest face.

"Bridget, I'm not sure that there'll be enough bread to last us till the baker comes tomorrow. When you have finished you'd better run out to Paley's and get another loaf."

"Yes, ma'am."

"There ought to have been sufficient, but it seems to have gone very fast today." There was a note of interrogation and disapproval in her voice, which Bridget ignored.

Mrs. Fitzroy sighed. "When you've got your things on, tell me, and I'll give you the money."

Bridget hurried up. It was a pleasure to go out by herself in the evening, even if only to post a letter, and ponder over the recipient. Now she shut the door behind her with alacrity, and it seemed to her that the lamps to her right and left threw a friendly regard her way. There were two young men standing at the corner as she passed, and one raised his hat, and said "Good evening."

Of course she didn't reply, but hurried on, her heart beating faster. The nerve of that one! But it was very gentlemanlike the way he raised his hat. Better class than when they just coughed. Not that she cared that much for any of them! Weren't all the men the same? A few soft words to wheedle you, "What wonderful eyes you've got!" and that sort of light chat, and then away, chasing after someone fresh. Oh, she knew them, the sort they were.

Still it cheered her up being out of the house on her own, and feeling the keen air against her face. And the little lighted shops looked gay. Would you believe it – the Christmas cards were out already! When she had got the bread she was loth to leave them, and sauntered slowly, looking in the windows.

How pretty the red apples and yellow oranges looked all piled up together in that tasty way! Those writing pads at threepence each were very cheap. A real bargain! Then the array of magazines and paper with their bright red and blue and yellow covers adorned with pictures of smiling girls and illustrations of frocks and cami-knickers[69] (some with patterns to be given away) held her eyes. That was a notion! She'd treat herself to "Home Notes" that evening. Sure, the way things were, didn't she need something to take her mind out of herself?

The woman inside was friendly, and said it was a lovely evening, very seasonable. "Indeed it is," replied Bridget heartily, and went out feeling really light-hearted.

As she had come so far she might as well slip along and have a look to see what was on the cinema. It was only a minute away; no one at all would be the wiser.

She walked fast now, feeling a little guilty; but when she got to the entrance she lingered, fascinated. "The Sins Ye Do," the big film was called; and there was a huge picture at the side of a beautiful girl standing outside a great palace of a house with a baby in her arms. She wouldn't be married, because she was poorly dressed, and looked desperately miserable. That would be where her mother and father were living, and they wouldn't have anything to do with her any more. Staring big blue eyes the girl had.

It would be a tragic film. Wasn't it a pity now she couldn't see it, for how did she know but that she wasn't going to be the same way as that young lady. And she might have got a hint or two from the film what to do. But, of course, that girl was extra beautiful, so that she'd be sure to meet someone after a bit who'd

---

69 See footnote 10.

fall really in love with her, and forgive her everything. There'd be a fadeout with a man in evening dress kissing her over a cradle with the baby in it, and saying that he'd never hold it against her.

Or if it were a really tragic film the girl would die a beautiful death with everyone sorry and weeping that they'd been so unkind, and hadn't known that she was more sinned against then sinning.[70] Or something. Anyway, it would be lovely to see it. It was after six and people were just starting to go in. She watched a young man clink money down while his girl stood waiting. They'd have a grand time inside with the orchestra playing sitting so comfortable on the red velvet seats, with the warm darkness wrapping them round. And after a while she'd put her head on his shoulder.... Well, no use standing there.

She found she had lost her light-heartedness as she walked quickly back. The picture had come as a sharp reminder of something she had almost forgotten. But she felt a little important, too, because the picture's subject had brought her the assurance that many people would regard her as a sad victim of man's wickedness. "She gave her all and he left her to pay the price." The sentence came into her head, and she muttered it to herself with a sort of satisfaction. She, Bridget Kiernan, was one of that sort of women, more shame to the man.

She was so deep in her thoughts that she was taken aback when she heard the sharp edge of Mrs. Fitzroy's voice: "Here you are at last. You've been long enough to buy out the whole shop."

"They were sold out at Paley's, so I had to go along to Bowen's," said Bridget glibly, and admired herself for the way she had found on the spur of the moment a feasible explanation. She'll hardly take the trouble to go to Paley's and see, she assured herself.

Mrs. Fitzroy looked disbelieving. "That's queer. I've hardly ever know Paley's sold out before. They always keep a few loaves for the next day. Some of their customers only like it when it's a day old. And in any case, I wouldn't have thought it took half an hour even to go to Bowen's."

Bridget was silent. She had said her say, and if Mrs. F. didn't like it she could lump it. She noticed that her mistress had changed into her brown crêpe de chine frock, and powdered her face. You could well see where the powder ended on her nose. If she only knew she needn't think it improved her, because it didn't. She was a plain-looking woman, and a cross woman, and she, Bridget, wasn't going to demean herself by answering her for all her disagreeableness and innuendos.

---

70 'I am a man /more sinn'd against than sinning'. *King Lear*, III.ii l. 59–60.

Mrs. Fitzroy turned angry. "Understand this, Bridget, when I send you out for bread, I don't mean you to go for a walk. This isn't your evening off, you know. Be quick, now, please. I want some coals taken up to the study."

Bridget went upstairs to her room without a word, and banged the door behind her. She sat down on the bed and thought murderously of Mrs. Fitzroy. She imagined her in hell, and the flames scorching her that she screeched out for mercy. But there wasn't one would have mercy on her. Wasn't it true that they said all Protestants had to go to hell? And it might be so. Certainly it would be true for a woman with a temper the like of hers. And meanness! And ugliness! And sneakiness! And her thin, pinched voice!

She mimicked it to herself. "Understand, please, I don't want you to go for a walk. It's not your evening off."

"I'll walk out of here, anyway, Mrs. Fitzroy. *And* I'll have my wages, if you please!" That would have been a great thing to have answered her with. And she'd say it, too, if there was much more of her impudence. Sure a black or a slave would get more decently spoke to. They would so.

She pulled off her hat and coat, and went down with a feeling of going into mortal combat. No one in the kitchen. SHE'D be up in the study with Paula. What was the time? Twenty after six. A bit more, for the clock was slow. Into the dirty cellar again, and yet was expected to keep as clean as a shining angel in Paradise!

She clattered about, and after a while her rage wore down. The joint was cold; that was a mercy. Potatoes on to boil. SHE'D brought in a cauliflower. When Mrs. Fitzroy came down to make what she described as a sweet, Bridget went upstairs to lay the table. Mr. Fitzroy had returned, and was in the dining room, measuring out a whisky and soda.

"Good evening, Bridget."

"Good evening, sir."

That was a nice smile he had given her! But it made her feel shy like, being there all alone with him.

Mr. Fitzroy observed Bridget without appearing to do so. She seemed a bit down in the mouth, he thought. Not bad-looking. Pretty hair, and good eyes. Irish, she was. Cheer her up a bit. No harm in a friendly word.

"Well, Bridget, how do you like London?"

Bridget knew she didn't know. She'd only been up to London proper twice. Once with Jim, for THAT! And then when she had had tea in a Lyons, near Oxford Circus, and been terrified of getting lost. Still he wouldn't expect her to hand out all that piece.

"I like it well enough, sir."

"I suppose it strikes you as very big and noisy after the country. So much traffic, and all that."

"Oh, indeed, you're right, sir. Very big.... And very smelly," she added thoughtfully, remembering her first impression on arriving at Euston.

Mr. Fitzroy was a little puzzled by the last word. But at the same time he thought he heard a sound on the stairs. "You'll soon get used to it," he said rather hastily; and went thoughtfully out of the room. It wouldn't do for Dorothy to hear him talking to the maid. She was always so suspicious. And he didn't want her to know he was having an appetiser. Women always called it, "Drinking again!"

Bridget knew why the master had gone out so suddenly. She could have told him the mistress was safely away for a few minutes. Ah, well, the poor man had a good heart, and you could only pity him, seeing the sort of woman he was married to.

Sadness came upon her as she smoothed the tablecloth. The room looked pretty now with the pink shade over the electric light. And the rose-coloured chrysanths. on the white tablecloth, and the glittering silver on the mahogany sideboard. But it didn't belong to her. It wasn't intended for her. There didn't seem anything that belonged to her in the whole wide world.

She went to the window to draw the curtains. The sitting room of the house opposite was lit up, and a piano was tinkling out a tune. It was meant to be gay; yes, "Where's my sweetie hiding?"[71] That was it. They played it at the pictures. But it was mournful sounding all the same, coming across the dark quiet road. The more the person playing banged it out, the more it caught at your heartstrings, because of the lonesome way the notes flowed into the silence.

There she was, playing the fool again! Standing, dreaming! Bridget pulled the curtains to with a determined hand, and went back to the kitchen.

Mrs. Fitzroy looked up from the table at which she was standing.

"Don't you think, Bridget," she said in a voice that sounded strained in her effort to speak pleasantly when she was moved by a spasm of sharp irritation, "that you might give your face a wash? There's a clean towel on the roller in the scullery."

Bridget did not trust herself to speak. She would have burst into tears if she had. And she couldn't disobey the old beast without saying one word. She put the tray down, and, glad to get her back turned, went into the scullery.

"Oh, God, can't she die? Kill her! Kill her! Kill her!" she prayed violently as she splashed a little water on her face down which tears of anger and mortification came rolling fast. "Bad luck to her in her life and in her dying and in her death. Oh, kill her, kill her, kill her, and may she suffer the tortures of the damned, the eternally damned!"

---

71 A jazz tune performed by the Paul Whiteman Orchestra in 1924.

She choked a sob in the towel. To be humiliated that way! To be spoken to like that! Told to wash! She, Bridget Kiernan! An Irish girl! She'd get her own back somehow, she would so.

She stood for a moment getting her breath under control. Paula came running downstairs and into the kitchen. Bridget turned back to the basin, and washed her hands noisily. Anything to give herself a few seconds more out of the sight of the mistress. She wouldn't give the old bitch – she didn't care; that was the right name for her – she wouldn't give the old bitch the chance to see she'd been crying.

She went back with the water jug filled. The mistress didn't turn round from the fire, but Paula stared at her, and said in her shrill voice: "You *have* got a red face, Bridget. You look as if you'd been crying."

"Run upstairs, Paula, till you're called to have our cocoa," said Mrs. Fitzroy firmly; and Paula, running after Bridget, pushed past her so that Bridget nearly stumbled. "Will you look where you are going, and don't push," said the girl so sharply that Paula was surprised into saying, "Sorry."

Ah, but the dining room had a blessed coolness with no one in it. If she could only lock the door, and stand there for ever by herself.

The piano across the road was still playing. She listened to it awhile, her lips apart and a dreamy look in her eyes. She and the pain inside her, and the little song in the night, and the silence that surrounded them were all part of one another, or seemed so in some queer fashion that brought its soothing message. After a while she stirred herself, and gave a little thoughtful nod. That was the way things were, God pity us all.

When dinner had been taken upstairs there was Paula to be seen to, and the cocoa made for them both. When they were drinking it the bell rang, and Bridget took up the pudding and clean plates on a tray. As soon as she got in the room she knew they had been talking about her because of the sudden conscious silence into which they were immediately plunged. She held her head high as she went out of the room.

Then Paula was sent for to say goodnight; and Bridget had to prepare her bath. She felt a sudden impulse to be determined and hasten things along.

"Will you come on now, Miss Paula," she called irritably from the bathroom.

Paula came running in with just her little vest on. "Didn't your mother say you were to wear your slippers and put on your dressing gown?" Bridget demanded mechanically.

Paula disdained reply. She put her fingers in the water. "It's too cold, turn some more hot on."

Bridget obeyed, testing the water with her hand meanwhile. Paula decided to be naughty. "I don't like you putting your dirty red hands in to my bath water," she said, wrinkling her nose with disgust.

Bridget turned off the tap with a jerk. Then she brought her face close to Paula.

"You don't speak to me like that. Do you hear me now? You don't speak to me like that."

There was so much passion behind her words that Paula, abashed, got into the bath without replying. She meditated bursting into tears, for she knew that in the ordinary way it was just because Bridget, like the previous maids, was afraid of her crying and bring up her mother that she got her own way. But Bridget was different tonight. Perhaps it wasn't worth it.

Going back to get Paula's nightgown and slippers, Bridget looked at herself in the wardrobe glass. She had a vague impression of a queer-faced girl with a lot of dark hair, eyes that seemed all black pupils, and a white apron over a black dress. It was strange and queer that that should be herself, Bridget Kiernan!

Paula was put into bed and left with her picture book till her mother should come and put out the light. Bridget went down, and cleared away the dinner things. Her brain had stopped registering anything; she felt very tired, and her back ached; only a dull hate burned within her.

As she cleaned the knives she heard voices in the hall. Were they after going out? Please God, they were! She stopped and listened attentively.

Someone had gone upstairs. She'd take the silver up to the dining room; that would give her a chance to see what was going on. Returning, she saw Mrs. Fitzroy come down the stairs with her hat and coat on. "Oh, Bridget, I'm going out. Have you washed up?"

"I have, ma'am."

"Wait a minute then."

She went into the study and lifted the coal box lid. "You'd better bring up some more coals." When Bridget came back, she found Mrs. Fitzroy still in the room. Mr. Fitzroy was sitting reading the evening paper. So *he* wasn't going out.

"If anyone calls, Bridget, tell them I'm out, but Mr. Fitzroy is in."

"Yes, I will, ma'am."

No one had ever called since Bridget had been there, except the mistress's brother. And once the master had brought home a friend. But SHE always told her to say that. SHE had told her to bring up more coal when it wasn't wanted, because she didn't want her to come in the room with the master there by himself. Oh, she saw through her well enough.

Bridget returned to the kitchen, and stood waiting till she heard the front door slam. There it was! She relaxed. The old devil was out of the house for a while. Thanks to be to God for it!

"Isn't it a pity she hasn't taken herself off for good?" she muttered to herself. "Begob, she's the worst vixen in the world; and it wouldn't hurt me at all to know that she'd fallen down where she stood and died. Not at all it wouldn't."

She shook her head, the sense of all her wrongs coming uppermost to her mind. Then she sat down in the easy chair, and buried her head in her arms. Soon she found herself shaken by sobs, the sobs that had been pent up within her for the last hour or two. They grew more and more unrestrained till she recollected herself in a fright, and, with her hand pressed to her mouth, got upon and closed the kitchen door. The master mustn't be let hear.

Now for a good cry. It would relieve her feelings. She sniffed and whimpered and gasped, while her nose became swollen, and her eyes grew small as they disappeared under her puffy eyelids. Sometimes her grief would slacken in its expression for a moment; but then the remembrance of one or another of her troubles and resentments would surge up again, and she would renew her sobs. It was a shame for her! A shame! And no one cared a tither.

At last she cried herself out. At first she was conscious of nothing but that her skin seemed pressed tightly over the top of her head, and that her body was giving little uncontrollable shivers. She poked up the fire and turned her chair round to it. For some while she sat thus, smoothing out the pain at the back of her forehead with her fingers.

Slowly odd fragments of thoughts began to drift to and fro in her mind. The delf[72] was still in the scullery, she'd have to put it away. Wasn't it very still? You couldn't hear a sound ... it was twenty to nine ... the big picture would about be on at the cinema; what would happen to the girl in it? Anyway there'd likely be a happy ending ... There was her "Home Notes," and she didn't feel like reading it at all ... she'd had all her pleasure spoilt ... would those two fellows have picked up two girls? ... were they having a good time? ... It was a shame the way she was put on by the mistress....

"Bridget!"

My God! Was that someone calling? Bridget went quickly to the door and opened it. It was Mr. Fitzroy. He was standing at the top of the kitchen stairs.

"Yes, sir."

"Are you there, Bridget? I thought you might like to look at the evening paper?"

Bridget went quickly upstairs, feeling the perplexity suggested by her temperament. Did he mean her to take the paper or not? He might be depriving himself.

"Ah, sure, it's all right, sir," she said hesitatingly.

---

72 Delf: A type of crockery.

"I've finished with it."

"Thank you very much, sir."

She took the newspaper and turned her back as quickly as possible, leaving Mr. Fitzroy to return to his chair disturbed. The girl had been crying. There was no doubt about it. Poor little soul! It seemed a bit thick for her to be crying down in the kitchen while he sat there. Was she homesick? Her home was a long way away, and the Irish, of course, were very patriotic. Or Dorothy might have been sharp with her? She had been complaining at dinner about her being stupid and dirty.

He went into the dining room, and poured himself out a whisky. It was a pity he couldn't go down to the kitchen and comfort the girl. But too dangerous. He'd never forget Dorothy catching him out kissing that girl – what was her name? Alice – they had had a couple of years ago. Never gave him a chance to forget it, she didn't. Ah, well!

He returned to the fire. Dorothy would be back soon. He'd speak to her about it. Or better not. Women were the devil to one another. The girl wasn't bad-looking either. Something soft and appealing about her. The way she spoke perhaps.

No good letting his mind run on women.

Bridget had carefully spread the paper out on the table. She stood for a moment, looking at it unseeingly, and feeling warmed by the kindness shown her. "That's a decent one," she thought to herself. "He deserves a better one for his marriage bed. Wouldn't it be grand now if I could get a place with a man by himself, as his housekeeper. Someone who'd know how to treat a girl polite."

She moved into the scullery and restored the crockery to its right place. Then she sat down again.

Well, she felt better now that she'd had her cry out. She wouldn't have minded a bit of a read. Nothing like a good story to take your mind off things. Only she ought to think of her position really seriously like. Suppose, strange and impossible as it sounded, she really was going to have a baby? She'd give herself another week, and then, God help her, if she didn't come on, she'd be sure she was in the way.

The terrible part of it all was that there wasn't a creature she could talk it over with. Now these London girls would be sure to be up to all sorts of tricks for stopping things. There was the girl next door that she'd passed the time of the day with. But could she go and say to her…ah, of course she couldn't. It wouldn't be decent.

There was her mother. "My dear mother, I take my pen in my hand to tell you I have bad news for you. There was fellow I met, and I am sorry to say he has got me into trouble…."

Oh, Holy Mary! What would her mother say, and she reading a letter with news the like of that. Oh, didn't it sound terrible when you came to put it into words. A disgrace to her poor mother she was, and a disgrace to herself....

Tears were unloosened again, but her mind was no longer still. It seemed to her she was weeping for remorse at her wickedness, and the thought vaguely comforted her. The first thing she must do was to repent. Wasn't there the Blessed Mary Magdalene?[73] She'd pray for her intercession. And she'd say an Act of Contrition[74] as if it were to the priest himself. First she'd confess.

Bridget knelt down on the floor and with folded hands repeated the Confiteor.[75] When she came to the words, "I have sinned exceedingly in thought and word and deed, through my fault, through my fault, through my most grievous fault," she had to pause for sobbing. The magnitude of her sin overwhelmed her, and it seemed to her that she had been hard and una-shamed up to now.

Then she repeated the Act of Contrition. That was better. Sure, God would forgive her if she truly repented and offended Him no more. And she did truly repent. Perhaps He'd let her off having a baby. Now a Hail Mary.[76] "Hail Mary, full of grace, the Lord is with thee: blessed art thou among women, and blessed is the fruit of thy womb, Jesus. Holy Mary, Mother of God, pray for us sinners, now and at the hour of our death."

The familiar words soothed Bridget. There's nothing so comforting as a Hail Mary when deep troubles come upon you, she reflected, and repeated the invocation several times. Then she said the "Hail Holy Queen,"[77] and then an Our Father. And then she turned back once more to the words which gave her the most healing, "Holy Mary, Mother of God, pray for us sinners, now and at the hour of our death."

Hadn't Father Reilly once preached a sermon – she remembered the time well, because she had been wondering if it would be right to pray for a bit of money so that she could get herself the new cute hat in Murphy's   hadn't he said then that the Blessed Virgin never denied Her intercession to those who approached Her in sorrow and contrition?

That was true. There were the words, "A contrite and humble heart, O God, Thou wilt not despise."[78]

---

73 Mary Magdalene: A follower of Jesus known for both her devotion and her status as a repentant sinner.
74 Act of Contrition: The prayer said by Catholics during the sacrament of Reconciliation (penance).
75 A prayer of repentance said during a Roman Catholic mass.
76 Hail Mary: A traditional Catholic prayer asking Mary for intercession.
77 Hail Holy Queen: Also known as Salve Regina, a traditional Catholic hymn.
78 Biblical reference, Psalm 51:17.

She blessed herself and rose. She felt tired, but there was a sort of happiness with her all the same. There was great help in saying a few prayers, and no one could say else. She had been brought up badly, and that was the truth. It was her father's blame. For ever cursing and swearing at the priests and saying they were the bane of the country. God forgive him! Well, he was dead and knew better now. God spare him and deliver him from distress and torments. "Deliver him, O Lord, from eternal death."[79]

In a fashion it was due to him and the way he'd never set an example that she'd lost her beads which Father Reilly had blessed. In the Isle of Man she'd never given a hoot. Well, indeed and indeed, it would be different from this time on. She'd be chaste and pure; she'd put away all thoughts of badness, kissing and such-like. She'd buy a new Rosary as soon as she got her money; she'd go to Mass every Sunday; she'd go to confession….

But that last wasn't too pleasant to think about. What would the priest be after saying at all? Would he tell her to confide in her mistress? She wouldn't do that. Never. After all, the mistress was a Protestant. Would he let her off if she told him that? He might.

You could never tell what an English priest would do. He might be poking his nose in her affairs all the time. Hadn't her father always said they were the meddlesome fellows, making trouble and bringing ill luck wherever they went.

What was she thinking? Ah, nothing! Nothing at all (She crossed herself quickly.) She wasn't meaning any harm. But it was difficult. The more you thought the more troublesome everything was.

A red bank of cinders broke and fell to the bottom of the grate. Bridget roused herself, and gave the fire a poke. Watching the flames dart swiftly upwards, she meditated whether she would put some more coal on. Better not. SHE'D march in, stare hard at the fire, as if she'd never seen such a thing in all her life before, and say something about wasting coals at nighttime. What was the time? Half past nine. She must mind not [to] forget she had the shoes to clean. Would SHE want hot milk when she got in? Another saucepan to clean. Never cared what trouble she gave.

Her evening off tomorrow. Nobody to meet. It might be a good thing to go up to the Church, and see if she could find anything out about a priest. Somebody might be giving her a tip about getting hold of the decentest one; someone with a bit of sympathy in him. Ah, there was no call yet. There mightn't be anything in it after all. And she worrying herself to flitters with no need. It was the thinking and worrying that had you driven distracted.

---

79 Possibly a reference to prayers sung or read during the Catholic Mass for the Dead, such as *Libera Me*.

A wind blew up, murmured, complained, and sank down. Bridget heard and shivered. You never knew your luck, of course, and it was a queer world to be in. Anything might happen to anyone at any time. God help us all!

It wouldn't hurt her at all to die at this moment. It would be a way out of all the confusion. No more getting dog's abuse from morning to night. No more cleaning out the grates. Eternal rest. She couldn't kill herself, or else she'd go to hell maybe. "The horrid darkness, the hissing flames, and the excruciating tortures." Ah, no! But to die quietly as she was sitting there. Heart failure. And then people would be sorry. Mrs. Fitz. would be shown up for what she was. Her mother and neighbours would be weeping and crying when they heard the news. "Is it Bridget?" they would say. "Is it Bridget Kiernan?" "She that went to the Isle of Man and London?" "Poor Bridget's gone." "Is she now?" "That's bad."

Was that the front door? Bridget sat up alertly. Yes, a key was turning in the lock. It was the mistress back. If she came down, she'd better look as if she'd been reading the paper. Oh, she'd gone in the room to the master. Better go and get the shoes done.

As she was knocking off the dry dirt into the coal bucket, she heard Mrs. Fitzroy call:

"Bring me up a cup of hot milk, please."

"Yes, ma'am."

She filled the saucepan and brought it to the fire. There was only a little fire left. What she'd best do was to hold a paper in front. The paper on the table would do well enough. The master had said he'd done with it. Unthinkingly, she held the newspaper to the fire, her heart heavy again with apprehension. There was no happiness possible when that one was about.

A flame singed the edge of the sheet, and Bridget was only just in time to prevent it catching fire. The fire would do now. But the milk wasn't near boiling. She tested it with her finger. Only tepid. Had she better go up, and tell the mistress that the fire was nearly out? But it was like taking poison to go near her. And she didn't like speaking in front of the master.

Her predicament was decided by the study bell going. That was terrible. Mrs. Fitz. didn't often ring the bell, at least not so late in the evening. It meant she must be in one of her tantrums again: would it be that she'd get herself scolded in front of the master for being so slow with milk?

When she opened the door of the room, Mrs. Fitzroy was sitting on the couch looking very solemn, while Mr. Fitzroy appeared to be reading some book intently. "Oh, Bridget, I should like to see the evening paper if you've finished it. And isn't the milk ready?"

"Yes, ma'am. I'll bring it up, ma'am. The milk's nearly ready, ma'am, but the fire isn't very grand."

"I suppose you mean there's no fire at all. Why didn't you say so before? Well, bring up the saucepan here, and I'll see to it on this fire. And a cup and saucer. On a tray. *On* a tray, remember."

"I will, ma'am."

Bridget went downstairs with her cheeks burning. She hated it when Mrs. Fitzroy put on that thin voice with no sort of expression in it at all. As if she were speaking to a piece of furniture, and as if she, Bridget, wasn't really flesh and blood, and couldn't be expected to understand things like other people. Those English airs!

She fetched the tray and pondered for a moment on the question of putting the saucepan on it as well as the cup and saucer. Perhaps not, because it would make a dirty mark. But if she didn't it would sure to be wrong.... And then the paper that was burnt! Arrange it so as not to show the singed place. Sure, she'd probably never look at it. Only wanted it out of spite. She went upstairs again.

Mrs. Fitzroy nodded. "All right, I'll see to it. Give me the saucepan, and leave the tray on the desk. That's right. You'd better get off to bed now. It's after ten. Is your alarum clock working correctly?"

"It is, ma'am."

"And you've cleaned the shoes?"

"Yes, ma'am."

Mrs. Fitzroy dismissed her with a nod. Mr. Fitzroy turned over another page.

She went back to the kitchen feeling guilty and yet triumphant. She had got out of that all right, so long as the mistress didn't take it into her head to walk into the kitchen and see the shoes only half done. Ah, well, it wouldn't take her long to polish them off. It was no use telling *her* that she hadn't finished them, and give her a chance to be disagreeable in front of the master.

Upstairs, Mrs. Fitzroy poured out the milk, and then started to read the paper. As she turned it over, she noticed the burnt place. "With all respect, Harry," she said suddenly, "I don't think Bridget does much newspaper read-ing. I am quite sure she has never looked at this the whole evening – just used it to get the fire going. Look! Newspapers are not in Bridget's line. She keeps incredibly dirty-looking paper novelettes for her reading purposes."

"Sorry, my dear. I won't give it her again."

Dorothy Fitzroy was unable to control a grimace of irritation. Men were so stupid; answering you as if you had said things you never had.

"It isn't that. I'm sure I should be only too glad if she showed an intelligent interest in anything. I don't want her not to get every consideration. But she's an absolute fool. And a liar. That's what I object to most."

Her voice grew shriller, and her husband didn't reply. Usually he was more sympathetic than this.

"You think I'm hard on her? Well, just take today. At twenty past seven there was no sign of her. That meant that I had to cook the breakfast myself so as to get you off in time. You ought to have seen her standing gaping at me, incapable of doing a thing. Just the same with luncheon; she's always wriggling out of doing things, so that it's simpler to get them done myself. And it makes me feel ill, positively ill, in any case, to see her dirty hands – she never washes unless she's told, and I *did* tell her this evening; unless, of course, she's going out for the evening, and then she's dressed up and powdered to kill – well, it makes me sick to see her hands poking into the food we're going to eat."

Mr. Fitzroy murmured agreement.

"It's the same with errands. She forgot to get the eggs this afternoon when she was out with Paula, until the child reminded her. And after tea, when I sent her to get some more bread – there's nothing wrong with her appetite, I'm always having to get extra bread and tea and potatoes in, and butter – she took over half an hour over it. And then pretended they were sold out at Paley's and she had had to go just a few doors further on to Bowen's. What do you think of that for a story? A child could see through her. Walking up, and down, staring at the shops, as cool as a cucumber, of course.

"And the way she throws food away! After all, we're not millionaires. When she was out I found in the dust bin a huge piece of toast she had thrown away. Burnt it, you see, and then sneaked it away, thinking I should never see. She's always burning bread. And she throws away half the potatoes with the peel.

"If she was only willing to learn, I'd never say a word. But she's not. She lets you do anything rather than do it herself. Just stands by and stares at you, without raising a finger. And if you speak a word to her, then she goes away and cries. Or else looks like a thunderstorm. I really sometimes think she can't be all there the way she goes on."

She paused, and Mr. Fitzroy saw a reply was expected. He moved uneasily, remembering Bridget's swollen tear-stained face. "Perhaps she's homesick?"

"If she hasn't got over that by now, she ought to. She came to me of her own free will, didn't she? And she'd been in the Isle of Man before that. Though she's obviously never been properly trained. You don't seem to bother about me, but I can tell you it's not very pleasant having a girl going about the house all day looking like a sick cow. As if she might burst into tears at any moment.

"And she hasn't gone up to bed now. I told her to go off, because I was determined she shouldn't have any excuse for not getting up tomorrow. But she calmly disobeys me. It's waste of time saying anything to her. But I believe I know what she's doing."

Dorothy got up suddenly and went to the door, opening it very quietly. She went a few steps along the passage, and then listened. Presently she returned and closed the door.

"As I thought," she said triumphantly. "She's cleaning the shoes. You heard her say, didn't you, that she had done them?"

Mr. Fitzroy pursed his lips gloomily, and nodded.

"Another lie! Then she was afraid I'd find her out. So she sneaks down, and does them on the quiet. That's the sort of thing I'm always having to put up with. You see for yourself now?"

"Why don't you dismiss her then if you're not satisfied?"

"I expect it'll come to that. But it's no joke getting girls in these days. They're nearly all as bad. Or unkind to Paula."

Mr. Fitzroy let his eyes return to his book. He wished Dorothy would go to bed so that he could have another whisky.

Mrs. Fitzroy observed him with resentment. He was not really sympathetic. You worked from morning to night to see that the house was run properly, and got no thanks for it. People seemed to think you *liked* being disagreeable. As if it wouldn't be far easier to let the maids do as they liked and not give a button, like some women. The house would be dirty, and bills run up, but it wouldn't matter to them. Or apparently it wouldn't. Just give Harry the chance to see how uncomfortable he would be if she didn't look after things. It would make him sing a different tune then....

But she was tired to death of it all. You wore yourself out coping with dirty ignorant lying sluts, and no one cared ... no one cared.

Bridget passed the door, and though she was going softly Mrs. Fitzroy, who had been waiting for the sound, heard her. There the girl was, she thought, creeping up to bed like a thief. Well, if she had any more trouble getting her up in the morning she'd give her notice. She'd made up her mind to that.

She turned her attention to the leading article headed "More Efficiency," and read it with approval. It comforted her, for it secured to her the feeling that she was in the right. Cleanliness, speaking the truth, punctuality, capability, were things that mattered. The whole country would be in the workhouse otherwise. And she and Henry would be in the workhouse, if she took her hands off the household helm (something like that the paper said, and very rightly). It was the individual's contribution that mattered. Well, she would go on doing her share, whether she got any sympathy or not!

Upstairs, Bridget was lying in bed wrapped round in a blissful feeling of security. She had made a discovery. She was safe after all. No baby on the way! Wasn't that the great mercy? God had answered her prayers. The Blessed Virgin had not interceded in vain. After this you couldn't say but that there was a great deal in religion. Oh, she'd keep her word to Our Blessed Lord, and be a good girl for keeps. Wait till marriage after this scare! It was she was the happy girl, with the relief of it. The mistress didn't matter, not at all she didn't. She'd give her notice one day soon, see if she didn't. It wouldn't be difficult to get another job. There was a great shortage of domestic servants, so the papers were always setting forth. A job now where she'd see a bit more life would suit her grand. She must mind and remember to get the beads all the same. Sure, God was good, and it wasn't a bad world, if a queer up and down one at that.

'MARY, PITY WOMEN!'

Norah Hoult

Any sensitive young woman starting out in life comes sooner or later up against the hard, and sometimes unpalatable, fact that it is one of her most important jobs as a woman to conciliate the man. He may be her father; he may be her employer; he may be her lover; he may be her husband – the point is that the great majority of women are economically dependent on some man.

Now this unequal state of affairs is not particularly pleasant to swallow. Most of us who are women, and particularly who are unsheltered women, have, I suppose, at one time or another, been moved to envy men the greater ease with which they can maintain their self-respect, and play their own hands without dissimulation; without niggardly fears for the future.

These stories are not propaganda; they are not attempts to solve the unsoluble [*sic*]. I wrote about the individual women, young and old, whom I have written about, because, very briefly, each of them happened to come my way; and it seemed to me that I was able to understand, at least in part, something about them: what they wanted, what they were unable to obtain, and the nature of the handicap against them. They are real to me, and I have tried to make them, and their problems real. That is all.

This text was appended as a preface to some, but not all, 1929 editions of *Poor Women!*, and sometimes numbered. The title references a Kipling poem, 'Mary, Pity Women!', which portrays the plaint of a lower-class pregnant woman abandoned by her lover as she asks him to 'give her the name' and marry her to make her again respectable. Hoult's intertextual reference here is ironic; whereas Kipling employs pathos, Hoult's stories maintain a sympathetic but often ironic distance from her flawed characters, thus suggesting not only criticism of them, but also sympathy for the cultural and social conditions that influenced their self-construction and plights.

NOTES ON THE TEXT

This edition is drawn from the 1929 edition, not the original 1928 London publication, because, as I observe in the Introduction, the former included two additional stories not originally published in the latter. I have also included the short piece, 'Mary, Pity Women!', which is inconsistently found in some of the 1929 editions, as well as select correspondence from the Hoult holdings at the John J. Burns library at Boston College (see Acknowledgements on permissions).

Footnotes to the text are either mine directly or, when necessary, generated through consultation with the *Oxford English Dictionary* or *Encyclopaedia Britannica*. References drawn directly from either are referenced as *(OED)* or *(EB)*, respectively.

Hoult's writing includes many ungrammatical elements, such as sentence fragments and curious usages of semicolons, many of which are employed to suggest characters' internal dialogue. She also tends to use many ellipses to signal ruminations. In almost all cases, I have left these, as well as grammatical oddities and errors like pronoun–antecedent disagreements and expressions – 'to think out something to do'; 'pressing to me to stay with him'; or 'pretence' fights instead of 'pretend' fights – as they were found in the original text. I have added missing apostrophes and removed many outmoded hyphenations (to-day, to-night) in keeping with Anthem Press style guidelines. Where I have added a word for clarity, I have signalled the change.

Appendix

LETTERS TO THE AUTHOR

A. Oliver St John Gogarty

Telegrams: HOTEL, RENVYLE   Telephone: RENVYLE 3

Station: CLIFDEN (12 miles)

RENVYLE HOUSE HOTEL
RENVYLE, CONNEMARA
CO. GALWAY

praises to you.Don't mention that there is
a bias against me .It may make it worse.
Boyd will see to that.I am sorry to have
told you this.Were it from motives of jealousy
you would not have been told.

    Ely Place is gone to the Royal Irish
Academy.I am here until I get a flat in
London for the family that remains :wife and
daughter and roomsin Wimpole St.for myself.
I am glad to be out of the mortician's
parlour which Dublin has become.It was once
an intellectual centre.Now it is a cemetry.
Bi-linguals who are unable to express themselves in any language and civil servants
and Seumas who is blessing cows in verse
in the Irish Times,having forgotten that he
has already blessed geese–are all that re-
main.Higginsof course who hasoutsoared the
shadow of Irish and is becoming more and more
coherent and competentin English and parts
of Yeats remain.All that puzzles me is to find
out if it be a shortcoming in me or not,to be
so devoid of regret at leaving my "home
town."Perhaps it is an act of patriotism:–
It would never do for the only independant
mindleft to set a bad examples to the remnant
by the spectacle of independance.
A bi-lingual morgue!

    "And deValera,a tremendous gloom" as Shelley
calls Demogorgon in Prometheus.
When you met little Roosevelt you should have
improved the hour by sellinghim a book.It's
a damned shame that the most realistic woman
writer living only can get £100 in advance
subject to their damned Federal Tax.I have
to loose that andanother ten % to Curtis

Browne.What a nation of "agents"they are!
I know that when I have to travel all through
the US and Canada that there will be "owing
to mail"arrears in my £70 per week.If this
occurs,I don't procede.AndI will warn the
boysin the bureau beforehand.Havingbeen left
stranded in the far West,lost for all he knew,
by Fond of the mistress with a double mastoid-
itis,I know something about their ways.
Duff Cooper,or rather Duffer Coop is engaged
by Colson Leigh's gang at a less fee than *Mine*
~~~.This,you will yell,is as it should be
for he is a poor skate who betrays his leader
in a crisis and in about the worst crisis
that beslet England since Wellington's
Blucher-arrested retreat at Waterloo.Of course
Duff Cooper is an agent to bring about better
feeling etc.etc.but the mere sight of the
mim-mouthed rat will enggnder contempt.Anyway
I "pull down"more.
    Dear Norah,what a dose for you this letter
has become.Here is lighter copy:your cottage
has been roofed with scalloped thatch by a
thatching master from Oughterard.A father and
son have it.Sentimental stuff maybe from
England,for the best thatch lasts on 12
years without re pairing.Wallace is dead and
leaves Mrs.Wallace sole owner of his estate.
They got an immense price for the heap of
~stΩones which you made famous:£260.
    Here I am all alone for aweek until the
family arrive with news of the auction of the
residue of furniture-and for Christmas.*My*
grammarv is givingout.I have written too
much.Don't think that it was that I had
nothing else to do.I would write to you
if I were atelephone exchange attendant in
medias res or,as Fanning says,in via media.
        Affectionaltely yours,

        Oliver Gayoffo.

A Happy Christmas to you.

Telegrams: HOTEL, RENVYLE   Telephone: RENVYLE 3
Station: CLIFDEN (12 miles)

RENVYLE HOUSE HOTEL
RENVYLE, CONNEMARA
CO. GALWAY

Talking of London burning.I had a letter
to-day reporting that Dr.Furlong the
Director of the Nat.Gallery(over Brindsley
who has a flat in London came back yester
day with the word that war is imminent
and inevitable."Nobody can stand Hitler".
Also that the Income Tax will rise to
8/6 in the£.

The modern Londoner who is alien
is very easily scared.It may be that
the Jews are making the wish father to
the war.Anyway,I'll join up for the
Nation that instituted and maintained to
long week-end which is the final measure
of freedom and civilisation.I could tell
you a secret anent this.It will keep.

I shall miss the easy access to
the heights above Jobstown where the

gorse is on the granite;and the well-meaning

shining foolish face of Mr.Clarke.But there

will,I hope,be compensations in London *if you*

do return in the Spring.

This afternoon I walked along to road

to the old castle.It was blowing hard from

the north west and the shore was piled with

long-stalked sea-weed which the troglodytes

were gathering busily for top-dressing.

The sea was very fine to behold all white

and light green, *more* whiter than green with

the far islands a faint amethyst in the

wet air.There will be cottages galore about

this part next year.A guest house is being

built at Lettergesh from stones of the old

Protestant Church was was such an unsightly

new ruin half demolished.

Just this minute this cable from Morrow:
"Duell on continent unavoidably until Dec 8th.
Having no idea of what passed between you
naturally can say nothing about your proposal
but very doubtful about increasing any offer mad
made by Duell"

I think that Duell is *the* likely to increase.
My unwritten works sound so immensely superior
to those published!

I am all for Peace! *Gay offer!*

B. Brigid Brophy

Dear Miss Hoult

It's so long since we saw you that I wasn't sure I'd have the chance to tell you this to your face, so I hope you'll forgive a letter. I have just caught up with Cocktail Bar. I don't want to be impertinent but I can't help wanting to tell you I think they're great stories. To my half foreign mind, you tell the whole truth about the Irish — but simply,

by just writing literature. You had me transfixed with them all, particularly Afternoon In Asylum which broke my heart. Thank you so much for breaking it.

Yours sincerely
Brigid Brophy

3 PARK HILL, W.S.   17 JANUARY 1954

www.ingramcontent.com/pod-product-compliance
Lightning Source LLC
Chambersburg PA
CBHW030646110726
47901CB00002B/589